Acclaim for *The Phoenix Endangered*

"[Expands our view of this] world's desert societies and the secrets hidden far beneath the sands. As the young characters learn to accept responsibility for their actions, their trials increase in difficulty. Solidly developed characters, appealing magical companions, and an intriguing tale make this a good addition, along with its predecessor, to any fantasy collection."
—*Library Journal*

"Lackey and Mallory continue to develop their intriguing characters and expand their world in the second book of the Enduring Flame series. The two protagonists grow while staying true to their roots, and their villain is complex and sympathetic. Shaiara, perhaps the best character in the series, gets a larger role and helps mold the satisfying plot in this enjoyable read."
—*Romantic Times BOOKreviews*

"Shaiara is a plucky and resourceful character, rising above the tropes common to multicultural fantasy. Readers can rest assured that Lackey and Mallory will not let them down."
—*SFRevu*

"Young adult readers will enjoy the action-packed *The Phoenix Endangered*. The exploits of the teen heroes and their camaraderie are fun to follow. Additionally, the two male buddies learn the destructive nature of unchecked or unbalanced power. An enchanting quest fantasy."
—*Baryon*

The Phoenix Endangered

Book Two of
The Enduring Flame

Mercedes Lackey
and James Mallory

TOR®
fantasy

A TOM DOHERTY ASSOCIATES BOOK
NEW YORK

This is a work of fiction. All of the characters, organizations, and events
portrayed in this novel are either products of the authors' imaginations or
are used fictitiously.

THE PHOENIX ENDANGERED: BOOK TWO OF
THE ENDURING FLAME

Copyright © 2008 by Mercedes Lackey and James Mallory

All rights reserved.

A Tor Book
Published by Tom Doherty Associates, LLC
175 Fifth Avenue
New York, NY 10010

www.tor-forge.com

Tor® is a registered trademark of Tom Doherty Associates, LLC.

ISBN 978-0-7653-5507-2

First Edition: September 2008
First Mass Market Edition: August 2009

Printed in the United States of America

0 9 8 7 6 5 4 3 2 1

FOR DENNIS—

—quare habe tibi quidquid hoc libelli, qualecumque quod, o
   patrona virgo, plus uno maneat perenne saeclo.

—CATULLUS

The Phoenix Endangered

Prologue

IN THE MOONTURN of Flowering Harrier Gillain's best friend had cast his first spell of the High Magick, something nobody in the Nine Cities had done in almost a thousand years. Because of that, Tiercel Rolfort had begun having visions of a mysterious Lake of Fire and a Fire Woman who—though beautiful—was terrifying as well. Hoping to put an end to his visions—or at least get an explanation for them—Tiercel went in search of a Wildmage, since a millennium after the fall of the Endarkened, there were no other Mages that anyone knew of.

And of course his best friend went with him. Harrier had known Tiercel since they were both small children; their friendship was a strong one, and Harrier was completely convinced (based on long experience) that Tiercel would only get into trouble if he went anywhere by himself.

As it turned out, he got into trouble even with Harrier there to try to talk sense into him, and the search for a Wildmage led them both farther than either could ever have dreamed, into the Veiled Lands where the Elves lived. There, Tiercel and Harrier met people who they had only known from wondertales of the ancient Time of Mages: Jermayan, and the black dragon Ancaladar, and even Idalia. The Elves had confirmed Tiercel's worst fears: the Dark, banished for so many centuries, was awakening again. And apparently the Light had chosen Tiercel to do something about it.

The Elves would tell him nothing more than that, fearing that if they did, they might cause him to reject some plan of action that might be the only hope of destroying the Darkness. Tiercel must choose his own path.

But they did not leave him entirely helpless. Tiercel had already learned that his Magegift was useless without the power to cast the spells, power that the ancient Armethaliehan Mages had harvested from the people of their city. In place of that, Jermayan offered him something unheard-of in all the centuries of the Bonding of dragons: Sandalon Elvenking would use the one Great Spell that each Elven Mage might cast once in their lives to transfer Ancaladar's Bond to Tiercel, granting him the power to fuel his magic, but at the cost of three lives: Sandalon's, Jermayan's, and that of Sandalon's dragon Petrivoch. Only the fact that Jermayan was dying—having reached the end of an Elf's long-but-not-infinite span of years—and the fact that the need was so very great—persuaded either Tiercel or Ancaladar to agree.

Though no one knew where the Lake of Fire that Tiercel needed to find might be, his visions suggested that it must be in a desolate and uninhabited place, far from the haunts of men. The only place the Elves knew that might be the destination Tiercel sought was the Madiran Desert, far to the south. And so Tiercel, Harrier, and Ancaladar set out on their journey. But the Gods of the Wild Magic were not yet finished with their weaving. . . .

One

Called to Magic

E'D NEVER THOUGHT he'd see a unicorn, Harrier thought crossly, and like so many things he'd thought he'd wanted to see when he was back in Armethalieh (like Elves and dragons and Wildmages) the reality was nothing like he'd expected it to be.

Oh, sure, Kareta was beautiful. In fact, she was the most beautiful thing he'd ever seen. But he hadn't expected her to sucker him into falling into the stream with most of his clothes on—and make him lose his shirt—and then laugh her silly head off about it just as if she were one of his idiot brothers.

Of course, maybe that was just what unicorns were like. How would he know? Nobody in human lands had seen one since . . . well, since the time of the Magic Unicorn Shalkan and Kellen the Poor Orphan Boy.

Thinking about Kellen, a hero out of the Nine Cities' most ancient legends, made Harrier shiver just a little, and not with cold (although he was soaking wet, and the walk back to the wagon from the woods wasn't that pleasant in wet clothes), but because only a fortnight ago, he'd been talking to the person who'd taught that very hero to hold a sword. Who'd helped the Wild Magic turn Kellen into a Knight-Mage, a great warrior who could defeat the Endarkened.

With that thought, the red leather satchel he had slung over his shoulder, small as it was, suddenly seemed incredibly heavy. Because it contained the Three Books of the Wild Magic, brought to him (*not to Tiercel, to* him) by the unicorn Kareta, and if Harrier could believe her (did unicorns tell lies?), he hadn't been granted the opportunity to become just an ordinary Wildmage—as if there could be such a thing—but a Knight-Mage.

Just like the hero Kellen had been.

Nobody knew how Kellen's story ended, though everyone knew how it began, and everyone knew the ending of his sister's, the Blessed Saint Idalia's. She married the King of the Elves (so the tales went), was granted immortality by the Light, and lived forever in the Elven Lands. But over the last several moonturns, Harrier had learned a lot about how the stories he'd always taken for granted as being, well, *wondertales* (which meant they were sort-of true and sort-of not) were completely wrong about all the important things. Jermayan wasn't King of the Elves, just to begin with. And Elves certainly didn't live forever.

And having fought Goblins, and seen magical things that he had no name for, met Elves and dragons and all sorts of Otherfolk that had left the lands of Men in the time of the Great Flowering, Harrier'd thought he'd gotten used to things being strange by now. He and Tiercel had left Armethalieh almost four moonturns ago, at the beginning of summer, looking for a Wildmage who could put an end to Tiercel's little problem, as Harrier had thought of it then. Tiercel said he was having visions. Harrier thought Tiercel was having bad dreams.

But they really *were* visions, and that was only the start of problems that just got worse and worse. At least they had Ancaladar with them now, because the Elves had cast an incredibly powerful spell (that they hadn't been sure at the time was even going to work) to transfer Ancaladar's

Bond from Jermayan to Tiercel, because otherwise Tiercel, whether he was a High Mage or not, wouldn't have the power he needed to cast his spells. So now Tiercel had the power, and all he had to do was *learn* all those spells, so when he'd gotten up this morning, Harrier had thought they only had two problems to deal with.

One was the fact that Tiercel kept saying that it took about twenty or thirty years to train a High Mage (and he also kept saying that they didn't have that long before the Darkness came back), and the other was that they really had no idea of where they were going to find it and fight it, because nobody recognized the landscape from Tiercel's visions.

Now they had a third one.

Harrier really didn't like magic. It was weird. It made him uncomfortable. It wasn't that it was wrong or evil or bad, but . . . he was the youngest son of the Portmaster of Armethalieh, for the Light's sake! And he would have made a really rotten Portmaster, and he was glad now that he'd left because that meant his older brother Brelt would be Portmaster instead, and Brelt would make a *wonderful* Portmaster, but what he was *supposed* to be doing out here was the same thing he'd been doing for moonturns: keeping Tiercel out of trouble, and watching his back, and making sure that there was food and that Tiercel came in out of the rain and that nobody took advantage of him because Tiercel was much too easygoing for Harrier's peace of mind. And sure, Ancaladar could do some of that, but not all of it. And how was Harrier supposed to do *any* of it if he was being a Knight-Mage?

Even leaving aside that he didn't know the first thing about being a Knight-Mage, except that if you were one you were supposed to be an incredible warrior and a great leader of men. And he really wasn't.

BY THE TIME Harrier got back to the wagon, Kareta was already there. Her pale golden coat shimmered in the late-morning sunlight as if it were actual gold, and the long spiraling horn that grew from the center of her forehead glowed with the soft white iridescence of the inside of a seashell. Even as irritated as he was, Harrier couldn't help stopping to stare at her for just a moment: an actual unicorn—most beautiful of the Otherfolk!

But she was tapping one small pink hoof in irritation as she waited for him, and kept glancing back over her shoulder toward him, interrupting her conversation with Tiercel and Ancaladar to do so. At least *Ancaladar* was having a conversation. Tiercel, Harrier was pleased to see, looked just as flummoxed as he had upon his first sight of Kareta.

Harrier wondered if the two of them had shown up of their own accord, or if Kareta had gone and gotten them— he really didn't put anything past her at this point, because even though he'd only talked to her for about five minutes, Harrier already knew that she was just as pushy and managing as any of his sisters-in-law. But maybe Ancaladar and Tiercel had just been drawn by—for lack of a better term—the *scent* of magic. Were unicorns magic in the same way that dragons were? He knew that they were Otherfolk, and creatures of the Light (as little as Kareta had been *acting* like one just now), but nobody really knew all that much about them; they hadn't been seen in human lands since the Great Flowering.

"*There* you are!" Kareta said, tossing her head. "Well it *took* you long enough—did you stop to take a bath after all? Come on! We've got a lot to talk about!"

"My clothes are wet. I'm going to change," Harrier said sulkily.

He wanted to toss the satchel with the Three Books down on the ground just to show Kareta what he thought of her bright idea that he should become a Knight-Mage, but he couldn't bring himself to do it. Whatever he thought of the idea of becoming one, a Knight-Mage was a Wildmage, and Wildmages were guardians of the Great Balance, and Harrier worshipped at the Shrine of the Eternal Light— the Great Balance as it was venerated in the Nine Cities—

just like everyone else in Armethalieh. The Light might be known by different names in different places: as Leaf and Star to the Elves, as the Herdsman to the Centaurs, as the Huntsman and the Forest Wife back in the Hills, and even in some places as the Good Goddess, but it was all the same Light, the same way as the sun was the same sun, no matter where you went. Without another word, he sighed, and settled the satchel firmly on his shoulder as he walked past the other three and climbed the steps into the wagon.

He ducked his head as he stepped up and inside. *"You don't have to like it. You just have to* do *it."* That was one of his father's favorite sayings, and it had gotten Harrier through many an afternoon of tedious chores. He wasn't entirely sure that Antarans Gillain had ever meant it to apply to his youngest son becoming a Wildmage, though.

Well, maybe there was a way out. He was sure Ancaladar would know.

He closed the door of the wagon behind him, and bolted it too, just to make sure he had a little time alone to think. He kept his head ducked; Tiercel could stand upright in here, but Harrier was a good half-head taller than Tiercel was, and he'd already collected more than his fair share of bruises from the ceiling and doorframe of the wagon.

THE TRUE PURPOSE of the wagon wasn't actually to provide him and Tiercel with a place to sleep, but to provide Tiercel with a portable workroom, for unlike the Wild Magic, the High Magick required a large number of ingredients, and research books, and tools. But at the moment it also held all their belongings, for though the boys had arrived at Karahelanderialigor, city of the Elven Mages, with little more than the clothes on their backs, they had left it fully provisioned, thanks to the generosity of House Malkirinath.

He sat down on one of the chests to remove his boots, setting the satchel carefully aside. The boots were durable leather, made for hard use (and even for wading into a stream, if need be), but it would take them hours to dry. He set them in a corner. He'd oil them later, to keep them from stiffening as they dried. Then he dragged off his overtunic (his shirt was floating downstream, but if he was lucky, it had caught on a branch, and he'd be able to retrieve it later; he had others, but that was his favorite) and got to his feet to rummage through the chest for a change of clothes. At least he'd packed up the camp this morning before he'd gone off for his ill-advised morning swim, so he was able to lay hands on a drying cloth and his camp boots without tearing the whole organization of the wagon to bits. All of Tiercel's High Magick stuff was carefully packed away out of reach, and he'd told Harrier over and over that it was completely harmless: without a High Mage's will and power, nearly all of it was nothing more than *objects,* and Harrier could do them more harm, actually, than they could do him. But Harrier still didn't like the thought of touching them. And it was the "nearly" part that bothered him. It would be just his luck to bump into the *one* item in Tiercel's collection of weird new gimcracks that could turn him into a tree, or something.

A FEW MINUTES later, dressed in dry clothes, but no more ready to talk about this than he had been before, Harrier opened the door of the wagon—and nearly skewered himself on Kareta's horn.

"Hey!" he yelped, jumping back. He hadn't expected her to be there. He straightened up quickly and fetched his head a painful thump on the ceiling of the wagon.

Kareta shook her head violently. A unicorn's face couldn't have much expression, but Harrier just knew she was trying—and not very hard—not to laugh.

"If I'd known that humans could be this much fun, I would have gotten one a long time ago," she said unsteadily.

Harrier glared at her until she backed up. He came down the steps, ducking carefully.

"You forgot your Books," Kareta said. She sounded just

like one of Tiercel's sisters when she was pretending to be helpful but actually trying to get him into trouble.

"They're fine where they are," he said. He walked around the side of the wagon.

Tiercel and Ancaladar were waiting for him. A dragon's face was even less capable of showing expression than a unicorn's, but somehow Harrier never had any trouble telling what Ancaladar was thinking. Right now, Ancaladar was waiting to see what would happen. Harrier supposed that when you got to be as old as Ancaladar was, you developed patience.

He didn't know precisely how old the great black dragon was, and he doubted that Tiercel did either. He knew that Ancaladar was at least a thousand years old, because he wasn't just *any* black dragon named Ancaladar, he was *the* Ancaladar: Ancaladar Star-Crowned, who had fought against the Endarkened. But Ancaladar had said once that he'd seen the start of the war that had come before that one, and Tiercel said that war had been a thousand years before the Great Flowering, so Ancaladar was . . . older than anything Harrier could easily imagine. Older, even, than Armethalieh, and Harrier had grown up knowing that he lived in the oldest and most famous of the Nine Cities.

He walked over and sat down, using Ancaladar's shoulder for a backrest. Ancaladar might be an ancient creature of magic, but in the short time he'd known him, Ancaladar had also become Harrier's friend. He glanced over at Tiercel, who still had the vague look on his face that meant he wasn't paying attention to anything in particular. Harrier stretched out a hand and snapped his fingers in front of Tiercel's face.

Tiercel jumped, and his eyes focused. He looked around for Kareta (who was standing facing them, and if she'd been human Harrier was pretty sure she'd have her arms folded over her chest and be tapping her foot) and then looked at Harrier.

"You're going to be a Wildmage," he said in tones of disbelief.

"A Knight-Mage," Kareta said. "And he can still refuse, you know. People *have* refused to become Wildmages."

Harrier wondered how she knew.

"But this is different," Tiercel said slowly. "A Knight-Mage isn't just any ordinary Wildmage. They're special. They do things no ordinary Wildmage can do. Wildmages keep the Great Balance, and do the work of the Wild Magic, but Knight-Mages . . . make things happen."

"Will you stop talking about this as if it were something interesting that didn't really matter?" Harrier demanded. "This is me! And I *can't* be a Knight-Mage!"

"Why not?" Ancaladar asked, before either Kareta could argue or Tiercel could ask the same question.

"Well," Harrier said slowly, "Knight-Mages have to be able to fight, don't they? That's why they're called *Knight*-Mages. And I don't know anything about fighting."

But Roneida—the Wildmage that they'd met on the Great Plains, the one who had told them to go to the Elves—had given him a sword. She'd brought gifts for all of them, but she'd brought only Harrier a sword. He wondered if she'd known, all that time ago, if this might happen.

"Foo! That's simple!" Kareta said. "Cast a spell and summon yourself up a teacher! The Mageprice shouldn't be too great for that!"

Harrier did his best not to recoil in horror. *Cast a spell?* Okay, that's what Wildmages *did* (and there must be *some* kind of directions on how to do it in the Three Books), but . . . he still hadn't agreed to any of this.

And that wasn't the only problem he had with becoming a Knight-Mage.

This morning, he'd known what his place in the scheme of things was. Take care of Tiercel. Take care of Ancaladar, too (as much as he needed taking care of). How was he supposed to do that if *he* had magical things to do too? He was thinking back to all the stories he'd ever heard about Kellen the Poor Orphan Boy—Kellen who'd had his own unicorn (and Shalkan had probably been much nicer than Kareta was, Harrier thought darkly); Kellen who'd been the greatest warrior—human or Elven—the world had ever seen; Kellen who had slain hordes of monsters with an Elven-forged sword that only he could wield; Kellen who'd gathered together a great army and led it against the Endarkened.

If anybody's safety depended on Harrier's ability to do anything even remotely like any of those things, the world was doomed.

"WELL, HE DOESN'T have to do that right this minute, does he?" Tiercel asked hesitantly.

The golden unicorn was the most beautiful thing he'd ever seen—well, next to Ancaladar, of course—and that made it slightly hard to concentrate while he was staring at her. But she did seem just a little bit . . . pushy.

And he'd gotten a good look at Harrier's face as he'd stomped off into the wagon to change clothes. He'd known Harrier almost all their lives, and that was quite long enough for Tiercel to know when Harrier was scared to death about something and would rather die than admit it. And Tiercel knew how Harrier felt about *him* having magic. He'd barely gotten used to the idea in half a year, and it still made *him* nervous.

"Of course not!" Kareta said sarcastically, tossing her head. "He can just stand around and *dither*—even though he's the first Knight-Mage chosen by the Wild Magic since the time of Kellen Tavadon!"

Harrier sighed. "Well, can't it just choose someone else?" he asked hopefully. He sighed again, more deeply. "Only . . . I don't know of *anyone* who's ever refused the Three Books. Do *you*?"

He stared firmly at Kareta, so Tiercel did too. He wasn't sure what made him think so, but Tiercel almost got the feeling she looked . . . embarrassed. Finally she looked away.

"Not . . . forever," she finally admitted.

"Well, there you are," Harrier said gloomily. He looked

at Tiercel. "We both know—the Light teaches—that the Wild Magic never gives you a gift if you aren't going to really need it. Which is why you've got that High Mage magick. But there were High Mages a lot more recently than there were Knight-Mages, weren't there?"

According to everything Tiercel had read back in Karahelanderialigor, High Magick had just sort of . . . died out slowly in the centuries following the Great Flowering. He'd told Harrier that, of course, but he hadn't thought his friend had been listening.

"I told you! You're the first one chosen since Kellen! You should be pleased!" Kareta said brightly.

"Yeah," Harrier said, sounding anything but. "Okay. Fine. But I'm not going to go around casting a bunch of spells just because you think I ought to. And I might change my mind. But . . . come on. We should probably get a move on. We've wasted enough of the day already."

He got to his feet and walked over to where the horses were waiting, hitched on a loose rope to the side of the wagon. He began harnessing them for the day's journey. In Harrier's mind, obviously, the discussion was over.

BUT TIERCEL KNEW that even if his friend didn't want to talk about it anymore, the matter was far from settled, and for that reason, Tiercel continued to brood about the morning's strange turn of events, even after they'd finally started down the road at last.

The world was a strange and beautiful place as seen from the back of a dragon. Tiercel had always been terrified of heights—even climbing a ladder would make him nervous, and as for climbing into a ship's rigging (something Harrier had often urged him to do, back in the days when, as children, they'd been able to amuse themselves by running around the Port of Armethalieh, not *quite* getting into trouble), well, that was something he'd found completely impossible. So logically, riding on the back of a dragon, hundreds of feet higher than the tallest ship or the tallest tower in Armethalieh, should have terrified him.

But it didn't.

He could feel Ancaladar's amusement through the Bond that they shared. Ancaladar could always tell what he was thinking, though he'd said (quite matter-of-factly) that Tiercel wouldn't live long enough for the opposite to ever become true. It was one more reminder that from Ancaladar's point of view, their relationship, even though it would last the rest of Tiercel's life, would be a brief one. And it would end in Ancaladar's death, for both halves of a Bonding died at the same moment. Without the Great Spell cast by Sandalon Elvenking, Ancaladar would be dead now.

"Do not think of such things, Tiercel," Ancaladar said aloud. "It is the nature of the Great Bargain struck on behalf of my kind by Tannetarie the White with Great Queen Vieliessar Farcarinon in the morning of the world. I do not regret the opportunity to know you. And you are more worried about another matter, I think, than this one, which is something we have discussed before," he added reprovingly.

"Harrier," Tiercel said, and Ancaladar snorted in understanding.

Tiercel glanced over Ancaladar's shoulder, down at the ground below. The road they were following was a pale tracery against the green of the landscape around. Through the trees, Tiercel could see the sparkle of the stream; the road paralleled it. In the distance, he could see a plume of smoke rising into the sky; Ancaladar said it was another Elven settlement—a farm—and that they should reach it tomorrow or the next day.

Almost directly below them (Ancaladar flew in great sweeping circles in order to pace himself to the wagon's slower rate of travel) Tiercel could see the wagon that contained all of his and Harrier's possessions, and, moving along beside it, the golden spark that must be Kareta. Harrier had done his best to convince her to *go away,* since she'd already delivered the Three Books, and Kareta had insisted (she was just as stubborn as Harrier was, Tiercel thought) that he was much too entertaining to leave behind just yet. So now they were traveling with a unicorn as well as with a dragon. He wondered how long that would go on. Did all Knight-Mages have unicorns? It wasn't really as if there were anyone he could ask. Ancaladar had been alive in a world filled with both Knight-Mages and unicorns—during the Great War—but he'd spent that war in hiding in order to keep from Bonding. Because in the Great War, dragons and their Bonded had died—quickly—in the fight against the Endarkened.

"And those who were not Bonded died as well," Ancaladar said. Even after two thousand years, his voice still held sadness. "I should have stayed to fight instead of hiding."

"If you had, you wouldn't have been there when Jermayan needed you," Tiercel said. It felt so strange to be talking about ancient legends as if they were ordinary people—and Elves—but of course they had been once.

"They were always ordinary people," Ancaladar admonished, changing the subject. "It is you who have made them into legends and wondertale heroes. Kellen was much like Harrier. At the beginning and at the end."

"What?" Tiercel said. "He refused to become a Knight-Mage? Or do magick?"

"He doubted his ability to be what the Wild Magic wished him to be," Ancaladar said simply.

But Tiercel knew that there was much more behind Harrier's reluctance than just doubt in his own abilities and distrust of magic. He knew that Harrier had "decided" that his purpose was to take care of everything in the way of day-to-day chores—and everything else he could manage to do—so that Tiercel "only" had to worry about turning himself into a High Mage.

And that was another part of the problem.

Tiercel knew he couldn't do that. Yes, he had Ancaladar, he had the Magegift, but what he didn't have was *time:* the decades to spend in study and meditation to make himself into someone who completely understood the complicated system of the High Magick; someone who not only had committed hundreds of spells to memory, but all the complicated details of how and when and *why* to cast each one.

Harrier didn't know this, of course, but Tiercel was pretty sure that he sensed it at some level, and that was why (Tiercel knew) Harrier hadn't argued longer or louder or harder against becoming a Knight-Mage. He wanted to be able to help Tiercel, and protect him, too. And because of that, Harrier was going to take on something he didn't want, and didn't feel ready for, and still try to do everything else as well.

Tiercel didn't have the faintest idea of what you needed to do to become a Knight-Mage, but what he *did* know was that Kellen the Poor Orphan Boy hadn't been trying to take care of a bunch of other people while he did it. He'd had a bunch of other people taking care of *him*.

Which is exactly what we need, and don't have, Tiercel thought with an exasperated huff. *An army.*

He knew Ancaladar could hear him, but the great black dragon said nothing at all.

Two

A Journey into Legend

THE MADIRAN DESERT stretched across the lands far to the south of the Nine Cities. Upon its border—deep within the lands that those in the Cold North would already name as "desert"—were the *Iteru*-cities, the walled Border Cities where most of those people who called the desert "home" lived. In the language of the South, *"iteru"* meant "well," for here in the south, one might live a round handful of years without ever seeing rain fall upon the land, and the *Iteru*-cities could only exist in places where wells had been sunk deep into the living rock to provide the ample amount of water that so many people living so close together required.

Yet the *Iteru*-cities did not hold all the desert's inhabitants. Further south, the Madiran turned to a trackless landscape of erg and dune-sea, a place known as the Isvai Quarter, a harsh and trackless sea of sand. To the people of the Isvai, the *Iteru*-cities and the land immediately around them seemed lush and water-fat paradises, for in the Isvai Quarter, the only sources of water were tiny desert wells and a few—a very few—oases. These sources of water were not only few and far between, but they might go dry at any moment. Not only skill, but luck was needed to survive in the Isvai, and both skill and luck were bound up in the Isvaieni's relationship to kin—not only the members of their own tribes, but to all the tribes that called the Isvai "home." For the first lesson any child of the Isvaieni learned was that there was no charity given or received between Sand and Star, for the lives the tribes led were too harsh and uncertain to allow them to expend food or water or shelter on any who did nothing to earn those things. But if there was no charity tendered upon the sands of the Isvai, then—equally—no person who lived between Sand and Star did anything to make another's burden harder.

Or so it had been once.

Now tribe was set against tribe, something that had never been so in all the days of the Isvaieni. And—worse, because somehow more unthinkable—the nightmare of *war* had come to the sands of the Isvai, and there had been no war anywhere in the world, from the Great Heat to the Great Cold, since the time of the Great Flowering, in that centuries-ago time when the army of the Light had smashed and sundered all the forces of Darkness—so the world had thought then—forever.

Shaiara, leader of the Nalzindar Isvaieni, knew otherwise, and she thanked the Gods of the Wild Magic for the forewarning she had been given. If she had not gone to Sapthiruk Oasis less than a moonturn ago upon what should have been a simple trading mission, she would never have seen something she had never imagined could exist: the tribes gathered out-of-season at the behest of the most powerful Wildmage to have been born among the Isvaieni in uncounted generations—Bisochim Bluerobe, who had been born to the tents of the Adanate Isvaieni, though he had left them long ago. The elders of many of the largest tribes had gathered at Sapthiruk Oasis to hear him speak, and that itself was odd, for the blue-robed Wildmages of the Isvai did not use the power that the Gods of the Wild Magic had given them to take for themselves a place of authority among the Isvaieni. Alone of all the desert peoples they claimed no tribe, wandering where the Wild Magic sent them, using its power for the good of all.

But when she heard him speak, Shaiara knew that Bisochim had stepped beyond the bounds set for all those who took up the Three Books and their teachings, for Bisochim spoke of the Balance being out of true; of armies coming down out of the Great Cold to destroy the Isvaieni. He named the Isvaieni as the last peoples who kept the True Balance, and said that only through Bisochim could they—and the Light—be saved.

At first Shaiara had thought that all who listened must know Bisochim's words for the dangerous madness that they were, for Shaiara knew the men gathered at Sapthiruk, knew them for cautious, prudent, sensible elders who had guided their tribes across the desert sands for many turns of the year. But to her horror, the tribal leaders into whose ears Bisochim spoke his tainted words merely nodded and smiled as if what they heard Bisochim speak were words of sweetest reason and sense.

And in that moment Shaiara knew that the greatest horror that anyone who lived between Sand and Star—who lived in all the *world*—could imagine had come to pass.

Bisochim was Shadow-touched.

She had not waited to hear the full details of Bisochim's purpose that day, lest she fall beneath the same spell that she had sensed Bisochim wove with unclean magic over the minds of the other Isvaieni. The Nalzindar Isvaieni had always walked a path apart from the other tribes, keeping no flocks or herds, living entirely by hunting, constantly upon the move over the face of the Isvai. For that reason, when the tribes were numbered, the Nalzindar were often counted as the last and the least.

And that, Shaiara hoped, would save them now. It was clear to her from what she had heard that Bisochim intended to gather up all the tribes—*"I have prepared a place for you, where we all may go, to await the day when we may scour them from the desert sands as the Sandwind scours"*—he had said, and certainly any who refused to accede to his madness and fall in with his plans would be counted among his enemies. The Nalzindar could not stand alone against his purpose; Shaiara's hope was merely to preserve her people, taking them into hiding before Bisochim and the rest of the Isvaieni thought to seek them out.

But where?

As she had ridden from Sapthiruk back to the tents of the Nalzindar, she had known this was a decision she must make immediately. Her people must be away and on the move at once. Every moment not spent in flight was a moment that could be woven into a snare to trap them, and the Nalzindar valued their freedom nearly as much as they revered the Balance.

For that reason, it did not even occur to Shaiara to seek refuge for her people in the *Iteru*-cities. The Thanduli and the Hinturi and the Aduzza and the Khulbana and half-a-dozen of the other tribes of the Isvai might go to the edge of the Madiran, to Radnatucca Oasis or even into one of the *Iteru*-cities themselves to trade their wares for that which the desert could not provide. The Nalzindar did not. And if Bisochim were naming all but the Isvaieni his enemy, surely the city-dwellers would be first among them.

Yet to remain openly upon the face of the Isvai was something the Nalzindar dared not do. Bisochim would count their absence as rebellion, and hunt them down.

Then inspiration came to her—perhaps a true gift of the Gods of the Wild Magic. She knew one place that no one would seek her or her people, for though all the Isvaieni knew its name, none but the Nalzindar believed that it was real.

THEIR TENTS WERE struck within hours, every trace of their presence here erased. That was the job of the youngest children; a child of the Nalzindar barely old enough to walk was still old enough to drag around a brush of desert grass to sweep the sand smooth, to pick up any of the droppings of the *shotors* that others had overlooked and carry them to the storage baskets. They did not do this only because now they feared pursuit; the Nalzindar had always moved through the world as if they were the wind upon the sand, taking only what they needed to survive and leaving no trace behind. Now this custom would serve them well.

Shaiara had not yet said where she was leading them; not even to Kamar, brother of her father, had she confided their destination. Her people loved her, and trusted her absolutely—in the bare handspan of years since her father's death, there had been none to dispute that she must guide them in Darak's place, and her decisions had always been wise ones, good for the Nalzindar—but the way to this refuge would be a harder path than any they had ever walked, and she wished to gather the right words in her mind before she spoke to them of it.

Were this any normal journey from one hunting-ground to the next they would have gone first to Sapthiruk for water. Many turns of the seasons ago, at a Gathering of the tribes, Shaiara had heard a tale that the People of the Great Cold thought their *shotors* ungainly and ugly, with their slim curved necks, long slender legs, and short round bodies with their thick humps of stored fat. But a *shotor* was riding beast and pack beast and wool beast and shelter from the Sandwind and sometimes even food; faster than the fastest horse over the shifting sands of the Deep Desert, and once one had drunk its fill, it could go a sennight with ease without drinking again, and longer if food was plentiful. And this was vital, for in the desert, the path between one place and the next was not measured in the straightness as of an arrow's flight, but was a matter of going where the water was, always, until at last one arrived at the place one sought to be.

But now, Sapthiruk was the last place they could possibly go; they must begin their journey without proper preparations. A sennight's passage over the sand would see them at Rutharanda Oasis; a difficult trek, but possible.

The tribe traveled through the rest of the day, and through the night as well. In the desert, few creatures were active in the heat of the day; the life of the Nalzindar tents was conducted at dawn and twilight. They were well-used to sleeping through the heat of the day, and doing the work of the camp, including its packing and moving, by night. Such an extended journey was little hardship to them, for the Nalzindar lived by hunting, taking their prey with spear and arrow and sling-stone and the aid of hawk and *ikulas*-hound. The narrow-headed long-bodied beasts were their greatest ally and tool, wise and clever, and though there was neither mercy nor charity between Sand and Star, many a Nalzindar, in hard times, had given up his or her last drop of water to the four-legged companion who had shared their sleeping mat since puppyhood. Though it would be difficult enough to find water for themselves upon the way they were to walk, no one suggested slaying the *ikulas* and making the journey without them. The *ikulas* were Nalzindar, and while hard choices must always be made with open eyes and open hands, only a fool called the future into his tent.

The children of the tribe too young to walk slept as easily slung from a *shotor*'s pack-saddle as they did on their sleeping-mats in their mother's tents: in fact, they were far more used to the slings and the saddle, for the Nalzindar never lingered long in one place. *Until now,* Shaiara thought grimly. *Now we must go to ground as if we were the* sheshu *pursued by the* fenec, *and pray that* this fenec *is not wily enough to dig us out of our burrow.*

As dawn broke over the sky the little caravan stopped and made the sketchiest of hunter's camps—only one tent erected to shelter them from the fierce light of the sun, and the *shotors* were made to kneel in a circle so that their bodies would shield the light of the small cookfires from the eyes of those who passed. Flour, the small sour desert plums, and dried meat were mixed together with water to make the flatcakes that were the Nalzindar's chief sustenance when the tribe was on the move.

Once the *kaffiyeh* that signaled the end of the meal had twice been brought to a boil and poured out into small clay cups, the children went off to their sleeping mats and the adults of the tribe gathered silently to hear Shaiara's words. Though the Nalzindar were a taciturn people, Shaiara knew that this was, as never before, a time for words.

"You know that I have said I believe Bisochim to be Shadow-touched. He gathers the tribes to him. He speaks of armies coming from the Great Cold to enslave us. This is madness, and I will not give my throat—or yours—to the yoke of madness. Time must burn out this fever. Until it does, I take us to where his sickness cannot reach us. To Abi'Abadshar."

None of the circle of watchers uttered a sound as they absorbed this news, as shocking in its own way as the knowledge that a Wildmage had been Shadow-touched. To most of the Isvaieni the city just-named was no more than an ancient legend; if the desertfolk had believed in ghosts or spirits or things of that nature, they would certainly have believed it was haunted, because those same legends that told of Abi'Abadshar's existence told that it had been built by creatures of the Endarkened countless thousands of years ago for some unknown purpose. Of all the peoples of the Isvai, only the Nalzindar knew that Abi'Abadshar was both legend—and a place as real and mundane as any of the *Iteru*-cities.

At last, after many long moments of silence, Kamar drew breath to speak. "The way to Abi'Abadshar is long," he said.

"It is," Shaiara agreed.

In truth, she was not absolutely certain how long the way was, for she had never been there, nor had her father, nor his father, back through many generations of the Nalzindar. Once, so long ago that the years could not be easily counted, a hunter of her tribe, driven far from Nalzindar tents by the Sandwind, had wandered many days in the Isvai, barely clinging to life, before he had stumbled upon the bones of the ancient city. There he had remained for a moonturn, recovering his strength, before finding his way back to the tribe. Rausi had brought with him the knowledge that Abi'Abadshar was more than myth, and that the way to it was arid and perilous. The rest of the Nalzindar, being a practical people, had seen no reason to go and see for themselves, but had passed Rausi's words carefully down through the generations, hoarded against a time of need.

"I tell you truthfully that all who begin the journey may not end it." Shaiara said nothing more. There was no need to. And when night came again, the *shotors* were saddled and laden, and the Nalzindar continued their flight.

As the Isvai was to the Madiran, so the Barahileth was to the Isvai: hotter, more arid, and even more devoid of life. Though the Nalzindar knew the location of every oasis in the Isvai, they knew of none within the Barahileth. Not even the Nalzindar dared attempt to explore its fastness—it was madness even to try. Water was life, and no one knew of any source of water within the Barahileth.

Save one.

Rausi had spoken of a deep *iteru* of sweet water that lay concealed within the ruins that were all that remained of

Abi'Abadshar. If they could reach it—if it was still there—the Nalzindar would survive.

Though Abi'Abadshar was only on the outskirts of the Barahileth—had it been any deeper within that region, Rausi could not have survived his journey back to the tents of the Nalzindar so many generations before—it was still a fortnight and no one knew how much more beyond the last water to be found upon the course which led to it. At Kannanatha *Iteru,* the last true water to be found before they reached (if they *did* reach) Abi'Abadshar, the Nalzindar first scouted carefully for enemies—and anyone they saw was now their enemy; they could believe nothing else and be safe—and then filled every waterskin they had. The *shotors* drank until they could hold no more, but Shaiara knew that would not be enough—if the refuge she sought for her people could be so easily reached, it would have been discovered long ago. On the next leg of their journey, some would die. She accepted that with desert-bred stoicism and set the thought aside.

The Isvaieni kept few books. Every child learned to read and to write and do sums—for in the desert, an accurate count must be kept of many things—but the only book most of the Isvaieni ever saw was the *Book of the Light,* which contained teaching stories of saints and heroes, and the Nalzindar did not possess even that, for they carried nothing with them on their travels that was not immediately useful. Yet they kept a record of the important events in the life of the tribe, and of the history of all the tribes, woven into songs and stories, and though the Nalzindar were known throughout the Isvai as the Silent People, their store of songs and tales was as large as any other's. Rausi's journey and all that he had learned on it had been woven into one such tale. From it, Shaiara had gleaned the knowledge of the direction in which to lead her people, and generations of Nalzindar ancestry told her what must be done to reach their destination alive. To lead the Nalzindar required much more than right of birth: it required the ability to husband the desert's meager gifts in ways that might seem miraculous to lesser souls. But it would take all that she knew, all that she was, to bring her people to safe haven.

At Kannanatha, Shaiara told her people to abandon all but what they would need to keep them alive and sheltered upon the journey. If Rausi's song was true, both water and shelter awaited them at the end of their journey. If it was not, then it did not matter, for they would never survive the return trip.

All but one of their tents they cut into pieces, leaving the desert winds to carry the strips of dun *shotor*-hair cloth where it chose. The wooden tent-poles they broke into pieces, scattering those that they did not use as fuel that day. Sun and scavengers would render the pieces unrecognizable within a moonturn. Shaiara was ruthless in her winnowing of the tribe's scant possessions—better to destroy more than was necessary here, than to have to abandon it later and leave a trail of detritus that would lead the enemy directly to their hiding place.

Even now it felt wrong to think of her fellow Isvaieni as her enemy, as those her people might have to fight in order to survive. Of course there was conflict between the tribes, even—sometimes—raiding and blood-feuds. But what the Nalzindar faced now was no matter that could be brought before a Council of Elders at the Gathering of the tribes, to be settled there if it was deemed to have gotten out of hand. This was something a thousand times worse: war. And Shaiara wanted no part of it. Better to risk everything on this desperate gamble than to allow her people to fall beneath the influence of the Shadow.

And so, in the hour before sunset, the Nalzindar did all that they could to erase the evidence of their presence from Kannanatha *Iteru,* and Shaiara led her people into the Barahileth.

They had camped two days at Kannanatha, not only to make themselves and their *shotors* as water-fat as they could, but so that Shaiara's hunters and scouts could ride forth a day ahead of the tribe, for this was the last part of her plan to get her people to Abi'Abadshar alive.

Their store of grain and fruit must go to feed the *shotors,* for the hardy animals were being taken far from their usual forage, and though Shaiara did not think that all the beasts would survive the journey, it was important to keep them alive as long as possible. Without those supplies, the tribe must rely entirely upon what it could catch—and game of any kind would certainly be all-but-nonexistent within the inhospitable furnace of the Barahileth.

A more pressing need even than food was water, and while there were no wells, and certainly no oases, on the path ahead, the desert held more sources of water than these, and Shaiara's people knew how to find them all.

The hardest part of the journey began.

As they advanced into the Barahileth, Shaiara's hunters scoured the desert for anything edible in a way that flew in the face of every teaching the Nalzindar held dear, for Shaiara's people not only kept the Balance, they *lived* it. There were no *sheshu* in the Barahileth, for the desert hare made its home in the roots of thornbush and daggerplant, but there were mice, and adders, and scorpions, and all could be eaten if one's hunger were sharp enough, and one knew the secret of preparing them.

Such an insult to the desert's balance would take more than one turn of the seasons to repair, but if Sand and Star was kind, the Nalzindar would never pass this way again, and the desert would have time to heal.

They rationed the water from Kannanatha *Iteru* ruthlessly, eking it out with what their scouts found—sometimes nothing more than a seep that had to be scraped clear of precious moisture and which collected only a few precious sips of water at a time. They spread cloths upon the ground to collect the scant desert dew, and set up little sun-stills to get more water out of their own urine. And when the time came—as Shaiara had known it must—for them to slaughter two of the *shotors* for food, they drank their blood as well.

If her people had not loved and trusted her absolutely,

there would surely have been rebellion long before they drew within a sennight of their destination. It was only upon her word that they were making this terrible journey into the Barahileth at all. Not one of them had seen what she had seen. They had followed her because she had told them they must.

It was the third sennight of their flight—the ninth day since they had entered the Barahileth. Here the heat hammered them mercilessly by day, leaching strength from their limbs, and by night they labored through powder-fine sand that slipped and shifted beneath the *shotors'* broad splayed feet, or trudged across *ishnain* flats where the fine white dust their steps raised burned skin raw and made lips and hands crack and bleed.

No Isvaieni expected to live to make old bones, for the Isvai was a harsh taskmaster, and no tribe could afford to feed and house any who did not contribute to the life of the tribe. If one did not hunt, or cook, or perform some other necessary task, one went from the tents to lay his or her bones upon the sand, for there was no charity given among the Isvaieni—they could not afford it. Only the youngest children were exempt from this law, since soon enough they would grow to take their place among the tribe's workforce. What might seem like cruelty to non-Isvaieni was merely necessity, and all who lived between Sand and Star accepted it from birth. There were no weak, no ancient aged, among the Nalzindar, nor among any of the tribes.

But even so, the Barahileth took its toll of them, as Shaiara had known it must. On the third evening of their journey, as the tent was struck, Katuil came to Shaiara.

Katuil had been a woman grown when Shaiara was but a child. Her daughter Ciniran was Shaiara's closest friend. Katuil had taught Shaiara how to hold a lance and string a bow. Age had caused her to leave the long hunts to the younger Nalzindar, and devote her time to leatherwork and the curing of hides, but she had remained a vibrant presence among them, sharing her wisdom and knowledge.

"I remain here," Katuil said quietly.

Shaiara bowed her head in acceptance, though this was bitter hearing indeed. Katuil nodded and began removing her robes, so that if by some mischance her body should be found, there would be nothing to mark it as Nalzindar. When she was finished, she unbraided her hair until it hung loose and free, and then walked barefoot, away from the others, out into the chill desert night.

On the fifth night of their journey into the Barahileth, Malib fell to his knees and could not rise. His partner Ramac knelt beside him as the long coffle of *shotors* passed slowly by them. When Shaiara walked back to them, Ramac looked up and shook his head. Malib would go no further, and Ramac would remain with him. She waited with them until Ramac had removed his and Malib's clothes and unbraided their hair. Then she bundled the robes in her arms and walked away.

As the second sennight of their journey into the Barahileth began, Shaiara began—quietly—to despair. She would have cut her own throat with her father's *peschak* before she let any of her people suspect her thoughts, but she began to believe that they were meant to die here. She had stopped sending out her advance scouts days ago. There was no longer any water to find, and none of her people had the energy left for hunting. This morning, when they stopped, Shaiara would order two more of the *shotors* slaughtered. Perhaps it would give them the strength to continue a while longer.

The last of the water had been measured out by careful cupfuls this morning. Not enough to slake anyone's thirst. They might survive another day, perhaps two, without water. Then they would die.

The moon rose into the heavens, turning the desert to silver, and automatically Shaiara glanced heavenward. She knew that she was following the directions set out by the *Song of Rausi* precisely: he had set his course by the stars, and so was she. She knew she was retracing his steps correctly. *And if you do not reach Abi'Abadshar before the sun sets again, Shadow will not need to touch the Nalzindar, for there will be no Nalzindar left between Sand and Star.*

But as the moon reached midheaven, the lead *shotor* raised its head, pulling its guide-rope from Shaiara's lax grasp. Its nostrils flared wide, and it began shuffling forward with renewed energy, the exhausted plodding gait of the last several days exchanged for a sudden desire to arrive at its destination quickly.

There was only one thing that could so galvanize a thirsty, exhausted, half-starved *shotor.*

Water.

Shaiara grabbed the guide-rope again and wrapped it firmly around her hand, hauling the *shotor* to a stop and tapping the animal on the knee so that it would kneel to allow her to mount. The other animals smelled the water too, now, jostling and fretting as the Nalzindar coaxed them to their knees. They'd been leading the beasts to spare their strength, using them to carry the hawks and the hounds and the youngest children, but now there was no more need.

Once mounted, the tribe rode in ghostly silence beneath the desert moon. Their few remaining pack-animals, more lightly laden than those bearing riders, raced on ahead. There was no need to lead them—they would go nowhere other than to the nearest water.

The moon had crossed very little more of the sky when Shaiara saw it. From a distance, the black shapes looked like nothing more than wind-worn stone. But there was grass growing around the edges of the stone, and she could see the large pale shapes of Nalzindar *shotors* browsing upon it.

They had reached Abi'Abadshar.

The Nalzindar allowed the *shotors* to lead them to the water. The *Iteru* was the largest Shaiara had ever seen, standing at the center of what was—now—an open courtyard, though surely it must once have been far beneath the ground, for it was reached by descending a long series of shallow terraces carved out of the ground.

The *Iteru* itself was a wonder, for here, in the depths of the Barahileth, it was open to the sky, allowing the wind to steal its moisture as it pleased. Yet the water seemed inexhaustible.

The thirsty *shotors* crowded forward, bleating and jostling in their attempts to get to the water, and the *ikulas*-hounds snarled and quarreled, pushing between them, their narrow bodies gaunt with privation. The Nalzindar shouldered through them, plunging waterskins and cups into the water to fill them, and passing them among the people. All the tribe drank carefully after so many days of privation, but no matter how much water they drew from the *Iteru* of Abi'Abadshar, its level did not drop.

At last, the thirst of all was slaked, and every waterskin was refilled, and the *shotors* were unpacked and unsaddled, hobbled and set to graze. For the first time since she had led her people upon this exodus, Shaiara's spirits rose. Grass meant something to feed upon it, for the Isvai wasted nothing. And there would be things to feed upon the feeders as well. Though she had long suspected that they would be forced to slay all of their *shotor*-herd—not only for meat, but because there would be nothing to feed them upon here in the arid waste—it might be possible to delay that time a little longer. And more than that, now that the way to Abi'Abadshar was known, hunters could return to the Isvai to seek food, so long as they carried enough water for the return journey.

"You have led us to safety, Shaiara," Kamar said.

"That is as Sand and Star will it," she answered absently. There were too many questions that must still be answered before she could know whether Abi'Abadshar represented true safety.

Without sand in which to anchor the tent-poles, it was not possible to erect their one remaining tent here beside the well, but Shaiara did not wish to pitch it upon the sand outside. Better it would be to seek shelter within, but though three archways led off into darkness from the *Iteru*-courtyard, and lamps and a scant bit of oil remained among the packs, Shaiara did not yet wish to risk a light. Light and fire could be seen at too great a distance in the desert. For such explorations as required a lamp to light their way, it would be better to wait until dawn. Meanwhile, she would explore that which could be seen by moonlight, for improbable as it was that any had traced their tracks, it was not impossible.

Once the people were settled into the great stone courtyard surrounding the *Iteru,* Shaiara took several of the most keen-eyed of the young hunters and set out to explore as much of the Nalzindar's new home as she could by night. Two of the *ikulas* followed them, obviously hoping for food, though most of the animals were content simply to lie beside their masters and rest.

Though the moon had passed its zenith, it still shone brightly enough to illuminate the scene sufficiently for a Nalzindar's keen eyes. Pale sand stretched as far as the eye could see, and nearly as far stretched the small outcroppings that were all that remained of what once had been a great city. Shaiara had never seen a city, but she thought that perhaps even those who lived in the *Iteru*-cities would be daunted by the vastness of Abi'Abadshar.

She walked on, watching carefully, her mind uneasy at the sheer strangeness of what she saw. Though the *Song of Rausi* had described all that he had seen and found at Abi'Abadshar, a part of Shaiara had not truly believed, for in all her young life, the largest work of human hands she had ever seen was the campsite of the Gathering of the tribes, when many tents were pitched together at the lushest oasis to be found within the Isvai. When so many Isvaieni were gathered together, it might take from dawn until midday to walk from one edge of the encampment to the other, moving at a pace politeness demanded, but only a few minutes' walk was enough to tell her that Abi'Abadshar was far larger than even such a vast encampment. An entire day—from sunup to sundown—would not be sufficient to take a person from one edge of the ruins to the other, even walking at the brisk pace suitable for journeys.

Here and there the capricious wind had exposed a stretch of flat smooth stone that seemed to be meant for folk to walk upon, though surely it would heat to burning within an hour, perhaps two, after sunrise. Elsewhere, broken cylinders, like the stumps of strange trees, jutted up out of drifts of sand; she could not imagine their purpose. It was not possible to see the true shape of what had once been, far longer ago than even the oldest story-memory of the most learned storyteller stretched, for Time had worn away the stone to the point that even the tallest pieces of what remained barely reached Shaiara's knee. As with the *Iteru*-courtyard, the desert wind had randomly scrubbed the ruins clean in some places—exposing deep pits and more of the strange shallow terraces—and covered them in others, so that in places where Shaiara was certain there must be more fragments of the ancient city, she could see nothing but mounds of soft sand.

As she stopped to peer into the distance, Natha pointed silently at the sand. There, sharp and clear, was the sinuous track of a desert adder, and beside it, a row of faint dots—the track of the mouse which was its prey. Shaiara's spirits lifted slightly. She had not dared to hope for antelope or wild goat here in the Barahileth, but she had feared she was leading her people to a refuge where they would simply starve to death. She was heartened, too, to see that tufts of the wiry desert grass had taken root in many places, kept alive by the moisture carried on the wind from the *Iteru* she had already seen. If Abi'Abadshar were as vast as she began to suspect that it was, there was grazing here to keep the *shotors* alive for moonturns to come.

Soon the *ikulas,* growing bolder and urged by instinct, began to hunt ahead. Shaiara did not call them back. Israf and Ardban were wise dogs, well-seasoned, and she would not begrudge them any prey they might find. Before she, Natha, Kamar, and Ciniran had walked on for much longer than it would take for a pan of *kaffeyah* to come to its first boil, Ardban came loping back toward them, with a small pale shape dangling from his jaws. He dropped it at

Shaiara's feet and looked up at her expectantly. She bent down and picked up the still-warm body of a *sheshu*. With a quick economical motion, she drew her *geschak* and cut off its head, tossing it to the eagerly waiting hound. Entrails, skin, and a hind leg followed, for Ardban had done well to bring the fruit of his hunt to her when his hunger must be as sharp as her own. She tucked the rest of the body into the hunter's pouch at her belt; they still possessed the largest of the cookpots, and both salt and spices. Meager fare this, to share among so many, but she did not wish to slaughter any more of their own stock if it could be avoided. And if the *sheshu* made its home within the ruin of Abi'Abadshar, the Nalzindar would survive here as well.

When the moon had crossed another handspan of the sky, they turned back toward the *Iteru*-courtyard. Such a vastness as this would not be explored all in one night.

WHEN THE SKY at last lightened toward dawn, Shaiara felt safe enough to take a lamp and begin to investigate one of the tunnels; fuel they would have in sufficiency once the well-fed *shotors* began to dung, but she disliked the thought of building a cookfire anywhere it could be seen. The Nalzindar were not unfamiliar with caves, for there were both cliffs and caves in the Isvai—and in the worst of the Sandwinds no other shelter would do—but the idea of a strange sort of cave that men had built was a thing that Shaiara had never thought to see.

The lantern she held in her hands gave only a little light, for she had made the flame as small as possible to conserve its little store of oil. Kamar and Natha accompanied her, for in such a strange place, no one thought it a good idea that anyone should go somewhere alone.

The ground beneath her feet was stone, as flat and smooth as the surface of an oasis pool, just as the ground in the *Iteru*-courtyard had been. Every few steps Shaiara squatted down and rested her palm flat against it, still mistrustful of what her senses told her was so: though the desert wind had covered it with a thin pale dust as soft as the finest flour, beneath that the stone was as chill as dawn-water, and as smooth as a polished *geschak*-blade. The great virtue of the dust was that it disclosed any mark made in it; as she looked behind her, Shaiara's fingers itched for a grass-broom to sweep away the traces of their passage, little need for it though there might be, but ahead of her, the powder held only the faint marks of such desert creatures who would naturally be drawn to water, and no sign of Man.

Though her senses were alert—for not all of those creatures that the desert could hold were as harmless as the timid *sheshu*—Shaiara could not help marveling at what she saw. This was only one tiny part of Abi'Abadshar, yet she believed it must be large enough to hold all of the Isvaieni within it. The path upon which she now walked was wide enough that four *shotors* could be led along it side-by-side, saddled and laden, and each would not jostle the next, and the roof above her was so far away that it was lost in darkness. On either side, the walls rose up as straight as the trunk of a young palm tree, and as smooth and unmarred as the surface of a pool of water when no wind blew. The Nalzindar loved decoration and ornament as much as any of the Isvaieni, trading hides and leatherwork at the Gatherings for bright rugs and colorful woven baskets, and this starkness seemed unnatural to Shaiara. If one made a thing, why not make it beautiful?

After a short time they came to the first break in the smooth walls: an archway, much like the one through which they had come—though smaller—but this one was blocked.

Shaiara handed the lantern to Kamar and stepped forward to run her hands over the barrier curiously. It fitted into the archway exactly, as if it had been made for it.

"It is wood," she said, startled into speech. She ran her hands over its surface again, more carefully, this time marking the places where the pieces had been joined together to make the whole. So few! She tried to imagine such a tree as this might have come from, and failed. But what was its purpose? Metal bands crossed its surface, and there was a large ring, larger than the largest bracelet, in the center of one side. She closed her hands around the metal ring, and tugged at it gingerly, but nothing happened.

There would be time enough later to solve this mystery. She took back the lantern, and the three walked on. They passed more of the blocked archways, but Shaiara did not bother to test them. Time for that later.

They walked until the lamp began to gutter, then returned. Shaiara had learned what she wished to know, and so, when she returned to the *Iteru*-courtyard, she ordered her people to lead the *shotors* down into the dark made-cave, and there to make their cookfire, and take shelter against the heat of the day. Tomorrow they would begin the task of turning Abi'Abadshar into their home.

IT WAS UPON the third day of their residence in Abi'Abad-shar that Shaiara realized that the Gods of the Wild Magic had truly taken the Nalzindar into their care. At evening on the first day, everyone but the children went forth to hunt, and after several hours, they returned with a startling bounty. Not only adders and scorpions and mice, but *sheshu* in abundance—all the more puzzling when Natha said that for every *sheshu* he brought to the cookpot, he let one escape, just as the Balance asked of them. But that night, all the Nalzindar ate well; the *shotors* grazing upon the rich forage that grew among the ruins, and the *ikulas* and falcons and every person of the tribe feasting upon the bounty of the day's hunt.

On the second day, Shaiara and her people went forth as soon as the sun had passed its greatest heat, for they must have light to see by if they were to properly explore their new home. The *ikulas* accompanied them; Shaiara hoped both that the hounds' keen senses might discern what the Nalzindar could not, and also, that they might flush more game, for keeping so many people fed was a constant struggle even in the Isvai, and here in the Barahileth, the task would be far more difficult.

Though no Isvaieni was a stranger to the heat of the desert, the furnace heat of the Barahileth in daylight was nearly too much even for the Nalzindar. If not for the fact that they possessed a copious supply of water, Shaiara would have turned back immediately. Even the *shotors* seemed uncomfortable in the heat; the Nalzindar brought them under cover, into the tunnels, during the heat of the day, of course, but now Shaiara was setting them loose to browse. She did not fear to lose them. No *shotor* would willingly travel far from water.

The people avoided the exposed stone road; as all of them knew from the experience of having to cross the *Iteru*-courtyard to reach the surface that it was far too hot to walk upon, and the sand was very little cooler. In the Isvai, Shaiara would have chosen to investigate by night, but in the Isvai, she would have been able to carry a lantern burning the liquid of the oilbark bush or a lamp whose wick was soaked in thrice-purified animal fat. They had not yet found any oilbark bush, and to gather and purify the amount of fat needed was a long and laborious process when they had cast away so many of their possessions. It would be long before they were once more able to light the few lamps they had retained.

Everyone chose a different path through the city, moving off into the distance in groups of two and four. In the Isvai, the Nalzindar hunted alone. In this strange land, it was as well for every Isvaieni to have assistance close at hand. Shaiara walked beside Ciniran, with Kamar a few steps behind them. Shaiara and Ciniran were age-mates, and they had done everything together from the time each had taken her first hesitant steps upon the twilight sands, sharing small triumphs and quiet sorrow in the way of their people. Ciniran had been bold where Shaiara had been quiet, and before their first hunt, when it had become clear that Shaiara was to be Darak's only child, there had been talk that Ciniran should be named his heir, or her

cousin Hauca. That was the first time Bisochim had come
to the tents of the Nalzindar, and said to them: *Wait. The
Wild Magic will make all things clear in time.*

Only a few years later, Darak had laid his body upon the
sand, and Shaiara had neither expected comfort nor received it. Now Ciniran's mother, Katuil, had chosen to re-
linquish her life upon the journey here, and Ciniran, too,
accepted that with the impassive response that Shaiara expected. Katuil had died as she had wished to, as Darak had
died, as all Nalzindar hoped to die: at a place and time of
her own choosing.

But life between Sand and Star was demanding, and it
did not encourage hope, for to hope was to live in a place
that was not of the here and the now, and the children of the
Isvai must live in the world upon which they set the soles
of their feet, neither in the dreams of the past nor the shadows of the future. Yet the wise hunter searched not only the
ground before his boots, but the horizon as far as his gaze
could reach, and now that—so it seemed—they were to
live, Shaiara's mind was busy with the future, and not just
tomorrow and next season, but such future as the leader of
the tribe must think on. If the Nalzindar were to survive,
there must be husbands and wives for them; Ciniran was of
an age to marry now, and Shaiara already knew that there
was no man of the Nalzindar who pleased her, nor was
Ciniran a one for women, nor yet to live alone all her days.
For one not born to the Nalzindar to come to their ways
was a delicate matter, yet in every generation, at the Gathering of the tribes, a handful of men and women made that
choice. Some left again, in a moonturn or a season or at the
next Gathering. Some became as much Nalzindar as if they
had been born within their tents. But now that Bisochim had
driven the rest of the Isvaieni down the path to madness
with the goad of smooth words, who would there be for any
of them?

At least she need not worry for herself. The Nalzindar
did not require the leadership of the tribe to pass to a child
of her body. Nor did it even need to remain in Darak's line

if another were more competent: in each generation, leadership of the Nalzindar went to the one best suited to rule, not the one born to it, though often those two things marched together. In any event, the child who would lead the Nalzindar in the next generation was known early, by his or her ways, and taken into the chief's tent to learn all those things that could only be learned by watching the leader of the Nalzindar lead the people. Shaiara's heir might not yet have been born, or still lie in swaddling clothes, or just be learning to walk. She did not need to concern herself with the matter of finding and choosing a mate. She did not think one existed for her anywhere between Sand and Star.

And that, she told herself with a small inward smile, *is so much the least of all your problems that you could number them all until the days grew long and short again and not reach that one!*

When the sun had moved two handspans more across the sky, a thing Shaiara had not imagined to be possible—in this whole moonturn of unimaginable events—occurred. Israf and Ardban, who had so far been content to pad along at her side, suddenly raised their narrow heads, quivering all over, and dashed off. A moment later she saw something—a *large* something—scurry over the top of a dune, pursued by the hounds, and a moment after that, she heard the single sharp bark the *ikulas* gave when they had taken down prey. Despite her concern, neither Shaiara nor her companions ran to see what it was. One did not run in desert heat unless life was at stake.

A few moments later they reached the *ikulas*'s side. The animals stood proudly, plumed tails slowly wagging, over the body of a fat young desert goat.

Ciniran knelt beside the carcass, running her hands over its flanks in wonder. She turned her face up to Shaiara, and Shaiara knew that the expression of grave concern on Ciniran's face matched her own.

The Nalzindar did not keep goats. Goats required water—much water—and good forage. Not so much as a sheep, but far more than a *shotor*. Certainly more than any of them had seen anywhere here in Abi'Abadshar. Nor could it have simply wandered here—the journey had been nearly enough to kill a *shotor*. A goat could not have survived.

She put her hand on Israf's collar. "Seek," she said, gesturing back in the way the goat had come. The two *ikulas* began moving in circles, searching out the trail. Shaiara walked after them, and Ciniran followed, as behind them, Kamar gathered up their unexpected prey.

But the trail ended only in another mystery: one of the empty openings in the ground, with terraces leading down into it. This one was small, and made of black stone, and heat radiated up from it as from the embers of a cookfire. Even though this was obviously where the path ended, the *ikulas* did not wish to go down, and Shaiara saw no reason to make them, for all that was there was smooth stone, and a small hole low in one wall that only a child could crawl through.

Or a goat.

With that thought in her mind, Shaiara redoubled her efforts to explore the caves-made-by-Demons in which the Nalzindar now lived. Goats must come from somewhere, after all. And if she shared this place with others, she wished to know about it.

THE GREASE FROM the flesh of the fat goat, carefully collected, could be used to saturate strips of fabric carefully cut from the edges of the remaining tent. Tightly braided, and forced over the head of a hunting-spear, the grease-soaked cloth made a crude if serviceable torch. Armed with a handful of these, Shaiara and several of the bravest hunters redoubled their explorations. This time they brought with them axes and hammers as well, for she was determined that the barriers of wood that blocked the archways to the sides of the tunnel would block it no longer.

Her people quickly learned the best method of releasing the barriers, especially once they discovered that they were hinged, like the lid of a wooden box. A few blows with an axe at the edge where the large metal ring was, and nearly all of them could be swung inward. Those that could not be, they left untouched, for Shaiara suspected that beyond those doors lay enough piled sand to bury them all, should those barriers be removed from their stone archways.

They had removed the first of the barriers entirely— before they had known about the hinge-mechanism—and when they had, beyond it all that there was to see was another tunnel, and at its end, sunlight. She had walked down that tunnel to its end, and seen more wooden barriers, drifts of sand and dust upon the floor, and then, at its end, a great round emptiness. She'd shrugged, turning back. It might well be the work of more than one lifetime to learn all of Abi'Abadshar's secrets.

The deeper they went into the tunnel, the colder it became, until it was as cold as a desert midnight, and Shaiara shivered, wishing for her warm cloak. They had been walking since dawn, and had come so far that now, when she looked back, Shaiara could no longer see the light of the entrance. None of them feared to make the return journey in darkness—should their explorations take as long as that—for the way was straight and smooth, and ears and noses could guide a hunter when eyes could not. And Israf and Ardban would sense far more than even the sharpest-honed senses of the Nalzindar, though, like any sight-hunter, the *ikulas* preferred the light to the dark.

Shaiara shivered once again in the cold, then sniffed at the air suspiciously and frowned, glancing at Kamar. He stepped to the nearest wall and ran his fingers over the stone, running the pads of his fingers together, and there did not need to be words between them for Shaiara to know what he had found. The stone was wet.

Was there another *Iteru* here within the tunnels? Shaiara had once visited a spring deep within a cave, and the air had been wet in just this way. But for the first time since they had begun exploring the tunnels, Israf and Ardban seemed eager to forge ahead instead of wishing to remain close at the heels of the five Nalzindar, and Abyaz and Zirah, barely out of puppyhood, were now straining at their leashes.

"Go," Shaiara said quietly, and with a bound, the two *ikulas* leaped ahead into the dark.

A few moments later, Shaiara could hear stuttering high-pitched yips echoing back over the stone. She nodded, and Kamar unleashed the two younger *ikulas*. They bounded eagerly after their elders. Holding her torch high, Shaiara led her band of hunters after them at a swift ground-eating lope.

They had barely covered more distance than might be compassed in three arrow-flights before strangeness abounded everywhere. The walls were no longer smooth, but covered with a web of root and vine, nor was the floor beneath their feet smooth stone either. It held a thickness of sand—far thicker than what they had found earlier in the tunnel—and not sand alone. Sand so mixed with water that it was as moist as uncooked griddle-bread, and so filled with the wet scent of plants that it was as if Shaiara stood in the middle of Sapthiruk holding a basketweight of figs and desert plums in the folds of her robes. All along the tunnel, where the floor met the walls, there were strange soft growths the color of the palest leather.

When they reached the place where the *ikulas* eagerly awaited them, Shaiara saw that more of the strange pale things covered the wooden barrier. The water in the air had rotted it, as sunlight rotted cloth, for the *ikulas*'s sharp nails had dug away deep curls from the wood where they had attempted to dig beneath the barrier. A click of her tongue summoned the hounds back to sit at her heel, and when Shaiara put her hand to the metal ring—reaching carefully among the growths—it came away in her hand, leaving her fingers covered with sharp black flakes and a thick coating of red. She dropped it, and the ring struck the sand with a dull sound. Cautiously, she pressed at the barrier. It scraped inward a double handspan, then stuck.

But no dangerous cascade of dry sand billowed out through the opening, and the *ikulas* were all but dancing with impatience to see what lay beyond. She passed the torch to Ciniran and set her shoulder to the door. Kamar and Natha joined her, and soon the barrier had been shifted enough that Shaiara could slip through. The four *ikulas* followed her immediately, and dashed off into the gloom.

For it *was* only twilight here beyond the barrier, and not true darkness. She paused to help the others force the barrier the rest of the way inward—kneeling down to dig away the thick mast of spongy sand-and-plant matter that covered the stone so that the barrier could move freely. Kamar doused the torch by rubbing it out against the inside of the barrier, and the five Nalzindar walked cautiously forward.

Only in the wildest tales exchanged around cookfires at the Gatherings of the tribes had she heard of anything remotely like this place, and those were of the "orchards" and "gardens" kept by the dwellers in the *Iteru*-cities. Here—impossibly—there was a whole garden beneath the earth.

They walked among trees the like of which Shaiara had never seen. She caught the familiar scent of figs, the less-familiar—but still-recognizable—scent of *naranjes*. Beneath the trees there were enormous bushes, but in contrast to the tiny gray-green leaves of the desert plants Shaiara was familiar with, the leaves of these were enormous and brightly colored, and between the leaves, their twigs were heavy with clusters of unfamiliar fruit. The very ground itself was covered with plants—a thick lush grass as shockingly green as if someone had spilled an entire vat of dye here. She stooped down and ran her hand over it. The blades were soft as fur.

In the distance, Shaiara could see bars of strong sunlight filtering down from somewhere above, though when she gazed upward, most of her view was blocked by branches and leaves. Through the few gaps between them, she saw the blackness of stone, and gained the sense of great space. As they walked—Kamar a little ahead, Ciniran beside her, and Natha and Turan following warily behind—she heard the sound of scuffling through the debris on the forest floor, and no matter how unfamiliar her surroundings, Shaiara was a hunter first. She recognized the sounds of small animals—mice, *sheshu,* perhaps others as strange as the trees and the bushes—fleeing from the approach of something large and unknown. Though it was difficult to see clearly here—the sight-lines were so oddly cluttered, unlike the familiar desert, and it was not possible to see clearly for even so much distance as would be covered by two tents of the Nalzindar—the farther they came, the more certain Shaiara became that this space was vast, larger than the largest oasis she had ever visited. Nor was the terrain beneath her feet level. It sloped downward as she walked, so gently that it was a handful of heartbeats before Shaiara realized that she walked along the side of a hill.

Even though her people had only begun to explore Abi'Abadshar, Shaiara doubted they would have discovered this hidden world from above no matter how long they searched through the sand and the ruins. She could now see that much of the ceiling above was intact, and the places where the sunlight filtered down were often tiny. Seen from above, it would be easy to dismiss them.

"There is much to hunt here," Turan said. He peered up into one of the strange trees. A small black-furred creature peered back, then grabbed a fruit from a branch and flung it at him. Turan caught it and sniffed at it suspiciously, tucking it into his hunting bag as Shaiara watched. She shared his suspicion. In a strange land, who knew what might be safe to eat?

She raised her hand, stilling Turan's chatter. She had not heard—or seen—the *ikulas* in too long. In the desert they were trained to run down prey and either kill it outright or hold it at bay until the hunter could come—in either event, to stay with what they coursed. She did not think that was prudent here, and so from beneath her robes Shaiara drew forth a small whistle carved of antelope bone. Any hunter who might need to call their hounds to heel wore one such; the sound it made could be heard by few Isvaieni and by all *ikulas*. And it carried over a great distance.

She put it to her lips and blew—Ciniran winced—and a few moments later, the four *ikulas* came bounding back through the trees. All four were filthy and blood-matted, and the Nalzindar quickly ran their hands over the animals' bodies, but the blood was not theirs.

It took nearly (so Shaiara judged) as much time to reach the place where the *ikulas* had been as it would have taken the sun to cross two handspans of the sky, for they moved carefully, and would not let the hounds run ahead. But when they reached it, Shaiara was certain at last that the Nalzindar had found not only a refuge, but a true home.

The bodies of six goats lay upon the grass, each one killed with the single efficient killing bite of an *ikulas*. The surrounding area was deserted, but it was plain to all that until the hounds had arrived, a great herd of goats had grazed placidly here, for the ground was thick with tracks and droppings.

Shaiara breathed a prayer of thanks to the Gods of the Wild Magic. Here was more than food. Here was *wealth*. Goat-hair to weave cloth—though her people were not weavers, there were one or two of them, born to other tents, who yet knew the skill. Food for more than a moonturn, more than a season, and every kind of plant and herb they could possibly need. Their only conceivable lack was salt, but the Barahileth was known for its deadly wastes where salt replaced sand, and even that, the Nalzindar could supply to themselves.

"Come," she said. "It is time to return."

Three

The World Beneath the World

BEFORE ANOTHER MOON had waxed and waned in the sky above, the Nalzindar had taken full possession of their strange new home. No longer did the *shotors* graze among the ruins above, for there was more-than-abundant forage here below. Now day upon day might pass without anyone venturing up to the sands of the surface, for all that anyone might need was here in the world below.

The long tunnel down which Shaiara and her people had ventured in their first days here at Abi'Abadshar was only the merest fingernail's-breadth of the city's subterranean realm. As her hunters had tracked the herd of goats, they had been led through a maze of passages that intertwined like the strands of a hunter's net. Some passages led to other open spaces such as the first one they had found, vast underground chambers that teemed with a shocking concentration of life. These underground gardens were filled with trees and grass and vines and bushes; with animals such as no one in the desert had ever seen, such as the large fat fluffy-tailed tree-climbing mouse and the chattering black-furred manlike creature the size of a young *ikulas* puppy. There were other animals here such as belonged in the *Iteru*-cities: the shaggy red-coated swine, the goats, the bright-plumaged birds larger than the largest and plumpest rock-dove. Doves there were as well, and bright tiny birds such as no Nalzindar had ever imagined could exist.

At first the hunting falcons were confused by this new place, a place that had no sky. But the Nalzindar trained their creatures well, and soon both falcons and *ikulas* were bringing down game in abundance. The Nalzindar tested each new beast cautiously before adding it to their menu, and the plants and fruits even more cautiously: what a goat or a *shotor* could safely eat might kill a man.

With the slaughter of fat goats, and swine, and fur-mice, and great-doves, there was fat for the lamps and wool to twist into wicks, and between the lamps and the creation of more and better torches—for the Nalzindar used the bounty of their new home to replace much that they had been forced to leave behind, weaving baskets and mats from twigs and vines and grasses, and harvesting wood to carve into bowls and cups in addition to creating new sources of light—the exploration of even those places which the sun did not reach continued. Beyond the refuge of the gardens, they found chambers where dry sand had drifted in through holes they could not find, and other places where great stone cylinders had fallen, and broken, and blocked further exploration. Seeing these, Shaiara was grateful that so much of this underground world seemed to have been carved from one piece of stone, much as an artisan might carve an object from a single bone. In any place they came to that was built from one stone set upon another, those stones had shifted and fallen.

Shaiara had moved the tribe down to live in the first of the garden-places they had discovered. Kamar had suggested, in the first handful of days after they had come to dwell here, that watchers should be set at the bounds of the city to warn them of discovery. Shaiara had held his words against her heart, then taken them to the tribal elders, speaking against them with a combination of fatalism and practicality. Upon the surface, sentries could be seen as well as see. In day, they would be punished by the fierce heat of the sun; in true night, there would be little to see.

But no hunter would go upon the hunt with only one bowstring for his bow, and the Nalzindar were master hunters. Shaiara was unhappy with the thought that there was only one entrance and exit from their underground home, and set her hunters to the task of finding others. Though her hunters found that there were many openings to the light and air on this level, most of them could only be entered and departed by birds, and the rest would only permit one person to climb out at a time, and that after scaling several feet of wall. If disaster struck, it was possible that all of the tribe could win its way to freedom through the many escape routes of this sort they had discovered in the time they had been living here, but they would have to abandon all of the *shotors* and all their supplies—and to do that would be to condemn themselves to a lingering death instead of courting a quick one. For that reason, each day Shaiara set a few of the hunters to searching out ways to the surface that the whole tribe at once might be able to use, ways that would allow them to take the *shotors* as well. Once such were found—and better more than one—then supplies could be stockpiled at each exit, and the exits carefully hidden again, and Shaiara would simply hope it was never necessary to use them.

But so far, their searches had been inconclusive. Though they had found what seemed as if they must be many upward-leading openings with terraces, all were choked with sand. Even if they could dig them out, there was no place to put the sand, and to shift it at all was to risk burying themselves.

And there was the hard truth that must be grasped in the hand as well: if this refuge were discovered by their enemies, there was simply no place for the Nalzindar to flee. While it was good to seek ways to escape, it was better still to follow the way of the *sheshu* as it evaded *pahk* and *fenec,* and trust that the Wild Magic that had brought them here would spread its cloak over them. Sentries at the mouth of the tunnel, yes, and at any other entrance they might find, for one did not grow to adulthood in the Isvai by having sand for wits. But for the rest, they would play the *sheshu* in its burrow.

And it was a more luxurious burrow than any of the Nalzindar had ever dreamed might exist. Here beneath the ground, the ground was soft and the air was warm, and there was arrow-cast upon arrow-cast of space. The first day's explorations had led them to the *Iteru* at which the creatures of this place slaked their thirsts, and there was not even any need to return to the *Iteru*-courtyard that was exposed to the heat and the sun in order to fill their water-skins. Only a few of the people hunted now, always careful, always watching to be sure that their presence did not upset the Balance of this strange and wonderful place, for it would bring sadness to all the Nalzindar were they to destroy the world beneath Abi'Abadshar, even if they did it to ensure their own survival.

Surrounded by so much bounty, there was more freedom for the Nalzindar than ever before, and in their new-found freedom, many Nalzindar followed terraced paths ever deeper beneath the earth, and there the explorers discovered the first traces of those who had been in this place before.

THEY HAD ERECTED their single remaining tent within an open space upon the flatness beneath the trees. The ground, so they had discovered in the few sennights of their occupancy, was unpleasantly damp, and it was Natha who had come up with the idea of bringing dry sand from one of the other chambers to lay beneath the skins and the sleeping-mats. Between the new woven mats and the sand, a growing carpet of well-tanned hides provided a further barrier to the damp ground—Shaiara had never imagined in all her life that there could be so much water in the world.

She sat cross-legged upon the ground, a flat piece of stone upon her knees, skinning and gutting a fur-mouse for the pot. Half-a-dozen more lay in a nearby basket awaiting her attention, and several *ikulas* lolled nearby, waiting to be thrown scraps. Marap had found a tree whose nuts looked very much like the ones for which the Nalzindar had once traded. Boiled, they made a bitter black brew, but combined with *shotor*-urine, they could render a scraped hide as soft as cloth, and the Nalzindar had used this liquid to cure those skins which they did not wish simply to peg out to dry in the sun. Marap said that adding salt to the liquid would make the hides even softer, but Shaiara was not yet ready to risk a journey to the salt-flats. Let the evil that Bisochim brewed within his heart distill itself yet further before any Nalzindar risked the open desert again. Perhaps the rest of the Isvaieni would waken from their poisonous dream.

Had Rausi but known these wonders lay here, and woven them into the *Song of Rausi,* Shaiara's heart would have lain lighter in her breast at the beginning of their journey, and perhaps those of her people who had chosen to lay their bones upon the sand would have drawn strength from the knowledge and been able to follow the path to journey's end. She shook her head, banishing such foolishness. Had Rausi known of these things and made them a part of his tale, they would have become known to all who lived between Sand and Star, for the *Song of Rausi* was a thing not known to the Nalzindar alone. Many would have quickly come to partake of Abi'Abadshar's bounty, and it would not have been a place of safety and secret at the time of the Nalzindar's great need.

As so often these days, Shaiara's mind turned to the future. Were they to live out all their days here? How might they know that it was safe to venture back into the Isvai once more? Would that day even come?

Today is in your hand, and tomorrow is upon your lips. That is all, she said to herself sternly. It was a thing her mother and father had both said to her—often—when she had asked after the future with a young child's impatience. No one could truly know what the future might bring, and to think upon it took the mind from the task of survival.

She worked carefully at her task—leader of her people she might be, but none among the Nalzindar expected to spend their days in idleness; it was as unthinkable as leaving the Isvai itself. Yet so many new things had happened in so short a time—and Shaiara knew that all her people looked to her to know best how to make sense of them— that she welcomed a chore that set hands to work and left mind free to rove. At day's end, the people would gather around—the hunters returning from their pursuit of game and their careful numbering of the herds and the flocks; the explorers from their travels deep within the secret hidden vastness of Abi'Abadshar—and all would share their knowledge together. Then they would eat, and sleep, and rise when the light came again to begin a new day. But if there were questions, then Shaiara must have answers—if not at once, then soon.

As Shaiara turned over in her mind what the new day—what many new days—would bring, here in a world where food fell into the hand and water was only a short walk away, she heard the muffled sound of running footsteps. She glanced up from her task to see Ciniran running across the grass, her bare feet green-stained.

The bag upon Ciniran's hip jounced and clattered with the sound of the bells that the foolish Isvaieni of other tribes hung upon the bridles of their *shotors,* and in her hands she carried an object of a familiar shape—round like a clay jug, but of a strange material, pale and glistening like water.

The *ikulas* all rose to their feet at her approach—all save Israf, who had lived at Shaiara's side long enough to be certain that whatever occurred, he would not be stepped on—and Ciniran slid to her knees beside Shaiara, holding out the strange jug.

Shaiara dropped the half-cleaned fur-mouse back into the basket—the *ikulas* knew better than to take that which they were not given—and set aside the skinning-stone. She took the jug onto her knees, running her fingers questingly over its surface. It was hard like stone, yet smoother than any stone she had ever touched. And it was as transparent as the *gauhars* which the Kadyastar took from a place in the desert they would reveal to no one and set into ornaments of gold prized even in the *Iteru*-cities. Yet it was clear instead of colored.

"It is glass," she said slowly. Yet she had never seen an object of glass so large and so clear.

"In a chamber three descents below, there are many

objects," Ciniran said, her voice troubled. She opened her hunter's bag and began emptying it onto the mat upon which she knelt.

A cup of yellow gold, with a bowl as large as Shaiara's two hands. It had a long straight stem and a disk-shaped base. There was another of white silver whose shape matched it exactly. Shaiara picked up the silver cup. The metal was chill in her fingers. The bowl of the cup was covered with a raised design of creatures that she did not believe had ever walked the earth: bird-winged cats; and creatures that were half adder and half something for which she had no name; and men and women with the heads of unknown beasts. The inside of the cup was studded with gems: not merely the red *gauhar* of the Kadyastar, but green and yellow and blue and purple stones as well.

When she looked up from contemplating the cup, Ciniran had finished emptying her bag. Small bowls of gold, and flat plates, and circlets for arm and head. All were ornamented—some with designs meant to depict creatures, however impossible, some merely with patterns.

Gold was prized by many of the tribes of the Isvai, and even more greatly—so Shaiara had heard—by the dwellers in the *Iteru*-cities. The Nalzindar had little use for it: it was soft, and heavy, and did not bring game to the pot or water to the waterskin. They did not accept it in trade when it was offered, preferring things which were of real use between Sand and Star. Here, Shaiara suspected, was enough gold to purchase a score of the finest *shotors* to be had among the Isvaieni, or perhaps six pairs of matched *ikulas* of proven lineage, or four fully trained falcons ready for the hunt. A frightening amount of wealth, for in a world where there was war, Shaiara did not doubt that the Isvaieni would soon be taught to kill for gold as well.

"How many?" Shaiara asked.

"I could fill the pack of every *shotor* of the tribe with what is there, and more would remain," Ciniran said. "And there are these. Many."

Ciniran reached into a fold of her headscarf and held

out her hand. On her palm lay a small disk of gold. Shaiara took it from her and studied it curiously. Both sides were covered with elaborate designs, but she could not deduce its purpose.

Ciniran watched her, and Shaiara knew she was awaiting her decision. Shaiara thought carefully. Gold, yes, and the Nalzindar had heard many tales at the Gatherings of how gold stole men's wits. But both gold and Nalzindar were safe within Abi'Abadshar, and should that change— well, Shaiara would meet that day when it dawned.

"Tomorrow you and I shall return to this chamber," she decided. "I shall see if there is anything there that is useful." She dropped the disk onto the mat and reached for the skinning-stone again. "Now come. There is work to be done if we are to eat."

UPON THE DAY that followed, Shaiara and Ciniran returned to the chamber which Ciniran had discovered. The two of them went alone, for Shaiara wished to see this place before she made a present of the knowledge of it to all the tribe. She had tucked the contents of Ciniran's hunting bag away in a basket in a far corner of the tent, and Ciniran, seeing that, had not spoken of what she had found.

Shaiara was certain that Ciniran would be only the first to discover objects belonging to those who had lived here before—not the last—and she wished time to consider carefully before laying her thoughts before the people. It was only truth that the world was filled with magic, and— as the Nalzindar now knew to their sorrow—the ancient Dark magic of long ago had merely slept, and not been sent from the world completely. While it was true that the spirits of men did not linger in the world after their bodies had been laid beneath the sand, Shaiara did not know if the same could be said for the Endarkened and those who had served them in the long-ago time, and there was no Wild-mage now dwelling among the Nalzindar who could— perhaps—answer such a question.

* * *

IT WAS FORTUNATE that the hunting had been good and
the Nalzindar were careful and provident. The lamps and
lanterns possessed by a people who worked and hunted by
the sun and the moon were few, retained upon the journey
across the Barahileth more for the heat they might give
than for the light, for the depths of a desert night were
cold, and it would be foolhardy indeed to arrive at their
destination unable to make fire, or light, or warm themselves. As it was, they had arrived at Abi'Abadshar with
the wells and reservoirs nearly dry, for oil was food for
people as well as lanterns, and until they had discovered
the rich treasures that lay beneath the surface of the sands,
there had been no fuel to bring life to their lamps and
lanterns once more. It was fortunate that they had kept
them, for the torches they could craft burned quickly, and
the place Ciniran had discovered lay so deep beneath the
ground that Shaiara did not think that the light from the
sky above could have reached it by any means at all, even
if all the stone ceilings that lay between it and the free air
were broken. It was a great wonder indeed that the air itself was so sweet, here in a place where the absence of the
lantern's small flame would mean suffocating blackness,
yet it was so.

The Nalzindar were a people who used whatever came
to their hand to make the path they must walk between
Sand and Star as smooth as it could be rendered, and so it
had not been long before they turned all the unfamiliar
bounty of Abi'Abadshar to their advantage. The strange
pale stone-fruits that grew in abundance in the damp darkness of the tunnels were not safe to eat: the goats shunned
them, and the *ikulas*-puppy who had eaten some had died a
lingering and painful death, her illness beyond the skill of
any of the tribe's healers to ease. But the stone-fruit was
not entirely useless. Some of the larger growths gave off a
faint pale light, and Merab had learned how to use them to
make a paste that—mixed with fat and white ash—could

be used to mark one's way in the passages whether one had light or not, for the marks made with this paste would shine against the rock even in complete darkness, and the white ash made them highly visible even in the dimmest light. Each Nalzindar who ventured into the Descents made his or her own personal mark upon the walls with the paste upon each journey, in much the same way as such a one might scratch hunt-sign into the hard-baked desert clay, for should one who explored fail to return in time for the evening meal, those who went in search must be able to trace the steps of the missing one. Upon returning, each hunter wiped away the marks he or she had made upon going, and after a few days, the faint gleaming smears left behind by their fingers vanished from the rock entirely.

Shaiara and Ciniran's descent was accomplished by means of sets of broad terraces—if Shaiara did not have great experience of these curious things by now, they would surely have tripped her, for the ones leading from one level to the next were wide and shallow—one must walk two or three steps between the edge of one and the next, and descend only a narrow handspan, and then walk again. Indeed, any *shotor* might have made such a descent in perfect comfort, could the stubborn beasts have been persuaded to venture into near-darkness, for the terraces were as broad as the passageway from which they led.

As Shaiara knew, the Descent below the first also held gardens, and water, and sunlight, though the growth was less abundant than upon the level above. There was more damage to the Second Descent, as the roots of plants and trees that flourished on the level above had worked their way through any tiny crack in the rock they could find, levering it wide over the centuries. In the Second Descent, no barrier remained in place across an entrance—if, in fact, any had ever existed. Those hunters who wished a greater challenge than their days now held came to the Second Descent to hunt, for the creatures lurking here were difficult to track and more difficult to capture, and the Nalzindar had come to believe that this was the Descent upon which most of the predators who lived within Abi'Abadshar made their homes.

Shaiara and Ciniran made their way carefully along the length of the great corridor. Their way was not unencumbered, for though it was as broad and as high as the one above, uncounted years had filled it with dung and debris and crumbled stone. With the weaving of many more baskets and the labor of moonturns, the passage could be cleared—just as the passage above was being cleared of wet sand and poisonous stone-fruit—but the material must be put somewhere, and they could not simply dump it on the sand outside. To do so would be to attract unwanted attention—and any attention at all would be unwanted. Though some of the rooms in the passage above were empty, and might be filled, Shaiara hesitated before ordering any action that would so disrupt the Balance of this place. For the moment, the Nalzindar were but guests. Bad enough that their necessity required them to hunt the *fenec,* the desert cat, and the wild *pakh*—not even for skins (for the *pakh* was a useless creature whose flesh was inedible even by the starving and whose skin could not be tanned), but because the Nalzindar now needed their prey to feed their own hunger. It was true that game was abundant here, but it was also true that the weight measured out by the Eternal Light into each pan of the Great Balance must tally exactly. When new predators arrived in a hunting ground, old predators must go, lest the prey be hunted to destruction. And the Nalzindar were predators.

They reached the end of the corridor, and the shallow terraces that marked the next Descent. Ciniran paused to light the second lamp, and Shaiara blew out the first, tucking it into her pouch to let it cool before refilling it. She and Ciniran continued on, following the marks left upon the walls—first those that many Nalzindar had left in the course of going forth for a day's hunting and harvesting, but as they went on, the marks became fewer.

* * *

THE THIRD DESCENT held little sign of life, though there was evidence here that the beasts that made Abi'Abadshar their home had occasionally ventured down here, most so long ago that their bones—all that remained—crumbled away to dust at the touch. For the first time, Shaiara's touch discerned ornament upon the walls, though the illumination she and Ciniran carried was not enough to show her the whole of the design. She held the lamp close to the walls, hoping to see.

Wide bands of something that might almost be carved letters—were it not for the fact that it held no shapes that Shaiara recognized—alternated with what might be more pictures like those upon the cups. But the carvings were too vast, and her lamp was too dim. There was not enough light.

Perhaps—if they discovered a way to make proper torches, and if the smoke did not suffocate them—Shaiara would be able to return, and see more clearly what stories these walls told. At last they reached the terraces that led to the Fourth Descent, the limit—so far—of the Nalzindar's explorations.

"Narkil did not wish to continue so far," Ciniran said quietly. "I went on alone."

Silently, Shaiara blessed Narkil's hesitation, little though she cared for the fact that it had led to Ciniran's continuing to explore by herself. "Not twice," was all she said, and Ciniran nodded. Shaiara made fresh marks against the carved stone, indicating clearly that two young female Nalzindar had come this way early in the day. Then she lifted the lamp high, and they continued.

SHE HAD TAKEN care to wear her heaviest cloak when they set out, for experience had taught her that the deeper one went into Abi'Abadshar, the colder it became, but they descended now into a bone-deep chill such as Shaiara had never experienced, and Ciniran, who had warned her of it, was just as uncomfortable.

"There is another Descent below this one," Ciniran said, and Shaiara understood the unvoiced question: *is it possible that they grow colder and colder until water could become ice?* Both of them knew that such a thing was possible, for at certain times of the year, ice could be harvested even in the deep desert, by leaving water out in a shallow metal pan overnight. It was a game played by the children of the Isvaieni at the Gatherings of the tribes, for the desertfolk had no need of ice.

And it was a question Shaiara could not answer.

The walls of the shallow terrace-passage leading to the Fourth Descent were carved as well, and Shaiara felt frustration at not being able to *see* what her hands discerned so clearly. In the distance, she could see the faint smears of Ciniran's marks upon the wall, angling down and away as the passage descended. While it was true that it would be hard to lose one's way upon the terraces—no passages led off from them, and one must go either up or down— Ciniran had marked the wall, with a true hunter's prudence, against the possibility that she might lose her lamp and have nothing but the small glow-marks of the stone-fruit paint to guide her. Such marks as those, simple arrows indicating that a passage had been explored—no more—were not erased when the explorer retraced his or her steps, but left to stand.

To finally reach the bottom of the terraces was a relief, for the careful counting of steps in the darkness was a great strain. Here in the Fourth Descent there was no sign of life at all, nor any sign that any creature between the city's desertion and the Nalzindar's arrival had ever ventured so deep. When Shaiara stooped down and ran her hand over the stone beneath her feet, it was as smooth and clean as if it were a fresh-scrubbed skinning-stone. Even the eternal dust—fine as the finest flour—which worked its way into every corner of the passages above had not made its way to this depth.

The barriers here were of a different kind than those Shaiara had seen above. There, all were the same. Here, each one was different. All were of the same shape, but each was elaborately decorated, no two alike: some inlaid with ivory or bone or metal, others carved. Here, too, the metal upon the barriers was different—not rings, but crescent shapes like a hunter's bow, or round balls, or only a flat disk. Holding her lamp up close by one of the barriers, Shaiara could see that it had once been painted, for flecks of color still clung to the deep furrows in the design.

Nearly every door opened at her touch, and though she could see, by Ciniran's marks upon them, which chambers had already been visited, Shaiara wished to see what lay within them for herself.

The first chamber was filled with dust. Ciniran's quiet warning stopped Shaiara before she entered, but even the opening of the barrier was enough to fill the air with a cloud that made both of them sneeze violently. With determination, Shaiara pushed the barrier through the debris upon the floor until it would go no further.

"I think—once—there was much paper here," Ciniran said quietly. "Long ago."

Shaiara nodded. Perhaps something remained—but if it did, would it be marked in any fashion she could read? She thought of the strange carvings upon the walls, and glanced at Ciniran. Her age-mate shrugged slightly. "I put my scarf over my face and went inside. The chamber is large, and its sides are filled with places where one might lay a body. Or even sleep. Now: dust." Her expression was plain for Shaiara to read: *how could there be so much paper in the world?* "And there are more chambers beyond."

Shaiara nodded. They left the barrier open, and continued.

The next barrier opened into a chamber so small that Shaiara's lamp lit every part of it. The walls were entirely covered in wood, and she could see that once they had been as elaborately inlaid as the barrier to the chamber itself, but now the walls were dried and cracked with age, and pieces of the inlay had fallen to the floor. She could not imagine what the purpose of this space had been.

The next barrier could not be shifted at all, and the next several chambers further along the passage, upon being opened, contained much the same as had the first—contents rotted away to dust by the passage of uncounted years. Though there might be some information to be gained by searching them thoroughly, their contents were not that which had disturbed Ciniran so greatly.

The barrier to that chamber slid inward easily, for in this chamber little had rotted away. Ciniran took the lamp from Shaiara's hand and stepped forward into the darkness. Shaiara had counted fifteen paces, watching the small flame strike gleams from gold everywhere around her, when Ciniran stopped and lowered the lamp. There was a surface before her, a cube of green stone as tall as a kneeling *shotor*, and it was not opaque, but translucent, for even the tiny flame of the lamp made the stone glow.

Shaiara reached into her pouch and withdrew the second lamp. In this room, she wanted all possible light. When she had filled it again and lit it, she set it beside the first.

Ciniran had selected samples of the items here to bring back to their camp, but knowing Shaiara would come to see for herself, had not brought one of every item that was here. Now Shaiara lifted a long heavy chain from the top of the green stone cube—each link was fashioned in the seeming of an adder, its tail held within its mouth, and each adder's eyes glinted with tiny gems. Beside it lay a dagger—cunningly wrought, but the blade was of soft useless gold. What manner of people were these, to have made weapons that could not be used?

There were more cups, both the tall footed sort, and the more familiar ones such as Shaiara might use herself—though hers were clay or wood, and not gold, silver, or glass. There was another bowl of gold, so large that Shaiara could not encircle it with both arms, and it was filled with what seemed, at first glance, to be fresh fruit—both the figs and sand-plums familiar to any desert-dweller, and the strange new fruits the Nalzindar had only found here in Abi'Abadshar. Yet when Shaiara touched them, all were stone.

There were tall footed cylinders of both gold and white silver, whose purpose Shaiara could not guess at, for though there was a small opening in the top, they would hold no more than a drop or two of liquid.

And this was only that which stood upon the top of the cube. Along one wall there were chests—some of metal, some of wood—piled four and five and even six high. Some of the highest had fallen down and broken open, and this was the source of the disks Ciniran had brought back. There were gold ones, and others of white silver, and still others in metals of other colors—green and blue and red—and many that the years had simply turned black. Not all were round: Shaiara held her lamp over one glittering spill of metal and counted more shapes than she had fingers and toes.

The chamber was not small, nor was the green cube the only cube within it. Shaiara saw things she recognized—a metal coffee-service; a broken *shamat*-set—and things she could not imagine the use of—something like a hunter's bow, if a hunter's bow had been made of gold and then savagely twisted. There were low tables of metal and of bone which had survived the passage of time, some of wood which had collapsed beneath their burdens, still others which had survived. And every surface, and the floor between them, was covered with *objects*. Here, in this single chamber, there were more *things* than were possessed by all the Isvaieni together, and after a while, Shaiara found herself doing nothing more than standing beside the nearest cube—one of clear yellow stone—resting her forearm upon it and gazing down at the objects that it held in confused exhaustion.

Behind her, Ciniran refilled the other lamp with deft motions. "I do not know what to think," she said.

Shaiara drew a deep breath. "*I* think," she said, "that should we need cups for drinking or bowls for washing, it would be well to remember this place, and return. But if we do not, there is nothing here that is of the least use."

Four

Magic's Cost and Magic's Price

WHEN THEY STOPPED to make camp that evening, Tiercel could see that Harrier was no closer to being settled in his mind about having received the Books of the Wild Magic, though he was apparently much closer to fighting with Kareta.

The golden unicorn either didn't notice Harrier's black mood or simply didn't care (which Tiercel felt was much more likely). If this were any evening such as they had spent in the sennight journeying from Karahelanderialigor with Elunyerin and Rilphanifel, Tiercel and Ancaladar would already have headed off for some nearby quiet spot so that Tiercel could practice his spells, but this evening Tiercel thought that a much better use of his time would be to stick around and make sure that Harrier didn't simply murder Kareta, and Ancaladar seemed to agree, because once they'd landed and Tiercel had removed Ancaladar's saddle and harness, tucking them carefully out of the way until they'd be needed again, the great black dragon merely folded his wings and curled up like an enormous—a *really* enormous—cat.

That didn't leave very much for Tiercel to do besides stay out of the way. Since he'd been studying as hard as he could from the moment he'd been Bonded—including during their entire sennight on the road—Harrier had pretty much been handling all the camp chores. Even though Rilphanifel and Elunyerin had been traveling with them up until this morning, the two Elves had let Harrier cope with the bulk of the daily tasks, since he'd have to be able to do them by himself once they left to return to Karahelanderialigor. Of course Tiercel could have offered to help; although he wasn't as handy as Harrier was at doing things like these, and never had been, they'd both been equally ignorant of how to deal with life on the road when they'd left Armethalieh, and Tiercel hadn't spent six moonturns sleeping on the ground without picking up *some* idea of what to do around an encampment.

But when Harrier was in a temper, the best thing to do was to stay out of his way until he cooled down. Only Kareta didn't seem to have any interest in letting Harrier cool down. As he unhitched the horses and turned them out to graze (after leading them down to the stream for their evening drink), as he unrolled the thick blanket of fine mesh quilted around heavy bars of fired clay that the Elves used to protect the earth from the heat of their fire-pots and braziers, filled both firepot and brazier with char-coal, filled the kettle with water and set it to heat, and began preparing the soup for the evening's meal, Kareta pestered him with incessant questions. Although, Tiercel thought, listening, they were really closer to demands.

"You really have more important things to do, you know. Don't you? Well, if you mean to do them at all. And I have to say, you don't seem terribly *interested.* Don't you know how many people there are who yearn all their *lives* to be chosen to receive the Three Books? And here you are: you've had them almost one entire day, and have you looked in them once? You aren't even carrying them! You could have spent the whole day reading *The Book of Moon:* I'm sure you'd at least be able to cast Fire by now if you had! It's a very sim-ple spell, you know, and doesn't even come with a Mageprice! But have you even read it? And you're going to need to know what's in them, you know, and how to cast spells. Isn't that what you want? After all, you're a Knight-Mage, now."

"Not. Yet." Harrier spoke each word very precisely, and if Kareta had been a boy their own age—and not a unicorn—Tiercel would have been certain that the next thing Harrier would do would be to take a swing at her.

"But you will be!" Kareta said, as simply as if the

decision had already been made. "And then you'll need to cast spells. *Lots* of spells. And you're going to need a teacher, aren't you?"

"I thought Wildmages didn't have teachers?" Tiercel asked hastily, because Harrier had the griddle-stone for griddle-cakes in his hand, and Tiercel thought that in another minute he might forget that Kareta was a unicorn and try to hit her with it.

Kareta stopped and looked at him, blinking as if she'd forgotten he was there. Tiercel stared into her glorious blue eyes and found it hard to remember what his question had been. He couldn't imagine how Harrier was not only managing to be mad at her now, but had evidently managed to stay mad at her for the entire day. She was so incredibly beautiful that it was simply hard to think about anything at all while you were looking at her.

"Huh," Kareta said, snorting rudely and switching her long tufted tail. "And he said you were smarter than he was! Everyone knows that the Three Books are where Wildmages learn all they know about the Wild Magic. But Harrier's going to need someone to teach him how to be a knight, too, you know. Of course, maybe you don't."

On the other hand, maybe Tiercel could see Harrier's point.

"Leave him alone," Harrier said flatly. "You're the one who said there hasn't been a Knight-Mage in a thousand years. Well, we don't see that many Wildmages in Armethalieh either. And . . . I've spent the last half-year finding out that everything I thought I knew was wrong, so . . . why shouldn't everything we think we know about Wildmages be wrong, too?"

Tiercel glanced at Harrier in alarm. Harrier had complained all the way from Armethalieh to Ysterialpoerin—and on to Karahelanderialigor—but Tiercel had never heard him sound quite so . . . tired.

"It is not wrong," Ancaladar said, speaking up for the first time that evening. "It is merely . . . incomplete."

"Why?" Tiercel asked. Partly because he really wanted

to know—and Ancaladar hadn't actually been in a mood to answer many questions so far—and partly because if he and Ancaladar were talking, it might mean that Kareta would leave Harrier in peace for a little while.

Ancaladar blinked slowly, and Tiercel got the impression the dragon was smiling. "Magic is . . . long," the dragon said slowly. "Humans are . . . brief."

"That is enormously helpful," Harrier snapped. He ran a hand through his hair and sighed. "Sorry," he said. "But—Ancaladar—it doesn't make *sense*. Um, okay, there are Elven Mages. But . . . I've never heard of an Elven Wildmage—and then there are—were—all these High Mages—like Tiercel—so . . . you just said that most magic is done by people who can't do it."

Tiercel did his best to keep from looking surprised. Harrier always said he hated to think, and back in Armethalieh he'd always done his best to give the impression that he wasn't very bright. But Tiercel had always known better: Harrier wasn't stupid. He was deliberate and methodical. Where Tiercel's mind skipped ahead, arriving at conclusions by intuition and instinct, Harrier's worked its way slowly and carefully toward a solution, weighing and judging each element of a problem carefully before he spoke. It had made Harrier's teachers think he didn't know his lessons and call him slow, and over the years, Tiercel knew that Harrier had started to believe them. It wasn't surprising that Harrier had reached the conclusion he had, merely that he'd been willing to say so.

"No," Ancaladar answered. "I do not say that the Children of Men cannot do magic, but that magic has its own purpose, which does not always align itself with the needs and desires of those whose lives are brief, and therefore, those whose lives are filled with magic, and those whose lives are not, will rarely have a great deal to say to one another."

"But the Wildmages keep the Balance," Harrier said, and now he just sounded puzzled.

"Indeed," Ancaladar answered. "And Men—and

Elves—are only a part of the Balance. Some Wildmages weave spells and pay Prices to set into motion events which their grandchildren will not see come to pass. I will set you a riddle, Harrier Gillain: does the weed thank the gardener?"

"That's not a riddle," Tiercel said instantly. "Of course not." No gardener wanted weeds in his garden: Tiercel's own mother uprooted them ruthlessly from their tiny back garden whenever they appeared.

But Harrier was looking thoughtful, and not as if he liked the idea of being either the gardener—or the weed.

At least Ancaladar's cryptic lecture had gotten Kareta to stop bothering Harrier for a while. She went wandering off on some mysterious business of her own and let them eat supper in peace. After dinner, Tiercel insisted on helping Harrier clean up. Most evenings he was so exhausted from practicing that he just rolled immediately into his blankets and fell asleep, but not tonight.

So tonight Harrier didn't need to carry a lantern with him to light his way down to the stream to wash up. Tiercel gestured, and a ball of glowing cerulean Coldfire appeared over their heads.

"I'm still not used to that," Harrier sighed.

"You—" Tiercel said, and stopped. *You can do it too, now. It's a Wildmage spell.* In Karahelanderialigor he'd learned that the High Magick had been created out of the Wild Magic during the Great War in order to fight the Endarkened, because the Endarkened could taint and subvert the Wildmages but not—or not as easily—the High Mages (who had originally been—at least until the war was over—called War Mages). The two magicks combined could slay the Endarkened.

Harrier shrugged irritably and said nothing.

With two pair of hands instead of one, the task went quickly. Neither boy was a stranger to hard work, though, back in Armethalieh, Tiercel was (technically) *"Lord"* Tiercel, a member of the minor Nobility, and Harrier was the son of the Portmaster (and so, in down-to-earth terms, from a family just as well-off and far more important). Because of the boys' friendship, and because of their fathers' professional relationship (Tiercel's father was the Chief Clerk to High Magistrate Vaunnel, the ruler of the City), the two families had been close since Tiercel and Harrier were children, in no small part because the families had shared a similar ethos: that rank, wealth, and privilege should not keep any of their children from learning the value of hard work or the satisfaction of being able to do things for themselves. Tiercel's father had told him over and over that true power came not from commanding people, but from leading them: that leadership grew out of respect, and respect grew out of ability; that to rule a city, one must be able to perform the tasks that any of its inhabitants could. Tiercel knew that Harrier's father must have said something similar to him: one did not reign over the Port of Armethalieh—a city within a city—without knowing how to keep it running smoothly.

When the plates and cups and cookware had all been scrubbed clean and set aside, Harrier sat back on his heels. There was obviously something on his mind, but Tiercel didn't think it was magic. Harrier's mind didn't work that way. Certainly he was brooding over the unexpected (and unwelcome) gift, but he wasn't likely to ask Tiercel's advice on what to do about it. Or at least not yet.

"How far to the Veil?" Harrier asked.

Tiercel thought about it for a moment. There were some things he knew without knowing how he knew them—thoughts caught from Ancaladar's mind, probably. Other things he knew simply because he could see so much more of the road ahead from dragonback. And the more he practiced his spellcraft, the more it seemed he could actually *see* magic. It was a little disconcerting.

"I'm not quite sure." He wondered why Harrier was asking. Pelashia's Veil was the Elven Ward that marked the boundary of the Elven Lands. Once they crossed it, they'd be not only in unknown territory, but very likely uninhabited territory as well, but he wasn't sure that was the reason. "I know we're going to reach a settlement of some kind tomorrow—Ancaladar and I could see it today. Beyond that . . . a sennight? Maybe ten days?"

"Huh." Harrier picked up a stone and tossed it into the water. "And we've been able to get provisions—for us, for the horses, for Ancaladar—wherever we stop in the Elven Lands. And House Malkirinath is paying for everything—which is nice of them, considering that they're sending you off to be killed. And considering how much Ancaladar *eats.* But what about when we leave the Elven Lands?"

Tiercel blinked at him in puzzlement. "Leave the Elven Lands?"

Harrier sighed in exasperation. "Leave. The Elven Lands. I don't know what you were doing when we were studying Geography in school, but *I* was paying attention. We're east of the Bazrahils. Which means that we are *far* to the east of Windalorianan, which is as far east as civilization goes. There might be a few other scattered villages east of the Dragon's Tail, but I guarantee they're all west of the Bazrahils. We aren't going to bump into another city until we hook around the southern span of the mountains and head west into the Madiran—and since I have no idea where we are, I have no idea how far away it is. Now, *you* may have some idea of what we're all going to eat between here and there, but I don't. The only thing I *do* know is that we can't possibly load up enough supplies before we cross the Veil."

"Oh." They were going to have a couple of other problems—big ones—the moment they crossed the Veil, actually, but Tiercel didn't want to bother Harrier with them just yet. Not tonight.

"Yeah," Harrier said. " 'Oh.' "

IN THE MORNING Tiercel was awakened by the sound of Harrier and Kareta arguing.

"It's a lovely morning—see? The sun is all bright and

shiny, and you don't have anything else at all to do! You could sit right down and read your lovely Books!"

"I have a lot of things to do. Feed the horses. Water the horses. Cook breakfast. Pack the wagon. Harness the horses. And maybe burn those damned Books if it'll shut you up."

"It won't do you the least good, you know! They can't be stolen, they can't be lost, they can't be taken from you, and they can't be destroyed. You'd have to give them up."

"I suppose you're going to stand there and tell me that *burning* them doesn't count?"

"I suppose it would depend on how you burned them, wouldn't it?" Kareta answered chirpily.

"In a *fire.*"

There was absolutely no point in trying to sleep through this. Tiercel groaned, rolled over, and sat up.

"Well, of *course* in a fire, silly!" Kareta was saying, "but *why* you burned them matters so much more than *how!* Really, if you'd just read a *little* bit of *The Book of Moon*—"

"Why would what you *meant* to do matter?" Tiercel asked, puzzled.

"Ask *him,*" Kareta said, tossing her head.

"*Don't* ask me," Harrier snapped.

"I want to ask *somebody,*" Tiercel said, now thoroughly awake. "Intention doesn't matter in magic. You do the spell, and you get the results. They're the same every time."

"Hah," Kareta said.

"Aren't they?" Harrier asked, looking as if he hated himself for asking.

"Yes," Tiercel said. Everything he'd studied about the High Magick said so.

"Read your Books," Kareta said.

"*DOES* INTENTION MATTER in magic?" Tiercel asked later.

It was with unaccustomed reluctance that he'd saddled

Ancaladar and prepared to fly that day. He'd really wanted to stay behind and ride on the wagon with Harrier, except that Harrier had all-but-thrown him onto Ancaladar's back. Tiercel only hoped that both Harrier and Kareta would both still be there—and in one piece—when they stopped for the midday meal.

"In House Malkirinath, you read the history both of the Great War, and of that which your people call the Flowering War," Ancaladar answered.

House Malkirinath in Karahelanderialigor was where Ancaladar and Jermayan had lived for, well, a very long time. Until Tiercel had come, and the Great Spell of an Elven Mage had transferred Ancaladar's Bond to Tiercel. He knew that Ancaladar had been Bonded to Jermayan for over a thousand years, and that the dragon still grieved for him deeply—even now he rarely spoke Jermayan's name if he could avoid it—though the magic of his new Bond made that grief less sharp than it could have been. Tiercel was grateful for that: without the magic that softened Ancaladar's sorrow it would have been unspeakably cruel to force him to live on without the man with whom he had shared so many centuries, no matter how necessary he was to the success of Tiercel's quest.

"Yes . . ." Tiercel said slowly. "That doesn't exactly answer my question."

"High Magick and the Wild Magic are not the same," Ancaladar answered, giving the impression of heaving a deep sigh of reluctance. "In nearly everything—save that they are both forces for Good—they are opposites."

"Which is why, when you put them together, they could kill Endarkened," Tiercel said, half guessing. "And that means—since I know intention doesn't matter at all in the High Magick—that intention must matter a lot in the Wild Magic. That's . . . the most ridiculous thing I ever heard."

"And *that* is precisely what Kellen Tavadon said many times," Ancaladar said, sounding amused now. "Long before he became a Knight-Mage he spent many years being trained to become a High Mage."

As fascinating as it was to hear about Kellen the Poor Orphan Boy's *real* past, Tiercel had more urgent questions right now. "But how can magic know what you want instead of what you do?" he asked.

"The Wild Magic—so I have been told—does not care so much what you want as much as what it wants. And what you need," Ancaladar replied.

"I don't think we should tell Harrier that," Tiercel said.

"Indeed," the dragon said.

BY THE TIME Tiercel landed at midday, Harrier had already lit the brazier and was rummaging through their supplies for bread and cheese and fruit. Tiercel was relieved to see that Kareta seemed to be in one piece. She looked amazingly cheerful, too.

He sat down next to the brazier with a groan—flying for hours was fun, but it left him stiffer than riding a horse did—and a moment later Harrier came back with a carrying basket. He set it down on the blanket, removed the teapot, mugs, and a canister of tea, shook a measure of leaves into the pot, and settled down to wait for the water to boil. While neither of them really thought that the "tea" the Elves were so fond of tasted like anything much more than boiled grass, they'd both gotten fairly used to it in the last moonturn, and it was actually pretty drinkable if you added enough honey. Tiercel rummaged in the basket, setting the loaf aside for the moment and lifting out the wheel of cheese. They'd stopped two days ago in the village of Wintercrown—at least Elunyerin and Rilphanifel had *said* it was a village; it certainly didn't look anything like any village Tiercel had ever seen—where they'd loaded up with supplies, and Ancaladar had enjoyed a hearty meal.

Tiercel drew his dagger and cut off a large chunk of cheese, then replaced it in the basket and reached for the loaf of bread. They had dry provisions to last at least a fortnight, and perishables for several more days, though this was (he was pretty sure) the last of the bread.

"You should be at the farm in a few more hours," he said around a mouthful of bread and cheese. He and Ancaladar had already overflown the farmstead several times that morning; there was no reason to fear that the sight of Ancaladar would disturb the inhabitants, since in the Elven Lands, dragons were actually a fairly common sight. Unfortunately, that would change as soon as they crossed the Veil; when he'd come to Karahelanderialigor Tiercel'd hoped that the Elves would be able to tell him exactly what place he was looking for, but in fact, neither Elves nor dragons had been beyond the Veil since the Elves had withdrawn eastward from the Nine Cities centuries ago. And that meant that whatever was on the other side of the Veil wouldn't be used to seeing dragons either.

"Huh," Harrier said without actual comment, pouring hot water from the kettle to the pot.

"And that will leave you all the rest of the day to read!" Kareta said brightly. "Aren't you the least bit curious about what—"

Without even looking up, Harrier reached into the basket, snagged an apple, and flung it at Kareta. The unicorn caught it neatly and crunched it with obvious enjoyment.

"The two of you might as well just go on ahead," Harrier said, as if Kareta hadn't spoken—and as if he hadn't just tried to brain her with an apple. "There's no reason for you to fly around in circles for the rest of the day just because Nethiel and Dulion aren't as fast over the road as Ancaladar is."

"Who is?" Ancaladar asked mildly.

"I am," Kareta said simply.

The dragon lifted his head, and Tiercel could almost swear he looked affronted.

"Easy enough to say," Harrier said, cutting his own chunk from the wheel of cheese. He pared a piece off it and flipped it over his shoulder. Kareta caught it neatly. "It's not as if we're going to be holding races any time soon. Or as if they'd settle anything. So why bother?"

"I'm faster," Kareta said sulkily.

"But go ahead, because it's not as if we can get lost between here and there," Harrier said, ostentatiously ignoring her. "And when you get there, be sure to ask them how far it is to the Border, and if there are any other settlements before we get there."

"Um," Tiercel said.

" 'It would be good to know, of your courtesy, were there anything you would care to say concerning what might lay between—whatever the name of the place is—and the border of the Elven Lands,' " Harrier rattled off around a mouthful of bread. The most difficult thing for both boys to master during their sojourn in Karahelanderialigor had been the maddeningly indirect forms of polite Elven speech, in which any form of direct question was considered the height of rudeness. Since Tiercel hadn't really talked to all that many people during his stay, Harrier was much better at it than he was.

"I shall remind you, Tiercel," Ancaladar said.

"It's not that hard," Harrier said.

"And you'll want extra supplies," Kareta said. "You'll need a lot more apples, just to begin with! And oat cakes. And maybe some of those—"

"I am not feeding you," Harrier said. "Don't you have someplace else to go?"

"Oh, no," Kareta assured him soulfully. "I'd be so bored anywhere else! And I'm not bored here. And . . . *someone* has to make you do the right thing."

Tiercel reached for the teapot hastily. Kareta might be a unicorn, and a creature of magic, but he didn't think there was anyone—or anything—anywhere who could *"make"* Harrier do something if he'd made up his mind not to.

THE ELVEN FARM (or village or whatever) was called Blackrowan. Kareta (in his mind he added "that stupid unicorn" every time he thought about her, until in his head her name was simply "Kareta-that-stupid-unicorn," and Harrier didn't really give a damn whether or not unicorns could read your thoughts or not; if she was eavesdropping, she deserved whatever she got) had mentioned that offhandedly once they were on the road again. She also mentioned that Blackrowan was famous for its fine fruit cordials, that the area wasn't suitable for rice but did well for silk, that the nearest city to Blackrowan was Tarmulonberan, and that it didn't matter anyway because they weren't going there.

In short, she just *didn't shut up*.

Harrier was pretty certain that he could get her to stop talking if he'd only say he wanted some peace and quiet in order to read the Three Books of the Wild Magic. And he was damned if he'd do any such thing. The harder she pushed, the harder he dug in his heels.

And the thing was, he *meant* to read them. Or at least take a look at them. He didn't want to—to be perfectly honest, the thought of even opening *The Book of Moon* scared him stiff. But he was pretty sure it was his duty.

The first Knight-Mage to be called by the Gods of the Wild Magic since Kellen . . .

Maybe some people would think that was just great. Harrier could think of half-a-dozen of his age-mates at Armethalieh Normal School who would be whooping with glee at the thought, brandishing imaginary swords and talking of the battles they'd fight. Harrier just felt sick to his stomach—he'd already fought battles, and as far as he could see, he'd lost every one.

He remembered Windy Meadows, the town he and Tiercel and Simera had stopped at. The one whose inhabitants had all been eaten by Goblins. That had been after the Wildmage Roneida had given him a sword, but it hadn't done him a lot of good. He hadn't been able to save Simera's life.

And in Ysterialpoerin, when *something* had chased him and Tiercel halfway around the city, he hadn't been able to do a single thing then either, even though—he was pretty sure—it would have killed them both if it had caught them.

He knew the Wild Magic was wise and good, and it

must know what it was doing by sending the Books to him. And he was reasonably sure that (that damned unicorn) Kareta wasn't lying when she said the Wild Magic meant him to be a Knight-Mage, because while Harrier didn't know very much about what Wildmages did, he was pretty sure that even if he'd make a really bad Knight-Mage, he'd make an even worse regular Wildmage.

The trouble was, that wasn't saying much. He'd watched Simera die, poisoned by the Goblins. And he was terrified that he was going to have to watch Tiercel die too, because what Tiercel was trying to find was a thousand times more dangerous than a few Goblins. And thinking of Tiercel dying was bad enough, but what was worse was the fact that according to everything they'd been told over the last several sennights, Tiercel was the Light's champion. And that meant that if Tiercel died, the Darkness would win. Or at the very least, have time to get stronger, until a new champion came along. And while it was getting stronger, it would kill more people. And all the stories Harrier had grown up with—about the Blessed Saint Idalia, and Kellen the Poor Orphan Boy, and the Great Flowering—told about how difficult the victory of the Light had been a thousand years ago, and how high a price the Armies of the Light had paid to gain it. And that made Harrier afraid that this might be their best chance to win, even if it didn't look like a very good chance at all.

And that brought him right back around to becoming a Knight-Mage.

I'm only seventeen; I shouldn't have to think about things like this.

But he didn't really have a choice. Any more than Tiercel'd had a choice about accepting Ancaladar's Bond. The Bond was the only way Tiercel could gain the power to work his High Magick spells. Becoming a Knight-Mage might be the only way Harrier could keep Tiercel alive long enough to use them.

"You're awfully quiet," Kareta said chirpily.

"I'm wondering if they know any recipes for roast unicorn at Blackrowan," Harrier muttered.

TIERCEL AND HARRIER had spent nearly two moonturns in Karahelanderialigor, one of the most important of the Elven cities, and it had been sennights before they had realized they were in a city at all, because the Elven notion of how a city should seem and the human one were quite different. The Elves believed that everything they built should exist in harmony with the world of Nature, and they were so good at what they did that (to human eyes) what they built often seemed to simply vanish into the landscape. Even great Elven cities were only discernible—to human eyes—as a few scattered cottages, and without the help first of Elunyerin and Rilphanifel, and later of Ancaladar, Tiercel and Harrier would simply have gone right past the villages and farms and steadings that lay along their road.

At least Blackrowan was easy to find. Not because it was visible, but because Ancaladar was. Harrier clicked his tongue at Nethiel and Dulion, urging them off the road and in the direction of the stand of trees where the enormous black dragon lay sunning himself.

As he drew closer, what had looked like a woodland underwent one of those odd transformations that Harrier was becoming used to. Suddenly, between one moment and the next, it was no longer simply a group of trees, but a long, low-roofed house in the midst of trees. Though there were great Mages among the Elves, there wasn't, as far as Harrier knew, any magic involved in the way Elven settlements seemed to appear out of nowhere—just the sort of misdirection and trickery the mock-Mages used to delight their audiences at the Flowering Fairs. But on a much grander scale.

"Do you suppose they'd . . . ?" he said, glancing around. He stopped, frowning in disbelief, and stood up on the step of the gently rocking wagon to get a better look around himself.

Kareta was nowhere to be seen.

"Huh," Harrier said, sitting back down again. That was odd. He would have been prepared to swear that she intended to stick to him until he read those Books and memorized every line. Instead, she'd vanished without a single word. There wasn't much he could do about it, though, so he concentrated on finding his way to where he was supposed to go. As he knew from experience, it wasn't all that easy; the Elves might be able to tell a farmhouse from a stables from a drying shed, but to Harrier, the buildings all looked pretty much alike. Fortunately Tiercel was there to greet him, along with an Elf he introduced as Aressea, the mistress of Blackrowan.

"Be welcome in my home and at my hearth, Harrier son of Antarans. Stay as long as you will, and when you go, go with joy," she said, bowing as he stepped down from the wagon's bench.

"To be freely welcomed is to be made doubly welcome," Harrier answered, bowing in return. "It would be good to know, of your courtesy, where I might see to my horses before I bathe."

He knew he wasn't being in the least presumptuous by assuming that a bath would be the first thing on the menu. Elves were fanatical about cleanliness when it was at all possible to be so, and Harrier knew perfectly well that cold baths in rushing streams weren't nearly as good as hot soaks in Elven bathhouses for getting a person clean.

Aressea waved her hand dismissively. "It would be a poor hostess indeed who asked a guest to labor. Siralcar will see to your horses while you refresh yourself. Come."

As another Elf appeared—seemingly out of nowhere, but Harrier had gotten over his astonishment at the way Elves mysteriously appeared out of "thin air" long before he'd left Karahelanderialigor. Once Siralcar took charge of the horses, Harrier turned and followed Aressea and

Tiercel along a path through the trees. He knew, since he'd driven the wagon past the main house already, that he was already in the middle of the farm, and if this had been a farm in the Delfier Valley, he would have expected to see an open farmyard, with open fields and low hedges surrounding the farmstead. But he'd long since gotten used to the idea that the Elves did things differently.

"I believe you shall find all that you require within," Aressea said, stopping at the door of the bathhouse. "Afterward, perhaps it would please you to come to my kitchen to take tea, and let it be known how Farm Blackrowan can best be of service to House Malkirinath."

Harrier bowed again. "It will indeed be my pleasure to take tea, and to share with you all that I know."

Aressea bowed again and walked off.

"How do you do that?" Tiercel muttered, shaking his head.

"It isn't any harder than calming down a boatload of Selkens who've convinced themselves that Da wants to cheat them on the Port fees," Harrier said. "And anyway, I *had* to learn to talk like that. Elunyerin kept hitting me if I didn't."

Tiercel shook his head again. "I guess there's just something about you that makes people want to hit you, Har. Because—remember?—Roneida kept hitting you, too."

"Don't remind me," Harrier muttered, rubbing his arm in reflexive memory. He pushed open the door to the bathhouse and stepped inside.

The interior of the bathhouse was much the same as the others he'd been in, even the one in House Malkirinath, though that one had been inside, rather than a separate building. Tiled walls and a tiled floor, one of the traditional ceramic stoves nestled in the corner (something neither of the boys had seen outside of museums before they'd come to the Elven Lands, as they hadn't been used in the Nine Cities in centuries), benches along the walls, small wooden tubs, and, filling most of the room, a deep tub filled with gently steaming water. Piled on one of the benches was a stack of fabric: scrubbing cloths, drying cloths, and a large soft house-robe for Harrier to wrap himself in when he was done (a nice gesture, but he was damned if he was going to go wandering around the farm wearing nothing but a house-robe). There was also a pair of wooden sandals tucked neatly beneath the bench, and Harrier noted with faint surprise that they were actually large enough to fit him. He wondered if other humans had visited here, because he'd never yet seen an Elf with feet as big as his.

"You can make yourself useful, you know," he said to Tiercel as he sat down on the bench to remove his boots. "Go out to the wagon and bring back a set of clean clothes for me."

Though he'd lost a shirt (actually his favorite shirt) in the stream when he'd met Kareta, it had been an annoying loss rather than a calamitous one, for House Malkirinath had sent them off more lavishly supplied than their own families had for the trip to Sentarshadeen. Of course, then they'd been taking a pack-mule for a fortnight's trip to another city, not a wagon for a trek to the end of the world, but thanks to Idalia's openhandedness, Harrier could actually afford to lose his shirt more than once—and his pants as well, if it came down to it.

"Sure," Tiercel said. "I think Aressea would even let us do the laundry while we're here, if you asked her."

"Beats banging the stuff on rocks in a muddy stream," Harrier agreed. "Maybe you can make something glow in the dark for her. That's always nice."

Tiercel snorted rudely. "Ancaladar will let me know if there's anything she'd like, but . . . I think the whole idea is that they do things for us, and then they get to ask House Malkirinath to do things for them. Isn't it?"

"Of course it is," Harrier said with a sigh. He shook his head. There were times when he wondered if Tiercel had actually grown up in the same city he had. "And even if—" He stopped, but there really wasn't any way to be tactful about it. "Even if House Malkirinath doesn't have an Elven Mage anymore, I bet a lot of Elven Mages still owe them favors. So House Malkirinath will pay back every-body who helps us with magic—which I bet is what they'll want—and then they can call on those other Elven Mages for help. So it's not like either of us needs to worry about taking charity in any of these places, because we aren't. Everything we get is being paid for."

"Just not by us," Tiercel said.

"Oh, we're paying for it," Harrier answered darkly. *By going off on this crazy-bordering-on-suicidal quest that's going to get us both killed.*

Tiercel frowned, as if he'd just thought of something. "I didn't see . . . Where's Kareta?" he asked cautiously.

"Your guess is as good as mine," Harrier said, shrugging. "She was there when I turned off the main road. At least I think she was. Then I looked around and . . . she wasn't. What? You think I murdered her? Tempting as the idea is, Tyr . . . no."

"You think she just left?" Tiercel asked.

"I *hope* she just left," Harrier answered. "Probably too good to be true, though."

He tucked his boots under the bench beside the sandals and stripped off his tunic and shirt. He was still annoyed at the loss of his favorite shirt—they never had managed to find it. He wadded up his tunic and tossed it at Tiercel.

"Go on. Make yourself useful. Unless the High Magick has spells for cleaning clothes."

Tiercel laughed, throwing Harrier's tunic over his shoulder, and walked out of the bathhouse closing the door behind him as he went.

There was a large ladle in one of the tubs, and Harrier picked it up and used it to scoop several dippers of water from the bath into the tub. Once he'd gotten the rest of his clothes off and folded them neatly out of the way, he stood in the tub with the scrubbing-cloth and the soap and washed himself all over quickly—Elven baths were more for soaking than for scrubbing, as he'd quickly learned. Once he was fairly clean, he stepped into the big tub, sink-ing down until the hot water covered him to the chin.

Half a year ago he wouldn't have even noticed things like this—hot baths, and soft beds, and hot meals (cooked by other people) and served on plates, at tables, where you sat on chairs. Half a year ago he'd been living in Armethalieh, with nothing more pressing to consider than the fact that he was going to be a really bad Apprentice Harbormaster. He'd taken all the comforts of his soft settled City life for granted.

It wasn't *precisely* that he missed them now. He missed his parents, of course, and his brothers, and (oddly enough) the hot ginger cider and roasted chestnuts that they sold down at the docks in the winter, and it hurt to know that in a few more moonturns he was going to miss being at home for his Naming Day celebration, and there was no way he could imagine that he could send a letter home to his family to tell them that he and Tiercel were still all right. But he didn't really miss the rest of it.

He would, he knew, if he were *actually* cold and hungry and really dirty, but so far he hadn't been any of those things—or at least not for long. And he was realistic enough to know that he would probably be all of those things before all this was over, and to still hope it wouldn't happen.

After he'd been in the bath for about a chime, Tiercel came back with a set of his clean clothes. "Aressea says she'll be happy to do our laundry," he said, setting them down on the bench, "and before you ask, no, I didn't *ask* her. I just said we looked forward to the opportunity—if possible—to get everything clean before we left."

"Huh," Harrier said. "Did you not-ask her how far to the Veil?"

Tiercel flopped down on the bench and ran a hand through his hair. "That would be a question," he pointed out. "And I know you told me what to say, but, well . . ."

Harrier sighed. "Fine. I'll do it. For the Light's sake, Tyr, they're only Elves."

Tiercel grinned at him. "Oh, listen to Harrier Gillain, the great traveler! 'Only Elves'! Nothing to concern yourself with!"

"Come over here and I'll hold you under water until you start making sense," Harrier invited.

"I've already got more sense than that," Tiercel said cheerfully. "Hurry up and come out of there and get dressed. They eat early here."

Harrier didn't need any more invitation than that.

Five

The Books of the Wild Magic

AT THE ROLFORT house in Armethalieh, the family ate in the dining room and the servants ate in the servants' hall. In the Gillain household, the family and the apprentices ate together in the dining parlor, and the servants ate in the kitchen. It was the difference between the organization of a Noble household and a Tradesman household.

In the Elven Lands, while both boys were fairly sure there *were* servants—or at least Elves who served in the households they'd guested in—it didn't matter whether the household was as grand as House Malkirinath, or as humble as a simple farm: at meals everyone gathered around the same table, and no distinctions were made between servant and master. Harrier had never found out if there even *were* servants and masters among the Elves, simply because he'd never figured out the right way to phrase the not-a-question.

The Blackrowan household gathered for its evening meal around two long wooden tables in a room just off the kitchen. The simple elegance of every item in the room, from the furnishings, to the serving bowls, to the elegant frescoes on the walls, would have marked this as the dwelling of one of the most aristocratic families in

Armethalieh, rather than as the home of simple country farmers. But—Harrier reflected—these "simple country farmers" had had centuries to think about how they wanted things to look and to be, so it was no wonder that everything looked as if it had been polished and tended for generations. It had been.

At least he didn't have any more to worry about than just regular Elven politeness. He didn't know whether it was because he didn't notice, or they made allowances for him not being an Elf, or they just didn't have the same kinds of differences among them that humans did, but he'd never seen any difference between the highest Elven households and the lowest. So all he really had to worry about was his table manners (which were excellent, since his ma had raised four boys with a long spoon and a quick hand) and not saying anything that resembled a question. And after Elunyerin's similarly forceful tutelage in Elven manners, Harrier was excellent at that as well.

As befit farmhouse fare, the food was hearty and filling, although Harrier still found Elven food odd. Fruit, in his opinion, did not belong in soup, and the meal began with a creamy soup that was thick with rice and cherries. By now Harrier had eaten weirder things without comment, though, and it wasn't as if it was actually *bad*. The main part of the meal was more to his liking: roast pork and roast fowl, served with an assortment of breads, some stuffed with vegetables and spices (and fruits) and some plain. There were other dishes as well: vegetables and stewed fruits and hot and cold pies—it was obvious that if you left the table hungry, it would be your own fault.

Once the meats were on the table, it was the signal for general conversation, and both Aressea and Aratari—who was probably Aressea's husband, though the Elves rarely specified relationships when making introductions—were happy to tell Tiercel and Harrier a great deal about the farm over the course of the meal. Just as Kareta had said, the main crops that Blackrowan produced were silk—which meant silk-houses where both the insects and their food was cultivated—and fruit cordials, which meant orchards as well as stillrooms.

By now it was nearly second nature for Harrier to steer an Elven conversation more-or-less in the direction he wanted it to go without asking any direct questions; it took a while, but as long as he kept reminding himself that he wasn't really in any hurry, he didn't find it too frustrating.

After their hosts had carried the brunt of the conversation as long as politeness demanded, it was time for Tiercel and Harrier to share their own news. Some of it was information that Tiercel—prompted by Ancaladar—had already passed on: Sandalon Elvenking's death, and the accession of Vairindiel to the rulership of the Elven Lands. Other things they spoke of were far less spectacular: the farms and villages they had stopped at between Karahelanderialigor and here, the weather, the travelers they'd encountered along the way.

"And we're going to be heading even farther south," Harrier said, "and so it would make good hearing to learn all that you may tell of the road ahead." While it was true that Ancaladar could certainly just fly ahead and *see* what was there, covering in a matter of hours a distance that would take the wagon days to traverse, neither Tiercel nor Harrier really liked that idea. They weren't quite sure what would happen once they reached the Veil—or whether Ancaladar could get back through it once he'd gone out.

The information he got in response wasn't as encouraging as Harrier could like. They were about a fortnight's journey from the Border, close enough that Aratari said that Blackrowan was the last settlement of any size to be found near the road. And worse, since that was the case, the road itself did not extend much farther. There was hardly any point, after all.

Harrier did his best not to look as disappointed as he felt. He'd suspected that the road would run out some time. He just hadn't expected it to be quite so soon. But the horses were strong and the wagon was sturdy, and if all else failed, at least Ancaladar could pull them out of a ditch. And Aratari and Aressea both announced themselves more than willing to provide all the provisions Tiercel and Harrier could possibly want. It would mean spending another day here, but it was hard to really feel their quest was urgent, when they didn't know where they were going or what they were going to do when they got there. And it was at least as urgent not to starve to death along the way.

After supper, Tiercel and Harrier brought their clothing to the room they'd been given to use while they were guests here—it would be washed tomorrow—and then Tiercel went off to find Ancaladar to get in a bit of practicing. At this time of year it was already dusk, and farmers, even Elven farmers, kept country hours. The household would be in bed soon, to rest in preparation for tomorrow's work. For now, its members occupied themselves with the small chores that filled their evening hours, for there was little leisure time upon a farm. Animals must be fed, clothing must be cared for, preparations made for tomorrow's breakfast. Harrier was just as happy to announce that he was tired and looking forward to his own rest; it was much less complicated for all concerned if the Elves didn't have to deal with having a human underfoot, since neither Aressea nor Aratari, nor, for that matter, any of the rest of the Elves Tiercel and Harrier had met along the way, appeared to have ever seen a human in their lives.

But once he was alone in the guestroom, he was alone with the Three Books.

He'd been surprised to find the small red leather satchel there in the pile of clothing he'd brought from the wagon. The last he'd seen of it, he'd wrapped it up thoroughly in his heavy winter stormcloak and stuffed it into a corner of the wagon. But here it was.

Harrier sighed. *"Unpleasant tasks are best done at once."* His mother had always said that when he'd been dragging his feet about something. And it wasn't as if this was precisely an *unpleasant* task. In fact, as far as Harrier understood things (which was, admittedly, not very well at all) reading or not reading the Three Books wouldn't really make a lot of difference to turning him into a Knight-Mage. It was all about him agreeing to be one.

Aressea had given him a small lamp to light the way to his and Tiercel's bedroom, a small comfortable room at the back of the farmhouse. The lamp didn't give much light, but there were a couple of larger lanterns here, one hung on a hook on the wall, the other set on the table between the beds. Harrier took the one off the wall and carried it over to the bed to set beside the other one. The guestroom lacked the sumptuous luxuries of a desk and upholstered furniture that their rooms had boasted in Karahelanderialigor—the only other furniture in the room was a chest built into one wall that could be used for both seating and storage—but Harrier didn't intend to write anything and he didn't need to lounge. He was just going to take a look at the Books, and he could do that lying on his bed as well as anywhere else. At least, once he had light to see by.

Just as he'd thought, the shallow drawer in the bedside table contained all that was necessary to take care of the lanterns: a clipper to snuff and trim the wicks, a flask of oil to refill the reservoir, and a number of long thin pieces of wood that could be used to light the wick safely. Harrier was interested to note that the drawer was lined in copper, so that even a smoldering wooden spill could be dropped back into the drawer safely with no chance of starting a fire. He'd already learned that strange as the Elves could be sometimes, they were also extremely efficient. He lit the two large lanterns, snuffed the small lamp, and settled himself comfortably on one of the beds.

As he picked up the little satchel again, he hesitated. But he certainly didn't want to think of himself as having less courage than Tiercel did—and Tiercel had participated in the spell to have Ancaladar's Bond transferred to him not knowing whether he'd survive it or not. Harrier sighed heavily. At least Tiercel *wanted* to be a High Mage. Or Harrier was pretty sure he did. A lot more than Harrier wanted to be a Knight-Mage, anyway. *Stop stalling,* he told himself sternly. He opened the satchel and pulled out the contents before he could think about what he was doing.

He hadn't examined them very closely the last time he'd held them—or if he had, the discovery of what they were had wiped all memory of it from his mind. He inspected them more closely now.

They were, well, *book-shaped* books. But small, really only about the size of his hand. All three were exactly the same size and thickness, bound in red leather, and they looked, not exactly old, but worn. Harrier wondered if someone else had owned these Books before they'd come to him, and who they'd been, and what had happened to them, and how the books had gotten from them to Kareta, and how she'd known to bring them to him. He wondered if the Books just sort of *vanished* when a Wildmage died, or if somebody had to do something with them, and if so, what. He wondered how three books that were so small could possibly contain everything that someone needed to know about the Wild Magic.

He held them up to the light and inspected them closely. There was no title on the covers, and no sign that there ever had been, but there was a small gold symbol stamped into the spine of each: a moon, a star, and a sun. *I wonder who makes these?* he thought idly, knowing he was doing his best to delay as long as possible the moment when he had to look inside.

Where to start? There were three of them, and it wasn't as though he'd known in advance that this was going to happen so that he could ask the only Wildmage he'd ever met for some useful advice. But Kareta had kept talking about *The Book of Moon* as if it were the logical starting place, and Harrier supposed it was as good a place to begin as any. He sorted through them, picked it out, and opened it.

The book was hand-written, and the writing, while clear and even, was tiny: Harrier was glad he'd lit both large lanterns, because he thought he'd need all the light he could get to read it. There wasn't a title-page or anything, either. The book just started.

He'd looked at some of Tiercel's High Magick books (mostly out of curiosity, and only after Tiercel had assured him that they couldn't hurt him) and at least they'd made a certain amount of sense to him. They were full of recipes and complicated directions. Harrier could *do* High Magick—assuming he had the patience for all those fiddling details. It just wouldn't work, because he didn't have the Magegift that Tiercel had been born with.

The *Book of Moon*? Wasn't anything like that. The beginning of it seemed to be more like . . . well, he wasn't quite sure. It was talking about how to behave, and why, kind of the way a Light-Priest talked on Light-Day, about how it was important for everyone to respect everyone else, and to believe that they acted from the best intentions even if you didn't understand why they did something, because just the same way that white light turned into a rainbow when it shone through a crystal, so the Eternal Light contained so many different things within it that you couldn't expect to know what they all were just offhand.

Except the Book wasn't talking about people, and it certainly wasn't mentioning the Eternal Light. It talked about acting in harmony with the Wild Magic, and understanding that you must always be ready to pay the price for anything you asked of it, and knowing that the less selfish you were, the more likely you were to get what you really needed.

It didn't really sound a lot like magic to Harrier—even though he'd be the first to admit he didn't know what magic was actually like. What it sounded like was the wondertales he read his young cousins to bed with. "Be good." "Be kind." "Be unselfish." And you'll get what you want.

The trouble is, I don't know what I want. Except for Tiercel and me to be safe back in Armethalieh, and for none of this to have ever happened. He thought for a minute. *No. For none of this to have ever needed to happen. For there to never have been any Fire Woman, or Lake of Fire, or Goblins, or Tiercel to have had to have visions because of them, or . . . anything. That's what I really want.*

He didn't think even the Wild Magic had a spell for that, though.

Only about half or maybe two-thirds of the Book was those closely written pages. Harrier didn't read them all. After the first several, he started skipping through, seeing if there was anything different. That was when he found the spells.

Each one took up a page—or at most, two. There was a name at the top—like in his Ma's cookbooks, like in Tiercel's High Magick books—and then a lot of writing underneath. But there the resemblance to both cookbooks and spellbooks ended.

The first one was *Fire*. That one just had a lot of instructions about thinking and concentrating—and on having something you wanted to light on fire close at hand. Harrier turned the page hastily. He didn't want to set any fires here. Next there was *Finding*—that one required a drop of his blood and the desire to find whatever it was he was looking for—and then there were *Summoning* and *Scrying*—which were a little more complicated, and required him to burn a bunch of leaves and cut himself (again!) or find a pool of water and a jug of wine, and as far as he could tell, Wildmages spent a lot of time poking themselves with sharp knives. Maybe it was so they didn't just do spells any time they felt like it. There were a couple of other spells, too: one was titled *Weather-Calling* (which was the first one Harrier had seen that looked remotely practical, especially if it could be used to summon a fair wind, since he couldn't count the number of times ships had stood in Armethalieh Port for sennights because they couldn't catch a favorable wind) and there was one for *Coldfire* (another one that just needed thinking and concentrating) and one that simply said at the top of the page: *To Know What Needs To Be Done.* That one was vague enough that Harrier vowed then and there that even if he *did* become a Knight-Mage, he would absolutely never cast it. The stuff he'd already read about Mageprices had been enough to thoroughly worry him. Everyone knew that the Wildmages paid for their magic by performing mysterious tasks set them by the Wild Magic Itself, and while Harrier might otherwise have dismissed such tales as one more thing the legends had gotten wrong, what Roneida had said to them back on the Plains seemed to confirm it. She'd made a journey of hundreds of miles to find them—all the way from Vardirvoshanon—because the Wild Magic had demanded it of her.

Which pretty much meant that any time a Wildmage cast a spell, the Wild Magic would make them *do* something, whether they wanted to or not. And that didn't sound very comfortable at all to Harrier. What if the Wild Magic wanted him to pick up and go traipsing off somewhere right in the middle of Tiercel's quest? And what if he said no?

He just wished there was someone he could ask about this stuff. He turned the page.

The last spell that was written in the book was one for Healing, and for that one, apparently he'd need not only as many different kinds of leaves as Ma would use to season a stew (and, apparently, something to burn them on, and he wondered—uneasily—if he ought to see if they had the right sort of thing here) but he'd need to cut a lock of his hair and a lock of the hair of the person he was going to heal, *and* take some hair from anyone else who was "participating in the spell." That sounded weird, and he had no idea how somebody who wasn't either casting the spell or having it cast on them "participated" in it. Maybe there was an explanation of that somewhere in the parts he'd skipped. But then again, he didn't intend to Heal anybody if he could help it. In fact, the more he read, the more he was sure he didn't intend to do any spells at all.

He closed *The Book of Moon*, grumbling under his breath, and tucked all three of them back into the satchel. He was just in time to get them under his pillow before the door opened and Tiercel walked in. His hair was damp from a ducking—probably in the watering trough, though there was a washroom down the hall—and he hadn't bothered to tie his hair back again. Since they'd left Armethalieh, Harrier had gotten his hair cut whenever its length started to annoy him, but Tiercel had simply let his grow. It was down to his shoulders now.

A globe of Coldfire hovered over his head, but by now, Harrier hardly noticed the things any more.

"If Aressea is anything like my Ma, she'll whale you for dripping on her clean floors," Harrier said.

"I'm not dripping," Tiercel said. He snapped his fingers, and the glowing blue ball of light vanished.

"You're wet," Harrier said.

"I'm damp," Tiercel corrected. "What are you doing?"

"Nothing," Harrier answered reflexively.

"You're reading your Books, aren't you?" Tiercel said. "Can I see them?"

Harrier felt an automatic impulse to deny that he'd been doing any such thing, but this was *Tiercel*. He dug the satchel out from under his pillow and tossed it across the room. "Knock yourself out," he invited.

Tiercel walked over and sat down on his own bed, where the light was best. He opened the satchel and pulled out one of the books. "It sort of tingles," he said as he opened it. He looked down at the first page, frowned, turned the book over, opened it from the other end, paged through it quickly. "Also, it's blank."

"What?" Harrier sat up hastily and reached for the book. Tiercel passed it to him across the gap between the two beds. Harrier glanced at the spine. There was a small cluster of stars stamped there, so—obviously—this was *The Book of Stars*. He paged through it. All the pages were covered with the same dense script as *The Book of Moon*. "No it isn't," he said.

"Well, *I* couldn't read it," Tiercel said. "I couldn't even see it."

"Maybe—" Harrier began, but Tiercel shook his head

quickly, rubbing his fingers against his pantsleg as if they still tingled.

"Maybe they're something only a Wildmage can read." He tossed the satchel back over to Harrier's bed. It landed beside Harrier with a thump, but he barely noticed.

He'd been able to read them.

Was that all it took? Did this mean he already *was* a Wildmage, or a Knight-Mage, or whatever it was he was supposed to be now? Did it mean there was nothing else he needed to do to be able to light fires just by thinking about it and summon up winds and make balls of Coldfire just the way Tiercel did? He didn't feel any different than he had when he'd sat down to dinner!

"I'm really not going to be a very good . . . Knight-Mage," Harrier said quietly.

Tiercel looked at him, and his mouth drew into the shape that it took when he was thinking. He started to say something, then he started pulling off his boots instead. "I'm not really the best High Mage," he said softly, when he'd gotten them off and set them aside. "Certainly not as good as First Magistrate Cilarnen. Or Jermayan Dragon-Rider, come to that. Even if he . . . was . . . an Elven Mage and not a High Mage. But." He stopped, and Harrier could tell that Tiercel was thinking carefully before he spoke. Funny, because usually Tiercel just charged right into things, especially with him. "But you know, Har, it's not like I *decided* to become a High Mage. Oh, sure, I went poking around the Great Library because of your Uncle Alfrin's book, and then I decided to go and do a spell, and those parts were pretty much up to me. But I was a High Mage before that, really, because I had the Magegift. And that was the Light's decision. And the Gods of the Wild Magic, because you know, I think I would have died when I was a baby because of the Magegift if there hadn't been a Wildmage in Sentarshadeen to make me better. So it's because of the Wild Magic that I'm here now, being a High Mage."

"You're a *good* High Mage," Harrier said, determined to defend his friend.

Tiercel shook his head. "Not really. I don't know. But the thing is, I was *picked*. And you were picked. By the Wild Magic. And, Har, you've kind of got to, I don't know, hope or believe or trust that the Wild Magic knows what it's doing to have picked us. Or . . . I don't know."

We'll be lost before we start. Harrier didn't know how good a High Mage Tiercel was—he had to be a good one, didn't he, with all the practicing he was doing and with Ancaladar to help?—and he knew exactly how bad a Knight-Mage he himself was going to be. Even if they weren't exactly like all the stories told about Kellen the Poor Orphan Boy, Harrier did know one thing: a Knight-Mage could fight, and probably even command armies. And he was strong, and good with his fists, and he'd never backed down from a fight—in fact he'd even started his share—but he'd seen Elunyerin and Rilphanifel spar against each other back at House Malkirinath, and he knew he couldn't do that. And as for leading an army . . . he wouldn't even know where to start.

Not that they *had* an army right now.

But Tiercel was right about one thing, even though Harrier was enormously reluctant to admit it. The Wild Magic had picked both of them. So he either had a choice between deciding it didn't know what it was doing and refusing the books—and while he'd like to do the second, the first was just terrifying—or just muddling on and pretending he thought everything would work out. Although no matter what Ancaladar said, Harrier was absolutely certain Kellen had *never* felt this way. Ever.

"I'm tired if you aren't," he grumbled. He stuffed *The Book of Stars* back into the satchel and stuffed it under his pillow, then bent over to remove his own boots.

AFTER SO LONG on the road they were both used to getting up as soon as it was light, and even if they were sleeping indoors in soft beds, habit woke both of them a few minutes before Talareniel—one of the Elves they'd met the previous evening—scratched on the door to let them know that the morning meal would be upon the table shortly. Both boys were up, dressed, washed, and in the dining room quickly enough to be able to help Aratari, Siralcar, and Talareniel bring the dishes to the table.

Today, Harrier discovered, Tiercel would be gone for most of the day, since at some point yesterday when he'd been out of earshot, Tiercel and Ancaladar had offered to assist with a number of tasks around the farm. "Ancaladar says it will be good practice for me," Tiercel said when the subject came up again at breakfast, from which Harrier figured out that the "tasks" referred to all had to involve magic in one way or another.

That left him to get everything ready for tomorrow's departure. Half a year ago he wouldn't have known where to begin, and now half his mind was occupied with lists of things they'd need, while the other half was engaged in framing his requests in accordance with the demands of Elven politeness.

Salt was the first thing on his list. If they could hunt on the other side of the Veil, they'd need to be able to preserve what they caught. Fishhooks, because he'd never thought to ask for any at their previous stops. Grain, because horses who pulled a wagon all day couldn't be asked to live on grass. Bacon and meal and tea—and honey for the tea—because they had some dried and preserved foods, but he wanted to load up on as much more as they could. Rope, because his Da had drummed into him that there was *always* a use for rope.

"I would be lacking in courtesy—and a very poor guest—did I abuse the generosity of those who had offered nothing but kindness," he said at one point. He wasn't quite sure if the Elves could refuse to give you things when you asked for them, even indirectly.

Aratari had assigned Siralcar to assist him for the day. Harrier had no idea at all how old Siralcar might be—he looked like a grown man, but among Elves, that could mean he was anything from a few decades to several centuries old. Siralcar regarded him, smiling faintly.

"I do not think that it would be possible for you or Tiercel Human Mage to exhaust the bounty of Farm Blackrowan, Harrier Gillain," he answered. "And Tiercel does us great honor by aiding us today as he does. The work come the Springtide will go more quickly with the fields cleared now. And calling the queen home to her own hive will mean more honey for all. Yet it would be good to know, should you care to tell it, what purpose could take you across the Veil."

Harrier knew that even if the Elves didn't ask direct questions, that didn't keep them from being just as curious as anyone else. And while he didn't intend to tell Siralcar everything about everything, there was no harm in telling him where they were going—especially since none of the Elves had the least interest in leaving the Elven Lands.

"Far to the south and the west there's a big desert called the Madiran," he answered. "Back home—in Armethalieh— we trade with them. And that's where we're going. I'm just not quite sure how far from here it is."

"It would be good to know what such trade might consist of," Siralcar said, after he'd mulled Harrier's words over for a few moments.

Harrier thought carefully, trying to picture in his mind some of the cargoes he'd helped to check aboard outbound ships. "Rugs, a lot of it," he said. "Nothing as fine as I've seen here, of course. Spices. Goldwork. Metalwork and pottery. Some stays in the City. Some is loaded onto ships and goes across Great Ocean, and is sold in other lands."

"Even here we have heard of Armethalieh," Siralcar said. "It is a very long way from here."

Harrier sighed. There wasn't much to say to that.

WHEN THEY'D BROUGHT everything Harrier wanted to take with him on the journey to the storage barn where the wagon was being kept, Harrier's heart sank. Even if Tiercel never wanted to be able to get at any of his High Magick *junk* ever again, there was no way they could fit all this stuff inside the wagon.

"Storage baskets may be attached to the outside of the wagon," Siralcar said quietly, seeing Harrier's expression. "They can be lined in oilcloth to keep their contents from the damp, and they will not add much to the weight of the wagon. It will be only the work of a few hours to attach them."

Harrier nodded. It was a good solution, and the load would only grow lighter as they used up the supplies. "I thank you for all your courtesy. It would be good if such a thing could be done. There is . . . one item more that I . . . I think . . ." he stopped.

Siralcar regarded him with obvious curiosity.

"It is difficult to describe something if you don't know it exists," Harrier said with a sigh.

"Things which do not exist can be made, if they can but be described," Siralcar said helpfully.

Harrier ran a hand through his hair. "It would be a sort of a brazier, I suppose. But very small. Just something that would hold one of those little cakes of charcoal that go into a tea-brazier to keep the water hot."

Siralcar frowned, considering. "Perhaps such a thing can be found."

GATHERING TOGETHER THE list of provisions had taken the entire morning, and even though it hadn't involved a lot of lifting and carrying—much less than Harrier would have done any afternoon on the docks in Armethalieh— he'd still worked up enough of an appetite to be more than interested in the midday meal.

The weather was mild enough that the meal was taken outdoors, even though as far as Harrier could remember, it should be Vintage or even Mistrise by now, and back home there would be heavy frosts at night and everyone would be watching the skies and predicting the date of the first snow. Several long tables were set up under the trees; Harrier had already noticed that for all that the Elves built so many things to last, they didn't build one more permanent thing than they needed, or leave something standing a moment longer than necessary. Where humans would have just left the outdoor tables up year-round—or at least during the moonturns of good weather—the Elves took them down and put them up between uses.

Interestingly enough, there were many more people gathered for the midday meal than there had been for either breakfast or supper. Harrier didn't have enough experience of farms in general (let alone Elven ones) to know whether this was typical—and whether it was or not, where *were* all the other Elves when they weren't here? As far as he knew, Blackrowan Farm was the only settlement for miles around. He knew it would be rude to ask the question even if he could figure out how to phrase it, though. Maybe Ancaladar could tell him later. At least the food was good and plentiful. He hadn't had a meal yet in the Elven Lands that wasn't, even if some of the dishes were a little strange.

He wanted to know what Tiercel had been doing all morning, but even though he was right there beside him at the table, Harrier couldn't exactly ask him a question—not at a table full of Elves—and Tiercel really wasn't picking up any of the indirectly phrased hints Harrier was dropping, so after two or three tries, he gave up. He'd get it out of Tiercel later. And nobody was dawdling over the meal anyway, any more than they would have been around the Gillain table at midday back home. There was always work to do.

After the meal, Harrier helped take down and store away the tables again, and by the time he was done with that, Siralcar came to get him to tell him the baskets were ready for the wagon. They hitched one of the farm's plowhorses to it to bring it out of the shed where there was better light to work by—no sense in interrupting Nethiel and Dulion's vacation—and Siralcar and two more craftworkers began the exacting task of fitting the six large baskets to the wagon's sides. Harrier was interested to see that no nailing or drilling was necessary, merely the removal of a few plugs in the wood that could easily be hammered back into place again later once the baskets were removed. It was as if the wagon had been designed to have hampers attached to the outsides. And for all he knew, it had been: it was an Elven-made wagon, after all, and Harrier already knew how efficient the Elves were.

Each of the baskets was large and sturdy, bound with leather straps, and could be buckled closed. And—just as Siralcar had said—was fully lined in durable oilcloth, making it entirely waterproof.

"It's too bad you don't trade with us any more," Harrier said wistfully, examining one of the baskets. "You make so many useful things. I'm sure we could use them. But I suppose we don't have anything you'd want in exchange."

"No single person can know the shape of all the world," Lanya said reprovingly. She was the elder of the two craftworkers—old enough that her hair actually had some gray in it, so Harrier couldn't even begin to imagine how old she must be.

"True," Harrier said, grinning. "But I find it hard to imagine that you wouldn't have everything you want right here."

Lanya smiled back. "You are young. And one may have all that one needs, and still not have all that one desires."

"I suppose you're right," Harrier said, surprised. The more he thought about it, the more he was certain that Lanya *was* right—back in Armethalieh, both he and Tiercel had seen lots of people—both Trade-class and Nobles—who were never satisfied, no matter how many possessions or honors they accumulated. He supposed it was lucky in one way—if people stopped buying things once they had what they needed, half the merchants in Armethalieh would starve. In another, it wasn't, because if you were never satisfied, then you were never happy. It wasn't the sort of thing he was used to thinking about. He frowned suspiciously, wondering if this was something to do with the Three Books. He thought, though, that it was probably more to do with walking halfway across the world and having to listen to Tiercel babble at him the entire time.

IT WAS MIDAFTERNOON by the time the baskets (hampers, really) were affixed to the sides of the wagon to both Siralcar and Harrier's satisfaction and the process of loading the supplies could begin. Of course, that meant *un*loading the entire wagon, and that was a task Harrier wanted to do himself. It wasn't that he didn't trust the Elves. It was that the whole wagon was full of Tiercel's *junk,* and if anybody was going to break it, it might as well be him. And for that matter, the best way to know where everything was in a load was to be the one who packed it. Morcia Tamaricans was Chief Cargomaster at the Armethalieh Docks—you didn't get a cargo onto—or off of—a ship without her approval as well as Da's. She'd saved many a ship from going down in Great Ocean simply by refusing to give them their Permit to Sail until they repacked their hull, and sometimes Harrier had helped her. It occurred to him—now, when it was far too late to do him the least bit of good—that he would have made a terrible Portmaster and hated the Customs House, but that he wouldn't have minded being Morcia's apprentice at all.

And while a wagon wasn't a ship, the bells he'd spent listening to her bellow at ships' crews about the proper way to stow their cargoes so they didn't get themselves killed before their ships cleared the mouth of Armethalieh Harbor stood him in good stead now, as he packed away sacks of grain and sacks of salt and sacks of meal and tins of tea and kegs of dried fruit and kegs of crystallized honey and jugs of cider and jugs of liquid honey and a large crock of butter that should keep until it was gone and wheels of cheese and fletches of bacon and a sack of smoked fish and another sack of dried beef and a coil of rope and a big sack of charcoal and some spare horseshoes and nails and a wooden mallet to set the pegs back into the wagon's walls again sometime. And then all the hampers hung from the sides of the wagon were full, and inside of the wagon was full, too, with clothes and bedrolls and a box that held fishhooks and line and a whetstone and a couple of extra knives, because Siralcar said you always needed one more knife than you had when you were on a journey. And Harrier knew that right now it seemed like an awful lot of food and supplies, and he also knew that it wouldn't get them even halfway to the Madiran, which was vaguely annoying.

Just as he was nearly done, Lanya appeared again. She was holding a small object between her hands, and had a large leather bag slung crosswise over her shoulder on a long strap. "I believe you will find this to be what you require. Siralcar told me of your need. It was a simple item to craft." She held it out.

Harrier took it and examined it. The outside was copper, but it seemed to be lined in clay. The bottom of the bowl was flat, with three small broad feet sticking out from it—the little brazier looked as if it would rest steadily on practically any surface. "Yes," he said, bowing. "I think this is precisely what I need."

"I have brought a bag as well, so that you may carry it in comfort. And herbs and leaves—the most common ones. For your spells," she added, seeing Harrier's look of incomprehension.

"I . . . Ah . . ." He really had no idea of what to say. He'd barely gotten used to the idea that he'd been given the Books at all. He really hadn't gotten much past that. And he had no idea at all what had given Lanya the idea (even if it might be true) that he might be a Wildmage now.

"If I am in error, I beg your pardon. But there are few other uses for such an item as this, young Harrier, than to husband the small fires which a Wildmage might need, from time to time, to light. It is true that the magic that returned to the Elves with Jermayan son of Malkirinath, An-caladar's Bondmate, does not run in this wise, but Elven memories are long. And we owe a great debt to the Wild-mages. We remember."

"I—" Harrier took a deep breath. Whatever else he did, he had to *stop stammering* as if he'd suddenly forgotten how to speak. "Thank you. I don't know yet if you're right, but . . . you aren't wrong." *Oh, that's clear as mud,* he snarled to himself.

"Then perhaps my gift to you will ease your way, hu-man child," Lanya said. "We are told, always, that human memories are short as human lives are brief, but my father was born at the Fortress of the Crowned Horns. I have of-ten thought he would not have been, were it not for Wild-mages."

"I'm sorry," Harrier said again, bowing. "I'm afraid what they've told you about humans is true. I don't under-stand what you're telling me."

Lanya smiled. "Then finish your task, and as you do I will tell you the tale, as I had it from my father, and he from his mother, and you will understand."

HE DIDN'T UNDERSTAND—not really—even after she told it, but it was still a fascinating story of the darkest days of a terrible war. The Elves hadn't known they were going to win. In fact, when Lanya's grandmother had been sent to the Fortress of the Crowned Horns, the Elves had been pretty sure they were going to lose, and were hoping against hope to save at least a few of their people from the Endarkened.

One part of the story was recognizable to Harrier, though: the moment when Vimaudiel had stood on the bat-tlements of the Fortress and seen nothing but green grass and flowers everywhere she looked, because all the En-darkened were dead and the Great Flowering had swept across the land. She'd gone home—Harrier was a little surprised to learn she'd lived in Sentarshadeen, but of course it had been an Elven city once upon a time—to find that her husband Anamitar had survived as well. And when Sandalon Elvenking of the House of Caerthalien had succeeded his father Andoreniel Elvenking of the House of Caerthalien and decreed that Elvenkind should withdraw beyond the mountains, she had settled here with her family to farm.

It was a long and fascinating story, and by the time it was done, not only was the packing done and the wagon returned to the storage shed, but Harrier had rinsed off in the watering trough and he and Lanya were sitting in the shade of one of the trees drinking large tankards of berry cider.

"You have a long history," he said, when Lanya indicated her story was finished.

"Ah, Harrier, were I to tell you a *long* story, we should be here for a sennight, perhaps more. Long stories are best saved for deep winter, when the days are short and time grows heavy." Lanya glanced at the sky. "But a long enough tale for now, I think, for your friend returns from the fields, and Aressea frets if we keep her waiting when she thinks it is time to serve supper." Lanya got gracefully to her feet and walked away, and Harrier got much less gracefully to his feet and followed.

"So, DID YOU have fun today?" Tiercel asked a couple of hours later.

It was after the evening meal, and both boys had retreated to their room once more. After breakfast tomorrow they'd be on the road again. Harrier tried not to think about the fact that this might be the last time he slept in a bed in *his entire life*.

"I arranged to keep us from starving. How about you?"

"Oh, I had lots of fun. I cast Mageshield to keep from getting stung by a swarm of angry bees, turned a bunch of rocks into water so the Elves could dig a new irrigation ditch, made *another* bunch of rocks come up out of a field—Har, you have *no* idea how many rocks there can be in a field—and then it was back to the bees. If this is what High Mages did with their time, no wonder they all quit."

"I don't see what you're complaining about. You spent the day casting spells."

That startled a laugh out of Tiercel. "You know, you're right. I did."

"And you didn't throw up or pass out or anything. So go to sleep."

THEY WERE UP as soon as it was light. Harrier had slept with the Three Books under his pillow. He wasn't quite sure why, because if what Kareta had told him was true, it wasn't as if they could possibly be stolen from him. He just had.

Both of them did a quick check of the room as they dressed, making sure they had everything, then once they were washed and dressed, Harrier took the pack with their gear out to the wagon and tossed it inside.

The bag Lanya had given him the day before was hanging on a peg just inside the wagon door, and Harrier lifted the flap and tucked the Three Books inside. He'd think of something else to do with the red satchel later. He looked around the wagon, and took a moment to think that if he and Tiercel were both Mages now (and apparently they both were—or could be—which was the scariest thought Harrier'd had in quite a while) it certainly seemed to be more *convenient* to be a Wildmage. At least he wouldn't need to drag a Flowering Fair's worth of junk around with him everywhere he went.

The only meal anybody dawdled over in any way at Blackrowan Farm was supper, so it wasn't long before people were leaving to begin the day's work. Before they went out to the stables, Tiercel and Harrier made sure to formally thank Aressea and Aratari for their more-than-generous hospitality.

"It is a gift to repay those gifts which our greatfathers were given," Aratari answered, bowing in return. "Leaf and Star watch over you until you pass this way again."

"And the Eternal Light guide your way," Tiercel answered simply.

Six

The Unicorn's Feast

IT SEEMED AS if Nethiel and Dulion were more eager to be on the road than the boys were—or at least *eager*. The Elven-bred draft horses frisked and skittered about as Harrier led them, one after the other, out of their stalls and lined them up with the wagon-tree to hitch them to the wagon. After so many days of doing this—although it was really only a sennight and a few days since they'd left Karahelanderialigor—it was nearly second nature to him, and Harrier was glad that Elunyerin and Rilphanifel had spent so much time making sure he knew what to do and then leaving him to do it.

As he tested the girths, making sure that each was firmly and snugly fastened, he saw Tiercel come walking out of the barn carrying Ancaladar's saddle and harness. Harrier was always impressed that Tiercel could carry it by himself, not because the saddle itself was particularly large (it wasn't), but because the straps—which were long enough to go around various parts of Ancaladar, after all—really weighed more than the saddle itself. If not for the fact that all the parts of the saddle were of Elven manufacture, and so both stronger and lighter than anything that could be found in human lands, Harrier doubted that Tiercel could have lifted it.

"See you at lunch, I guess," Tiercel said, and Harrier lifted a hand in salute.

He was just about to climb onto the seat of the wagon when Siralcar and Lanya came hurrying out of the house, carrying a large hamper between them. He got down quickly, looping the reins around the hand-brake at the corner of the wagon step. Dropped reins, as he'd learned from bitter experience, tangled, and were Darkness Itself to *un*tangle.

"Food for the early part of your journey," Lanya said as he came forward to meet them. "It will not keep above a day or three, but I do not think that you and Tiercel High Mage will find it a hardship to consume it in that time."

"No," Harrier said, bowing. "I'm sure we won't. I thank you again for all your kindness to us."

He quickly went around to the back of the wagon and opened the door, then helped the two Elves settle the hamper into place on the floor, shoving a few items out of the way to make room. From the look of it, there was quite a bit of food inside, and he was tempted to open it and peek, but that would be more than rude. He shut the door and bowed again.

"A safe journey to you," Siralcar said.

"Come back to us, if it pleases you. To hear all that you may wish to tell would make good hearing," Lanya added.

"Thank you," Harrier said. "I will, if—If it works out that way," he finished awkwardly. Both Elves nodded, as if what he'd said seemed perfectly reasonable to them, and Harrier mounted up to the bench of the wagon, collected the reins, and headed the team up the path back to the main road.

IT TOOK HIM almost a chime to get the wagon settled down the main road again and he had to rein the horses in the entire way. Usually they were slow first thing in the morning, which was fine—you didn't really want a draft-horse that was going to take off down the road at a canter and jounce the wagon behind it to kindling—but this particular morning they were frisky with a day and a half of rest, and Harrier thought they *might* think about cantering. Or at least trotting.

When he reached the road, he could tell from the position of the sun that it was still several chimes before Morning Bells. Ancaladar made a low pass over the wagon, and Tiercel leaned down from the saddle and waved energetically. Harrier waved back, but if Tiercel had something to say, it was going to have to wait until lunch, since there was no way for them to have a conversation: Ancaladar could do many wonderful things in the air, but as far as Harrier knew, hovering wasn't one of them. The dragon veered away, sliding up into the sky again, and Harrier watched him go. The air was sharp and cold with early morning chill, but the day was clear, and later it would be warm enough for Harrier to bundle his heavy stormcloak behind the seat and enjoy the sun. He wondered how much colder it was up in the sky. Tiercel had often offered to take him for a ride on Ancaladar's back—the saddle was built for two—but he'd always refused. Maybe—

"*There* you are! I thought you were supposed to be in a hurry to get wherever it is you're going! I almost got tired of waiting! At least you took the time to read your Books!"

Harrier's automatic startled tug on the reins brought the wagon to a halt. He took a deep breath—grateful he hadn't yelped in shock—and glanced down at the side of the wagon. Kareta was standing there looking up at him.

He resisted his first impulse—which was to deny having read any of the Books at all—and his second one—which was to climb down from the step and try to chase her away. He had the feeling that neither one would work out very well. "Why didn't you come to the farm?" he asked.

"You don't know much about unicorns, do you?" Kareta asked in return.

"Are they all as annoying as you are?" Harrier asked.

"I'm not annoying," Kareta denied. She sounded hurt,

but she'd fooled Harrier thoroughly the first time he'd laid eyes on her and he was determined she wasn't going to do it again.

"Sure you aren't," Harrier muttered. He slapped the reins on the horses' rumps to get the team moving again. This was probably what Tiercel had been waving at him about a few minutes ago—he'd certainly have been able to see Kareta coming a lot further away than Harrier could. Even if he'd been looking for her.

"So did you get apples?" she asked, once the wagon was moving again. "And oat cakes? And—*oh!*—chestnuts for roasting, because roast chestnuts—"

"And why in the name of the Blessed Saint Idalia would I have been asking for a bunch of things like that, considering that you vanished without a word and I had no idea you were ever coming back?" Harrier demanded.

"You missed me!" Kareta exclaimed in delight.

"I hoped you were gone for good," Harrier growled.

"No you didn't. You missed me."

"You wish I missed you. And I didn't. And now you're mad because pulling that mysterious unicorn disappearing act means I didn't ask the Elves for a bunch of things you could stuff yourself with," Harrier said. Now that she was back he was sure he'd wanted her gone, though he hadn't been as certain of that when she'd actually *been* gone. And he knew Kareta was a unicorn, but if he closed his eyes, she really sounded a lot like Hevnade Rolfort, the oldest of Tiercel's younger sisters, who was fourteen and incredibly annoying.

"I do *not* stuff myself!" Kareta protested.

"Well you won't be doing it now, because I didn't take your provisions list to the farm," Harrier pointed out.

"I'm sure you got at least *some* good things to eat," Kareta said hopefully.

"And how in the name of the Eternal Light do I know what unicorns like to eat?" Harrier demanded. He sighed. "Yes. Probably. Maybe. We'll see."

"Oh, good!" Kareta galloped up the road for a short

distance, stopped in the middle, and, well, *capered* was the best way Harrier could describe it. The early-morning sun gleamed off her golden coat, and her spiral horn sparkled like the inside of a seashell. And even while Harrier was trying to be cross, he had to admit she was beautiful.

The legends and wondertales all said that Kellen had ridden the Magic Unicorn Shalkan into battle. Looking at Kareta, Harrier just couldn't imagine it. Until he'd seen the Light-Temple at Imrathalion, he'd always just assumed that unicorns were the size of horses, but Kareta was about the same size as the ones depicted in the carved wall panels at the Temple (the size of a small deer), and those dated back to the Time of Mages, so Harrier had to imagine that they were fairly accurate, and that unicorns hadn't changed much in the last thousand years. He still couldn't see how you'd ride something that size, though. Fortunately, he thought it was going to be one of the few problems he wasn't going to have.

She came trotting back, tossing her head and looking very pleased with herself. "It's a beautiful day," she announced.

"Would you rather it was raining?" Harrier asked, just to be difficult. He pulled the hood of his stormcloak up and tugged it as far forward as it would go. He didn't really need it, but he wasn't exactly in a position to go stomping off and slamming a door between him and Kareta right now.

"Humans don't like to get wet," Kareta answered loftily, just as if she were an expert on the subject of humans.

Harrier decided to ignore that, as the only things he could possibly do would be to agree with her—which would make her unbearably smug—or try to argue that he *did* like to get rained on. And he didn't. And he wasn't quite sure whether or not unicorns could tell when you were lying.

"So," Kareta said brightly, when the wagon had rolled along in silence for a few more minutes, "how do you like being a Knight-Mage?"

"I'm not a Knight-Mage," Harrier said, because this was a point he *was* willing to argue.

"You've read your Books, haven't you?" Kareta said, as if this were all that was necessary.

"I *looked* at part of *one* Book," Harrier said.

Kareta didn't say anything.

"What?" he demanded. "It isn't like that makes me . . . anything. I've read books before. Lots of them."

"Why are you arguing with me?" Kareta asked ingenuously.

Harrier slumped down on the bench and didn't reply. Arguing with Kareta—even *talking* to Kareta—was like juggling with a ball of tar. You ended up with it all over you and no idea of how it had happened. And no way to get easily unstuck, either.

UNFORTUNATELY, IT WASN'T possible to simply *ignore* her. If she wasn't asking him idiotic questions—like what sort of armor did he think he'd like to have as a Knight-Mage—she was pointing out things along the way that were actually almost *interesting*—like exotic sorts of trees, or the flocks of sheep grazing on the distant hillside, or mentioning that in another day or two, when they were beyond the edge of the land held by Blackrowan Farm, they'd be in country as wild and uncultivated as any part of the Veiled Lands got. Since he couldn't shut her up, and couldn't outrun her, Harrier was very grateful to see Ancaladar on the ground up ahead, meaning it was time to stop for lunch.

He drove the wagon off the edge of the road, onto the grass. It was always a mystery to Harrier how everything in the Elven Lands could be so neat and tidy, as if armies of invisible gardeners were everywhere, clipping the grass and raking the ground beneath the trees. Of course, for all he knew, maybe they were.

He climbed down from the bench and stretched. Elunyerin and Rilphanifel had said there was no need to unhitch the team if they'd only be standing for an hour or so, but it would still be a good idea to get them a drink if that could be arranged. He opened the back of the wagon. He'd go and see if it was possible to lead them down to the stream without unhitching them after he'd gotten the brazier set up. "You want to get off your lazy tail and help me with this?" he called to Tiercel. He wasn't sure what was in the hamper the Elves had given him this morning, but he knew it would take two people to manage it.

"What do you—oh," Tiercel said, peering into the wagon. "It's full."

"Of course it's full. There isn't another farm or village that we know of between here and the Madiran," Harrier said.

"But how am I going to get at my books? Or our clothes? Or—"

"We'll move things, Tyr," Harrier said, sighing. "And most of this is going to be gone in a sennight or two." *You wouldn't believe how fast it's all going to disappear, in fact,* he thought darkly. "Now come on. Lanya and Siral-car packed us some special stuff this morning, and we'll need to eat that first."

Once the extra hamper was out of the way, Harrier was able to get out the heavy blanket to spread on the grass, and the tea-brazier and pot, and the basket with the rest of the supplies for the meal—napkins and plates were vital when they couldn't just hand over their clothing to household servants to get it washed. Once everything was out of the wagon, and Tiercel was setting it up, Harrier decided he had time to take the water bucket and go looking for the stream. "And don't let her stuff herself!" he called over his shoulder, since Kareta was hovering greedily over Tiercel's shoulder as he unbuckled the straps of the hamper.

Elven roads always followed the landscape. Harrier wasn't sure what this road was called—possibly "Road That Goes Nowhere in Particular," since it went in the general direction of the southern border of the Elven Lands and then just sort of stopped—but what he *did* know about it was that there was a stream here, and the road went along beside it, and it wouldn't stop doing that, well, as long as there was a road at all. He supposed if you lived as long as the Elves did, you weren't ever in a hurry to get places. At least it meant he never had to spend half the day looking for water.

There weren't many trees on this side of the stream at all, and he decided he wouldn't have to unhitch the team to bring the horses down for their drink. He'd let them cool off a bit first, though. They'd been working all morning.

He knelt on the bank, automatically checking to be sure that the water was clear and running freely before filling his bucket. Simera had taught both him and Tiercel, moon-turns ago, how to be sure that you were taking good sweet water out of a stream.

Even now, thinking of his dead Centaur friend made Harrier's chest hurt. She would have loved to have seen the Elven Lands! And she'd so much wanted to know what she'd always called "the end of the tale"—the reason for Tiercel's visions, and what he was going to do about them. Discovering that Harrier was to be a Wildmage—well! He couldn't know for sure, but he imagined the thought would have made Simera laugh until she couldn't stand up. Light knew *he'd* be laughing, if it weren't happening to him. He felt like the Mock-Mage in the Flowering Festival Plays. Only the Mock-Mage thought he had magic and didn't, and Harrier . . . well, it looked like it was going to be the other way around. He had magic—or he would—but it didn't feel like it.

When he walked back to the wagon with the bucket of water, Tiercel looked up at him in helpless exasperation. "I just set it down for a minute," he said.

Kareta had her face in a pie dish gobbling up its contents enthusiastically. Harrier sighed. There wasn't even any point in being angry. "You probably couldn't have stopped her," he said. "Unless you, you know, hit her with a lightning bolt or something. You couldn't do that, I suppose?"

"It's good!" Kareta said, raising her head. Her muzzle was covered with what looked like blackberries. She was purple halfway to her eyes.

"You look ridiculous," Harrier said flatly. "And you're a thief." He walked over, picked up the pie dish, and skimmed it a few feet away. It hit the grass and slid.

"Hey! I wasn't done with that!"

"Then go finish it," Harrier said unfeelingly. He sat down on the blanket and filled the kettle. Tiercel had already lit the fire in the brazier, and the water would boil soon. "You didn't let her get into anything else, did you?"

"No, I . . . no," Tiercel said. He shrugged again. "She—"

"And you with four sisters," Harrier scoffed. He'd have thought that Tiercel could manage one pesky unicorn, after riding herd on a house full of younger sisters all these years.

"But she's a unicorn!"

"Okay, so none of your sisters has hooves and a tail. As far as I can see, that's about the only difference." He opened the hamper and began to investigate the rest of the contents.

The Elves of Blackrowan Farm had certainly given them a luxurious send-off. In addition to the pie that the two of them hadn't gotten any of, there were several loaves of fresh bread, a couple of cold roast chickens, apples, and some loaves of the spicy fruit-bread that had been served at breakfast both days the boys had been there. There was a large piece of cold mutton as well—Siralcar had been right; the contents of the hamper would keep them for several meals. Harrier tore off a large chunk of chicken and a piece of bread, grabbed a plate and a napkin, and began to eat.

"I'm still hungry," Kareta said a few minutes later, coming back.

"Go eat grass," Harrier said heartlessly.

"You're mean," she said.

Tiercel laughed—nearly spilling hot water on himself, since he was filling the teapot. "I suppose there are all kinds of unicorns," he said after a few moments. Harrier recognized the sound of Tiercel hastily backpedaling when he recognized that he'd said something that might hurt someone's feelings.

"What do you mean by that?" Kareta demanded, rounding on him.

"Well, I mean, there are all kinds of people, you know," Tiercel said. "Some that are . . ."

"Yes?" Kareta said dangerously. She was swishing her tail back and forth, and Harrier could tell that she had no intention of letting Tiercel get out of the conversation gracefully. So be it. Tiercel might worry about hurting her feelings, but *he* didn't.

"He means some that are mature and reasonable—like him—and others that steal people's lunches when their backs are turned," Harrier said bluntly. Kareta rounded on him, her blue eyes wide. The effect would have been a lot more dramatic if her nose weren't purple. Harrier snickered.

"You're mean!" she cried. "You're mean and hateful and I don't like you anymore! All I've ever done is help you! I brought you your Books and, and—everything!"

"And you stole our pie," Harrier said mercilessly. He'd grown up on the Armethalieh Docks, and spent a good portion of that time with people trying to wheedle him into one thing or another. It would be different if he thought her feelings were actually hurt. But he didn't think they were. "It's not as if you asked. Or *waited* to be asked," he added.

"That's not *fair*!" she burst out.

"Actually, it probably is," Tiercel said meditatively, as if the idea had just occurred to him. "I know you and Harrier argue all the time. But he's always shared his food with you. And so would I."

"All right," Kareta said, stamping her foot. "I said I was hungry. Give me some of the bread. You've got a lot."

"No," Harrier said around a mouthful of chicken.

"And that's fair too," Tiercel said, as calmly as if he were the High Magistrate herself.

There was probably a long explanation that would have followed that, but Kareta didn't stick around to hear it. Tiercel had barely gotten half his next sentence out before she wheeled away and galloped off, and in only a few seconds she was only a bright spark in the distance.

"She *is* fast," Harrier said calmly, reaching for the teapot.

AFTER THEY FINISHED their meal and packed the food away again, Harrier led the horses carefully down to the stream edge. He could wash the cups and plates while they had their drink, and then pack the last of the gear away. Then he'd be on the road until dusk. Ancaladar would have mentioned if he was likely to run out of road today, so he knew he wouldn't, but he knew the road would end in a few days more at best. Then he'd be steering by the sun and the stars and whatever landmarks Tiercel and Ancaladar could provide on their overflights.

He was kneeling on the streambank, setting the last clean dish on the grassy verge, when he felt a sudden sharp blow between his shoulder blades and went sprawling into the water. Fortunately the stream wasn't that deep, but he inhaled enough water that he came up coughing and choking, blinded by a faceful of mud. He scrubbed it hastily out of his eyes—smearing it everywhere—and spun around. He didn't know what had hit him, and he'd never forgotten that Tiercel had enemies even if he didn't.

Kareta was standing on the bank laughing her fool head off.

For a moment Harrier was so furious he couldn't breathe. Then he took a deep breath. *"Always pick your fights,"* his Da had told him. Of course, his Da had also whaled the living daylights out of him on the few occasions he'd ever picked them with anyone smaller or weaker than he was. Or a girl. And while Harrier doubted very much that Kareta was weaker than he was, she was definitely a girl. And if he chased her, he couldn't catch her anyway, so he guessed keeping his head right now would fall under the heading of picking his fights.

He stood in the middle of the stream, thinking all this through—because he didn't quite trust himself to remember all of it if he got within reach of her. And he thought about being cold and wet and how his back hurt—*she must have kicked me,* he realized. "You're a bully," he said slowly, and the last of his hot anger faded. "That's all you are."

Whatever reaction she'd been expecting from him, it wasn't that one. "You look funny," she said hopefully.

"Yeah, right." He walked carefully out of the stream and up to the bank. Kareta backed away as he approached, but he ignored her. He picked up the dishes and dropped them back into the basket. The horses regarded him curiously. He was lucky they were placid, well-trained beasts, because if they'd spooked and tried to bolt when he'd gone flying, they could have hurt themselves and smashed up the wagon as well.

He tucked the basket into the back of the wagon, and then backed and turned the team carefully until he could lead them back up to the road.

"You aren't mad, are you?" Kareta asked, trailing after him.

Harrier stopped. "You know what?" he said. "I was wondering why you were here—well, mostly, why you kept hanging around. And I think it's because you really don't have any place else to go. Because if you act this way with everybody, it's hard to imagine that you've got any friends."

By the time he'd led the team back up to the side of the road, Kareta had vanished again. Tiercel and Ancaladar were already gone—off up into the sky, Harrier guessed. It took him the better part of an hour to unpack the wagon enough to find fresh clothes and a towel, towel himself dry, and pack things up again. His boots were soaked through, so he left them inside the wagon where they'd dry slowly, and put on his camp boots. The rest of his clothes he spread out over the tops of the hampers on the sides of the wagon to dry as he drove.

HE DIDN'T SEE Kareta for the rest of the day. When the shadows started to lengthen, he picked what looked like a good place and pulled the wagon off to the side of the road—he hadn't seen any other travelers, but that wasn't any reason to block the road if someone came along—and unhitched the team, and got out their feed buckets, scooped grain into them, and set them out for the horses. A few minutes later, Tiercel and Ancaladar landed.

"You've got mud in your hair," Tiercel said, walking over with Ancaladar's saddle in his arms. "And you changed your clothes." He glanced around curiously, obviously looking for Kareta.

"I haven't seen her," Harrier said. He ran a hand through his hair, dislodging more flecks of dried river bottom. "She kicked me into the stream after you left, so I kind of had to. Change my clothes, I mean."

"She did what?" Tiercel said. He sounded shocked.

"Kicked me into the stream," Harrier repeated, sighing. "I guess she wanted to pay me back for saying she stole the pie. And for refusing to hand over the rest of our lunch."

"She could have hurt you!" Tiercel said.

"Tyr, I don't think that even occurred to her," Harrier said fair-mindedly. "She just wanted to pay me back."

"What did you do?" Tiercel asked cautiously.

Harrier shrugged—and winced, because it certainly felt as if there was a bruise back there. "Called her a bully. Unicorn or not, people who sneak up on other people and knock them into streams because they don't get their own way are bullies."

"And she ran off?" Tiercel asked, looking around again.

"I guess so. If she's going to pull stunts like that, it's not like she'd be the best company anyway," Harrier pointed out. And it wasn't entirely fair, to his way of thinking, for

Kareta to expect them to feed her when—as far as Harrier knew—she was perfectly capable of finding her own food. And they hadn't asked for her company in the first place.

With the wagon as fully loaded as it was, they needed to move a number of things before Tiercel could get at the items he needed for the evening's practice session. Harrier took the opportunity to get out the big brazier, the bedrolls, and a number of the other items they'd need for evening camp, doing his best not to wince and swear, because he'd been sitting for long enough to stiffen up nicely, and moving hurt. At least he didn't need to bring out the ground tarp—they'd be needing it to sleep on in another sennight or so, but right now they only had to deal with a heavy morning frost, and the ground was still dry. Still, they were heading into winter, and sooner or later the ground would be wet when they stopped to camp and he had no intention of sleeping on wet ground.

When all that was done, he led the horses down to the stream for their drink, taking the bucket he'd need to bring back their own water. He'd hobble the horses when he got back and let them graze, then go and gather wood for the fire while it was still light (only felltimber, since Elunyerin and Rilphanifel had been very insistent that he must never cut down a tree anywhere in the Elven Lands) and get the evening fire going. It was cool enough, now that the sun was setting, that a fire would be welcome, even though Tiercel could provide all the light they needed. When those chores were done, he'd clean the tack. All of those things (along with getting the meal ready, most evenings) usually occupied him until Tiercel was done with his evening's practice, and by then it was dark, and when Tiercel came back from practicing he was too worn out to do much besides eat and fall into his blankets, and there wasn't much else to do around the camp at night, really, after he'd cleaned up after the evening meal. If Harrier wanted he could sit up and talk to Ancaladar; Ancaladar said that dragons *did* sleep, but not as often as humans, and when they did sleep, it was usually for a lot longer.

Ancaladar had said, in a sort of offhand fashion, that he was probably going to be awake for the rest of Tiercel's life, which gave Harrier the creeps, just a little, although it was nice to know that no matter where they were, there'd be somebody awake and on watch.

But assuming he actually intended to read the Books of the Wild Magic, Harrier wondered when he was supposed to do it. And if there was any practicing involved. Not of the Knight-Mage fighting and stuff. He assumed there had to be practicing there. But of the magic and casting spells part. All the wondertales just said that the Wildmages got their Three Books and then they "had" their magic—but of course, none of those stories had been written by Wildmages. And Harrier didn't feel one bit more magical than he had a sennight ago.

No son of Antarans Gillain was a stranger to hard work, and he'd had plenty of time by now to settle into the routine of setting up camp for the night. Once Harrier got Nethiel and Dulion settled, the longest part of things was always finding wood for the fire, since he could never count on finding some without a long hunt. Some days—if he didn't have to spend too much time at it—he gathered up some during the midday stop. Of course, today he'd been more than a little distracted. . . .

Thinking about Kareta made Harrier growl with irritation, though it wasn't her he was irritated with just now. He'd been careless not to at least consider the possibility she might come sneaking up on him. It was true she hadn't pushed him into the stream the first time, but she'd been happy enough to see him fall in. It was also true that unicorns were Otherfolk, and he certainly couldn't even begin to imagine how a unicorn would think. But he'd been around Kareta for long enough by the time she'd kicked him into the stream to know, if not what she was really like, then what she wanted him to think she was like. And that person (if it was only an act, and not who Kareta really was) was just the sort of person who'd come sneaking around to pay him back for making her look stupid. Light knew Harrier'd faced down two-legged bullies who thought exactly that way often enough. He should have expected it.

But you didn't. Just because she's a unicorn. He snorted rudely. *Harrier Gillain, just listen to yourself! True, though. She's the most beautiful thing I've ever seen. Prettier than a three-master full-rigged heading out for Deep Ocean. And oh, Light Defend Us, you* can't *let things like that matter—not if you're going to keep your head on your shoulders, and Tyr's head on his! Because he says that Fire Woman he keeps dreaming about is beautiful, too, and I'm scared to death she isn't just a what-you-call-it, a* symbol. *I think she's real, and it stands to reason that means we're going to see her before this is all done. If we live to get that far. . . .*

He'd learned his lesson, though—or he hoped he had— and he certainly had an aching back to set the lesson firmly into his mind. He didn't go too far from the wagon as he looked for kindling, and he kept an eye and an ear open for trouble the whole time he was gathering wood. He was lucky enough to find a whole tree, too—a sapling, really—that had been uprooted in a storm and had fallen against two live trees. It had died—and dried out—in place, and would make fine firewood now. He dragged it, along with the rest of his gatherings, back to the campsite, and used the small axe to help him break the longer branches he'd gathered into short chunks suitable for burning. Of course it would have been easier to start the fire if Tiercel had been there just to point at it, but Harrier had been starting fires with flint and steel most of his life, and it only took him a couple of minutes to strike sparks into tinder and then ignite the smaller twigs. Once the fire was burning, he lit the lanterns—though he didn't quite need them yet—then quickly chunked the sapling into logs. It was enough wood so that he probably wouldn't need to go looking for more tomorrow.

All that was left to do was wash his hands and light the tea-brazier, then wrestle the hamper out of the wagon, since he knew perfectly well that Tiercel would be too tired to help with it when he got back. It was heavy, but he managed. He added a jug of the fruit cordial from Black-rowan Farm to the evening's provisions—Lanya had said that if you mixed it with hot water, it made a soothing evening drink, and he thought it might be a good thing to try.

In the distance, across the road, he could see the intermittent flashes of light as Tiercel practiced. He was a little more curious about what Tiercel did now than he had been. Tiercel said he was mostly practicing "spells of protection," and Harrier had no idea of what he meant by that. Whatever it was, apparently it took a lot of practicing.

He poked around in the hamper, and ate an apple or two, and finally—about the time it was starting to get really dark—Tiercel came walking back, with Ancaladar following him. You couldn't exactly say that Ancaladar moved "ponderously," but it was hard to see something that large moving at all and think of him as moving gracefully, even though Ancaladar did. The ball of Coldfire that hovered above Tiercel's head as it always did on his way back from practice gave the parts of Ancaladar it shone on a foggy bluish gleam, and in the dusk, the black dragon looked almost insubstantial.

When the two of them reached the wagon, Ancaladar folded himself up neatly and settled himself on the grass. Tiercel flopped down onto the blanket beside Harrier and sighed. "It doesn't get any easier," he said.

"Oh come on," Harrier scoffed. "You haven't even been doing this a fortnight yet. Complain when you've been practicing for a moonturn at least." He poured hot water into the waiting pot, then poured more into one of the mugs already half-filled with berry cordial. "Drink this."

"What is it?" Tiercel asked, taking the wooden mug.

"Poison, of course," Harrier answered promptly, and Tiercel snorted in amusement.

"It's good," he said, when he set the mug aside.

"Lanya said they drink the cordial that way in winter. It

isn't winter yet, but you're always cold after you practice," Harrier said. "Now eat before you fall asleep."

Harrier divided up the second chicken and set it out on plates. He knew he really didn't have to—and Tiercel tended to complain if Harrier spent too much time nurse-maiding him—but if he had to choose between listening to Tiercel complain, and trying to bandage him up in the dark when he cut himself with his own eating knife, Harrier would take complaints every time. And no matter what the Elves had said about a dragon taking the place of the mysterious "something" that a High Mage needed to power his magic, Tiercel was always dead tired after practicing.

About the time the tea was ready, Ancaladar raised his head. "H'm," he said, in thoughtful tones.

Kareta was walking slowly toward them. Her head was down, and her tail practically dragged on the grass. Even her ears drooped. She stopped a few feet away.

"I know you won't believe me," she said in a low voice, "but . . . I'm sorry."

"For what?" Harrier asked. He was surprised at how calm he felt. Not the least bit angry.

"For kicking you into the water. That was wrong."

"Yes it was," Harrier agreed. His back still ached. "Is there anything else you're sorry for?" He had the bizarre sensation that he'd suddenly become his father, because he'd been on the receiving end of just such a series of questions so many times when he'd done something he shouldn't have. Both his parents thought that punishing their children didn't do any good if they didn't know ex-actly what they were being punished *for*. And Antarans Gillain was a fair man; if any of his children could prove either that they hadn't known what they were doing was wrong, or that it wasn't actually wrong, they wouldn't be punished for their actions. And because he'd always lis-tened first, no matter how angry he was, they'd repaid that faith in them with honesty.

Kareta's head drooped even lower. "I'm sorry I took your

food without asking. I . . . I'm sorry I *took* it. Because that wasn't right."

"Okay," Harrier said. Tiercel opened his mouth to speak, but Harrier held up his hand. "I'm glad you apologized for both those things—" he really *did* sound like his father, right now "—and I'm glad you're sorry. But what we both—what we all—need to know is that you aren't going to do them again."

"I won't," Kareta said. "I promise."

"Okay," Harrier said, trying not to sigh with relief. "We'll say no more about it then." He really didn't like laying down the law to a unicorn, even an incredibly annoying one. And he couldn't imagine what he would have said if she'd told him she was just going to go on and do the same things again.

Kareta seemed to be just as relieved as he was. "What are you eating?" she asked hopefully.

"Chicken. Bread. Cheese," Tiercel said. "There are apples."

"May I have an apple?" Kareta asked politely.

Tiercel scrambled forward to dig into the hamper and find one for her. Harrier grinned to himself. He didn't think that Kareta's extravagant politeness would last—but he didn't think she'd go back to snatching food out from under their noses, either.

Seven

Beyond the Veil

WE'RE ALMOST THERE," Kareta said cheerfully.

It was a fortnight later, and the last two sennights had been peaceful to the point of boring. Harrier wondered who kept *order* in the Elven Lands, because unless they were a lot different than humans, someone had to. When he'd finally gotten curious enough to ask Ancaladar about it (and to explain something of what he meant), the dragon had told him that the Elven Knights did much of what he was thinking of, and the Forest Rangers did the rest. Between them, the two groups protected trade caravans, succored lost travelers, and dealt with the extremely infrequent cases of actual violence.

"The Elves have been a peaceful people since long before your kind built cities," Ancaladar had said. "I do not say that there is no strife or unhappiness here in the Elven Lands, for there is unhappiness everywhere. But violence such as is common in the Lands of Men . . . that would have to come from outside. And no merely mortal enemy can pass Pelashia's Veil."

"Then why are there Elven Knights at all?" Tiercel had asked. "I mean, if they don't have anyone to fight."

"Because Elven memories are long, Bonded," Ancaladar had said.

Three days after they'd left Blackrowan Farm, the road had simply come to an end. Harrier had been a little worried at first, but the wagon was sturdy and well-sprung, and the ground was still fairly level, and since Ancaladar said that the stream continued in the direction they needed to go, he'd simply followed that for the next few days.

After that, the stream had taken a sharp bend away from the direction they needed to go. They weren't making as much progress each day as they had been on the road—at least the wagon wasn't—because they'd moved out of open country and into woodland. While it was true that the trees weren't so close together that Harrier couldn't get the wagon between them, he *did* have to spend more time searching for a suitable path than he had when they'd been on the road.

Kareta, to his great surprise, was actually useful. It was true that she had no real notion of what paths the wagon could take and which it couldn't, but once they'd stopped following the stream, the other thing they needed to do on a regular basis was find water, and Kareta was eager to help.

One of the items that had been a part of the wagon from the very beginning—unused until now—was a set of barrels lashed over the forward axles. The two barrels could hold enough water to take care of their needs for several days. Of course, Harrier had to find a water source in order to fill them—and to his amazement, the first time the level in the barrels began to drop, Kareta volunteered to go look for water.

"Don't you know anything about unicorns?" she'd demanded, tossing her head.

"You know exactly what I know about unicorns," Harrier had answered gruffly. "If you find water, kindly remember I'd like to be able to get the wagon next to it."

She hadn't quite been able to manage that. But when she'd found a spring, he was able to get the wagon close enough that he didn't have to haul the buckets too far.

"Don't worry if the water's muddy," Kareta said. "Or if it goes bad."

"Why not?" Harrier asked, and when she opened her mouth to reply, he added, "And *don't* just tell me again that I don't know anything about unicorns."

"Because I can purify it for you," Kareta said, sounding indignant at having to explain.

"Okay. Fine."

A few days later she had to do just that, because the water she led him to was a deep pond completely covered with green slime. It stank.

"I'm not going to drink that," Harrier had said simply.

"Wait," Kareta had answered. She'd knelt down, and touched her horn to the pool. A blue shimmer had spread out from the point at which her horn touched the water, and a moment later the entire pool was crystal clear. She'd looked smug—or as smug as she *could* look, anyway—and at the evening meal, Harrier had brought out the last of the apples and fed them to her.

"You earned them," he said simply.

* * *

AND NOW THEY'D reached the edge of the Elven Lands. Ancaladar had seen the Veil yesterday and had told Harrier that they'd cross it today. He hadn't flown beyond it, as he wasn't entirely sure, he'd said, if he'd be able to get Tiercel back through. Certainly an Elven Mage could pass back and forth through the barrier with ease, and Ancaladar could travel back and forth through the Veil alone, but he didn't want to risk what might happen to Tiercel if he attempted to bring him back through the Veil.

"I don't see anything," Harrier said dubiously, looking where Kareta was pointing. There were trees all around them—trees ahead, trees behind—and somewhere in the next mile or so, the edge of the Elven Lands. In Harrier's opinion, there ought to be a marker stone, or something.

"*I* do," Kareta said pertly. "Look! I'll show you!" She dashed off through the trees and then stopped. Eventually, the wagon rolled up to join her.

"Right *there*," she said.

Harrier had stopped the team. He looked where she was pointing. All he saw was more trees—and, maybe another mile or so in the distance, Tiercel and Ancaladar, on the ground, waiting for him. That meant that somewhere between where Kareta was standing (probably *right* where she was standing) and where Tiercel and Ancaladar were, was the Veil that everybody had been talking about for the last several sennights—the thing that kept people like him out of the Elven Lands. But since he was *in* the Elven Lands right now, it shouldn't stop him from getting *out*.

He clucked to the team again, and they started forward.

He tried not to wince as the wagon passed Kareta, or to imagine he felt something. Because he didn't feel anything, any more than he saw something. He'd been poking half-heartedly at the Three Books whenever he was sure Kareta was out of sight, but he didn't feel any more like a Wild-mage than he had before he'd gotten them. And whether he was one or not, apparently his so-called Wildmagery didn't extend to sensing Elven magic, because he didn't notice anything at all, and by the time he reached Ancaladar, he was pretty sure he was on the other side of the Veil. About the only difference he could see was that the forest here looked scruffier than the forest in the Elven Lands, and he wasn't even sure if he was imagining that. He pulled the wagon to a halt again. "Did you feel anything when you went through?" he asked Tiercel curiously.

"No," Tiercel said, looking both disappointed and relieved. "You?"

"Not a thing. But I'm hungry now. Let's eat."

AFTER THEY ATE, Harrier packed up and then spent almost an hour gathering a good solid load of firewood. He was a little uneasy about wandering around looking for wood at the evening stop, and even though anything that might be prowling around these woods probably wouldn't come too close to Ancaladar, it was starting to get cold enough that it certainly wouldn't hurt to be able to keep a good fire burning all night. There was already enough empty space in the storage hampers for Harrier to be able to load a good amount of wood into them before he left. And—Harrier brightened—now that they were out of the Elven Lands, he'd be able to cut trees down for wood, assuming he wanted to, although unseasoned wood didn't burn particularly well. It was always nice to have the option.

THEY WERE STILL in the forest when the light began to dim; tonight, at least, Ancaladar would be able to give him a good idea of how much longer he'd have to travel through it, and what lay beyond. There might have been another hour or two of light if they'd been out in the open, but not here in the depths of the forest. Harrier was starting to decide he hated trees.

"Far enough," Harrier said aloud, reining the horses in. He swung down from the bench and began the work of making camp. Eventually Ancaladar would notice that they'd stopped and bring Tiercel back for the night.

It took him a while to notice that Kareta was hanging around watching him work.

It wasn't as if she was always either particularly close by or completely absent during the day. It was true that she tended to kind of pace the wagon as it traveled, but she frequently wandered off entirely. And it was also true that she always showed up at mealtimes, but at the end of the day, Harrier had gotten used to being pretty much left to himself while he got the camp ready for night. Having her hover like this was . . . unusual.

It took him until the horses were fed and watered—and Ancaladar and Tiercel had showed up, and Tiercel had collected his *stuff,* and the two of them had gone off for Tiercel's practice session—to figure out what was going on.

"You've never actually been outside the Elven Lands, have you?" he asked.

"Of course I have!" she answered indignantly, tossing her head. He knew better, though, than to believe her just because she told him something—or denied it, for that matter.

Harrier sighed, and leaned against the wagon wheel. "Look," he said. "You've brought me the Books. I've even—okay, I've done some looking into them, all right? So you can go on back now. Go on. Shoo. Scat."

"Harrier Gillain, don't you dare *shoo* me as if I were a—a—a *housecat*! I'm going to go precisely where I want, and stay there as long as I want to! Besides, you need my help!" she answered huffily.

"Exactly what do I need your help for?" Harrier demanded, exasperated now.

"In the first place, you need me to help you find water—"

"Tiercel can do that!" Harrier was almost sure of that.

"—and in the second place, if you've actually looked at your Books—which I doubt—I'm perfectly certain you haven't done one single spell. Have you?" she demanded.

"What does that—"

"*Have* you?"

"No! And I'm not going to, either!"

"*Why not?*" Kareta challenged, now sounding just as irritated as he was.

"*I don't want to!*" Harrier bellowed at the top of his lungs.

"Oh, that's a *very* good reason," Kareta said, snickering.

A moment later Tiercel came charging through the trees, waving his Wand as if it were a sword, and looking worried and out of breath. "What's wrong?" he asked, looking from Harrier to Kareta.

"Nothing," Harrier muttered.

"He doesn't want to do magic," Kareta answered, managing to sound as if she were personally offended by Harrier's refusal.

"Well did you think he did?" Tiercel asked after a long pause. "Light deliver us, this is *Harrier* you're talking about."

"Thanks a lot, Tyr," Harrier said.

"Well," Tiercel said, shrugging as if the statement needed no further explanation. "From the way you were yowling, I thought someone was being murdered."

Kareta snickered again.

"Go away," Harrier said. "You, too," he said to Kareta, once Tiercel was gone. "Back through the Veil, I mean." Because it wasn't fair to make her go off into the forest by herself alone, especially now that it was getting dark. "I mean, in the morning."

"No," Kareta said simply.

He didn't waste breath in arguing with her. In the morning, he'd get Tiercel to talk her into it. Right now, he had dinner to make.

Ancaladar didn't have to eat every day, but he did have to eat. And while he didn't like having to hunt for himself, he could. When Ancaladar had accepted his Bond to Jermayan, Jermayan had promised him he would never have to hunt his own food again, but certainly Ancaladar was willing to be reasonable. If Tiercel had been in a position to feed him, Tiercel would have; since he couldn't, Ancaladar was willing to hunt. It was not, after all (he'd explained), as if there were Endarkened hunting for him now, so it didn't matter too much if he were seen. And Ancaladar's willingness to hunt for himself extended to hunting for them as well, which meant venison stew for dinner.

Ancaladar had taken down a buck three days before. They'd eaten fresh meat that night and the next day, and then Harrier had cut up the rest of the meat into strips and cooked it thoroughly. Packed in salt to dry it out further, it would keep for a week or so, and the salt could be brushed off and reused. Of course, that also meant a certain amount of work was involved if you wanted to eat it later (and have anything palatable), but Harrier was firmly convinced that eating was better than not eating. Once the stew was started, he got working on the flatcakes. They'd never rival his Ma's breads and biscuits, but they were edible. The first couple off the griddle always burned, but Kareta never seemed to mind eating them.

"You know," she said, chewing, "if you'd just learn to make Coldfire you wouldn't need to light all those lanterns. Or wait for Tiercel to come back with his Magelight (because he doesn't make Coldfire, you know, he makes Magelight). And it wouldn't be as dark."

"It's not that dark," Harrier said, just to be difficult. "And I'm about as likely to start making things glow in the dark as dinner is to get up and walk again, so don't hold your breath."

Kareta made a rude noise and said nothing.

Tiercel and Ancaladar showed up about the same time they always did; Harrier had the idea that all of Tiercel's practices took just about the same amount of time for the same reason any other training session would; no matter what you were practicing, you had to be careful not to overtrain.

Harrier refused to admit that the additional brightness from Tiercel's Coldfire (or Magelight or whatever) was welcome in the darkness beneath the trees, and he refused to ask Tiercel to refrain from dispelling the globe of light the way Tiercel always did every night once he'd finished eating and went to climb into his bedroll. After the meal was over, Harrier washed up, using as little water as possible. He'd be just as glad to get out of the forest—Ancaladar said another day or two and they'd be back in open country. He also said that in another sennight or so they'd be back on a road, and maybe that meant they could find another stream.

"A road?" Harrier had said indignantly. "Why would there be a road out here if there aren't any people?"

"*I* never said there were no people here," Ancaladar had answered primly. "You did."

And Tiercel had laughed, and even Harrier had to admit that was true. But on the other hand, he *knew* they were east of the Bazrahils, and the only thing beyond Windalorianan—so he'd always been taught—was empty wilderness and the Elven Lands. A thousand years ago, there hadn't even been any humans living as far east as Valwendigorean, and that was one of the cities of the Dragon's Tail today. While Harrier didn't think he would have been notified *specifically,* he was certain that if there was a momentous historical fact in the history of the Nine Cities available to bore him with—such as settlements extending beyond the ancient bounds of the Nine Cities—his teachers would have done it some time in the last twelve years of his school days.

He'd know soon enough.

TIERCEL WAS ASLEEP from nearly the moment that he rolled himself into his blankets. He wasn't sure whether he ought to try to feel guilty about leaving all the work of the camp to Harrier, or ought to try *not* to feel guilty, because he was certainly working hard, even if what he was working on was magic, and not on keeping the two of them fed. It wasn't fair to Harrier to leave Harrier to do all the day-to-day work now that Harrier had his own magic to figure out. But Tiercel knew that Harrier didn't really want to figure it out just yet. In another moonturn maybe. Harrier usually took at least that long to make up his mind about something. Tiercel knew he ought to talk to him about it soon.

But he'd been able to practice—really practice—the complex spells of the High Magick for barely a moonturn, and he was just starting to master the fifty-two glyphs of the High Magick by themselves, and they had thousands of combinations, and practicing them and memorizing them and *getting them right* was exhausting. And all of that was only the *foundation* of the High Magick: the glyphs and cantrips and wards and the incredibly basic spells like Magelight and Fire and some of the Lesser Summonings and Transmutations. If he ever wanted to become a *real* High Mage . . .

Well, he never would be. He was willing to face that fact squarely, even if Harrier wasn't. He would have to have begun his training ten years ago. With different teachers. In a different world.

He didn't blame Ancaladar for the fact that he could never become the thing that he'd been born to be, the thing that having the Magegift said he *could* have become. Ancaladar knew that—it was one thing Tiercel could be sure of, thanks to the Bond they shared. Ancaladar was a wonderful teacher—probably better than he deserved. It was just that Tiercel was trying to learn something starting too late. And trying to compress what would be (or have been) a lifetime of study—decades and decades—into . . . well, he didn't know how long he had before he was going to need as much as he'd been able to learn, but he doubted he had even as much as *one* year, let alone decades.

And he didn't think that—no matter what happened—he and Harrier were going to survive looking for the Lake of Fire, let alone finding it. And that meant Ancaladar wouldn't survive either. He'd left a letter with Idalia back in Karahelanderialigor, for her to try to get to his family if—and only if—she was sure he was dead. He was fairly sure Harrier had left a similar one behind for his family. And he really didn't want to think about that at all. Because he was sixteen and Harrier was seventeen and thinking about dying was unbelievable and planning for it was somehow worse. It was just as well that he never had the energy to stay awake to brood about it for very long at the end of the day.

Since he'd left Ysterialpoerin for Karahelanderialigor, Tiercel hadn't had one of the horrifying prophetic dreams that had begun at Kindling. Normally he didn't remember his dreams—he remembered that he dreamed, but not what his dreams were about. Not for long, anyway. The ones about the Lake of Fire were different, but of course they weren't really dreams. He hadn't thought about them much lately, except to think that perhaps they might be over for good—their purpose had been served, after all. So he wasn't worried about falling asleep tonight any more than he had been on any of the other nights.

SINCE HE'D LEFT Armethalieh, Tiercel had seen lakes. Blue with reflected sky, their surfaces ruffled by the wind. Sometimes edged with reeds. Usually filled with fish.

This lake was orange, its surface veined with brighter gold. Its surface didn't shimmer, but the air above it did, because the lake wasn't filled with water, but with fire. He could smell burnt rock, and sulfur, and scents that came from things burning that should never be able to burn at all. And standing in the middle of the lake—on the surface of the fire—was a woman.

The ancient books Tiercel had read so many moonturns ago in the Great Library of Armethalieh had said that Elven women were dazzlingly beautiful and dangerously seductive, and he had to admit that the ones he'd seen in Karahelanderialigor were very pretty. Prettier than anyone he'd ever seen in Armethalieh, or (for that matter) in all his travels beyond it. And the Fire Woman was more beautiful than the most beautiful of the Elven women.

But the Elven women were . . . just beautiful. And you might not know what you could possibly say to them, and it might be impossible to imagine them ever saying anything to *you,* but they weren't actually terrifying.

The Fire Woman made Tiercel want to run as far away from her as he could run.

The fire of the lake gleamed off her naked skin, so that Tiercel couldn't tell what color it was, and the heat rising from the lake's surface made her long hair lift and swirl. Her hair was the same color as the surface of the lake; he could tell that much. She stood in the center of the Lake of Fire, on the surface of the fire—she'd never, in any of his visions, so much as *moved* one step—and he didn't understand why the sight of her filled him with the need to escape. It was as if just seeing her was the most dangerous thing that had ever happened to him; as if the sight of her was as toxic as poison. All Tiercel knew was that dangerous or not, poisonous or not, there was something so *wrong* about the Fire Woman—something he couldn't see, but could sense—that the sight of her made him ill with revulsion.

He wondered how the Other could bear it.

Because the Other wasn't just dreaming about her—Tiercel knew that somehow—he was wherever she was. *He* was the one she was calling—or perhaps he was calling her. But there was something she wanted from the Other, something more horrifying than she was herself.

The Fire Woman raised her arms, beckoning to that unseen Other. She wanted the Other to come to her. That was what she always wanted—what she'd wanted from the beginning, and the Other never would. And because—this time—Tiercel wasn't alone, he was actually able to wonder why.

Are you ready at last to accept the gifts I have for you?

It was the question she always asked. And though the answer was still "no," it was so much closer to "yes" than it had ever been before that the knowledge was enough to thrust Tiercel into terrified consciousness.

He sat up, looking around groggily. *I'm not there. It isn't really happening. Not here. Not yet. Not to me. I'm here.*

Harrier was on his feet, rumpled and barefoot but clutching the sword Roneida had given him. Kareta was standing, staring at him, coat fluffed out . . . and her horn was *glowing.*

Even Ancaladar was up. He hadn't actually moved, but he'd lifted his head enough to crane around the wagon to peer down at Tiercel.

"I woke everybody up," Tiercel said tentatively.

Harrier made a rude sound that might have been laughter, and Kareta simply shuddered all over—possibly in sympathy to what Tiercel had seen in his dream; he couldn't quite tell.

"I have been expecting this, Bonded," Ancaladar said.

"You might have said something," Harrier snarled, and went to build up the fire.

A few minutes later Tiercel was sitting with a cup of warmed cordial in his hands. He could tell by the way that the air felt that it was an hour or so before dawn; under the trees it was too dark to see. Slowly, haltingly, he told the details of what he had dreamed, but he knew that telling it couldn't convey how it had *felt.*

But there was one person here that he didn't have to explain anything to. He and Ancaladar were Bonded, and Tiercel knew that meant Ancaladar had a certain amount of access, not only to everything he saw, but to his thoughts as well.

"You have a difficult task ahead of you, Bonded," Ancaladar said quietly.

"Did you . . . ?" Tiercel asked hopefully, but Ancaladar blinked slowly in denial.

"I did not recognize the place you see."

"Wait—wait—wait—" Harrier sputtered. "You—He—Ancaladar could *see* what you were dreaming?"

He sounded outraged, Tiercel thought, as if Ancaladar

had been spying on him while he slept. Tiercel knew that Harrier had accepted his Bond with Ancaladar, and called Ancaladar a friend—something Harrier didn't do either easily or lightly—but Tiercel didn't think that Harrier really understood what the Dragonbond *was*.

"Yes," Ancaladar said simply.

"Fat lot of good it did," Harrier said. He got up to get the tea-things.

"It did some good," Ancaladar said. "I have seen, through my Bonded's mind, the nature of the enemy which you face."

"Dark magic," Harrier said dismissively. "We knew that already."

"Worse," Ancaladar said, and Harrier stopped.

"Tell me how it can be worse than the Dark coming back," he said tightly.

Ancaladar seemed to sigh. He stretched out his neck, so his chin rested on the ground beside Tiercel's knee, and Tiercel shifted around until he could reach the place behind Ancaladar's eye to stroke it gently.

"It is the way in which the Dark returns, Harrier. I will explain, if you like."

"Oh, no," Harrier said. "I'd much rather not know a thing about what we're facing. Let me get dressed first."

A few minutes later Harrier came back, dressed for the day. He made another cup of hot cordial for Tiercel, refilled the kettle and started the water brewing for tea, and set some dried fruit to soak for griddle-cakes. "Okay. Now. Ruin my day," he invited.

"You have known for some time—as did the Elves since before Tiercel was born—that Darkness is returning to the world."

"Oh, don't tell me you're actually going to *tell* us something?" Harrier said mockingly.

"Shut up, Har," Tiercel answered affectionately.

"I just—" Harrier began, but Tiercel found a pebble on the ground and threw it at him, and Harrier broke off to dodge.

"Anybody would think you didn't *want* to know what's going on, you know," Kareta said.

"Not if it's bad," Harrier said untruthfully.

"No one knew what form it would take," Ancaladar continued imperturbably. "Or what form it *had* taken, for it was clear to the Elven Mages that the Darkness had begun its return to the world before Tiercel's parents, even, had met."

"Someday I'd like to know how they knew *that,*" Harrier interjected irrepressibly. Kareta shoved him with her shoulder.

"But there are many expressions of Darkness. Unfortunately, I now know which one you face."

"Get to the point," Harrier muttered, but quietly now.

"This magic, and its manifestation, is Demonic in nature," Ancaladar finished. "I have seen the works of the Endarkened twice before, for though I would not Bond in the Great War, and spent most of its decades asleep and in hiding, still I knew much of what they did in that time. And I saw far more of their evil in the war that came after, the one which ended in the Great Flowering."

Harrier sighed. "Yeah. About that. Ancaladar, it *can't* be the Endarkened. The Blessed Saint Idalia destroyed all of them forever. That's why the Great Flowering happened at all. I mean, I'm no Preceptor of the Light or anything, but . . . everyone's always said so. The Endarkened are all dead. And even, I mean, the *real* Idalia . . . when we met her. She said she killed the Queen of the Endarkened, so . . . it *has* to be true."

Tiercel looked down at his enormous friend, continuing to rub gently at the soft skin behind the eye socket. What Harrier said was nothing more nor less than what Tiercel had heard every Kindling when the story of the Great Flowering was retold: the Blessed Saint Idalia had destroyed all the Endarkened.

Ancaladar blinked again, slowly. "There's destroyed, and then there's destroyed. Yes, all the offspring of Shadow Mountain that were placed into the world thousands of years ago by He Who Is were destroyed. If not at once, then soon thereafter. And no matter what the Endarkened themselves might have chosen to believe, they were never anything more than perversions of the Elves, as the Darkness cannot create, merely distort that which has been created. And yes, He Who Is was locked out of the world forever by Idalia's willing sacrifice at the Place of Power and would never choose to meddle in the World of Form again even if he could: to have been defeated by time-bound creatures grates too heavily upon him. But so long as there is Life, it can be touched and twisted by the Elemental Quality of Darkness, because Darkness Itself is impossible to remove from the world. And that is what is happening here: the Darkness that is the essential nature of He Who Is and his creations touching Life once more to create a new race of Endarkened, identical to the original Endarkened only in intent."

"That doesn't make any sense," Harrier complained, after thinking for a moment.

"No," Tiercel said. "It does. The original Endarkened were made from Elves by He Who Is. And he's locked out of the world, but he still exists, right?"

"Correct," Ancaladar said.

"And the Endarkened are all gone, but the way they were made . . . it can be done again, right?"

"Nobody's that stupid," Harrier said. He thought for a moment. "And how could it be? Ancaladar said that He Who Is made the first set."

"Yes . . ." Tiercel said slowly. "I think that's why it's taking so long. I think a *person* is trying to do it. Being tricked, somehow. I don't know. But the Fire Woman . . ."

Despite himself he shuddered, and Harrier got up to drape an extra blanket around his shoulders. Even sitting next to Ancaladar's radiant heat, Tiercel felt cold.

". . . she must be the, well, the *piece* of Darkness. The thing that's going to bring the Endarkened back if she gets what she wants."

"But you said she wasn't dark," Harrier said plaintively.

"It's lying," Kareta said, sounding exasperated and stamping her hoof. "Leaf and Star, Harrier Gillain! If the thing looked like Darkness Personified, do you think it could fool even *you* for a moment?"

"Well, I wouldn't be stupid enough to want to call back the Endarkened," Harrier snapped, sounding cross. "So . . . now that we know that, what do we do?"

"I do not know," Ancaladar said, sounding troubled. "My memory is long, and the histories of the Elves are longer, but this is something not contained in either. It is new, and so I cannot predict what you must do. It is why, you know, no one wished to tell you their thoughts and suspicions. You would have made plans to fight the old, and you do not face the old."

Harrier sighed, and stared up at the trees. "Fine. Great. So we've got a lot of new information that isn't really useful right now. I'm going to make breakfast."

After they'd eaten, Harrier tried one last time to convince Kareta to return to the Elven Lands. He had as little success as he'd had the previous night. He gave up. If unicorns could go into battle against the Endarkened a thousand years ago, he supposed one unicorn could take care of herself now.

Eight

On the Shore of the Lake of Fire

EVEN BEFORE THE Great War that had turned nearly all the world into a wasteland in which nothing grew, that part of the land which later became known as the Barahileth had been as it was now: hot, arid, and without any form of life that needed water to survive. But in those ancient days not all Life had required water, and millennia ago, the

Barahileth had been home to a flourishing civilization: creatures whose form and nature was Fire.

The Firesprites were only one of many races which had been destroyed utterly by the Endarkened because they had fought for the Light. The Barahileth had been their home, for water had been as destructive to them as fire was to those they named the Children of Water, and though rain might fall elsewhere in the Isvai—scantily, and at rare intervals—there was never rain in the Barahileth. Even the most powerful Wildmage could not coax water to the surface of its sands, and as hot as it was elsewhere in the desert, it was hotter here. This was a place over which hawks did not fly by day, for the heat was too punishing, and owls and bats did not fly through the air by night, for there was nothing in its skies, or upon its sands, to hunt.

When the Isvaieni Wildmage Bisochim had begun his quest to restore the Balance, this was where he had come, for here, in the only Firesprite Shrine to survive the devastation wrought by the Endarkened, lay the knowledge he sought. The Shrine itself lay far beneath the surface of a lake of fire, and standing upon its shore, Bisochim drew upon his dragon's power and created something the Barahileth had never seen in all its millennia of existence: a great fortress filled with fountains and gardens. With the inexhaustible power of Saravasse to draw upon, he had done what no other before him had ever been able to do, and called water up to the sands of the Barahileth from the deep rock beneath. Water to fill wells, water for irrigation canals to make the desert blossom, water for the fountains that cooled the air of the home he built for himself. Bisochim had first seen the light of day upon a rug in a tent of the Adanate Isvaieni, but with the power of his magic, on the cliff overlooking the Lake of Fire he had built a palace that would have dazzled the ancient Kings of Men.

Its walls and terraces were of pale glistening stone fused together out of the desert sand, for the sand had once been rock and could easily be made to remember its former state. His stronghold was merged indissolubly with the black cliff, and many years before, though in those days Saravasse had spent more time at the palace than she did now, he had conjured a long curving staircase out of the stone to the land below in order to be able to leave his sanctuary without waiting for Saravasse to come and carry him forth.

Though she was still subservient to his will by the magic that bound them both, were he to be dependent upon her to come and go from his fortress, there would be a long wait between his desire and its fulfillment, for Saravasse wandered far these days. But Bisochim did not leave it often. Long ago, the gold his magic had summoned from beneath the desert sands had allowed Bisochim to purchase everything his magic could not create. The palace was filled with everything he needed to survive: gardens, and animals, and spell-animated servants to tend them both, and as the years had passed, he had extended his gardens until the plain which had once been named Telinchechitl when its masters were creatures of living fire became filled with orchards and meadows brought forth from what had once been lifeless desert sands. The air of these gardens was made sweet and cool by a hundred fountains—it was a profligate waste of water, but the power he commanded allowed Bisochim to summon an inexhaustible supply of water from the deep earth. Without it, nothing that grew could survive the heat of the Barahileth by day. Now he had reason to be grateful for so much foresight.

For many years—since he had first come to the Firesprite Shrine to begin his studies on how to restore the True Balance—one vision had haunted him.

He stands upon the ramparts of his fortress, looking out over the sand. Below him, two vast armies gallop toward each other, their weapons glittering in the sun. One is his. One belongs to the Enemy. He raises his hands, summoning up the Sandwind. It is their only hope: it will destroy the Enemy's army.

But it will also destroy his own.

He hears Saravasse scream, and knows, in that terrible

moment, that an army of merely human warriors is not the
Enemy's only weapon. . . .

No.

While he lived, that day would not come to pass.
Bisochim had done all that he could think of to do to pre-
vent it: he had conjured up the shadow of the Great Power
that the Firesprites had once worshipped here and sent the
shade of the Firecrown forth to destroy his enemy while
that enemy was still confused and weak. But just as the
prudent hunter had more than one string to his bow,
Bisochim knew that the Light had more than one huntsman.

He knew that there were many who would name him
foolish and even wicked for setting his will against the
Light. Everyone was taught—*he* had been taught—that
the Light was always good. But the children of the desert
should know better. Light scoured. Light blinded. Light
killed. It was Darkness that was the friend and ally of the
desertborn, and the truth that all Wildmages should have
understood without any need for Bisochim to teach it to
them was that both Light and Darkness were vital to the
Balance. It was for this reason first of all that he worked to
restore the true Balance by bringing Darkness back into
the world. The fact that he could save his Bonded from dying at the end of his brief life—because he would not die
at all—only added urgency to his task. For Saravasse's
sake most of all, he must succeed.

And to protect the Isvaieni from becoming the army that
would face the Light in futile battle, he would hide them
here, where they could not be found. To accomplish that
task, Bisochim had once more donned the blue robes of an
Isvaieni Wildmage and gone forth among the tribes,
something he had not done in many years. He had spoken
to the leaders of many of the tribes—urgently, persua-
sively. But not of their own safety. No. Desert life itself
was a battle for survival; there was no battle from which
the Isvaieni would run. Instead, he had spoken of war, had
spoken of the sanctuary in the Barahileth as a place of

only temporary retreat, a place where the tribes could gather and make themselves strong against the day when they would sweep the enemy from their desert home. It was the only way he could gather them together, the only way he could lead them to safety. And for the sake of what he had told them, they had agreed to follow where he led.

If not for the numerous wells Bisochim had summoned up out of the sand, his people would have died upon the journey to the Lake of Fire, for never had so many Isvaieni— with all their flocks and herds—attempted to travel together. Survival in the desert meant not overtaxing the desert's scant resources by gathering too many people in one place: the only time the tribes came together was for the yearly Gathering, when they spent a few short days at one of the largest oases to be found in the entire Isvai. For the rest of the year, each tribe followed its own path between Sand and Star, hunting, tending its flocks, and perhaps meeting occasionally to trade. Now they moved across the desert as if they were in fact the army of Bisochim's vision, but this army journeyed not to war, but to a paradise such as none of them had ever imagined, a place where they might spend all their hours in idleness and play.

Bisochim had dreamed, once he had settled his Isvaieni on the meadows and fields at Telinchechitl and returned to his fortress, of going back at once to his greater task, for the work of building the bridge, slowly and with infinite care, that would allow him to make that vital adjustment to the Great Balance. He must allow the *possibility* of Darkness to reenter the world without doing anything that might summon up the full hideous manifestation of it that had once nearly scoured the world bare of all life. Once he had accomplished that task, the waning power of magic would be revived and refreshed. He could bind his years to Saravasse's. He would share in her immortality, not she in his mortality. The Wild Magic would be reborn, a proper measure of the world it shaped, as it had not been for centuries.

This task had occupied him for years, and at last he was close enough to hope that another turn of the seasons, or two, or three—five at the most—might see his work completed. He begrudged every instant he spent away from that precious labor, even on the most necessary of tasks, but he had been resigned, even before he had arrived, to the knowledge that there would be one last problem to solve before returning to the work of setting the Balance back into true would be possible.

In the Isvai, the tribes looked for aid in the ultimate problem of their survival to the Wildmages. Those who wore the blue robe were members of no tribe, and of all. In service to the Wild Magic, they went where they were needed: protecting the people from the ravages of the Sandwind, leading them to new wells when the old ones failed, finding the lost, healing the sick and the injured when they could, and providing counsel to help the Isvaieni live the lives the Balance asked of them. Between Sand and Star, no tribe trusted the lone traveler, for one who traveled alone might be a thief or an outcast. In the Isvai, tribe met only with tribe for the safety of all. Only those who wore the blue robes of the Wild Magic were exempt from this law; a Wildmage might travel with this tribe or that for a season, but all knew that those who held the Three Books walked alone upon the sand, listening always for the voice of the Wild Magic.

For many years, Bisochim had hoped that others who bore the Three Books would see what he had seen. That he would gain allies. Bisochim had never approached any of his brethren openly, but he had watched them carefully. Should any of them even begin to question the insidious doctrines of the Light, he had vowed that he would seek them out to offer his friendship and support. But such a day had never come, and so he had realized that those who had once been his brothers would someday become his enemies. The other Wildmages did not understand, as he did, that the Balance was flawed.

It had not surprised him that there had been no Wildmages among his Ingathering. He would have been more surprised if there had been: undoubtedly the False Light

that they served had led them to keep themselves far from
him, lest he show them the truth and gain powerful allies.
He knew that once he took the tribes beyond their grasp,
they would begin to move against him. They must. The
Light would demand it. They would, in that moment, become his enemies as much as that unknown champion
against whom he had sent the shadow of the Firecrown.

He made one last bargain with himself. If the other
Wildmages had merely fled the Isvai for the safety of the
Iteru-cities, he would leave them in peace. The Wildmages
of old had lived in harmony with a Balance that encom-
passed both Dark and Light. Surely—when his work was
done—his brethren could strike such a balance as well.

But this hope was disappointed as well.

It took almost a fortnight after his return to the
Barahileth before Bisochim could leave the tribes to their
own devices. It took that much time for the Isvaieni to believe that a place so unlike anything most of them had ever
seen could be real, and a place that they were meant to
stay. And it took nearly all the days of those sennights for
the tribes to settle the places where they would place their
tents, for there must be places found for tents, and flocks,
and cookfires among the fountains and the trees. But at
last Bisochim was able to leave the Isvaieni to the care of
their leaders, return to his stronghold, and descend to the
deepest chamber within it.

Even Bisochim was not certain of how far beneath the
earth that chamber lay, for it was not a place he had made,
but one he had found: a perfect bubble of black glass cast
up by the Lake of Fire at some point in the distant past. He
had made only two changes to what he had discovered
here: he had smoothed the floor so that it was perfectly
even, and in the center of the chamber, he had called a
small pool of water from the deep earth. The pool was still
and black, and he used its water for no purpose but his
magic. Now he cast blood and powdered bone upon its
surface, for he had spent a moonturn and more leading the
tribes to this place, and sennights before that convincing

them to come, and he must know what the other Wild-mages had decided to do.

The spell he cast did not show him the present. There were other, simpler, means of seeing that. And to see where a man or woman was in the world at the moment he looked upon them would not tell Bisochim what they meant to do. Only Time could tell him that. He gazed now into the pool, and saw the Wildmages of the Isvai gathered together, an army of grim purpose. They were mounted upon *shotors*, and led many more, and the *shotors* that they led were heavy-laden with waterskins. Enough, perhaps, to let them make their way across the Barahileth in pursuit of their people, if their magic was strong enough to permit them to sense the Isvaieni through the wards that Bisochim had set around his stronghold. And it would not even require magic—just now, and for sennights to come—to discover the way to the Lake of Fire. The passage of thousands of people and their herds across the desert had left a trail that it would not need magic to follow.

But why and when and how they meant to follow did not matter. The intent was enough. Their plan must not be allowed to come to pass.

And so Bisochim cast a second spell, a spell that would show him not What Would Be, but What Was. He saw the Blue-Robes as they sought one another across the sands of the Isvai. And he drew upon the power he had gained to send storm after storm across the Isvai, harrowing and scouring the desert with lethal Sandwinds until not one of them remained alive.

To accomplish this task was the work of many days, for to call and control a Sandwind—many Sandwinds—with such precision required constant attention, and Bisochim had no desire to harm the desert or its creatures any more than he must. But his enemies must be destroyed for the good of all.

Bisochim slept only rarely now, for stronger and stronger spells sustained him, and the day did not hold enough hours. To listen for the subtle voices of the fire took all his concentration and skill, yet those voices contained the information to guide him—both to restore the Balance, and to keep his people safe. In gathering the tribes, he had been too long away from them, lost precious time. But when he was done with this task, exhaustion claimed him, and Bisochim surrendered to a rare period of true and precious sleep.

"MASTER? MASTER?"

The soft voice of one of his inhuman servants woke him. It had taken all his art to give the creature a voice, for it was simple enough to give stone the shape of a man and the semblance of life, and nearly as simple to conjure watchers and guardians out of the air itself, but to give either the power of speech was a skill that had eluded him for years. He had only bothered to do it for one of his servants, for what would they need to talk to him about? Now he was grateful that he had.

"Yes?" He sat up and regarded the stone statue he had named Zinaneg wearily. He knew the creature would not have roused him except for something he himself would consider urgent.

"Your kinsmen fight among themselves. There is blood," the creature said in its soft inhuman voice.

Bisochim rolled quickly from his sleeping mat and flung on his blue robes. For so many years he had refused to wear them, for he disliked the deference the tribes had given him. The deference, he had thought then and still believed, should be accorded to the Gods of the Wild Magic, and to the Balance, not to those who only did what they could to keep the Balance. Now the robes had become necessary once more.

By the time he reached the garden below the lake, the fight was over. The ring of watchers—a mixture of Laghamba and Tabingana Isvaieni, with a few scattered watchers from other tribes—parted like a dune before the Sandwind at the sight of his blue robe. At its center, one man stood over another, his blood-smeared *geschak* in his hand.

"Tharam, what have you done here?" Bisochim kept his voice calm and level as he walked forward and knelt at the side of the blood-stained body lying upon the grass. Breath yet remained in the still form, though the wound was deep and had been meant to kill. He stretched out his hands, slowing the bleeding, drawing upon Saravasse's power to begin the work of healing. Around him, he heard the watchers murmur in amazement, for he had asked no aid, called upon none of the watching Laghamba Isvaieni to contribute power to the Healing, as would have any of the other Wildmages they knew.

"Limrac insulted me, Wildmage," Tharam said. "How could I let such a thing go unpunished?" His voice was troubled now that his anger had passed, for while quarrels and feuds were as frequent among the Isvaieni as among any people anywhere, they began and ended in harsh words. For a man to shed the blood of another of his own tribe was cause for immediate banishment. At the Gathering of the tribes, all were bound by the Gathering Peace, and to shed the blood of a member of another tribe would be cause for the same instant banishment.

But this was not the Gathering, and the Gathering Peace did not bind the Isvaieni now. Now, for the first time, the thousands of Isvaieni were forced into each others' company not for days, but for moonturns.

On the march it had not mattered, for no Isvaieni was fool enough to brawl with his neighbor on the move, when the desert lay all around them, an eternal and unsleeping enemy. And when they arrived at their new home, amazement at so much luxury—endless grass for the flocks, and sweet water, and unfamiliar trees bearing delicious fruit— had kept the Isvaieni quiet for a few sennights more. Thus it was that, in the first days after their arrival, Bisochim saw none of the things that he saw so clearly now, kneeling beside Limrac's Healed body.

As soon as the shock of reaching their unfamiliar new

home wore off, the trouble would have begun. There were nearly three dozen tribes who called the Isvai "home." Some tribes counted their members in the hundreds, and their tents would fill even Sapthiruk Oasis when they came to water their flocks. Other tribes—like the Nalzindar— could not number even two score among their people. All were used to days spent in hard labor. The Isvaieni were not accustomed to idleness, and there was little for them to do here. There was nothing for them to hunt in the Barahileth, and there was food in abundance—even for so many—from Bisochim's flocks and herds and fields and orchards. Nor need the Isvaieni tend them, for Bisochim's magical servants did that work. And the Isvaieni's own beasts need not be herded and guarded either, for they would not wander away from the water and rich forage— there was nothing beyond it but sterile sand.

Without the fountains that constantly misted the air with water, all that grew would wither away and the air itself would be too hot to breathe. And for this reason, there was as little place for the people to go to escape each other's company as there was reason for their animals to stray. In deep night, when the sands cooled, the Isvaieni could leave the protection of the gardens and their fountains and go out into the desert, it was true, but during the day they must remain packed into intolerable closeness to one another. Grievances that could be ignored during a Gathering, or set aside during a chance meeting at an oasis, festered and grew until they must be answered in blood. This might be the first such quarrel, but he knew—with sinking heart— that it would not be the last. He must craft a net for the anger of the young warriors—and quickly.

"How could you do the work of our enemies for them?" Bisochim said quietly, rising to his feet.

As Limrac sat up, groaning, two of his kinsmen hurried forward to lift him to his feet and carry him back to the Laghamba tents.

"Hear me—all of you," Bisochim said, raising his voice. "You have followed me here because I spoke truth to you and you listened. The Balance of the world is out of true, and because we alone, of all the world, can see this, we are in danger. Because we see the truth, the enemies of the True Balance seek to place us in bondage.

"I have told you that the road to success and freedom would be as long and as hard for us as it once was for the Blessed Saint Idalia and Kellen the Poor Orphan Boy. I told you that in order to win our freedom we must set aside the differences between tribe and tribe—to become, not many tribes, but one. Would you rather squabble like children until the armies of the north sweep down upon us to destroy the Isvaieni forever? I do not wish to see that day."

"No one wishes that, Bisochim." It was Calazir who spoke, the leader of the Tabingana Isvaieni. His hair and beard were gray, and he had led his people with wisdom and justice for many years. "Yet are we the fat dwellers of the *Iteru*-cities, to pitch our tents so close by one another that one need not even leave his tent to have a conversation with a neighbor? Such closeness and idleness wears upon us all. We would hear of the battles we must fight."

"Your words have wisdom, Calazir," Bisochim answered, though the last thing he wanted was to either lead or send the Isvaieni into battle. "I will think upon them until the counsel I may offer is as wise as yours."

Calazir bowed and retreated. The circle of watchers were retreating as well, returning to their encampments. As Calazir had suggested, none of them had far to go.

Bisochim could double—even triple—the area protected by fountains, and it would not be enough—not for a people who had once roved over the entire Isvai. And a life of indolence did not suit the Isvaieni temper. Nor could he forbid them to fight among themselves—they knew him as a Wildmage, but the Wildmages counseled the Isvaieni, they did not *lead* them. Nor was there a Chief of Chiefs among the tribes—there had never been. Each tribe looked to itself alone. And even if all the leaders of all the tribes together agreed that their people must not fight among themselves, even that would not be enough: should the members of a tribe dislike the counsel of the one who led them strongly enough, that one would be banished from their tents.

He must think of something else.

As Bisochim brooded upon what he must do, he walked through the encampment. He had not attended a Gathering of the tribes since he left the tents of the Adanate, but all around him now he saw the tents of the peoples who lived between Sand and Star, each distinct in its patterns and weaving: Adanate, Kamazan, Khulbana, Barantar, Binrazan, Fadaryama, Thanduli, Laghamba, Hinturi, Kadyastar, Tabingana, Kareggi, Aduzza, Tunag, Tharkafa . . .

But—as he had known before this journey began—the tents of the Nalzindar were not among them.

He pondered for a few moments, then sought out Liapha, who ruled over the Kadyastar Isvaieni. Liapha had left the bodies of three husbands upon the sand, and borne a dozen children, but it was her cousin's son, of all her large family, who would follow her as leader of the Kadyastar. The Isvaieni could not afford to let the leadership of the tribe pass to the weak or the foolish. The day was near when Hadyan would take the staff of office from her hands, but it had not come yet.

And so Bisochim came to her tent, and bowed low, and waited to be welcomed inside, and sat upon the rug at her side, and allowed her granddaughter to serve him *kaffeyah*. And he ate dates, and patiently drank three cups of the hot bitter black brew, as Liapha shared the gossip of the enormous camp.

"I say, Wildmage, that I am not surprised that there was blood. Tharam was ever a fool. I would not let any daughter of mine go to that tent. Nor is Calazir overprudent. He has too many young men without wives within his walls. Well! He was ever shortsighted, asking too high a brideprice but never giving one. That is no Balance."

"It is not," Bisochim agreed.

They spoke a while longer of problems he could not yet

see a way to solve. The desertfolk chafed at such close proximity to one another: tempers flared and they had no understanding of how to live together in peace.

At last, Bisochim was able to broach the actual matter that had brought him to her tent. "I believe I see the tents of every tribe which calls the Isvai home . . . save one," he said.

Liapha regarded him shrewdly. "The Nalzindar have not come," she said. "Well, they were never ones to go where others led." Her expression turned sober. "I fear for them, Wildmage."

"As do I," Bisochim answered somberly. But he did not fear *for* the Nalzindar as much as he feared them. The sennights of the Ingathering had been time enough for the message he had preached among the tribes to reach Shaiara. He had not sought out each chieftain himself—there had not been time—but he had persuaded many, and they had convinced the rest. He had been certain that one of them must have sought Shaiara out.

He knew her. If she had doubts of what she heard, she would have come to him. He would have convinced her.

But she had not.

The Nalzindar were a tiny tribe, the smallest between Sand and Star. They kept no flocks, and only such *shotors,* hawks, and *ikulas* as they needed for hunting—and perhaps as many more *shotors* as might be needed to transport such tents and possessions as the *shotors* ridden on the hunt could not accommodate.

"Though . . . it has been many moonturns since the last Gathering," he said slowly. Such a tiny handful of people might vanish between one season and the next, through the harsh mercy of the Isvai, and leave no trace of their passage.

Liapha nodded. "So I had thought at first. And the Nalzindar are not ones to seek out the company of others at this *Iteru* or that. Yet their absence troubled me enough that I asked among the tents, for surely someone must have seen them since that time. And so word came to me that

Malbasi of the Tunag traded many fine robes to Shaiara of the Nalzindar at Sapthiruk Oasis for a great parcel of green-cured *fenec* skins. Nor, so she said, did Shaiara tarry to bargain overlong. I do not know why she did not stay to greet you, Wildmage, for you were there upon that day." Now Liapha looked even more troubled.

"Do not concern yourself. All goes as the Wild Magic wills." The words he had heard and spoken all his life fell easily from Bisochim's lips, but for the first time they tasted bitter. If Shaiara had been at Sapthiruk upon that day—as Liapha said—the Nalzindar had not simply vanished.

As soon after that as good manners permitted, Bisochim left Liapha's tent. She had given him much to think about. Three moonturns ago the Nalzindar had been alive between Sand and Star. Worse, Shaiara had been at Sapthiruk when he had been there to speak to Calazir, to Bakuduk, to Fannas, to half a handful of other leaders among the Isvaieni. And she had not made her presence known to him, nor had any among the Isvaieni seen her after that. Nor did what he had observed in his spells of foreseeing comfort him. The Wildmages had not gone to the Nalzindar *now,* and they would not have done so in the future. None of Bisochim's spells—of what was or of what could be—had showed him the Nalzindar at all.

Shaiara had taken the Nalzindar somewhere—but where? She would no more leave the deep desert for the *Iteru*-cities than she would raise a hand to the people she had sworn to shepherd and protect. Bisochim knew Shaiara as well as he knew himself—she was a creature of silence and the open sand, and could no more live within walls among the herds of city-dwellers than she could slit her own throat. Yet even if some unimaginable necessity had taken her there, it was impossible that she would have been absent from his vision of What Might Be, for the Wildmages would have sought out the only remaining tribe of the Isvaieni that they could find, just as the Nalzindar would have sought out their only possible allies.

He returned to his stronghold and paced through the vast stone chambers, the open courtyards, the gardens. He stood upon the battlements as the hot wind blew—from the desert, from the lake. The gusts of droplets from the fountains that kept the air breathable spattered over his skin like the rain he had heard of but never seen. And he thought of what he must do.

The Nalzindar were in hiding. No man hid from a friend.

Some Wildmage, some enemy—perhaps the Light Itself—had sought out the Nalzindar and filled their hearts with poison as a tainted well was filled with salt. They would not believe the truth now, even if he came to them and told it.

Yet even though they were in the service of the enemy—pawns at least, but no less dangerous for that—Bisochim could not bring himself to hate them. He had spent too many years sworn to protect the Isvaieni, as were all who held the Three Books. If the other Wildmages had forfeited their trust, he had not. There must be a way to protect the Nalzindar without endangering the other lives in his care. There *must*.

But to do that, he must find them first. Find them, and remove them from their bondage to whatever enemy had seduced them. Once he had done that, he would find a place where they could be safe. Protected. Where their tragic delusions could not spread to his true and faithful Isvaieni.

When the True Balance had been restored . . . the words the Nalzindar might speak to his faithful would not matter then. And when his battle was ended, they would see the truth. Shaiara was wise and long-sighted. She would not persist in error when she could embrace truth, and her people would accept her counsel. Or that of her successor, should she have left the tent of her fathers to give her body to the desert sands.

He must only find them.

* * *

IT HAD BEEN many years since any task Bisochim had set his will to had been beyond his means. There were only two things Bisochim had not yet accomplished. He had not yet restored the True Balance. And he had not yet won back Saravasse's love.

Both, he was certain, could be accomplished with time. And if he succeeded in the first, he would have all the time he needed to accomplish the second.

To find the Nalzindar was a matter, he now realized, as vital as discovering a way his Isvaieni could live together in peace, so once again he set aside the vital work of listening for the voices in the fire. His duty to his people must come before even that, for there was no one else to care for them now.

And so he summoned Saravasse to his side.

She came when he called her—as she must—but she would no longer speak to him. She had not spoken in years, even when he spoke to her, even when he begged her to speak. Her silence filled him with a dull heavy anger. How dare she mock him with silence, she who had once been so bright and clever, sharing her stories of far lands and centuries in the hours they had spent together in a thousand places upon the sand?

He loved her. Even now.

Through the Bond they shared, he felt her grief, as she felt his anger. Grief and anger bound them where once there had been only love and joy, and Bisochim dared not ask, even in the depths of his thoughts where he knew she could not hear, what had brought them to such a place in their lives. Sometimes he almost thought it would be better to abandon his grasping at the future in the name of what was. But to do that would be to betray the Wild Magic and to kill Saravasse, for when she had bound herself to him, she had bound her years to his. In two handspans of years—surely not three—he would be dead. And she would die with him.

And so when she came, he held his temper and his tongue, and set himself upon her back, and sent her soaring out over the desert, searching for the Nalzindar—and for a solution to a problem that magic could not solve.

Even three moonturns after the last time anyone had seen any of them, traces of their presence should have been easy to find, for one who rode upon the shoulders of the wind itself. The Nalzindar moved as the shadows of shadows, but hawks rose upon the sky, even the smallest cookfires made smoke, and no one could conceal tents and *shotors* upon the open desert—and the Nalzindar hunted with hawks, cooked their dinners, and slept in tents as did any other Isvaieni. Though the wind would wipe their footprints from the sand—and they might keep to the dunes for just that reason—if they ventured across the hard-baked clay, the faintest trace of sandaled foot or *shotor*'s pads would take many seasons to wear away, and those traces would be visible from above.

There was nothing.

Wrapped in spells of invisibility such as any hunter might envy, Bisochim and Saravasse ranged over the whole of the Barahileth, the Isvai, and even beyond, to the Madiran and the cities which edged it like the ornaments on a scarf.

There was no sign of the Nalzindar. Not a tent, nor a footprint . . . or even a body.

It took him a sennight to be utterly certain. Each time he returned to his fortress, there was more tension, more uncertainty, in the tents of the tribes. He knew that if he did not do something—soon—he would not have to wait for the war he saw in his visions to destroy his people. They would destroy themselves. And so he called an unprecedented council of the leaders of all the tribes. He spoke to them, not of the trouble in their own camps, but of another thing they all knew: the absence of the Nalzindar from among them.

Even before this past sennight, the tribes had accorded Bisochim respect and deference beyond that they had ever accorded to any Wildmage of the tribes, beyond anything

he had ever sought or wanted. But then he had led them
into the Barahileth and called water out of the arid sands
to slake their thirsts. He had brought them to a garden beyond any paradise in their story-songs. And then he had
summoned a dragon—creature of ancient legend—down
from the heavens, and rode forth upon its back. They
whispered now behind his back, linking his name with
those of Kellen the Poor Orphan Boy and the Blessed
Saint Idalia. Saying that poor Saravasse must be Star-
Crowned Ancaladar come again.

He did not want that. He did not want any of it. But he
would use it, to keep them safe. And so he spoke to them
of the Nalzindar and their mysterious absence.

"Forgive me, Wildmage, but—with all your power . . ."
Bakuduk, headman of the Hinturi, spoke hesitantly. Around
him, the other leaders of the Isvaieni shifted uneasily. These
men and women, unafraid of anything that lay between
Sand and Star, feared now to ask one of their own a simple
question, and it angered Bisochim further.

"Have you not asked to do battle with the enemy?"
Bisochim said sharply. "Now—when I tell you that I have
discovered that he has swept your brethren from the sand—
you ask me to do your work for you. Have I and my Bonded
not searched for them? That we found no sign of them tells
me that they are hidden by magic more subtle than my own.
Yet magic hides most of all from magic. I hope that if you
seek for them, you will discover them."

It was not a lie, for unless a spell was truly designed to
conceal a thing from all—which took great power—it
would work simply to turn aside the gaze, to misdirect. And
it was a thing nearly impossible to manage if many watched
at once.

But Bisochim did not truly believe the other Isvaieni
could find the Nalzindar where he had not been able to. He
hoped merely to give their restless energy a focus and an
outlet. Let the young men and women of the tribes scour
the empty desert while their more prudent elders settled
into this new life he had made for them. Let the absence of

so many cool tempers and bring wisdom to hearts—for there were few aged among the Isvaieni, and did all whom he hoped go forth upon this search, where once seven Isvaieni now stood among the tents of this new encampment, only one would remain. And when the young warriors tired of searching, in a moonturn or even six, they would be ready to embrace safety and security here upon the plains of Telinchechitl, and would have their elders to counsel them as to its desirability.

It would be a longer road to his goal than he had hoped to take, but the result would be the same: the Isvaieni would become one tribe, and settle here at the foot of the cliffs which bordered the Lake of Fire, and Bisochim's vision would never come to pass.

"To cross the Barahileth even once more will be a thing which will leave the bones of many upon the sand," Fannas said slowly. The headman of the Kareggi Isvaieni led a large and wealthy tribe, one that had traded frequently with the *Iteru*-cities. One did not survive in the Isvai by being rash, but it was sometimes said that Fannas did not act when action would be best.

"I shall make a safe road for our people that will take them securely as far as Kannanatha Well," Bisochim said. "The Barahileth shall be our guardian, the path into it known only to us, and may the Gods of the Wild Magic grant that we may soon share that secret with the Nalzindar."

IT WAS ANOTHER sennight before that part of his plan was ready to be set into motion, for it required the creation of wells in the Barahileth. Not the temporary summoning of water as he had done before, but deep permanent wells that would not fail, for if they did, the people who depended upon them—his Isvaieni—would die.

The water to fill these wells must come from somewhere, and Bisochim arrived at an elegant solution. The water would come from the Isvai. The new wells of the

Barahileth would flourish, and the old wells of the Isvai would decline.

Not all at once. Not overnight. But slowly the springs and oases of the outer desert would fail. Slowly enough so that the creatures who depended on them for water would go elsewhere in search of it. To the desert verge, the comparatively fertile land of the Madiran. He wished to harm no innocent creature.

But by the time the Armies of the Light came in search of the Isvaieni—long after his people had abandoned their search for the Nalzindar (they must)—there would be no water to sustain their great armies. Not for hundreds of miles. No army could possibly carry enough water with it to cross the Isvai *and* the Barahileth, and as soon as he knew they had first set foot upon the sand, he would turn the wells of the Barahileth to dust.

As Bisochim prepared the stone-covered wells in the Barahileth, eradicating as he did so every trace of the Ingathering from the fragile surface of the desert, the young warriors of the Isvaieni prepared themselves. With such a holy mission to undertake, tribal rivalries were set aside. Blood-oaths of fellowship were sworn, that each of them would hold all the others as dear as the kin of their own tents. *Geschaks* were honed to razor sharpness, bows restrung, hunting spears tested for soundness, *shotors* chosen for speed and stamina. And when Bisochim returned to tell them all was in readiness, the search parties began to depart, a few score at a time, to begin their hunt for the missing Nalzindar.

Another sennight passed before all of those who wished to join the quest had departed, for though each hunting party was small in number, even a full water-jug could be emptied drip by drip, and Bisochim had gathered thousand upon thousand of his people upon the plains of Telinchechitl. Less than two thousand Isvaieni remained among the tents when the last of those who wished to search had gone forth once more into the Isvai. In that time, the encampment became as peaceful as Bisochim could have hoped. It was the only contentment he had found since he had been forced to execute the rogue Wildmages, for in the days of waiting for the camp to become calm he had sought the Nalzindar with his strongest magic . . . and he had not found them.

If the Enemy had slain them, he would pay the greatest price Bisochim could exact. But Bisochim did not believe Shaiara and the Nalzindar were dead. Their deaths would have left traces his magic could sense.

No.

They were hidden from him.

Prisoners of the Enemy.

Or his willing—deluded—slaves.

Nine

A Feast for Crows

TO HARRIER'S RELIEF, he was finally able to drive the wagon out of the forest four days later. Ancaladar had thought he would make it in two, but the wagon's progress was slower than any of them had hoped. After the first day, Harrier started sending lunch along with Tiercel—the forest canopy on this side of the Veil was a tangled mess, and expecting Ancaladar to take off and land through it twice a day wasn't fair to him. Or to Tiercel. As Tiercel pointed out rather crossly, "Ancaladar has an armored hide, Har—but I don't, you know."

Each night Ancaladar told Harrier what lay ahead of him on the following day—since a dragon's eyes could penetrate the mass of tangled branches, old nests, and dying leaves to see what lay beneath—and Tiercel drew crude maps in the dirt of the forest floor to show Harrier what he could expect when he finally managed to get the

wagon free of the trees. And though Harrier didn't doubt
what he heard, he still argued.

"Are you sure it's a road? There can't be a road."

"You said that the first time," Tiercel said patiently. "It's
a road. It pretty much heads south, too, which is good. We
didn't see any sign of settlements. There's a lake, though.
Unfortunately, you'll have to leave the road to get to it."

"Worth doing," Harrier said. "Everything we've got could
use a good scrubbing."

"Don't I know it," Kareta said, wrinkling her nose fastidiously.

"Hey!" Harrier said, wounded. "You're welcome to—"
he waved his hands, pantomiming everything from
"leave" to *"stand upwind."* "It hasn't been *that* long since
I've had a bath."

"It hasn't been that recently, either," the unicorn answered
pertly.

"And I'm not really looking forward to a cold swim in
this weather," he added. Even though they were heading
south, it had to be either Mistrise or Frost by now—he'd
lost track—almost the end of the year, and it seemed to be
colder by the day now that they'd crossed the Veil. A fire
at night wasn't a luxury, it was a necessity, and Harrier
was wearing his warmest clothing. Tiercel must be freezing up in the sky.

"We'll just have to build up a couple of big fires," Tiercel said with a heavy sigh. From his expression, he wasn't
looking forward to a cold bath any more than Harrier was.
"I could probably heat the whole lake, but . . . it wouldn't
be that good for the fish."

"Unless you want poached fish," Kareta suggested.

"A lot of poached fish," Harrier said, resigning himself
to the inevitable.

It took Harrier another sennight to reach the lake. When
he finally rolled out of the forest, he spent a day in scrub
woodland—worse than the woods, because the wagon's
wheels caught in everything, and he worried the whole

time that either one of the axles would break, or one of the horses would put a leg down some badger hole—before getting out into really open country. Now he could see where they were going, and the ground was solid, but it wasn't level. Or smooth. The wagon jolted and jounced all day along the ground. The horses had to work hard if there was even a little upward slope, and Harrier had to be careful to catch any downward slope in time to set the brake before the wagon rolled over the team. He supposed he was lucky it was winter, not spring. The ground was hard-frozen, at least. In the spring, he probably would have had to convince Tiercel to coax Ancaladar into pulling the wagon. And at night they had to be more careful than ever before when setting up camp that a stray wind-borne spark didn't fly off and set the grass around them on fire, because it was tinder-dry. Tiercel thought he could probably stop a fire if it started, but neither of them wanted one to start.

Not only that, before he got to the lake, Harrier'd had to make one more detour—to a spring Kareta found for him—to spend most of one afternoon refilling the water barrels because they were out of water. The spring was tiny, but it was the only source she could find. And then he spent the rest of the afternoon—and the evening—listening to Kareta preen about how indispensable she was. At least when she was rejoicing in her own cleverness, Kareta wasn't nagging at him to do a spell. Harrier might be willing to *read* the Three Books—when he could get the light and the free time to do it—but he was damned if he'd do any magic. Tiercel could make all the Coldfire and light all the fires that they needed—Harrier had no intention of doing anything that would involve him with this mysterious "Magedebt" and "Mageprice." He didn't understand it very well, but Mageprice sounded a little like a mortgage: you got something—a spell—and then you had to pay for it later. And what he knew about mortgages was that the captain who couldn't pay one lost his ship. Harrier didn't think the Wild Magic worked quite the same way, but he didn't know how it *did* work. He was sure (pretty sure) that it couldn't be anything *bad,* but at the moment, he and Tiercel couldn't even afford something *inconvenient.*

When he finally reached the shore of the lake, Harrier chopped wood while Tiercel washed everything they owned—dishes and cookware and clothing and odds and ends of linens. Unfortunately, Ancaladar had been able to assure Harrier that the lake *did* indeed contain fish, so all there was to do to keep from freezing was build up two large bonfires. Their heat would help to dry the clothing as well; since Ancaladar hadn't gone along with Harrier's first suggestion that they just drape everything over him and let the radiant heat from his body dry it quickly. As he undressed, Harrier groused that apparently magic couldn't be used for anything *useful.*

The only reason he was willing to get into the water at all—the day was overcast, and the water looked gray and cold—was that it was more than a fortnight since they'd left Blackrowan Farm, and even in winter, that was entirely too long to go between baths. It would have been nice if they'd been able to bring a washtub along with them, but there really hadn't been room in the wagon, even if he'd thought to ask for one. The next time he had to go haring off into the middle of nowhere, Harrier vowed, he was bringing *enough stuff.*

At least he was able to entertain himself once they got into the water—and keep warm—by trying to duck Tiercel, who howled loudly about it. Harrier pointed out mercilessly that *he* wasn't the one who'd decided to grow his hair as long as an Elf's, and he was just doing Tiercel a favor by helping him rinse it. Even with the horseplay, though, they were both in and out of the water in less than a chime, and standing huddled between the fires, rubbing each other dry (and snapping at each other's legs with the damp towels) before struggling into sets of fresh-washed clothing. They were still a little damp, but neither of them wanted to wait. Besides, they still had to wash what they'd been wearing today, which meant the clothes they had on would only get damp again anyway. Perhaps by the time they were finished with the laundry something else would be *completely* dry.

Ancaladar caught them fish for dinner, and Harrier cleaned and cooked it.

"Can you read me something out of your Books?" Tiercel asked that evening. "I mean, is it allowed?"

Harrier supposed Tiercel must miss books. Back in Armethalieh he'd never been without one—or two, or half-a-dozen—for as long as Harrier had known him. But the only books he had with him now were High Magick books, which were, well, about as interesting as tide-charts. Which fascinated Harrier and every captain he knew—because you had to know the tides if you were going to sail—but they didn't have a lot of *plot*. And, really, only one use. Sighing, Harrier reached for his shoulder bag. It was never far from his side these days.

"Tyr, how do *I* know what's allowed or isn't? It's not like I've ever had a Wildmage to teach me anything about this . . . stuff." *Stupid stuff,* he'd wanted to say, but couldn't quite bring himself to. The Wild Magic wasn't stupid. It was just that he really wasn't cut out to be a Wildmage. At least in his opinion. He opened *The Book of Moon* at random. He half-expected the pages would have suddenly turned blank, but they hadn't. He looked around warily.

"Expecting to be struck by lightning?" Kareta asked. Her face might not be able to smirk, but her voice could.

"Shut up," Harrier said absently. He chose a passage at random and began to read. " 'The Knight-Mage is the active agent of the principle of the Wild Magic, the Wildmage who chooses to become a warrior or who is born with the instinct for the Way of the Sword, who acts in battle without mindful thought and thus brings primary causative forces into manifestation by direct action.' " He stopped. Nothing happened.

"Huh," Tiercel said. "Well, 'without mindful thought' pretty much describes you."

Harrier didn't even bother to reach out and smack

Tiercel. He was mulling over what he'd just read. "Okay," he said. "You—" he nodded at Kareta "—say I'm a Knight-Mage."

"That's right," she said brightly. "The first one born since—"

"Ah!" he said, holding up a hand. "Not now." Being compared to Kellen the Poor Orphan Boy just made him feel creepy. "So what this sort of . . . says, is that Knight-Mages have an, um, *instinct* for 'The Way of the Sword,' which is, I guess, sword-fighting."

"That's what it sounds like," Tiercel said seriously.

"Aren't you sorry now you didn't take lessons from those nice Elves when they offered?" Kareta asked.

"Aren't you sorry you didn't show up sooner to tell me I should?" Harrier sniped back. "Because I'm sure that Elunyerin and Rilphanifel would have been *happy* to stick around longer if they'd known they got to train an actual Knight-Mage."

"It doesn't work that way," Kareta muttered.

"What? You being helpful?" Harrier demanded.

"Elunyerin and Rilphanifel were not chaste and virginal," Ancaladar said, in tones indicating that he had no interest in listening to another argument tonight. "Kareta could not approach you while they were near."

Harrier thought back. What were practically the first words Kareta had said to him? *"I thought those two would never leave."* That must be why. He couldn't make up his mind whether to turn red or burst out laughing in disbelief, and from Tiercel's expression, neither could he. "Oh," he finally said.

"I wish you people—" Kareta said huffily.

"I wish you unicorns—" Tiercel said, echoing her tone exactly.

Harrier did laugh then.

I'M NOT QUITE sure where we're going, but we're making good time.

A sennight later, they'd settled into a comfortable—and peaceful—routine. Up before dawn, breakfast, horses harnessed, and onto the road in the dark. Why there was a road, and where it went, and who used it, were questions none of them had answers to yet. If there were any villages here, they weren't near the road—and "near" was a pretty relative term for Ancaladar.

If it was a trade-road, who were they (whoever "they" were) trading with? Not the Elves, because neither Aressea nor Aratari nor anyone else at Blackrowan Farm had seemed to have much notion about humans—or, in fact, anything on the other side of the Veil.

"Could be for a lot of things," Kareta said, continuing one of their usual conversations. "Could be only used in summer. Maybe people just come and *live* here in summer. Or come here to gather tasty berries."

Harrier looked around. " *'Tasty berries'?"* he said in disbelief. "They'd have to be pretty damned tasty." The road wended along through fairly open country. A few hundred miles away on his right hand, the Bazrahils rose up into the sky, their slopes white with snow. There were a couple of miles of open country to either side of the road, but beyond that it became hilly and—soon thereafter—forested again—Ancaladar had looked.

The only water they'd found since they'd left the lake was up in the hills. The last time they'd needed to fill the water barrels, Tiercel had needed to fly them up to a stream one by one, strapped to Ancaladar's saddle. There'd be water near the road soon, but the wagon wouldn't reach it for another sennight, Ancaladar calculated. Sometimes Harrier wondered how he'd gotten so good at guessing how many miles the wagon could cover in a day, but it wasn't that hard to figure out. Ancaladar had traveled with Kellen's army. He knew exactly how slow a freight wagon went.

"Well, you're grumpy today!" Kareta said, tossing her head. "It's probably because you aren't doing magic," she added confidentially. "If you were doing spells, I'm sure you'd feel better."

"Wrong," Harrier said comprehensively.

"You have to do some sometime," she said coaxingly.

"No I don't."

"What about just one nice little one? You could summon up a sword teacher for yourself. You know you need one."

If a Knight-Mage had to know anything about swordsmanship, then yes (Harrier knew), he did need one. But that wasn't the point. "And what would the Mageprice be for that?" he asked. "Do you have any idea? Light, Kareta, I don't even know whether all the things I *think* I know about Wildmages are even true! I know—I guess—that there are two prices to pay for every spell: the energy it takes, and then the Mageprice that's for, I guess, the *right* to cast it at all. Or for the Gods' help in keeping it from going wrong. And the first price is why Wildmages ask people to lend energy to a spell, and that's okay—not that I've got the first idea of how to take or use what they'd give me. It's the second part I'm worried about."

"Well, in that case," Kareta said pragmatically, "why not just do the ones that don't carry Mageprice? There must be some."

"Figuring that out in advance is—huh." He broke off. "That doesn't look right." The wagon had just rounded a bend in the road, and ahead, a good distance off the road itself, there was a fluttering movement. Ravens. A whole flock of them. "Something's dead. Something big." He clucked to the team, urging it to move faster.

By the time the wagon reached the place, Tiercel and Ancaladar had already spotted what Harrier had seen and landed. He jumped down from the wagon and ran over—Harrier didn't *actually* worry about Tiercel's safety when Ancaladar was right there to watch over him, but now that Tiercel's nightmares were back, Harrier was pretty sure Tiercel's enemies weren't that far behind. And whoever this was had certainly had enemies of his own. His robes were filthy and blood-soaked, and *something* had killed his horse, though by now it was hard to tell what and how.

The dying beast had rolled onto the dead man, trapping him beneath it, and Ancaladar had fastidiously plucked it free and set the body aside.

"I guess we should bury him," Harrier said, crouching down beside the body. The man was wearing a strange armor that didn't seem to be made out of metal—the face-piece had protected his eyes from the ravens, not that that really mattered much.

"Best not," Ancaladar said soberly. "He's still alive."

At Ancaladar's words, Harrier eased the helmet off. The face he saw was dark—both naturally, and burned dark by the sun. He looked a little like the Selkens Harrier had seen at Dockside Armethalieh, and his age was hard to estimate. Harrier felt for a pulse and couldn't find one at first. It was slow and weak, and the man's skin was cold. "Won't be for long," he said reluctantly. The horse hadn't died today, or even yesterday, and its rider had been lying trapped beneath it since it had gone down. And he'd been hurt even before that.

Harrier looked up at Tiercel hopefully. "Unless you can, uh, do a spell?"

"A Healing spell." Tiercel's voice was flat. He shook his head fractionally. "I don't know whether the High Magick didn't have them, or . . . if Jermayan just didn't have those books. But I don't know any. You have to."

"*Me?*" Harrier's voice rose to a near-shout.

"He'll *die!*" Tiercel's voice cracked on the second word.

"How much water do we have?" Apparently he'd made up his mind to do this without thinking it over. Or at least to try.

"Three-quarters of a barrel." Tiercel's voice was rough and quiet.

"Bring a blanket. The heavy ground one."

While Tiercel went to fetch it, Harrier unbuckled the man's belt and started cutting open his clothes. There was more armor beneath the robes he wore—still no metal, but a heavy quilted shirt sewn with disks of what looked like bone, and buckled arm-guards of thick leather. The shirt

wasn't enough to stop an arrow going into his shoulder—
Harrier saw when he cut the shirt open—but that wasn't
what had taken him down, because there was a crude bandage over it. He pulled the dressing away and caught the
unmistakable whiff of infection. The wound was red and
angry, too inflamed for him to be able to tell if any part of
the arrow was still in the shoulder.

Tiercel got back with the blanket.

"Help me lift him onto it," Harrier said.

"You'll kill him," Tiercel protested.

"Then I won't need to Heal him, will I?" Harrier answered brutally. "I can't do anything here."

He wasn't sure why he said it. He wasn't sure he could
do anything anywhere. It just felt right.

When they lifted him to move him, Harrier saw that
he'd been lying on a set of long curved swords. They
looked familiar, but he didn't have time to think about it
just now. He swept the swords and their harness aside and
then placed them on the blanket beside the man when they
laid him down again.

"Is he . . . ?" Tiercel asked.

"Still alive," Harrier said. "And probably bleeding all over
the blanket, now, so come on."

They carried him back beside the wagon. At least some
of the wind would be cut here. If it got much colder, he
and Tiercel were going to have an argument about actually
sleeping inside the wagon, even if that did mean messing
up all of Tiercel's *stuff*.

"What do you want me to do?" Tiercel asked nervously.

"Nothing," Harrier said shortly. "Start tea. I don't know."

"You cannot lend power to his spell, Bonded," Ancaladar said quietly. "You do not yet have the skill."

"It takes skill?" Harrier muttered. The man's long black
hair was matted with dried blood, and there was a crude
bandage on one thigh; nothing more than a torn rag wound
several times around the leg and hastily tied over his
trousers. It was black with blood, and the fabric of the
man's pants below the wound had been so sodden with

blood that it was still damp enough to stain Harrier's fingers. He decided to leave the bandage where it was.

"Skill," Ancaladar said, "to set aside the shields every High Mage must learn to place about himself, in order to share his power with another. To have such shields is important for the spells." The dragon sounded regretful, but at the moment, Harrier was just as glad that the High Magick had one more weird requirement.

"Fine. Find me a piece of charcoal, would you?" He wiped his hands as clean as he could, and started digging through his bag. He'd pulled out the tiny brazier—he thought he was going to need it—and then *The Book of Moon*. Real Wildmages might know how to do these things off the top of their heads, but he didn't. *Okay. Okay. I've got this. Willow, ash, and yew. Burn them. Hair and blood. Oh . . . yuck. And here are the words. It looks simple. If it was this simple, everyone would do it. Eternal Light, this isn't going to work!*

But when Tiercel came back with the charcoal, all Harrier said was: "Looks simple enough. Now, if you don't mind, light that for me, because I'm damned if I'm going to learn two spells in one day."

That made Tiercel smile, just a little. Harrier put the cake of charcoal into the brazier, and Tiercel set it alight. It would take a few seconds to burn down to the point he could use it. Then they both looked up and saw Kareta standing several hundred yards up the road, shivering and looking miserable.

"Why is she . . . ?" Tiercel began.

"Probably because this guy has a wife and kids somewhere waiting for him," Harrier snapped. "Why don't you go get a handful of honey disks and keep her company?" He was really trying hard to not think about what he was going to have to do next.

Tiercel shrugged and walked off. Harrier saw the wagon rock as he climbed in and out of it, and a moment later saw Tiercel trudging up the road, carrying an entire tin of honey-disks under his arm.

"You did not need to do that, you know. There is no danger to him," Ancaladar said.

"Fine," Harrier repeated, hardly paying any attention to his own words. He got up and got one of the buckets, opened the water-keg and ladled out some water to wash his hands. He would have tried to get the guy to drink if he could, but he wasn't conscious. He rinsed his mouth and spat; thirsty but too nervous to drink. *Should have had Tyr make that tea,* he thought, but there wasn't time.

He went back and knelt on the blanket and sorted through his bag again. All the leaves Lanya had packed for him were in tiny bags, labeled in a language he couldn't read, but he recognized them by sight and smell. Half of them were familiar from his mother's kitchen, the other half, from half a year of trudging through forests. He pulled out the three he needed, then picked up his knife.

"A circle," Ancaladar said quietly. "You will need one."

Harrier took a deep breath and nodded. He folded the heavy blanket in around the stranger as much as he could, exposing the pale packed earth of the trail, then drew the heavy knife Roneida had given him. He scraped a ragged circle around them both. It wasn't all that circular, but he was careful to make sure that the line of the end and beginning met exactly. He sheathed his knife again. "Thank you."

"I wish there were more aid I could provide," Ancaladar said.

"Just take care of Tiercel," Harrier said.

"Forever," Ancaladar promised, but Harrier had already stopped listening. He was concentrating too hard on his task.

Hair from the person to be healed. Blood from the person to be healed. Not hard to get when the stranger was covered in it, and to top it all off, moving him had started the shoulder wound bleeding again. Hair from the Wildmage (him). Not too hard.

His blood.

Harrier took a deep breath and ran his thumb over the

blade of his small belt knife. Not his eating knife—that wasn't very sharp—but the one he wore to use for any little task that needed doing. *A sharp knife is a safe knife,* his Da always said, telling him that more fools cut themselves on dull knives than ever did on a properly honed blade. *Oh, Da, if you could see me now. . . .*

He was nervous, so he pressed harder than he meant to, and he only realized he'd cut himself when he felt the blood running down his wrist. He swore, scrabbling to soak the ball of hair in his blood and then throw it onto the charcoal. Almost as an afterthought, he added the leaves.

Light blast it, this had better work!

As the hair spat and crackled, Harrier realized that wasn't exactly what he was supposed to say.

Um, Light? This is Harrier. I want you to Heal this guy. And I guess there's a Mageprice I'm supposed to pay. And I'm supposed to pay it willingly, and I don't want him to die, but I don't want anything to happen to Tiercel, either, and I've known him longer, and, so, if I could just help Tiercel first before I have to go off someplace else to do something for you that would be great, because then I'd be happy to do, okay, anything, all right? But this is so important—

For a moment he was sure it hadn't worked. He *knew* it wouldn't work—who was he, Harrier Gillain, son of the Harbormaster, to be casting spells? He closed his eyes tightly in pure frustration.

And he thought about his Da, in the kitchen teasing Ma, and the way she'd look when she'd turn and laugh at him, and he thought of the man lying on the blanket in front of him, and sure, he didn't know anything at all about him, and maybe he was a bad man, but maybe he had a wife somewhere, or a sister, and oh, Light, maybe he just wanted to go *home,* and certainly he didn't want to just die, and all Harrier could feel was panic and something like anger, and the need to be able to help, if it was at all possible to help—

And suddenly the constant cold wind that he hadn't even noticed, because he'd gotten so used to it after almost a moonturn on this side of the Veil . . . stopped. And there was stillness and warmth all around him, and that should have frightened him, but it didn't. Cautiously, Harrier opened his eyes, and saw that he was completely surrounded by a dome of shimmering green. And that didn't frighten him either. He just felt . . . purposeful.

He needed to know what to do now, but even as he wondered, he knew. It wasn't as if he was being told, but as if he was—somehow—*remembering*. He reached out and placed both hands gently on the stranger's chest.

The moment he did he felt as if a great weight settled on his shoulders, but only for a second. Then it broke through, and the weight was still there, but now Power was flowing through him, through his hands, into the stranger, as if Harrier had become a narrow harbor-mouth and the tide was racing in. It was power and Power, strong and sweet and wild, and he didn't have to tell it what to do—it wasn't a Power you *told*—he'd asked, and that was enough. All he had to do now was offer himself as its hands in the world, to do what needed to be done.

That was all any Wildmage did. Ever. What needed to be done. They—the Wildmages—offered themselves to the Wild Magic, and the Wild Magic gave them . . .

Everything, Harrier thought. *It gives you everything.*

He could still watch. He could still think. In this moment, Harrier could see the body beneath him as clearly and starkly as the drawings for a new sailing ship in the hands of the shipwright: how it should be, and how it was damaged. The Power raced through him, into the stranger, knitting up broken bones, closing open wounds, curing infections, healing damaged flesh.

He didn't know how long he spent, watching the body beneath his hands come back into true, but he knew—he sensed, he saw—that the work was nearly done. In moments the Power would depart.

Tell me! he thought. *What do you need? What do you want?*

He didn't know what he expected to hear. He didn't

hear anything at all. He just had the same sense of remembering, and a feeling like a key turning in a lock.

You must become an Apprentice.

That was the last thing Harrier knew for a very long
time.

THE FIRST THING Harrier noticed was that he was lying
down. The second was that he smelled woodsmoke. He
tried to sit up and managed—with infinite effort—to open
his eyes.

"He's awake!" Kareta cried.

A moment later Tiercel was tugging him into a sitting
position and trying to get him to hold a mug. When that
didn't work out—he couldn't quite get his hands to close
around it—Tiercel held it up to his mouth. Harrier drank
greedily. He was thirsty—and as soon as he stopped being
thirsty, he realized he was *starving.*

"You—I—what?" he said.

Tiercel laughed with relief. "Oh, Light, Har, you've been
asleep for *two days!* Kareta wanted to wake you up, and Ancaladar said it was better to let you wake up on your own,
and—I didn't know what to do."

"Yeah. Well. Next time you become a Mage, learn healing spells." He felt strong enough to hold the mug this time,
and drained it. "More."

After a second cup of broth he was ready to take stock
of the situation. They were still right where they had been.
They now had a big woodpile. There was a pot of stew
hanging over the fire, and the tea-brazier was steaming.
The stranger was wrapped up in blankets, lying next to
Harrier. And still breathing.

"He been asleep, too?" Harrier asked. He was so
thirsty!

"I got him to wake up a couple of times to drink some
broth," Tiercel said. "But he just went right back to sleep.
He hasn't said anything. We, uh, *Ancaladar* took the horse

back up into the pines and dumped it, and brought back a couple of dead trees. I cut them up to keep you both warm. We filled up the water barrels, too."

"What's in the pot?" Harrier asked.

"Rabbits," Tiercel said. "Hares, actually. I didn't want to have to deal with a whole deer, so I set some snares in the woods yesterday. They worked fine."

"Tiercel the Bunny-killer," Harrier said, grinning.

"And I've been very bored," Kareta said, "because he's been no fun at all! He's either been chopping wood, or cooking, or had his nose in one of his silly books. Him and Ancaladar both!"

"I'm pretty sure Ancaladar couldn't fit his nose into one of Tyr's books," Harrier said. He yawned.

"You aren't going back to sleep, are you?" Tiercel asked. He sounded worried.

"No," Harrier said. "I think I'm done sleeping." He yawned again. "I'm hungry, though."

By the time he'd eaten two full bowls of stew—which had a lot more things than rabbit in it, and he just hoped Tiercel hadn't poisoned both of them with all these wild-gathered vegetables—he felt almost like his old self again. He was a little unsteady when he got to his feet, but not so unsteady that he couldn't wave Tiercel off.

As soon as she'd seen he was all right, Kareta had retreated to what she obviously felt was a comfortable distance again. Harrier was touched that she'd been willing to come close enough to the stranger to see that he was all right—not that he'd ever tell her so, of course. And if she was passing up the opportunity to stick around and tease him now, it was clear that not going near people who weren't, well, "chaste and virginal" wasn't just a matter of personal preference for unicorns, but something they really couldn't do. At least not for long. He wondered, not "why" exactly, but what it was that stopped them. Did it hurt? Or was it some kind of barrier like the Veil around the Elven Lands?

He wanted to walk down the road to tell her that everything was fine, but it actually seemed like that might be a little too far to go just now. Maybe later. He settled for walking around to the back of the wagon and sitting down on the step.

Tiercel—of course—followed him.

"What was it like?" Tiercel asked.

"Getting knocked flat on my ass for two days? I'm pretty sure whatever I did, I did it wrong," Harrier said.

"Ancaladar says he thinks that happened because you didn't have anyone to share the—the *other* price of the Healing," Tiercel said. He looked a little embarrassed.

"Well, you couldn't, and Ancaladar couldn't, and Kareta sure couldn't. And hey, it worked." He knew it had. He didn't even have to ask.

"So I just . . ." Tiercel said, and stopped.

Tiercel wondered what it was like. And Harrier couldn't tell him. Not because he felt he was forbidden to. He just didn't have the words to explain it. Nice? Awful? Terrifying? Wonderful? Somehow they were all true at the same time. And the High Magick wasn't anything like it— somehow Harrier was certain of that. What had Tiercel kept calling it back in the beginning? *"A magick anyone could learn."* But you didn't *learn* the Wild Magic. You just sort of said: okay. And then *did* it. It was . . . it was *just* like being a Harbor Pilot. Watching the water constantly for every shift and change, so you could bring the ship you were guiding safely to port—or out to sea. Listening to the wind. If you did that, your ship was fine. If you didn't . . .

"Harrier?" Tiercel said doubtfully.

"I've never been that good at listening," Harrier said, half to himself. He blinked, focusing on Tiercel again.

"Are you okay?" Tiercel asked suspiciously.

"I'm . . . um. It was probably nothing like that stuff you do, okay?" Harrier said, because he knew he needed to say *something*. "And I don't know if I could say what it *is* like. You're the one who reads all those books."

"Which say next to nothing about the Wild Magic. And

nothing particularly useful about the High Magick, come to that," Tiercel pointed out.

"Don't look at me. *I* didn't write them. But if I had, there'd be a whole chapter about how a guy who shows up stuck full of arrows was probably being chased by somebody who was shooting the arrows," Harrier said. He was starting to feel more himself by the minute.

"Believe it or not, we actually managed to think of that ourselves. Ancaladar took a look around—'around'; meaning 'for about a moonturn by wagon down the trail.'" Tiercel shrugged. "He found about a dozen dead bodies scattered through the hills, and more tracks leading south. He says it looks like two groups, chasing each other and stopping to fight a couple of times. He said there was a fight where we found the injured man, and another horse ran away, but the man who was riding the horse was dead."

"Useful. What happened to the horse?"

Tiercel made a face. "It was tasty."

"Just as long as *I* don't have to eat it. Well, I guess we'll find out the whole story when he wakes up, won't we?"

"I guess so. Har?"

"Yeah?"

"The Wild Magic's going to want you to do something now, isn't it?"

Harrier sighed deeply. "Yeah. But it isn't urgent." *I hope it isn't urgent.* He also hoped he'd get more details about whatever this . . . *Mageprice* . . . was when the time came to pay it, or else there might be a real mess.

HARRIER HAD WOKEN up around midday. After a couple more hours of being up and around, he decided he felt well enough to go see Kareta. He wrapped up in his storm-cloak, filled his pockets with cold flatcakes, and walked up the trail.

"It's about time somebody thought about me," she said sulkily.

"I did," Harrier said. "I thought about how you wouldn't want to have to carry me back to the wagon if I fell on my face."

Kareta snorted rudely. Harrier looked around until he saw a likely looking rock by the side of the road—there were enough of them all along the edges of the road to make him think they'd been rolled out of the roadbed itself by whoever'd made the road, and *that* made him think this might have been a riverbed at some point—and sat down. He dug around in his pocket, pulled out a piece of flatcake, and offered it to her.

"Yours is better," she said, chewing.

"My Ma's is *much* better," he said, taking a bite of the other half of the flatcake. He thought for a moment. "Don't know what we're going to do when it's time to move on. Maybe Tyr can cast some kind of a spell." Something so Kareta wouldn't have to trail the wagon by a dozen horse-lengths or more.

"Huh," Kareta said dismissively.

"Well, we *could* have just given him a horse and sent him on his way, but . . . Ancaladar ate the horse."

"You don't even know who he is," Kareta said, after a moment.

"Doesn't matter," Harrier said.

"It does so! What if he's an—an—an—a bandit?"

"Oh, like you'd know anything about bandits?" Harrier scoffed.

"I've heard stories," Kareta said darkly.

"I bet you have," Harrier said. He sighed. "If he's a bandit, or—somebody who was being chased for a good reason, and we ask him about it, he'll just lie. I wonder, though."

"What could *you* possibly be wondering about?" Kareta demanded.

"Well, what he was doing here. What they were *all* doing here. Ancaladar said it was two groups, chasing each other and fighting. And he's the only one left. And there's nothing out here—Ancaladar looked. No villages, no towns . . . no people but them. So what were they all doing here? Why come this way?"

"Obviously so you'd *finally* do a spell," Kareta said.

"Do you want more flatcake or not?" Harrier demanded.

"I don't see why the truth annoys you."

"If it's truth that several dozen people had to die so I could be tricked into doing a spell, then I'm annoyed whether it's truth or not. And it better not *be* truth," Harrier said darkly.

"Well, of course *that* part isn't," Kareta said, as if it should be self-evident.

Harrier didn't bother to pursue the conversation any further. Figuring out Kareta's logic was a difficult task at the best of times, and he still felt as if he'd put in a full day's work on the docks. He supposed—in a way—he had. Because the stranger was alive, and if *making* him live was something that could be done by fetching and carrying, Harrier had done it. And like any job of heavy lifting, it would have gone easier if there'd been others there to help.

It was easier to think of the Wild Magic in terms like that. He still didn't quite understand it, but he had the vague idea that he might be able to *do* it. If he absolutely had to.

He spent a while longer with Kareta, then walked back to the wagon. By the time he got there he was so tired his muscles were shaking, but he tried not to let Tiercel know. He just sat down on the blanket again with a thump. "This really isn't the place I'd pick to spend a lot of time," he said, looking around.

Tiercel tossed another log on the fire and laughed. "Ancaladar says you'd have to go a pretty long way to find any place that *isn't* like this place. Unless you want to go up into the hills."

"No thanks."

* * *

ABOUT THE TIME it started to get dark, the stranger woke again. Tiercel helped him to sit up, while Harrier watched warily.

"I am . . . alive," the stranger said slowly. He looked first at Tiercel, then at Harrier, his dark eyes confused. "You do not wear the blue robes."

"Uh . . . no," Tiercel said, sounding equally puzzled. "Who are you? What's your name? What happened to you?"

"I am Telchi," the stranger said.

"Were the people in the blue robes after you?" Tiercel asked.

The man stared at Tiercel as if Tiercel had lost his wits. "Why would Wildmages pursue me?" he asked. He regarded both of them with sudden suspicion.

"Wildmages wear blue robes where you come from," Tiercel guessed.

"No," Harrier said. "They don't."

Suddenly both Tiercel and the stranger were looking at him.

"I thought I'd seen those swords he carries before. I had," Harrier said. " 'Telchi' isn't his name. It's what he *is*. He's *a* Telchi. The Selkens hire them to guard their ships. They're . . . some kind of warrior caste among the Selkens. And as far as I know, there aren't any Wildmages in the Selken Isles."

The Telchi smiled at that. "No, young master. There are not. But I have not seen the shores of home since I was a young man, nor shall I again, I think. And in the land I now call home, those who bear the Three Books wear the blue robe so that all may know and honor them."

"Well, that's dumb," Harrier said flatly. "If everybody knows you're a Wildmage, wouldn't they be bothering you all the time to—I don't know—*do* things?"

The Telchi smiled faintly. "In the Madiran, we depend upon the Wildmages for life itself. It would be foolish to offend one of you." He glanced from Harrier to Tiercel, obviously certain that one of them was a Wildmage, but not knowing which of them it was. "But perhaps you would tell me to whom I am indebted for my life?" the Telchi prompted.

"Oh." Harrier could tell that Tiercel would much rather be asking questions than answering them—especially once the Telchi had mentioned the Madiran—but he also had the good grace to be embarrassed at his lapse of manners. "I'm Tiercel Rolfort, and this is my friend Harrier Gillain. We're from Armethalieh. He's, um . . ."

"I'm sort of the one who Healed you," Harrier said awkwardly. He wanted to add: *But I'm not really a Wildmage,* only that wouldn't really be true. It was just that saying he *was* a Wildmage seemed awfully close to lying.

"Alone?" the Telchi asked. He looked more impressed than Harrier was really comfortable with.

"There was no one to help," Ancaladar said, craning his neck over the top of the wagon to regard their guest.

Confronted by this unexpected sight—for Ancaladar was on the far side of the wagon, his massive body out of the Telchi's line of sight—the Telchi uttered a choked cry and scrabbled backward.

"Light and Darkness, Ancaladar, do you want me to have to Heal him all over again?" Harrier snapped. "It's all right. It's just Ancaladar. He's Tiercel's dragon."

"Sort of," Tiercel muttered.

"One of the ancient Shining Folk," the Telchi said. He'd recovered his composure quickly, and was regarding Ancaladar with both curiosity and awe.

"Well, he's a dragon, anyway," Harrier said. He was just as glad that the Telchi was more interested in Ancaladar than he was in him, really.

Though Tiercel might have—in fact, definitely did—want to hear all about the Madiran, their guest had just awoken from a long sleep, and even now was far from fully recovered. He drank several mugs of broth, and then accepted a bowl of stew, but before he'd finished more than half of it, he was already asleep again. Harrier was barely in time to catch the bowl and keep its contents from spilling stew all over him. At least before he slept, the Telchi was able to tell them that he and his men had been following bandits into the Tereymil Hills, and that of all his men, he was the only survivor.

"WELL, WE KNOW where we are now," Tiercel said. "That's something."

They'd moved away to keep from disturbing the Telchi's rest, going around to the other side of the wagon to sit leaning against Ancaladar. The dragon spread a wing over them both to shelter them from the wind.

"Not that knowing that is particularly helpful," Harrier pointed out. "I could call this place 'Garnodin' or 'Bordron' and it wouldn't tell you anything."

"But—" Tiercel said.

"Knowing he's from the Madiran, now *that's* useful," Harrier said. "Because we're going there, and he can tell us about it."

Tiercel regarded him curiously. "Do you trust him?"

Harrier shrugged. "He's a Telchi, and . . . I kind of want to know why he's here, instead of back in the Selken Isles. But if he says he was chasing bandits, then . . . yeah. He probably was."

Ten

The Paying of Prices

IN THE MORNING, Harrier felt pretty much like his normal self again, and the Telchi was ready to take his first careful steps.

The clothing and armor that had been taken off him days before were too filthy and blood-soaked to clean, even if there'd been all the water in the world to wash them in. The armor might be salvageable, though not without work. For now, the Telchi was wearing a spare set of Harrier's clothes. He was several inches shorter than Harrier, but so broad-shouldered that nothing of Tiercel's would fit him.

The first thing he asked for was his swords.

Harrier was the one who found them and brought them to him, since with Harrier up and (he swore) fine, Ancaladar had insisted that Tiercel resume his practicing. Tiercel hadn't wanted to leave Harrier alone with the Telchi, but Harrier had pointed out that he was probably—at least for the moment—both stronger and faster than a man who'd been all-but-dead three days before.

The swords were the same sort Harrier had seen the Telchi guards wearing on the Armethalieh docks—long, slim, and curved. One was a little longer than the other. They were worn crossed upon the back—as he remembered—and he thought of watching Elunyerin and Rilphanifel spar. He couldn't imagine how you'd even draw swords worn this way, let alone fight with two at once.

The Telchi reached for the swords the same way Harrier had seen Tiercel reach for his Wand. Or for Ancaladar, sometimes. As if they were a part of himself that had somehow gotten too far away. He carefully fitted the harness on over the tunic and buckled the straps into place. Then he reached up—

There was a flicker of movement too fast for Harrier to follow, and suddenly both swords were in his hands. Harrier stepped back, his hand going automatically to his belt. He was wearing the sword Roneida had given him, of course, but he knew perfectly well it wouldn't do him any good if the Telchi meant to kill him.

"Do you think I would harm you, Wildmage?" the Telchi asked. "I could never enter the Hall of Heroes burdened by such shame."

"Ah . . . right," Harrier said. He didn't let go of his sword-hilt, though.

THE PHOENIX ENDANGERED {181}

"But I see that you, too, are a warrior," the Telchi added. He looked both interested and pleased.

Harrier couldn't repress a grimace. *I'm not. That's the problem.*

The Telchi cocked his head, regarding Harrier. "You disagree?"

"Let's say that I'm probably about as good a warrior as I am a Wildmage," Harrier said. He didn't want to tell a flat lie, but he didn't want to come out and say that he knew nothing about using a sword, either. Not when he wasn't quite sure why the Telchi had drawn his.

But the answer seemed to satisfy the man, because he nodded, and took a few steps away, and began a slow series of movements with the twin blades. The forms were unfamiliar to Harrier, but their purpose wasn't. He'd seen Elunyerin and Rilphanifel do something similar often enough: a kind of warm-up; a stylized version of all the moves that might be used in actual combat, performed much more slowly.

But after only a few minutes of careful exercise the Telchi sheathed his swords with shaking hands, and would have slumped to his knees if Harrier had not rushed to catch him.

"I am . . . perhaps . . . not as . . . strong as I might be," the Telchi said, when he was seated on the blanket once more.

"Give it a little time," Harrier said. He found a mug and ladled out some broth. The nice thing about being stopped for a long time was being able to cook things that took more than an hour or two. The bad part was that this wasn't getting them any closer to the place they needed to be. Or even to the place where they needed to start looking for it.

"Had I possessed such patience in my youth, we should never have met," the Telchi said, taking the mug.

"Yeah, well, I'm kind of wondering why we've met *now*," Harrier said. "If you don't mind me asking."

"My debt to the man who returned my life to me cannot

be easily or simply repaid," the Telchi answered. "My story is yours to hear."

"Um . . . great," Harrier said, getting his own mug of broth and settling down on the blanket opposite the Telchi. "Because Tiercel's kind of worried about the bandits and everything."

The Telchi smiled faintly. "The tale begins long before that. Before—I think—either you or your friend first saw the light of day, when I was young and rash and thoughtless. Had I been less of any of these things, I would not have accepted an oathbond from Inzileth to sail across Great Ocean. But in those days I was certain I knew better than my elders, and those who would offer guidance and advice. And I was curious to see the land which lay beyond Great Ocean.

"By the time we had reached Armethalieh, I knew Inzileth for a dishonorable man, fit to hold no Telchi's oathbond. I weighed—so I thought—the matter carefully in my mind, and chose to break my sworn contract with him rather than stay one more hour upon the deck of his ship. Of course, no other Selken captain would bond a Telchi who had broken his oathbound contract." The Telchi shrugged. "I was young and foolish, as I have said."

None of this made real sense to Harrier—he didn't know much about the Selkens, only about their ships and their cargoes. But he knew that a broken contract was a serious matter—and might even be a *deadly* serious matter in some places—and by now he'd traveled widely enough to know that there were a lot of different ways of doing things besides the way that they were done in Armethalieh.

"What did you do?" Harrier asked.

"I sought work. But your Nine Cities are a peaceful place, with little occupation for a swordsman from a far-off land. If the Sword-Giver and the Lady of Battles meant me to learn humility, They taught me well indeed. After some years of wandering, I came to the Madiran, and there I found suitable employment at last, for caravans travel frequently between the *Iteru*-cities, and there is always work for one of my talents. I settled in Tarnatha'Iteru, and my fortune was as good as it had once been ill."

"Until you ended up under a dead horse," Harrier pointed out.

"She was a fine animal. I shall miss her," the Telchi said with a deep sigh. "Yet it is some consolation to know that the task we set upon was accomplished."

Harrier leaned forward, frowning a bit in concentration. The rest of the story of the Telchi's life was interesting of course—and Tiercel would probably have found it all fascinating—but it was all ancient history, and Harrier wanted to know about the here-and-now. That was the important thing, after all.

"The trade-caravans have always been plagued by banditry. I do not know if you are familiar with the cities of the Madiran . . . ?" the Telchi asked.

"Not really," Harrier said, shrugging. "But my Da is Portmaster at Armethalieh, so I know about Madiran trade-goods."

"Then you know their value," the Telchi answered, satisfied. "Some loss was always expected: petty thievery; the dishonesty of the caravan masters; merchants figured such losses into their price, and if it did not rise above a certain level, all was well. But in the past year, the losses the trade-caravans have suffered have become far worse than ever before. Now it is not a matter of mere raids and midnight thefts and a few rugs or caskets of spices vanishing between one *Iteru* and the next—bloodlessly—but of entire caravans vanishing, and no man able to say where the bones of the guards and the drovers lie. For this reason, the Consul of Tarnatha'Iteru engaged me to stop it."

"Those dead guys Ancaladar saw on the road," Harrier guessed.

"Perhaps," the Telchi replied. "Once the task was placed in my hand, I collected a troop of fine fighters—sound experienced swordsmen and archers—and we disguised ourselves as a rich caravan. We were attacked by the raiders just as I hoped. When they saw we were not fat merchants, they fled, just as we had expected, and we gave chase." His expression turned grim. "We slew many, and pursued those we did not kill at once, thinking to finish the task and end the matter there and then."

Harrier already knew how this story ended. Even knowing that the Telchi had survived, he almost didn't want to hear the rest. Almost.

"We tracked them for sennights, as they headed north into the uninhabited wilderness. We would have overtaken them sooner, but they had the foresight to conceal fresh horses along their way, and we fell behind. But they were unable to escape us—so we thought. In truth, the bandits' numbers were far greater than anyone had imagined, and the survivors of the attack meant to lure us into a trap. We followed them into a narrow passage in the hills, riding hard on their heels as the sun rode low upon the horizon, thinking to finish them before nightfall. We outnumbered them, and they were—many of them—injured. Easy prey. And then, as we spurred our mounts to close with them, their brethren swept down from the slopes above, where they had lain in wait. They were many."

For a moment the Telchi paused in his narrative, looking grim. "Despite their advantage, we overcame them, but the cost was high. All of my men were slain that day, and when the leader of the bandits saw that he was not to claim the easy victory he had expected, he gathered a few of his followers about him and ran from the battlefield. They headed north, into the Tereymils, and I followed. To leave him alive would mean that in time he would gather another such force of malignants about himself, and the deaths of all my men would have been for nothing. One by one I stalked them and slew them, taking them under cover of darkness, until only the chieftain remained. And you say that he is dead?"

"Very," Harrier answered. He thought—from the way the Telchi had been injured when they'd found him—that he must have been wounded in that second battle, and had tracked the remnants of the bandits while slowly bleeding to death.

"Then my final blow struck true," the Telchi said, satisfied. "And yet—had you not found me—such a victory would have been a great defeat."

"Okay," Harrier said dubiously.

"I think that you know little of the Telchi caste," the Telchi said.

Harrier did his best to repress a groan. It seemed as if every time he turned around, somebody was telling him he didn't know something about something, whether it was Elves, or unicorns, or dragons, or Wildmages. And now apparently he didn't know anything about Telchis either.

"There is no shame in that," the Telchi said. "Were a Wildmage to visit the Selken Isles, your ways and customs would be as strange to us as ours are to you. But there is this that I would have you know: even though I may never see my home again, I still have obligations that I may not set aside. Upon the day that each Telchi takes up his swords, he also takes up an oath that he will train up at least one student, so that all that he has been taught, and all that he has learned in the course of his life, can be passed on to another. Always, I thought there would be time. That I could travel north to Armethalieh, purchase passage across Great Ocean, return home, do penance for my youthful crime, and then—*then*—seek a student." The Telchi smiled ruefully. "Now I know there is no more time."

"But—you can still do that," Harrier said. "I mean, you didn't do anything really wrong. And it was a long time ago—I'm sure they'd understand. . . ."

"I broke my oathbond," the Telchi said softly. "I swore myself to the service of one who was unworthy to be served, and then I yoked myself to my own pride rather than seeking the counsel of the Sword-Giver and the Lady of Battles. Here in the east you have a saying: *The Wild Magic goes as it wills.* In the west, we would say that all roads lead to the Hall of Battle, for all men die in the end.

And I would not die without discharging this obligation. So I shall train a student here. In the east. And it will both fulfill my oath, and discharge my debt—should the student agree."

Harrier regarded the Telchi with sudden deep suspicion. Not only did he have an inkling of the direction in which this conversation was going, he was also starting to feel oddly prickly all over, as if a storm was rolling in. He glanced up at the sky, but the clouds were high and thin—and anyway, Ancaladar would never have taken Tiercel off for a practice if a storm was brewing.

"You have given me my life, Wildmage, when I should otherwise have died. I am in your debt for the worth of my life, and I do not know how I can discharge that debt save by giving you the most valuable thing I possess."

There was a long moment of silence as they both looked at each other—the Telchi expectantly, Harrier with slowly growing suspicion.

"You want to train me as a Telchi Warrior," Harrier said in disbelief.

"If it can be done," the Telchi said, sounding just as doubtful as Harrier felt. "In all the years I have lived here in the east, I have never taken an apprentice. And I did not think that a Wildmage would be my first."

Apprentice. In the moment the Telchi spoke the word, it was as if Harrier heard the first note of First Dawn Bells ring out. The sound-that-wasn't-really-a-sound made him shiver. He knew what it was—how could he ever have imagined not knowing? This was how you felt when it came time to pay your Mageprice. *"You must become an Apprentice."*

He felt a combination of relief—because at least he knew what his Mageprice was to be, now, and it didn't involve him having to go off to the other end of the world, because the Telchi was *right here* and going back to the same place they were going themselves—and irritation—because he'd been worried about what paying his Mageprice would involve, and he realized (now) that that was the last thing in the world he'd needed to worry about. If the Wild Magic had given Tiercel the High Magick and his visions so that he could, well, at least *try* to do something about the Darkness, and for some incomprehensible reason of its own had made Harrier a Knight-Mage for the same reason, it certainly (probably) wasn't going to set him a Mageprice that would drag him off to the other side of the world to plant petunias in somebody's garden while Tiercel got himself killed. He hoped.

"Yes," Harrier said. "All right. Okay. I'll become your apprentice. And, um, it's okay, because I'm kind of not exactly a regular Wildmage. I'm sort of, well, a Knight-Mage." He winced, just a little, because it still sounded unbelievable and arrogant every time he said it. "And, actually, I've never held a sword in my life."

"Good," the Telchi said. "Very good. There will be less for you to unlearn."

THE FIRST TASK the Telchi set his new apprentice was to cut two short straight sticks, each a little longer than his arm. This meant Harrier had to go trudging off the side of the road in the direction of the nearest stand of trees, and hope he found something suitable.

Of course Kareta followed him.

"Well?" she demanded, as soon as she caught up to him.

" 'Well' yourself. Don't tell me you weren't eavesdropping."

"Of course I was! But I want details!"

Harrier sighed, but he wasn't irritated. For Kareta not to be . . . Kareta . . . would be like Ancaladar suddenly becoming small and fluffy and white. Or for Tiercel to suddenly stop asking questions. He explained as much as he remembered about the entire conversation—the Telchi's story, and about the bandits, and about how his Mageprice was to learn everything the Telchi could teach him about fighting.

"And you will?" Kareta asked.

"I told him I would," Harrier said. "And, well, I guess I promised the Wild Magic I would, too. Do you know what happens to a Wildmage who doesn't pay his Mageprice?"

"No," Kareta said promptly. "What?"

"If I knew," Harrier demanded, "do you think I'd be asking you? But I'm pretty sure it isn't anything good. Anyway, he's going back to the Madiran, and we're going *to* the Madiran, and he wants to show me what to do with a sword, so . . . I guess it all works out."

"I guess it does," Kareta said. "And you didn't even need to cast a spell to find him."

"I had to cast a *spell*," Harrier pointed out.

"But not to get a teacher," Kareta argued. "You just wanted to keep him alive. You didn't know he'd want to give you a reward."

"It isn't like that," Harrier complained. He didn't really think of learning Selken sword-fighting techniques as much of a reward. And he didn't want a reward in the first place.

"Well, if it isn't a reward, what is it then?"

"Almost as much of a pain in the butt as you are," Harrier said.

Kareta snorted rudely.

It took him nearly two hours to find what he thought would probably be two suitable pieces of wood. He thought longingly of all of the *extremely* suitable pieces of wood he'd passed in the last sennight—before, of course, he'd had any idea he'd need them. The two pieces he selected would need more work—smoothing and polishing—before they looked like much of anything but kindling, but there was a knife and a couple of files and rasps and some beeswax back at the wagon. He ought to be able to make do.

"All right then," Kareta said briskly, when Harrier turned to head back to the wagon.

"Um . . . what?"

"Well, I have to admit that you've been very entertaining, and really almost nice, but you don't need me now."

"Huh," Harrier said. He was about to say that he'd never needed her at all, but she was still talking, and what she was saying alarmed him too much.

"After all. You cast a pretty big spell. You've gotten yourself a *very* good teacher—a Telchi! Just imagine!—and I have no intention of following behind your wagon all the way to the Madiran as if I were a tethered goat. Besides, what is there in the Madiran besides cities full of people?" Kareta shuddered all over. "I don't think so! No, my Price is paid."

"I—Wait—What? Your Price?"

"Hmph," Kareta said. "I suppose you think that Wildmages are the only ones who have Prices set? A lot you know!"

"Buh—But—Are you—"

"Going to tell you about it? No. But maybe—if you're good—and if it's convenient—and if I haven't got anything more interesting to do—I'll look in on you again someday. Or maybe I won't."

"*Kareta!*" Harrier bellowed.

But it was too late. She'd already turned away, trotting, then running, then bounding in the effortless deer-like bounds that were a unicorn's fastest gait. In only moments she was a tiny golden speck in the distance. Harrier stood and watched until she was out of sight.

He stood there looking after her until he decided she wasn't coming back, and that he was cold, and that he should probably get back to the wagon and see if he'd picked out the right sticks, and see what he needed to do about the evening meal.

WHEN TIERCEL AND Ancaladar arrived back at the wagon a couple of hours later, the Telchi was cleaning his quilted mail shirt with rags and a small knife and a bowl of water—the stains would remain, but perhaps some of the stiffness could be worked out of the heavy quilted cloth—and Harrier was making flatcakes. He'd added some of the bacon and a little of the dried beef to the stew, and it was cooking down nicely. Tomorrow, the Telchi told him, they would begin their lessons.

Tiercel peered up the road, then looked around in all directions, frowning.

"Don't bother," Harrier said, not looking up. "She's gone."

"Gone?" Tiercel echoed, startled.

"Gone, left, said I could take care of myself now, said her Price was paid, wouldn't tell me what that meant, and . . . gone."

"Oh," Tiercel said.

"Yeah."

THE NEXT MORNING, Harrier hitched up the horses, and Tiercel saddled Ancaladar, and they started out again. It was interesting and a little strange to have company—*human* company—during the long day of travel. At their stops, Harrier found that the Telchi was a welcome extra pair of hands for all the chores involved in setting up and taking down camp. By the end of a sennight, their days had settled into another new routine.

At midday, and in the evening, there was practice for Harrier. He'd been worried—at first—that it would involve something like what he'd seen the Elves doing, but Macenor Telchi told him that it was far too soon for him to begin such practice. For now, Harrier was learning to stand, to move, to turn—and most of all, to keep his balance while doing all of it. It was much harder than he'd thought it would be, especially while holding a stick in each hand. And even more difficult once the Telchi armed himself with a long wooden spoon out of their kitchen utensils and started sneaking around behind Harrier and poking him with it at odd moments.

In self-defense, Harrier quickly learned to develop a *sense* of when someone was behind him. To move out of the way of the irritating poking. To keep the unexpected sharp jabs from pushing him off-balance—though that took longer.

With Kareta gone (he refused to admit that he missed her) Harrier felt an odd guilty sense of *duty*. With the addition of Macenor Telchi to share the workload, he had more free time than he had when it was only him to do all the work of keeping up the camp, so he combed through *The Book of Moon* for simple spells that didn't require him to pay a Mageprice. There were only three he was certain of: Scrying, Coldfire, and Fire.

It made no sense at all to Harrier why Scrying (a spell the book described as "a spell to show the Wildmage those things he needed to see" and which didn't seem a lot like Tiercel's High Magick distance-viewing spells) would be lumped in with two spells that seemed to him to be actually simple useful spells that someone would actually want to do, but even if he wanted to try it, he didn't have any of the necessary materials—wine, fern-leaf, and a spring of water.

He could practice Fire and Coldfire, though, and he did.

His first attempts at each were disappointing. If he hadn't already had the experience of Healing the Telchi, he would have given up on Fire long before he managed to make his first stick of wood burst into flame—it took him an entire sennight, spending every spare moment he could snatch in concentration, before he got his first results. As for Coldfire, while Tiercel's problem had been in making the blue globes of shining mist *go away* once he'd created them, Harrier's Coldfire tended to vanish the moment he forgot about it—which meant he'd be using a ball of Coldfire to light his way down to the stream to get water after supper, start thinking about something else, and suddenly find himself plunged into complete darkness.

The odd thing was, when Harrier used his power, it bothered Tiercel. Not in the sense of making him cross or anything—Tiercel *wanted* him to use his Wildmage gifts. But the first time Harrier had tried to Summon Fire, Tiercel had been a couple of yards away with his back to Harrier, and he'd made a *"whoof"*-ing noise and sat down on the ground suddenly. They'd quickly determined that any time Harrier tried using his magic, Tiercel felt weak—but that it didn't work the other way around. Tiercel muttered something about this being a good chance to practice his shielding, but Harrier noticed he still moved down to the other end of the camp any time Harrier practiced. And he guessed (now) that it had been a good thing after all that he'd sent Tiercel out of the way when he'd Healed the Telchi, or else all three of them would probably have been lying around on the ground out cold.

But no matter how inconvenient it was to make sure Tiercel was safely out of the way (or well-shielded), Harrier kept working at both spells. He supposed he should practice at more and different spells of his new magic (whether he wanted to or not), but it seemed somehow *ungrateful* to the Wild Magic to just play around with it as if it were a toy sent to entertain him. He decided that for right now he'd mostly stick to practicing the thing that he knew needed to be practiced—getting better at flailing around with a pair of wooden sticks.

And the days passed.

Macenor Telchi was a reliable and even-tempered companion. Nothing flustered him—not even the information that they were heading to the Madiran to seek out a place where the Endarkened sought rebirth.

"THIS DOESN'T BOTHER you?" Harrier asked.

They were sitting cross-legged in front of the fire. It was several hours before dawn, but Tiercel'd just had the vision again, and he never wanted to go back to sleep afterward, and neither did Harrier. From the position of the moon, Harrier thought it might be almost First Dawn Bells, and if he were home he'd be getting out of bed and dressing up warm and heading down to the docks for the day. Before Tiercel had his latest vision, he and Harrier hadn't quite made up their mind whether or not to tell Macenor Telchi everything about who they were and where they were going, but Tiercel's nightmares really did require a lot of explaining, and they always reminded Harrier that there might be *something else* out here after them. It wasn't fair not to give the Telchi as much warning as they possibly could. And so far, he'd taken everything calmly: Ancaladar, and the news that Tiercel was a High Mage, and—now—the news that they were following Tiercel's visions into the Madiran in search of Darkness Reborn.

Harrier stared at the sky again. He wondered if it was Kindling already, and if he'd missed his Naming Day and Flowering Fair.

"It would bother any man of sense," the Telchi replied calmly. "But it would bother me more if no one were doing anything at all."

Harrier laughed shakily. The idea that he and Tiercel were actually "doing something" required more of a leap of faith than he was capable of at the moment.

"I think, my apprentice, that you value yourself and your friend too lightly. I cannot speak to the magic which either of you may hold. But I know something of courage, and of honor. And I know that both of you have left the safety of your homes to set yourselves against a peril thinking that you have little hope of victory, merely because you feel that you must."

"I just—" Harrier protested.

"Have followed your friend past the end of your world. Risked your life to help a dying man. Go now, into what you believe is certain death, for friendship's sake. Have taken up obligations which you did not wish, because you felt they were your duty. I am proud to teach you all that I can."

Harrier ducked his head, embarrassed into speechlessness.

Macenor Telchi made it sound as if he was a hero. As if he was someone like Kellen the Poor Orphan Boy. And he wasn't. He was just . . . him.

"WE'RE GOING TO have to figure out what to do about Ancaladar," Tiercel said seriously.

They'd been on the road for another moonturn and a half. The Bazrahils would soon be behind them completely, and Macenor Telchi said that another moonturn after that—at most—would see them at the walls of Tarnatha'Iteru. Though he had not recognized the Lake of Fire from Tiercel's description of it, he had agreed that such a place might well exist. There were many learned men in Tarnatha'Iteru who might know for certain, and—better than scholars— traders. Scholars might wish to know the history of a place, but traders wished to know its geography. If anyone had ever seen such a place as Tiercel described, the tradesmen of Tarnatha'Iteru would know of it.

"Why is it that I must have something done about me?" Ancaladar asked with mild interest.

Tiercel and Harrier exchanged looks. Harrier smirked.

"It's not as if dragons are exactly . . . common . . . outside the Veiled Lands," Tiercel said carefully.

Ancaladar blinked slowly, amused. "You fear my presence will disturb them."

"Send them running screaming in all directions, more likely," Harrier said bluntly. "Until you open your mouth and say something. Then they're likely to just drop down dead from shock."

"You do not feel I could convince them of my peaceful intentions?" Ancaladar asked innocently.

"Ah . . . eventually," Tiercel said. "I'm sure you could convince them eventually. But maybe you won't have to. I mean, if we find out we aren't staying in Tarnatha'Iteru very long, we . . ."

"And perhaps, Bonded, it is best if you go first to this

city and see what you may see," Ancaladar said. Harrier knew perfectly well by now that Ancaladar possessed his own odd dry sense of humor, but the great black dragon also never teased Tiercel for very long. "Indeed, I am well aware that it has been many centuries since my kind has been seen in the lands of Men, and it is kind of you to concern yourself with my safety."

"Which brings us right back to the question of what we do with you," Harrier said firmly, because he'd learned from bitter experience that if he let them, Ancaladar and Tiercel were perfectly capable of discussing a subject for hours and never *coming to the point*. "It's not as if we can stuff you inside the wagon. And the Telchi says that from here south, we could start to run into people."

"I'm pretty sure I could keep them from seeing us," Tiercel said. "At least, from seeing Ancaladar and me. People don't look up, you know. And—at night, while we're camped—Ancaladar could just take off."

"Tiercel," Harrier said warningly.

Tiercel sighed and ran a hand through his hair. It was damp, and clung to his forehead and neck—even though it was deep winter, they were far enough southward that even their lightest clothes were too heavy. "I know," he said, sighing. He looked up at Ancaladar. "You must have had this problem before."

"Not precisely, Bonded," Ancaladar said. "But I remember how to hide."

Harrier saw Tiercel wince. "I don't want you to have to—"

"Be practical?" Ancaladar and Harrier said, almost in chorus—though in entirely different tones. Harrier stopped, and Ancaladar continued.

"This time, my concealment shall serve quite a different purpose than it did a thousand years ago. I shall merely make it more . . . convenient . . . for you to enter a city you have never visited before, and to learn all it may have to teach you. And when you are ready to proceed, it will be a simple matter for you to let me know, for you and I can never truly be separated. I shall know when it is time to rejoin you."

"But . . . what will you *do*?" Tiercel asked. Harrier thought he sounded a little bewildered.

"I shall take a nap," Ancaladar said reassuringly. "I have seen many promising caves in the landscape over which we have flown. I shall find one and wait for you to summon me."

"See?" Harrier demanded.

BY A FORTNIGHT later they'd left hills and trees and anything that looked even remotely familiar to either Tiercel or Harrier far behind. The landscape was broad, and dun-colored, and *hot,* and the fact that the Telchi said that it was winter—and comparatively cool—didn't make either of them feel any better at all. They rationed their water carefully, and were fortunate to have the Telchi with them, or they would never have found the traveler's wells along the way, for they were nearly always covered with a large slab of stone to keep the precious water from evaporating. While this wasn't the Trade Road that led across the Armen Plains, into the Delfier Valley, and—eventually—to Armethalieh the Golden—it *was* a road, and a well-traveled one. The Telchi said that rich merchants from the *Iteru*-cities often sought the cool of the Tereymil Hills in high summer, and that healers and perfumers would send apprentices there to gather the ingredients of their mixtures.

All traffic along the road depended upon the wells for its survival, and Harrier had no trouble understanding why. At midday the air shimmered with heat, and the only ones who were really comfortable were Ancaladar and the Telchi. Ancaladar had taken to spreading his wings to give them all a little sheltering shade through the midday heat, and they'd adopted what the Telchi said was the local custom of a long midday halt to spare the horses, starting earlier in the morning and going on for several hours after dark. At night, Harrier led the team, because no matter how much more sensible it was to travel at night, horses were happier when they could see where they were going, and they just couldn't see very well at night.

The idea that they were going to have to—eventually— go someplace that was even hotter than this was now was worrying Harrier, but there wasn't much he could do about it at the moment. He couldn't imagine why anybody would want to live here if they had a choice. Sometimes, he thought, people were idiots.

But apparently goats had more sense than people, because twice now they'd encountered boys heading northward on the road insisting—upon encountering the wagon—that they were in search of a lost goat.

On the first occasion it had been early in the morning, and Ancaladar and Tiercel had been airborne, so their unexpected company hadn't been much of a problem. And the boy had certainly *smelled* like someone looking for a lost goat. Possibly for a whole herd of them. But the second time they'd all been stopped for their midday meal, and Harrier had cause to be grateful that apparently all of Tiercel's practicing had been of some use, because even though he and Ancaladar were in plain sight—and Harrier could see them clearly—the boy who gabbled out his panicky explanation of seeking the goat of his master plainly didn't notice them at all.

"Do you think there *was* a goat?" Harrier asked curiously, when the boy was gone and the wagon was moving again. He hadn't even stayed long enough to be fed— Harrier would have at least given him a piece of roast meat. It was about all they had left after so long on the road, and while it was better than starving, Harrier was looking forward to arriving somewhere that he didn't have to eat roast meat for breakfast, lunch, and dinner.

"It is possible that there *is* a goat," the Telchi answered after a moment's consideration. "Or perhaps the boy has fallen out of charity with his master for some reason and feels he will have a better life elsewhere. It is not often that such a resolution endures beyond a moonturn or so."

"What will happen if he goes back?" Harrier asked. The idea of someone running away from his indentures was hardly a new one to him—Da had always grumbled that half the duty of the Port Watch seemed to be keeping the disgruntled youth of Armethalieh from stowing away on anything that would float, and the other half involved keeping them from stealing anything that wasn't nailed down.

The Telchi shrugged minutely. "Certainly he could not expect to escape punishment. If he is a bondservant or apprentice, he may be turned out of his place, and his family will forfeit what they have paid—or been paid. If it is his own family that he runs from, he may, if he has the wit, throw himself upon the Consul's mercy. Such children are taken from their families and set to a trade in another household. But perhaps he has already done that."

"Maybe," Harrier said. He was just as glad Tiercel wasn't here for this conversation. Tiercel would have insisted on going after the boy, and finding out everything about him, and *doing something about it*. And Harrier wasn't sure that would work out at all.

"It is just as conceivable, you know, that he is on a secret errand for his master that he does not wish us to know," the Telchi said reprovingly. "You must learn to look beneath surfaces, young Harrier. All things are possible."

"I'd rather not," Harrier said glumly. "I liked everything a lot better when they had surfaces. Lots of surfaces."

But that was the evening that Ancaladar—gently but firmly—said that he must go. He had already delayed longer than was absolutely safe.

"We have been fortunate twice, Bonded. We cannot hope for as much a third time—and should you be seen in my company, questions will be asked that you will perhaps find it uncomfortable to answer. Harrier and Macenor Telchi will keep you safe while you discover where we must go next."

"Be careful," Tiercel said. He wanted to say more—a *lot* more, to tell Ancaladar to stay, that they'd come up with a different plan, something that didn't involve Ancaladar having to go off and hide in a cave somewhere for Light only knew how long. But he just couldn't think of anything. Ancaladar was right. And this had seemed like a good idea when it wasn't happening *right now.*

Ancaladar turned away and trotted a mile up the road in an unlikely silence, and then the great shimmering wings swept out—a darker shadow against the darkness. There was a faint *snap* as they filled with air, and then Ancaladar sprang into the sky. Tiercel wanted to think that he heard the sound Ancaladar's wings made as they beat against the air, though he knew he didn't. The moon hadn't risen yet, so he didn't even see him as he flew away.

And that night he dreamed again.

At first he thought it *was* an ordinary dream, because he was dreaming about a dragon. He hadn't wanted either Harrier or Macenor Telchi to know how much letting Ancaladar leave affected him. Having Ancaladar *gone.* He knew Harrier and Ancaladar were friends, but it wasn't the same. Not for Harrier—Harrier thought of Ancaladar being gone the way Tiercel was supposed to think of it: that Ancaladar was going off to stay out of sight for a few sennights, and as soon as the two of them had finished their business in Tarnatha'Iteru, he'd come back.

But for Tiercel, it was more as if something that was supposed to be *right there* suddenly . . . wasn't. And the feeling was made all the worse by the fact that he could still *sense* his Bond to Ancaladar. But—not being either a dragon or a great Elven Mage—that was about all there was to it. A faint reassuring *thrum* in the back of his mind. Not like having Ancaladar here to see and talk to.

He knew it would hurt Harrier's feelings if he said any of that aloud, because, well, Harrier was still right here. And he and Harrier had been inseparable for as long as

Tiercel could remember, and for Tiercel to say that he felt *alone* now would be more than rude, it would be *insulting*. So he'd just gone off to bed and hoped he could get used to this as quickly as possible. And that it wouldn't last very long.

And he dreamed.

He was flying over the desert—alone, alone! *Only he wasn't exactly alone. That was—somehow—the problem. He was alone, and he wasn't.*

And he was terribly, terribly unhappy.

He soared through the hot winds that rose off the baking sands. During the day, the heat made strong updrafts, childishly easy to ride—alone, alone!—*but at night, it took skill to ride the upper air, for the temperature dropped fast and hard. Safety lay in height, but to hunt one must fly low. And alone. Grieving, hoping, unable to die, unable to rebel. Trapped, oh,* trapped, *perhaps forever, helpless, and alone, alone,* alone. . . .

He woke up with a yell because Harrier was shaking him.

"You were making noises," Harrier said tightly.

"I was . . . a dragon . . . ?" Now that he was awake, the dream was hard to hold onto. It hadn't quite been a dream, but it hadn't been his vision either. Something strange and in-between.

"Well, that's new," Harrier said gruffly. He sat back on his heels and ran a hand through his hair. "Any particular dragon?"

"I don't know. I mean . . ." He tried to remember the dream, but all there was, was the sensation of flying— nothing new there, after so many hours spent on Ancaladar's back—and the feeling of wild desperate grief. He rubbed his eyes.

"Hey, are you okay?" Harrier asked. "Is *Ancaladar* okay?" he added in an entirely different tone. "Is this some kind of, I don't know, High Magick vision or warning or something?"

"Ancaladar's fine." Tiercel didn't even have to think

about it before answering. He just knew. "And bizarre as I know you're going to find this, I've never found one single thing anywhere in anything I've read about the High Magick about visions of the future. Seeing over distance yes— and no, I can't do it except under certain conditions. Seeing the future with dreams and visions and warning prophecies, no."

"So the prophetic visions you've been having . . . you aren't having," Harrier said, perfectly deadpan.

Even barely awake from a highly disturbing dream, Tiercel had to laugh. "I wish," he said. "I didn't say they don't exist. But I think they're more your kind of Wild-magey thing than mine—didn't Roneida have to have had one to know where to find us? And I guess anybody who wanted to could send me all the prophetic dreams they wanted to."

"And they are," Harrier said, sighing. But he sounded more reassured now. "Why you? Tiercel, out of all the people in the Nine Cities—why *you*? And don't say it's because of the Magegift. Because yeah, that made sense—until the Light decided to turn me into a Knight-Mage."

Tiercel rubbed his eyes wearily. A few feet away there was a quiet clatter and a shower of sparks as the Telchi built up the fire and began to brew tea. They were down to their last canister—when it was gone, there wasn't any more, but they'd probably be at Tarnatha'Iteru by then. Probably.

"I've thought about that a lot, believe me, Har," he said. "I'm not sure you'll like what I've thought of."

Harrier snorted rudely. "Well, I haven't liked a lot of things since we got to Karahelanderialigor—I mean, I could go back farther than that, but we'd be here till dawn. So why not tell me anyway?"

"Ass."

"Book-nose."

"Lout."

"Noble-brat."

"Dock-rat."

"Proud of it," Harrier said promptly. "Where were we?"

"I was about to explain, and you were about to ignore me. As usual."

"Not ignoring," Harrier protested, smirking.

"Right. As far as I understand it—and remember, you're the only Wildmage I know, and I know *exactly* how much you know—the ability to do the High Magick—the ancient War Magick—is innate. You're either born with the Magegift, or you aren't. If you aren't, you can do the spells forever, and they won't work. Why this should be, when as far as everyone knows, the War Magick came *later* than the Wild Magic, don't ask me, because you know everything I know, just about. Maybe once upon a time *everyone* had the Magegift, and later they didn't. I have no idea. Anyway, that's the High Magick."

"The War Magick," Harrier supplied helpfully.

"Right. Which was invented because the Wildmages were being corrupted by the Endarkened. Through their magic, apparently, which is about the scariest thing I've heard about the Endarkened yet. And—at the same time— the Endarkened couldn't get at the High Mages in the same way."

"Just kill them," Harrier interjected.

"As far as I know, the Endarkened could just kill *everybody*," Tiercel said grimly.

"And now you're going to tell me what something that happened about a million years before the Great Flowering has to do with us," Harrier prodded.

"You won't like it," Tiercel warned.

"Get to the point."

"Well, in the first place, when I started having the visions, you weren't a Wildmage—Knight-Mage—yet. And Kareta couldn't exactly come walking into Armethalieh carrying the Three Books of the Wild Magic to hand them to you. Besides, even if she could have, you wouldn't have taken them."

"You've got that right," Harrier muttered.

"In the second place, from everything I know—and I could still be wrong—you can refuse to become a Wildmage, but you can't refuse to be, well, born with the Magegift. So you're pretty much *born* a High Mage, and the only difference is whether or not you're trained."

"Of course, if you aren't trained—or don't run into the right kind of Wildmage—you kind of die," Harrier said. Tiercel looked at him in surprise. As often as Harrier demonstrated that he did think—and think well—and listened—despite his constant complaints whenever people started explaining things to him—it was always a surprise to Tiercel when he came out with a comment like this. Not so much because Tiercel didn't think Harrier knew these things, but because Tiercel knew Harrier didn't want people to know he knew them. "Is there a third thing?"

"Yeah." Tiercel hesitated for just an instant. "It has to be me having the visions instead of you because I'm a High Mage and not a Wildmage."

"It is never not going to sound ridiculous hearing that," Harrier complained with a reasonable amount of good-nature under the circumstances. He shook his head.

And Tiercel was grateful that he didn't ask any more questions just then, because he hadn't quite figured out a way to explain to Harrier that just in case he was wrong about Dark magic not being able to corrupt a High Mage, it was going to be up to Harrier to try to see this through.

Whatever the cost.

Eleven

The City on the Edge of Forever

TEN DAYS AFTER that they reached the gates of Tar-natha'Iteru. It was the northernmost-but-one of the Border cities, and—according to the Telchi—one of the largest *Iteru*-cities in the Madiran. The *Iteru*-cities—*"iteru"* meant "well" in the Old Tongue of the desert-peoples—were the cities that lay along the edge of the Madiran.

What the Telchi called the true desert lay farther south and west of here, a place called the Isvai, a barren and in-hospitable wilderness that was home to nothing but a few nomadic tribes. Some of the Isvaieni came to the *Iteru*-cities to trade their crafts and the harvest of the deep desert—gold and gems, furs and resins, even salt—for the products of the *Iteru*-cities. Others never ventured out of the Isvai itself.

In Tiercel's opinion, if the Telchi thought this *wasn't* an inhospitable wilderness, he wasn't quite sure he wanted to see something that was. He thought this place must look a lot the way the whole world had before the Great Flower-ing. Only—probably—worse. But he'd listened closely to everything the Telchi had told them as they'd headed here, and so he already knew a little about the Isvaieni. He knew, for example, that the merchants from all the various *Iteru*-cities would trade with the Isvaieni throughout the desert winter, and then when spring came, would send their caravans of trade-goods from both city and desert to Akazidas'Iteru, a city north and west of here. Caravans would gather in Akazidas'Iteru to follow the Trade Road north to Armethalieh the Golden, reaching the city moon-turns later with their cargoes of rugs and spices and exotic

trade-goods. And caravans from Armethalieh would venture south, throughout the moonturns of fair traveling
weather, with everything that Armethalieh and the lands
across Great Ocean could offer in exchange.

The city itself, Tiercel thought, looked very much like
Armethalieh must have looked a thousand years ago. It was
entirely surrounded by high walls—the Telchi said they
were made of bricks of unfired clay that had been layered
over with sheets of wet clay to give them a smooth appearance. Tiercel really wished he could have been here to see
it built, because the wall on this side stretched for nearly a
mile, and he remembered, years ago, dragging Harrier all
through Armethalieh trying to trace the boundaries of the
ancient City Walls. He didn't think Tarnatha'Iteru was
quite as large as ancient Armethalieh had been, but it was
pretty big. And the walls, the Telchi had said, were so wide
that three men could walk side-by-side upon their tops.
There was an enormous set of bronze gates in the wall. The
Telchi said this was the main entrance to the city: each wall
had a gate, but the others were smaller.

"Those look as big as the ones back home," Harrier said,
peering up at them. "They've gotta be heavy." He glanced
up at the noonday sun. "And hot, too."

"Not solid bronze, young Harrier," the Telchi said,
amused. "Such would tax the strength of the men who
must open them each time someone wished to come or go.
Bronze-covered wood, merely—but good solid oak from
the Tereymil Hills. And they are not in direct sunlight for
nearly all the day—nor from inside the town at all—so
your fears are groundless."

"Why do they keep closing them?" Tiercel asked curiously. "If they're just going to have to open them again
every time somebody wants to come in?"

"Were they to leave them open, anyone might enter or
leave Tarnatha'Iteru just as they chose. Petty thieves, Isvaieni, even strangers unknown to the Consul."

"Like us," Harrier said.

"Indeed," the Telchi answered. "But I am perhaps not unknown to the Consul, or to those he sets to guard the walls of his city, and I believe we may be granted entry."

"I still think—" Tiercel said mutinously.

"It is also necessary to keep the gates barred to provide protection to the city from the winds of the desert," the Telchi continued smoothly. "Small winds on most occasions—though the dust they carry is unwelcome. But should a Sandwind come up out of the Deep Desert, it is as well that the gates be closed in advance of its arrival."

"What's a Sandwind?" Tiercel asked, but Harrier had already pulled the wagon to a halt beneath the walls, far enough back so that he could see the men standing above the gate. They didn't have any weapons that either of them could see, but they hardly needed them—they didn't have to open the gates if they didn't want to. They wore armor like the Telchi's—it had looked odd to Tiercel the first time he'd gotten a good look at it, but now that he was actually *in* the Madiran, he saw the point of it. Armor like the kind he'd seen the Elves wearing—or even the Armethaliehan City Guard—would leave someone roasting alive here.

The Telchi climbed down from the seat of the wagon and walked forward, removing his helmet so that his face was clearly visible.

"Telchi! We thought you'd left your bones for the wolves in the Tereymil Hills," one of the men called down.

"Come, now, Batho, have you ever known me to misuse an animal? I would make a poor dinner for even a starving wolf. No, by the grace of the Sword-Giver and the Lady of Battles, the enemies of our city have received proper payment for their deeds, and I have received my life from these travelers, whose kindness I am now eager to repay."

Batho stepped away from the edge of the wall—vanishing entirely from sight—and shouted down to someone inside. A few moments later, the gates began to open inward.

"They ought to open out," Harrier said meditatively. "If

you were actually being attacked, someone could force them easily."

Both Tiercel and Macenor Telchi regarded Harrier with the expressions of faint surprise—Tiercel, because it was the last thing he'd expected Harrier to say, and the Telchi, because . . .

"Who would make war upon us, young Harrier? No *Iteru*-city would force the gates of another. There has been peace in the land for a thousand years. Even the Darkness you seek was stripped of its great armies long ago."

Neither of them answered. Tiercel because he didn't know how, Harrier because the gates were now standing open, and he'd started the wagon moving forward.

Just inside the gates there was a long passage that ran the depth of the wall itself. The horses' hooves clopped sharply, for the floor of the passage was stone. The wicker hampers had been removed from the sides of the wagon long ago—dismantled, and used as fuel—but even if they had not been, there would have been plenty of space for the wagon to pass through the short tunnel. It was high enough that there was no danger of any of them bumping their heads on its curved ceiling, but even so, Tiercel felt the urge to duck. As soon as the wagon was all the way inside, the gates were closed and barred behind them.

Just the other side there was a large open space, also flagged in stone. Not the cobbles that Tiercel would have expected to see on Armethaliehan streets, or even the large flat slates or blocks of granite that ornamented the public plazas in the Golden City. Here the courtyard was floored in large octagonal pieces of sandstone. At the far side of the square, he caught sight of the first buildings of the city: one- and two-story buildings, flat-roofed and wood-shuttered. There were awnings stretched before them—not solid cloth, but an open weave—and more of the same, hung between the houses across all the streets he could see.

There was a watering-trough just inside the wall. The horses pulled toward it eagerly, and Harrier swung down from the wagon bench, going to their heads and pulling them away before they drank too much. Tiercel and Macenor Telchi climbed down as well—Tiercel, because he wanted to see everything at once, and the Telchi to go to speak to the guards. After a few moments, he returned.

"We will go, first, to the stables, where you may leave your horses and your wagon. Then we will go to my house. Tiercel must be my guest for as long as you both remain in the city. And certainly my student would live nowhere else, though any house in Tarnatha'Iteru would be honored to host one of the Blue Robes."

"Don't say that," Harrier begged.

"What about our things?" Tiercel said. "Can't we just—"

"We will bring them," the Telchi said. "But as you will find, the streets of the city are not as broad as those of the cities of the North. Your wagon would not . . . fit."

THEY LED THE wagon across the square—although to be perfectly accurate, the Telchi led the horses, and Harrier led Tiercel, who showed a strong tendency to stop or wander off whenever he glimpsed something new and interesting. Harrier had a certain amount of sympathy—there was so much to see, and all of it was exotic, in a slightly-more-familiar way than Karahelanderialigor had been. He wanted to explore almost as much as Tiercel did.

As they moved across the city, Harrier realized the Telchi had been right about the wagon just not *fitting* through most of the streets of Tarnatha'Iteru. To reach the stables, they took a long roundabout way along wide streets that were obviously in the "public buildings" part of town, and even so, when there was anything else on the street, whatever it was needed to turn down a side-street or back up and huddle against a wall until they could inch by with their wagon. Along the way, they saw not only the familiar horses and mules—some with riders, some with packs—but a strange new beast that Macenor Telchi called a *"shotor,"* a creature particularly well-adapted to the arid heat of the south. Harrier thought they were the ugliest things he'd ever seen.

As they walked, the Telchi told them what they were seeing. Here was the Consul's Palace—the Palace was a residence, but it also held the city's Law Courts, where cases were heard just as they were heard back home (though there it was done in a separate building). The official moneychangers for the city were in the Consul's Palace, too, but northern coins and precious metal could be exchanged for the coinage of the Madiran in the city markets as well.

"We'll need to pay for our horses' keep," Harrier said uneasily at the mention of money. "And for storing the wagon."

"It is not a matter with which you need to concern yourself," the Telchi said. "You are my student. These expenses are mine to assume."

"No," Harrier said firmly. "That's not right."

"Or you could simply tell the Stablemaster that you are a Wildmage, and receive the stabling of your horses and the storage of your possessions as a gift," the Telchi added.

"And that isn't right either," Harrier said. "People shouldn't give you things just because of what you are."

"Very well," the Telchi said. "We will discuss it later, when you have had time to know Tarnatha'Iteru better. For the customs of the south are not those you know."

"He's right, Har," Tiercel said.

"I do not need to hear from you just now," Harrier snapped. But he gave in—temporarily—because he could always find out how much things cost and pay for them later. They still had almost all the money Tiercel'd withdrawn from the bank back in Ysterialpoerin, after all, and the Telchi said they could change it here. Knowing the customs of other places was all very well and good in Harrier's opinion—and he knew perfectly well that it was silly to expect Selkens (or for that matter, *Elves*) to behave like Armethaliehans. But there was a difference between *hospitality* and *charity*.

At last they reached what the Telchi had simply called "the stables"—an enormous two-story building with another sweeping open plaza in front of it. A deep colonnade provided the entrance with shelter from the sun—Harrier would already have found it unusual to see a building here that was not designed to provide such protection—and beneath its shade, grooms curried horses, and walked them to cool them down after exercise, and simply sat and gossiped. After the stables at House Malkirinath, the grandeur of Tarnatha'Iteru's "stables" didn't impress Harrier, but their size did: this was a building larger than the Great Library at Armethalieh.

"Uh," Tiercel said intelligently.

"The animals of the Consul, of the City Guard, of the merchants, of the nobles, of all travelers to the city are housed here," the Telchi said. "Where else?"

"They don't just keep them locked up all day?" Harrier asked. Nethiel and Dulion were used to regular exercise, and any animal left stalled day after day became fat and weak and ill.

"No," the Telchi reassured him. "Those which are here for more than a day or two are exercised by the stablemen, if they are not ridden by their owners. Your beasts cannot be ridden of course, but I shall leave orders. They will not be neglected."

Everyone who was not otherwise occupied came out to stare when the wagon drew up before the stables. After a short discussion with the Telchi, one of the grooms—at least, Harrier supposed they were grooms, since they would have been back home—stepped forward.

"I am Castuca. It is my honor to conduct your . . . conveyance to the place where it may be kept until you have need of it again." From the disbelieving look Castuca was giving the wagon, it suddenly occurred to Harrier that no one here had probably ever seen anything even remotely similar.

"There are some things inside that we need to take away with us," Tiercel said. He sounded a little worried.

"Of course," Castuca said cheerily. "Porters will be arranged."

"I don't—" Tiercel said, and that was when Harrier kicked him.

"Shut up," he said, when Tiercel looked at him. "We'll make it work." He knew Tiercel didn't want people getting their hands on his precious High Magick *"junk"* any more than—than—well, than Harrier wanted to be given things he hadn't earned. This wasn't the time for that argument, though. Fortunately, Tiercel seemed to agree, because he didn't say another word about it as Castuca led them all the way to the end of the colonnade and then around the end of the stable block. Now they were in a second, smaller, court. The doors at the end already stood open, and Harrier could see a large room containing a number of odd things— small two-wheeled carts, and several somethings without any wheels at all that looked as if they were meant to be carried—but nothing that looked very much at all like the Elven wagon.

Castuca wanted to unharness the horses in the courtyard and move the wagon into the storage room by hand, but Harrier was pretty sure the man had no actual idea of how *heavy* the wagon was. Instead, Harrier turned the team and used them to back the wagon into the storage area before unharnessing the horses (something he did himself since it was obvious Castuca wasn't familiar with their tack). They stood quietly while he put their halters and lead-ropes on and led them out again. More grooms arrived to lead them away, and Harrier took particular pains to assure them that both Nethiel and Dulion were gentle, well-mannered, and used to strangers.

And then it was time to unload the wagon. If Castuca was unfamiliar with the wagon itself, he had a good eye for calculating just how much might be packed into a volume of space, for the number of porters he summoned was nicely judged.

In Armethalieh, a "porter" carried his load upon his back. Here, apparently, his cargo was conveyed in a small three-wheeled cart, similar to the ones the gardeners used at home to shift heaps of dirt from someplace to someplace else. They stood patiently for nearly an hour as Tiercel and Harrier emptied the wagon to the walls—clothes, chests, bedding, books, Ancaladar's saddle, all of Tiercel's High Magick *junk,* and all the other odds and ends they'd collected, accumulated, and forgotten about since they'd left Karahelanderialigor.

"It looks bigger now," Tiercel said, staring into the empty space. All that was left inside the wagon now was the stove in the corner—something they could have used a time or two along the way, if only they'd been able to *get at it.*

"Well, if you weren't such a Light-blasted packrat, we might have seen the walls of this thing sometime before we got here," Harrier grumbled.

"Who insisted on filling up every available square foot of space we had?"

"With *food.*"

Tiercel didn't argue further, which Harrier felt meant he'd won. He knew he'd only won *technically,* because Tiercel probably wouldn't have noticed a lot if they'd run out of food two moonturns ago, as long as he still had his books or something interesting to poke at. Which was why Harrier needed to follow him around, especially if Tiercel was planning on going off somewhere nobody'd ever heard of before to do something completely crazy. Even if going there was a really good idea, he'd probably starve to death while he was doing it.

Now they were finally ready to actually *go somewhere,* and it was a good thing that they didn't have to do so without anybody noticing, because they and their baggage made up an embarrassingly large parade: first the Telchi, then Tiercel and Harrier, then a string of eight porters all pushing identical wheeled carts.

It was all right at first—they all stayed together and didn't have much difficulty in working their way through the people on the streets. Away from the public areas, the streets were paved with clay brick, not stone, and it had been done long enough ago that the surface had worn down in a gentle slope toward the center of the street. These streets were as narrow as the narrowest streets in the poorest, oldest quarters of Armethalieh, but glancing skyward toward the awnings stretched overhead, and looking all around at the brightly painted doors and walls, and the happy healthy people all around him, Harrier thought that might have more to do with a desire to protect themselves from the sun and the wind than it did with being poor. The Elven cities, after all, were nothing like the Nine Cities either.

They'd arrived in Tarnatha'Iteru at midmorning, but the sun was rising toward midheaven now, and Harrier already had the idea that everything pretty much stopped here in the Madiran in the middle of the day. There were already fewer people on the streets than there had been when they'd arrived, and he suspected that in an hour or so, the streets would be completely deserted. Unfortunately, even though there were few pedestrians about, as soon as they'd moved a few streets away from the Tarnatha'Iteru stables, the line of porters began to stretch out so far behind them that Tiercel started twitching about something happening to some of his precious *stuff,* and ducked back to bring up the rear of the line. So of course Harrier had to drop back too, because no matter how intent Tiercel might be on watching the porters to make sure nothing fell out of one of the carts—or one of them didn't get lost—Harrier knew good intentions wouldn't last.

Here and there a door stood open, and as they passed, both of them could catch glimpses of what was going on inside.

"What do you think he's—" Tiercel said, slowing down to peer into a house where a man sat bent over a table, working hard at something neither of them could see.

"Later," Harrier said, grabbing a fistful of Tiercel's tunic and yanking him forward. "Unless you want them to toss your books into the nearest midden."

"You know they won't do that," Tiercel said. But he hurried after the line of carts anyway.

They walked, Harrier estimated, about the same distance they would have from the Port to Tiercel's house before the line of carts stopped, and when Tiercel and Harrier walked back up to its head, they found the Telchi standing outside a blue-painted door. On the first several streets they'd gone down they'd seen two- and three-story houses set side by side right at the street edge, but in this district all there was to see along the street was smooth wall with occasional doors. The walls only went up one story, but the streets were still too narrow for Harrier to see what lay beyond the tops of the walls.

"This is my home," the Telchi said. He pushed open the door and stepped inside.

To Harrier's surprise, on the other side of the door there was another courtyard. It was a small one, but he'd started to get the idea that there weren't any private open areas like this here. It was a pleasant space, with an awning above and benches along the walls. The ground was laid with baked clay tiles, and in the center there was a large copper fire-dish, scrubbed to gleaming. As the porters began lining up their carts neatly along one wall, a man came rushing out of the house itself.

"Master! By the fortune of Sand and Star and the grace of the Blessed Saint Idalia, you have returned!"

The Telchi laughed. "And I do not doubt that you deafened her with your demands, Latar. Now bring my purse, for these men must be paid for their hire."

Harrier cleared his throat.

"Did I imagine for a moment that you were as yet possessed of the copper *adhmai* of Tarnatha'Iteru instead of the demi-suns of Armethalieh, there would be no question that you would pay their hire. Instead, let it be my gift to you," the Telchi said.

Harrier opened his mouth to protest, and this time Tiercel kicked him.

The Telchi told the porters to return for their carts in a

few hours, and the men bowed and departed. It took far less time to empty the carts than it had to fill them, for the Telchi's servants took charge of every item Tiercel would let them handle. In the end, all of Tiercel's High Magick items—shuffled and reshuffled—fit into two of the carts—precariously overfull, but they fit—and Harrier stood guard over them while Tiercel made trip after trip to carry them into the house. He really couldn't imagine what Tiercel thought was going to *happen* to them out here, and Tiercel had spent the entire journey from the Veiled Lands to here telling Harrier that all of them were completely harmless. Sometimes he didn't understand his friend at all.

He patted the bag on his hip with a certain feeling of smugness. Books, brazier, herbs, and all, and it was still something he could pick up, sling over his shoulder, and just *go*. Tiercel had enough stuff here to stagger a strong mule, and he said he still had less than a tenth of what a proper High Mage would have had.

Harrier frowned, thinking. How could that be right, if the High Mages had been running around fighting wars? He wondered if maybe they didn't need as much equipment later, once they'd finished learning everything. Or if maybe they'd all shared the big heavy things. It was too bad there wasn't anyone to ask.

He carried the last load—all books—in with Tiercel, who by now was looking both sweaty and excited. Harrier was looking forward to the chance to actually see this place, because Tiercel's brief descriptions—in between trips—had involved not-very-useful remarks like "a lot of rugs" and "a lot of swords" and "there aren't any chairs," none of which gave Harrier a really clear picture of what lay beyond the door Tiercel kept going in and out through.

He already knew that the Telchi was a wealthy man—by the standards of Armethalieh, at least, though he didn't know if the Madiran's standards were different. Just to begin with, he'd seen at least half-a-dozen servants, and that was about what Tiercel's family had. When he was finally able to follow Tiercel inside, they went through the house-door and then down several steps. The air was immediately cooler, and smelled of growing things. They were in a small antechamber lined with large colorful jars with bushes in them.

"These are *naranjes*," Harrier said in surprise.

"Well, sure," Tiercel said. "Where did you think they came from?"

"The Armen Plain," Harrier said promptly. "It's filled with farms, and with farmers who scream blue murder to Da the moment there's the least hitch in shipping their precious cargoes across Great Ocean. I don't know why everyone else doesn't grow their own *naranjes* instead of making us ship them ours," he finished darkly.

"Maybe they can't," Tiercel said. "But they came from here originally. *Naranjes* like heat. Come on."

Tiercel pushed open the inner door—carved and inlaid with an ornate pattern in colored stone—and they were in a much larger room. Finally Harrier understood what Tiercel had meant. The room's floor was covered in carpets that, while not quite as exquisite as those of Elven weaving, were magnificent enough to fetch the highest prices in the markets of Armethalieh. The walls were hung with swords, and while none of them were of the type the Telchi carried, all looked well cared for, and Harrier suspected that the Telchi could use every weapon here.

There wasn't a chair—or even a couch—in sight. Instead, large colorful cushions were set on the floor around the walls.

"We have to sit on *those?*" Harrier demanded.

"Har, you've been sitting on the *ground* for most of a year," Tiercel pointed out.

"Hmph," Harrier said. "Well, I'm not walking on those," he said firmly, indicating the rugs.

"I didn't want to either," Tiercel agreed. "Someday we'll manage to be guests in a house where they don't cover the floors with a Magistrate's treasury of carpets. Come on.

We can go around the edge and take off our boots in the back."

The two of them edged around the carpets, along the thin expanse of tiled floor and down the hall. The hall, fortunately, wasn't covered in more priceless works of the rug-weaver's art, but with plain woven grass-frond matting, which was nice enough, but Harrier's Ma had it in the entryway, and it had to be replaced every couple of years, so Harrier wasn't worried he was destroying something priceless and irreplaceable just by walking on it.

"This is the room he gave us," Tiercel said, opening another door. Harrier followed him in.

"Yeah, and I see it's already a mess."

"It's not like anyone put anything away," Tiercel said defensively.

"Or that you'd let them," Harrier answered promptly.

Tiercel shrugged.

The room had whitewashed walls—and, Harrier was relieved to see, no carpets in sight. The floor was covered with more matting, and there were two low—*very* low—cushioned objects that Harrier supposed must be the beds. There were round holes high in the walls on all sides, and a set of shutters folded back to expose one window. Harrier went over and looked out; he was looking out over another courtyard. This one was covered entirely in sand that someone had raked; he could see the marks of the rake clearly. He shrugged. After living with the Elves, he'd seen weirder things.

He came back and sat down on the nearest chest and began pulling off his boots. It was just about the only clear surface in the room; the contents of the wagon were piled on both of the beds. Harrier frowned, wondering if he could possibly figure out what they'd need for the next part of their journey and what they could throw out or give away now. He decided he couldn't. Not without some idea of where they were going.

"Do you suppose we can get a bath?" he asked.

"I'm pretty sure our host is going to insist on it," Tiercel said, wrinkling his nose.

A COUPLE OF hours later, Harrier reclined on his new bed in his new room, entirely content, watching as Tiercel fussed and fretted, sorting all his possessions into some kind of mysterious order. Their traveling gear—at least the parts they weren't going to need right now—had been taken off to storage elsewhere once they'd been able to sort through it, and everything that could possibly be laundered had been taken off to be laundered. They'd also both been measured for clothing in the local style, since everything they owned was too heavy and hot.

They'd bathed, and Harrier was cleanly close-shaven for the first time since Blackrowan Farm. He'd gotten his hair cut short again too, since he hated it when it got long and straggly.

And they'd eaten.

Food that he didn't have to cook—didn't have to *catch*—bread and vegetables and soup and none of the dishes was in the least familiar and he hadn't cared. Traveling was all very well—and Harrier had developed a taste for it—but he also knew exactly how close they'd come to just plain starving to death or dying of thirst on the road during the last part of the journey. If they hadn't run across the Telchi . . . if Harrier hadn't been able to Heal him . . .

The lid of the chest he was filling slipped and banged down on Tiercel's fingers before he could snatch his hand away. He yelped, then swore.

"You could get into so much trouble for language like that," Harrier said.

"From who? You?" Tiercel demanded. His words were a little muffled since he'd crammed his bruised fingers into his mouth. Harrier snickered.

"Good point. Hey, Tyr?"

"What?" Tiercel asked sulkily. He sat down on top of

the chest—he'd filled it with his books; there weren't really many other sorts of storage space here—and glared at Harrier as if banging his hand had been Harrier's fault. Harrier could have told him that the lids of the chests wouldn't stay up by themselves and needed to be held in place, but Tiercel didn't pay attention to things like that.

"It ever occur to you that us finding the Telchi was lucky?"

"For him?" Tiercel asked.

"For us."

Harrier waited while Tiercel thought about it, though he wasn't quite sure Tiercel would reach the same conclusion he had. The fact that they'd had to lose Kareta because the Telchi had joined them still hurt—not the way Simera's death hurt, but in a sort of nagging *unfinished* way—and possibly with Kareta but without the Telchi they could have made it to Tarnatha'Iteru, since Kareta could have located water for as long as she could have safely traveled with them, but Harrier wasn't sure they could have gotten into the city without the Telchi. Certainly not as easily, anyway.

"Yes," Tiercel said, frowning. "I guess it doesn't happen the way it does in the wondertales, does it? I mean, when the Gods of the Wild Magic help someone."

That wasn't exactly what Harrier had been thinking. "You mean the Gods of the Wild Magic killed off all the Telchi's men and nearly killed him just to make things easy for us?"

Tiercel made a face. "Idiot. No. It's like a . . . puzzle. And all the pieces interlock. The Telchi's men died because they fought the hill bandits, and there were a lot of them, and they needed to be stopped. I think the Telchi *survived* because we needed him."

Thinking about it that way bothered Harrier just a little. More than a little, really. It seemed so . . . large. And while it was silly to think that the Wild Magic and the Light Itself would be anything small, he'd never had to think about what that really meant before. It bothered him more than he had words for to have to trust something he couldn't see or touch, something he couldn't have a conversation with, the way he could talk to Tiercel or his Da or one of his brothers. And if he *could*—he remembered the not-quite-voice in his mind when his Mageprice had been set—that idea bothered him even more.

"Yeah, right, okay," he muttered.

OVER THE EVENING meal, the Telchi discussed his plans for Harrier's immediate future. Now that they had arrived in Tarnatha'Iteru, Harrier's training could begin in earnest.

"What about him?" Harrier demanded, pointing at Tiercel.

"*I* am going to be trying to figure out if anybody knows anything at all about any place that looks like the place I've been seeing," Tiercel said, just a little huffily. "And trying to figure out how to get there."

"If it is indeed somewhere in the deep desert, you will need to hire Isvaieni guides," the Telchi said, scooping a large portion of some kind of pickled vegetable onto a piece of soft flatbread. Harrier had discovered that while the main dish at a meal was usually hot, nearly all the side-dishes were cold. He supposed that made sense if you lived in a desert.

"We ought to figure out where we're going first," he said, trying the idea on for size. "I mean, otherwise, we won't even have any idea of what supplies to buy."

"Indeed, that is so," the Telchi said. "Your horses will certainly fetch a good price, for they are very fine animals, and a buyer can undoubtedly even be found for your wagon."

"Sell them?" Tiercel said, and Harrier said: "Why?"

The Telchi smiled slightly. "To journey deeper into the Madiran—and especially into the Isvai—you will need *shotors,* not horses. And while wheeled carts may make the journey between the *Iteru,* and upon the Trade Road, your wheels will be useless in sand."

"Sand?" Tiercel said.

"You've heard of it, Tyr. It's like mud, only dry." Harrier frowned. It hadn't occurred to him that they wouldn't be able to take the wagon with them wherever they went. He sighed, and thought about the fact that the wagon would come in handy for their trip north again, and realized that if Tiercel found what he was looking for, they probably wouldn't *be* heading north again. "We can sell the horses now, but let's wait to sell the wagon until we're ready to go." He'd seen mules here, after all, and if it turned out that what they were looking for wasn't out there in the desert, they could buy some to draw the wagon and go somewhere else.

Tiercel nodded, frowning faintly.

IN THE COOL of the morning and the cool of the evening, Harrier practiced with the Telchi in the sand-covered courtyard at the back of the house. Both of them used only wooden swords—the Telchi promised that proper swords would be ready for Harrier when the time came, for Harrier was learning the Selken two-sword style.

It was a little frightening to him—when he let himself think about it at all—how fast he was learning. He knew he was *tired* all the time, and the Telchi said he must not worry about that, for he was retraining his muscles so that he no longer staggered through life like a drunken *shotor*— a remark that Harrier thought was enormously unfair (not that he'd ever seen a drunken *shotor*), because no one had ever called him "clumsy" before, even by indirection. But the Telchi also told him that once his muscles caught up with his skill, he would perhaps be nearly formidable, since after even a handful of days, his skills surpassed those of students whom the Telchi had had in his teaching for many years.

For as Harrier quickly discovered, he was not the Telchi's only student. During those seasons of the year in which caravans did not make their way between the *Iteru*, the Telchi taught sword skills to any who wished to learn, instructing them in the heavy curved southern *awardan*, and in the Southern fighting style—which involved, as far as Harrier could tell, hoping your enemy wasn't armed.

"Why do you teach them, if none of them are very good?" he asked one day, when they'd been in Tarnatha'Iteru for nearly a fortnight. Just as he'd said he would, Tiercel spent his days wandering around the city trying to find things out, but Harrier didn't worry too much, as Tiercel was accompanied by a man named Ophare, who was one of the Telchi's servants. On the first day the two of them had set out together, Harrier had heard the Telchi tell Ophare that if any sort of misfortune befell Tiercel as he wandered about the city, Ophare shouldn't bother to return home.

"It entertains me. It passes the time. It adds coin to my purse. Perhaps I looked for one I could make into an apprentice."

"Perhaps you didn't," Harrier said pleasantly, knowing that this last remark had not been made in true seriousness. None of the Telchi's students was good enough—Harrier watched them when he wasn't practicing himself. Not dedicated enough, or not capable enough, or just . . . not *good* enough. He wasn't sure how he could tell just by looking at them, but he could. And he was also pretty sure that even armed with nothing but a pair of light wooden practice swords, he could disarm—and then *hurt*—any of the Telchi's other students any time he wanted to. And thinking that was a little disturbing.

"Perhaps I did not," the Telchi agreed, his tone just as easy. "Undoubtedly I was waiting for the Lady of Battles and the Sword-Giver to lead you to my side."

Harrier shifted, a little uneasy now with the turn the conversation had taken. They were sitting on cushions in the main room of the Telchi's home. It had become too hot to practice, but it was not yet time for the midday meal, which meant it was time for Harrier's other lessons—lectures on what to do in every possible situation that might involve killing somebody. Since he didn't want to kill anyone at all, he usually did his best to distract his teacher at this point, sometimes with more success than at other times.

"You know we'll be leaving, don't you? As soon as Tiercel finds whatever he's looking for?" He didn't want the Telchi to think he'd be here forever, and he knew—*now*—that a normal apprenticeship to a Selken Master of Swords lasted years. Of course, it also began when the apprentice was a child, first presented to the Sword Temple as a promising acolyte.

The Telchi picked up his cup and sipped. The drink was called *kaffeyah*—they had it in Armethalieh, but it wasn't popular there—and Harrier had tried it and loathed it. Fortunately, the Telchi didn't insist he drink it.

"Yes. And I know—too—that no one to whom your friend has spoken, whether they be scholar or trader, recognizes this place he speaks of. But I know another thing that disturbs me more, that perhaps you should be mindful of."

Harrier sat up straighter. "What?"

"You know that this is the season for trading with the desertfolk."

"Yes. It's winter. You trade with them all winter and when spring comes and the snow melts in the Delfier Valley, the caravans head north."

It wasn't really winter. It was actually *spring*—it was already Rains, so he'd missed his Naming Day, and Flowering Fair, and everything else pretty thoroughly. In a sennight or two, the caravans would begin going north.

"Not this year. Tiercel does not know how to weigh the information as he should, but I do. It has been almost three moonturns since any Isvaieni was seen here in the Madiran, or lit their signal fire at Radnatucca Oasis to say they wished to trade. Ophare brings me the household gossip, and so I have the gossip of the marketplace, and thus I am told that it is so elsewhere as well."

"So they're all . . . gone?" Harrier asked, baffled.

The Telchi shrugged. "They are not here, nor in Kabipha'Iteru, nor in Laganda'Iteru, nor, one must imagine, in any of the rest of the String of Pearls either. And so they will be difficult to hire as guides."

"WE COULD SEND letters home," Tiercel said hesitantly one evening a few days later. Even without the goods usually provided by the Isvaieni, there were more than enough items to make up a payload, and the first caravans would be leaving Tarnatha'Iteru for Akazidas'Iteru in a sennight or so. The Telchi had already turned down several offers of employment as a caravan guard.

"A caravan takes about a moonturn on the Trade Road, maybe a little more," Harrier said meditatively, staring at the ceiling. "A dispatch rider showing the Magistrate's Seal could cover the same distance heading the other way in a sennight—less, if he rode straight through and didn't mind killing his horses under him. Do you want to bet the future on the idea that your father wouldn't write to the Consul here to yank you home the moment he knew where you were? Or that we'll be gone in that time, and far enough away that we can't be followed?"

Tiercel sat up and stared at him. "You don't think . . ."

"What I think is that first you were sick, then you vanished, and whatever letters home our families have actually gotten out of all the ones we've written—and there haven't been all that many—haven't been all that reassuring. And if your family got the last one, the one you wrote from the Elven Lands, well . . . I know what *I'd* think." *I'd think you'd written it while you were out of your head with fever somewhere, that's what I'd think. Light knows that would be more comfortable than believing it's all real.*

"But it's all true! I can prove it! Well, I mean . . . there's Ancaladar. And you've got the Three Books." Tiercel sounded as upset as if Harrier had said that *Harrier* didn't believe him.

"Yeah, and if I have to choose between being eaten by

the Endarkened and telling my Da I'm a Wildmage, I'm not sure which I'd pick. But what I'm saying is, having to try to prove anything is going to slow us down. A lot. And attract a lot of attention. And were you *listening* when Macenor Telchi said the other day that all the Isvaieni just upped and vanished a while ago?"

"I was trying not to," Tiercel answered simply. "Because I keep thinking of that . . . town."

Windy Meadows. Where the Goblins had come up out of the ground and devoured all of the inhabitants. Where Simera had died.

"Maybe we should call Ancaladar back now," Harrier said, frowning at the ceiling. Ancaladar's saddle was built for two. He could carry both of them.

"I don't want to . . . wake him up . . . until I know where we need to go. Or until I'm sure we can't possibly find it," Tiercel said.

"Okay. Fine."

TIERCEL HEARD HARRIER turn over, and a moment later, heard the not-quite-snoring that indicated he was already asleep. It was just as well that Tiercel had an entire city to occupy him, because all Harrier seemed to be doing these days was getting up before dawn, going off to spend several hours banging away at straw practice dummies (or at their host) with a pair of wooden swords, and then doing the same thing in the evening. As far as Tiercel could tell, Harrier wasn't even practicing Fire or Coldfire any more—not that he really could without giving away the fact that he was a Wildmage, because (as Tiercel knew perfectly well) there was no privacy to be had in a house filled with servants.

Tiercel wasn't quite sure why they'd both come to the conclusion that it was so important to, well, hide what they were. The fact that *he* had the ancient Magegift, yes. That would be awfully hard to even begin to explain. But Wildmages were revered everywhere, and the Telchi said that they wandered around the Madiran, wearing blue robes that were practically a *uniform* and nobody bothered them because their magic was so necessary to everybody's survival.

Tiercel frowned, momentarily distracted. He hadn't seen anybody at all wearing blue robes, and he'd walked up and down and through what he was willing to bet was every single street and alley of this city.

Anyway. The *point* was that Harrier wasn't practicing his magic (which was kind of a *sub*-point of the fact that both of them were pretending that they didn't have any magic at all, because Tiercel had been careful not to do any spells either, at least not where anyone could see him, at least not any spells that anybody would recognize as spells) and all he said when Tiercel asked him what he was doing was "nothing." If Tiercel hadn't known that Harrier was a Knight-Mage, and that the Telchi was teaching him everything he knew about fighting, Tiercel might actually have believed it.

But he'd watched the two of them spar one evening. Harrier hadn't known about it. But their bedroom window overlooked the practice area, and Tiercel had come in from another fruitless day trying to chase down some kind of clue to where they needed to go, and heard an odd clattering sound coming from outside the window. He'd gone over and looked out, and the two of them—Harrier and the Telchi—had been out there, training.

While they'd still been on the road, Tiercel had seen Macenor Telchi practice by himself many times, doing the exercises that he called "sword-dances." When he'd still been recovering, they'd been slow and stately, but later he'd moved through the forms with blinding speed.

As he was now. Only now they weren't forms. Now the dance had a partner, for outside, in the twilit courtyard, Harrier circled and moved and feinted with him. The wooden swords they both carried moved almost too fast to see, as the two fighters spun and turned and blocked. Tiercel didn't know all that much about sword-fighting—he'd never even watched the Elves practice back in Karahelanderialigor—but it didn't seem to him that Macenor Telchi was holding back much.

And Harrier was *fast*. No matter what the Telchi tried, Harrier's swords were there to block it, until at last Harrier stumbled, and the Telchi's sword caught him a sharp *"thwack"* along the ribs. Harrier yelped, and the Telchi laughed, and that seemed to indicate the end of the match.

Tiercel ducked back inside the room before either of them saw him. What he'd just seen troubled him more than he liked to admit even to himself. Harrier had only been doing this for a few sennights, and he was good enough to challenge a man who'd been a master of swords since before he'd been born. Somehow doing weird things himself seemed almost natural to Tiercel. He didn't have to watch someone else doing them, after all. But watching Harrier turn from, well, *Harrier*—his best friend, someone who hadn't even wanted to *touch* the sword Roneida had given him—into the person he'd just glimpsed in the courtyard was more unsettling than everything that had happened to Tiercel in the past year.

Harrier has been Called by the Wild Magic to be a Knight-Mage. Just like Kellen the Poor Orphan Boy. This is what it means, Tiercel reminded himself. He thought, for the first time, that back when Kareta brought him the Three Books, Harrier might have had a better idea of what they would mean than Tiercel had, and maybe that was why he'd fought this so hard. Because Tiercel suspected, down deep inside, that becoming a Knight-Mage might be a greater change for Harrier than becoming a High Mage had been for him.

It wasn't something they talked about, because Harrier didn't like to talk about things that made him as uneasy as the Wild Magic did. Tiercel really didn't have any idea of whether or not Harrier was reading the Three Books he'd been given, or had any notion of how uncanny his sudden ability with the sword was, but he *did* know that Harrier wouldn't thank the person who brought those things to his notice. And so Tiercel devoted his attention to other things.

With Ophare's help, he'd managed to make a pretty good start on searching every possible place in the city where possible information on The Lake of Fire might be found. To his surprise and his enormous disappointment, there were no public libraries in Tarnatha'Iteru of the sort he was used to finding in the Nine Cities, but Ophare had been able to direct him to other sources of information. There were scholars who were willing to share their knowledge of the past with him, especially when they discovered how much he already knew about pre-Flowering history. And while one of them—Master Arapha—was able to tell Tiercel of an ancient race of Otherfolk who had been made of and lived in fire, that information was interesting rather than immediately useful, since the Fire-sprites had been swept out of existence long before the founding of Armethalieh.

For a while Tiercel held out hope that the archives of the merchant traders would be able to provide him with the information that he sought, for the records they kept stretched back for centuries, to the time when the String of Pearls, as the eleven *Iteru*-cities were called, had first been built and the first trade-routes had been mapped across the Madiran. If not for the fact that many of the rich merchants of Tarnatha'Iteru owed the Telchi favors, and the fact that the Telchi was willing to call upon that goodwill to gain Tiercel access to the records stored in the Merchants Guildhall of Tarnatha'Iteru, it would have been difficult for Tiercel to do that research. The merchant traders of each city guarded their secrets jealously for fear that their rivals from the other *Iteru*-cities might try to gain access to their information, whether of sources for rugs and spices, or of the fastest route from one place to another.

Tiercel could have gotten into the Guildhall by himself—before he'd left Armethalieh (it seemed like a lifetime ago) his father had told him that he could call upon Chief Magistrate Vaunnel's name in an emergency, and even Consul Aldarnas owed allegiance to Chief Magistrate Vaunnel. But if Tiercel did that, word that he'd done so would get back to Armethalieh, and he knew Harrier was right: they didn't dare attract that kind of attention to themselves. He vowed to repay the Telchi—somehow, sometime—for all he was doing for them.

It was more than disappointing that after all that work and trouble, Tiercel's answers weren't there either, though it took him more than a fortnight of daily visits to figure that out. By then, his head was stuffed with information about cities and wells and oases and camps and Isvaieni tribes and their affiliations and their chief products and what they should be offered in trade. He felt he could probably draw a map of the entire desert, from the Madiran to the Barahileth.

But there was nothing, anywhere, about a Lake of Fire.

"I THINK WE should go," Tiercel said to Harrier.

It was a bit over five sennights now since they'd arrived in Tarnatha'Iteru, and it was slightly entertaining to Tiercel that here in the depths of the desert they'd both managed to almost entirely lose the sun-darkening they'd picked up on the way here. But in the Madiran, nobody went out in the harsh desert sun without protection—or at *all* during the hottest part of the day—and Tiercel had gotten used to keeping the hood of his light desert robe pulled well up whenever he left the Telchi's house.

It had taken him a couple of days to plot out the best time to grab Harrier for a discussion of their future. It wasn't—exactly—that he didn't want the Telchi involved in it. It was just that he wanted to talk to Harrier privately first, because he knew that the Telchi wanted Harrier as his apprentice, and that Harrier was paying his Mageprice by being trained, and if they had to talk about that, he didn't think Harrier *would* talk about it in front of somebody else. So Tiercel needed to find a time when he could catch Harrier alone. Mornings weren't good, because that was when Harrier went off to practice. Evenings weren't good either. The evening meal came late—it was served far later here than it was ever served in Armethalieh—and after it, all Harrier wanted to do was sleep. The middle of the day involved other lessons for Harrier, and Tiercel was usually out then anyway, since he was still asking a few last questions around the city.

About Wildmages, for example. In the Madiran, they moved about freely and openly in both city and desert. But he hadn't seen any in all the time he'd been here, and when he'd started asking questions he discovered that there hadn't been one seen in Tarnatha'Iteru in over four moon-turns. Nobody he'd talked to was willing to say whether that was unusual or not, but Tiercel needed to *know*.

Meanwhile, if he actually wanted to talk to Harrier while Harrier was awake it had to be now. Early in the evening, after Harrier had finished his evening practice and come back to his room after his bath, but before the evening meal. He'd made sure to get back to the house extra early just to be sure to be here.

"Go where?" Harrier said. He flopped down on his bed, still rubbing at his hair with a towel. "You've found something?"

"No," Tiercel admitted. "I'm not going to, either. But I still think what I'm looking for is here. In the desert, I mean. Somewhere."

"So, what? We just . . . go? We'd need guides, and there aren't any."

"You can find water with the Wild Magic. Ophare says so. The Wildmages here find wells all the time."

"Do I look like one of the local Wildmages to you?" Harrier asked in long-suffering tones.

"What they can do, you can do. If you have to."

"And why would I have to, if we stay here?"

"Because we can't stay here, and you know it. We got a good price for the horses. I changed out my money for the local currency, and I've been asking what things cost. We have enough to buy *shotors* and supplies. We'll ride out into the desert—Radnatucca Oasis isn't far from here. I'll call Ancaladar. We'll search from the air."

"And do what with the *shotors*?" Harrier asked.

"He'll be hungry when he wakes up."

"Great. Fine. So we ride lunch out to this oasis, and when Ancaladar gets there, we fly all over the desert looking for this place, and then what? Tyr, what about all your *stuff*? Ancaladar doesn't exactly come with saddlebags, you know. And what about supplies? Okay, *maybe* I can find water without needing to sleep for three days afterwards—which I'm not promising. That doesn't mean I can find *dinner*."

Those were good points, but what Tiercel saw right now was that Harrier was coming up with reason after reason to not continue their search, and he began to wonder if it was because the Wild Magic wanted Tiercel to go on alone and leave Harrier behind. Maybe it was keeping Harrier from thinking of leaving.

"We can bring extra *shotors*. Supplies. Set up a base camp. Har, we've got to try something!" Tiercel said urgently.

"Yeah. Let me think."

Tiercel groaned in frustration. When Harrier wanted to "think" about something, it usually took days—if not longer—for him to reach a conclusion. But to Tiercel's surprise, this time it didn't take long at all.

"This oasis. Where is it, exactly?"

"Exactly? Um, Radnatucca Oasis is about a day from here, into the desert. It's where the merchants meet the Isvaieni. Most of them won't come into a city."

"And it's got water?"

"It's an oasis, Har."

"So you could take Ancaladar there, and set up a base camp, and keep a couple of *shotors* there—not for eating—and fly around in circles until you found the place, right? And when you found it—or were sure it wasn't here—*then* we could actually do something. That makes a lot more sense to me than just charging off into the desert—without food or water or—you know—*guides*. And all you'd actually have to worry about is if whatever made the Isvaieni disappear came after you, but Ancaladar would be right there. And I could come out and bring you—I don't know—goats or something."

"I could go by myself," Tiercel said, because this still sounded to him a lot like Harrier wanted to stay here in Tarnatha'Iteru.

"Go *where?*" Harrier demanded, and now he sounded irritable—and a lot more like the Harrier Gillain Tiercel knew. "You have no idea where you're going, or even if what you're looking for is *there!* We don't even know how big this Dark-damned desert is—you've told me yourself that the maps just sort of . . . stop . . . in the middle of the Isvai and past that they're guessing. And I could tell you what the coast looks like all the way to the Southern Horn, but that's a few hundred miles west of here, so I don't think it's terribly helpful just at the moment. You and Ancaladar can cover hundreds of miles from the air, and see everything there is to see. And protect yourselves if you run into something bad. Isn't that what he's been teaching you all this for? Time to use it."

Tiercel stared at Harrier in something like shock. Sure, Harrier could plan things. But his plans usually involved things like lunch. Or a lot of lunches, because of course Tiercel knew that Harrier had been the one to pack and plan for most of their travel so far. But this went far beyond that.

"So while I'm flying around in circles in the desert, what will you be doing?" He tried very hard not to think about Knight-Mages or Kellen the Poor Orphan Boy or how much Harrier had changed just in the few sennights since they'd been here, and he must have succeeded because when Harrier answered, he wasn't at all defensive.

"Finishing up as much of my education as I have time for, of course. You don't think I'm going to let you go off to the real trouble without me, do you? And I'll tell Ancaladar, too—he'll listen to me, even if you won't."

Tiercel let out a breath he hadn't known he'd been holding in. Harrier didn't mean to leave him to go on alone, and the Wild Magic wasn't going to ask it of him.

NOW THAT THEY had a plan—or the beginnings of one—it was easy enough to tell it to the Telchi and enlist his help. The first thing they'd need to do would be to purchase beasts to ride to Radnatucca Oasis. Though so short a journey could be accomplished on horseback, the Telchi recommended the purchase of *shotors*, for the ugly sturdy creatures were far more dependable in the desert. If Tiercel meant to stay at Radnatucca for an extended period—with or without Ancaladar—he would need copious supplies as well, which meant at least six beasts: two to ride, and four to carry their supplies. ("Are you going to tell him you're going to feed most of them to Ancaladar?" Harrier had asked.) The Telchi could guide them to Radnatucca with ease, for he had been there on several occasions as a caravan guard, and the sight of Ancaladar would hardly be a surprise to him. It would take, at most, a few days to make those preparations, and purchase what they would need, and then they would be ready to go.

But they were already out of time.

HARRIER WAS ALWAYS up-and-out before dawn, a combination of new habits and old. Tiercel didn't feel the same need to go rushing into the day; he usually arose in a more leisurely fashion (when the sounds of practice outside his window became too persistent to ignore), dressed, breakfasted on the cold dishes still set out from the meal Harrier and the Telchi had enjoyed earlier, and then collected Ophare and went off on his day's errands.

Today, however, he'd barely begun his second cup of

tea—there was proper tea available here, which in Tiercel's opinion was one of the most welcome things about the place; while he loved *kaffeyah,* he'd missed tea—when there was a wild flurry of activity. First Latar went rushing out into the streetside courtyard, then he came running back the other way with Niranda in tow. Tiercel had never quite figured out her place in the Telchi's household—she seemed to do most of the cooking, but she also did most of the marketing, and the cook Tiercel's mother employed to keep the Rolfort household fed would have quit on the spot if asked to do his own shopping.

"What's going on?" he asked, getting to his feet, but both Niranda and Latar ignored him as they ran to the back of the house where the practice courtyard was. Now thoroughly concerned, Tiercel set down his mug and followed them. Before he got there, he heard wailing—Latar—and the sound of Niranda speaking low and fast.

He stepped out into the yard. The sun was starting to slant down into the courtyard, but it wasn't too hot out here yet. Harrier and the Telchi were both in armor, or what passed for armor down here in the Madiran: a heavy quilted surcoat sewn with disks of horn and braced in places with boiled leather. The protection was enough to stop an arrow, but probably not to turn a sword-strike. It was impossible to wear steel in the desert, though. Its heat and weight would kill its wearer faster than an enemy attack.

"Again," the Telchi said, speaking to Niranda. "More slowly. And Latar, if you do not compose yourself, I will personally hang you from the walls until you learn that silence is the greatest of the virtues."

"I went this morning to the Spice Market," Niranda said, obviously slowing her words with an effort. "And there I heard that there had been travelers from Laganda'Iteru camped below the North Gate all night, waiting until dawn when they could be permitted into the city. They begged immediate audience with the Consul—and sanctuary!"

Tiercel was puzzled for a moment, until he remembered that the Spice Market adjoined the Moneychangers' Court, since spices were so costly and valuable. Niranda had been inside the outer courts of the Consul's Palace.

"I was not there for the audience," Niranda continued, "but Musa was delivering pepper and rose oil to the Court Chamberlain for the afternoon banquet, and he heard everything. He says these men and their families asked sanctuary of the Consul because Laganda'Iteru is gone. They said it had been burned to the ground by an army that came from the desert like a plague of ghosts, saying they would cleanse the desert of all those who did not follow the True Balance."

Harrier looked up and met Tiercel's eyes. Tiercel thought he looked more puzzled than anything else. "There's only one Balance," he said slowly.

The one the Wildmages keep, Tiercel finished mentally.

"The rest," the Telchi said imperturbably.

"One of the refugees was a man Musa knew, or so he said. Piaca was a spice merchant in Laganda'Iteru. The two of them had corresponded for years, engaged in trade. Piaca would never have left his home or his business were he not convinced that his life was indeed in danger. If Piaca says that Laganda'Iteru has been destroyed, then it has been." Niranda folded her arms across her chest defiantly, but her eyes were frightened.

"It seems our lesson is finished for the day," the Telchi said mildly. "I shall go, and see what other news I may discover."

"What about us?" Tiercel asked.

"Come if you wish," the Telchi answered.

TIERCEL HAD HALF-EXPECTED the Telchi to go directly to the Consul's Palace for his answers, but he quickly realized that was a naïve assumption. It would be like expecting one of the Armethalieh City Watch to go stomping into Magistrate Vaunnel's private chambers to demand that she answer his questions.

Unfortunately, it was much too easy for them to get all

the information that they wanted. Before they had gone more than a few streets from the front door of the Telchi's house, even Tiercel could tell that the city was uneasy. There were more people on the city streets than he'd ever seen at this time of day before, and all of them seemed to have some bundle in their arms. Some of them were filling the ubiquitous three-wheeled carts with household possessions—apparently planning to leave the city as soon as possible—others were arguing with their neighbors, equally determined to stay. It was quickly apparent that the refugees that Musa had told Niranda about had only been the first wave of those who had fled from Laganda'Iteru—the ones who had possessed swift mounts and had fled early. More survivors had arrived in the city, but not to seek sanctuary. The new arrivals meant only to stop in Tarnatha'Iteru for long enough to purchase supplies for the longer journey north—not simply as far as Akazidas'Iteru, so the gossip had it, but all the way to Armethalieh. For as they told anyone who would listen, if this mysterious army truly meant to "cleanse the desert of all those who did not follow the True Balance" . . .

Then Tarnatha'Iteru would be their next stop.

It took the three of them longer than any of them liked to find someone who was actually from Laganda'Iteru, someone who'd *seen* the enemy army. Even so, Kinalan had only seen it from a distance. He was an ordinary tradesman who had arrived in the city only an hour ago—his mule, he said, had died beneath him on the road. He'd heard the shouting and boasts of the enemy, yes, but the only people who'd escaped Laganda'Iteru were those who'd heard and remembered the story of Rasan the Stableboy.

For Laganda'Iteru was not the first city to be destroyed by this mysterious army.

A moonturn less five days before Laganda'Iteru fell, a boy had arrived at its gates, filthy, terrified, and on foot. The story he told was madness itself, but as he'd had family living within the city, he had not been turned away. He claimed to have been exercising a string of horses outside

Kabipha'Iteru—a city south of Laganda'Iteru—when a vast army had marched upon it. Young Rasan had fled in terror, riding north as fast as he could, changing out mounts from the string of horses he'd been exercising as he went and abandoning the exhausted ones behind him. It had only been when the Laganda'Iteru City Watch had been roused to the sound of drums, and looked out over the wall to see a vast army approaching, that young Rasan's wild tale had finally been believed by those who remembered hearing it.

Listening to Kinalan's tale, Harrier began at last to get an idea of how far apart the *Iteru*-cities were. Kinalan said he had been on the road for a sennight without pausing for anything but water from one of the roadside wells. He looked haggard and wild-eyed and ready to drop from exhaustion—but he also looked unwilling to remain in Tarnatha'Iteru one moment longer than was necessary to buy a *shotor* and supplies for the next stage of his journey. If Macenor Telchi had not offered him several gold *uiqat,* he would not have paused to speak to them at all.

"But you saw this army?" Macenor Telchi asked.

"I saw them," Kinalan answered grimly. "More men than I could count, mounted upon *shotors* saddled and bridled in the deep-desert style. Now we know where the Isvaieni have gone—for they have been gone where no man may say since the beginning of the winter rains—though never would I have thought that the tribes would band together that way. I thought young Rasan was sun-touched, when I first heard his mad tale. Would that he had been."

"What happened to him?" Tiercel asked. "Rasan?"

"I know not," Kinalan answered wearily. "At first he would tell his story to any who asked—he worked at the stable where I kept my mules, for I was a launderer, and must tend my drying fields. One day I went and heard he had run off."

"Maybe he got away," Harrier said.

"I know not," Kinalan repeated. "I hope he did, for I owe my life to his warning. And I wish . . . but it does not matter. Even if the Consul herself had believed him, what could she have done? A handful of city guards against hundreds upon hundreds of madmen? Those of us who fled before they reached the walls were fortunate. The city burned for days." Kinalan turned away, walking off into the marketplace without another word. There was nothing more he could tell them.

Everywhere they went in the city in the next hours, it was the same: mounting fear and confusion as the refugees' story spread. No one knew anything more than Kinalan had told them—Laganda'Iteru had been roused at dawn to the sound of drums and the arrival of an army of Isvaieni warriors. A few people had moved quickly enough to seize mounts and flee before the army reached the city. If the tale brought by a young boy several sennights before was true, Laganda'Iteru was not the first *Iteru*-city that had been so attacked, nor would it be the last.

Even though it was nearing the hottest part of the day, a steady stream of people moved through the gates. There would have been riots in the city if Consul Aldarnas had barred the gates to keep people from leaving, but he was far too wise for that: instead, for the first time since Harrier and Tiercel had come to Tarnatha'Iteru, the main gates of the city stood open. "They would do better to wait a few hours and make better preparations," the Telchi said quietly, watching the exodus.

"How did they get out of the city?" Harrier asked, frowning. He'd been quiet after they'd spoken to Kinalan, as the Telchi found and questioned others about the destruction of Laganda'Iteru. So had Tiercel. There hadn't seemed to be much to say.

"What do you mean?" Tiercel asked, answering Harrier instead of Macenor Telchi.

Harrier shrugged. "If the other city's like this one, the gates are barred until a couple of hours after dawn. And guarded, too. And if *I* had an army coming toward *me*, you can bet I wouldn't open them."

"Desperate men can be very persuasive," the Telchi said.

"It is why, I am sure, that Consul Aldarnas is allowing all who desire it to leave now."

Tiercel swallowed hard, imagining just *how* the refugees had gotten out of Laganda'Iteru. Harrier just looked grim.

"So what do we do now?" Harrier asked.

They'd returned to the Telchi's house. He'd sent his servants to the marketplace with orders to buy all the food they possibly could. There was no point in trying to buy *shotors*—not if they weren't going to use them immediately, the Telchi had told them. The prices of the beasts would rise and continue to rise because of the frantic demand, and after a certain point, any animals in the stables would simply be stolen. Both Tiercel and Harrier wondered how he could know so much about what would happen in a city under siege—or under the threat of one. Not even the wondertales trotted out each Kindling, or the histories Tiercel had read in the Veiled Lands, had given much detail about what happened during wars and battles. But the Telchi seemed very sure.

"I cannot say what any of us should do next," the Telchi said somberly. "Much that we do in the next days depends on what the Consul chooses to do. I believe he will take this threat more seriously than Laganda'Iteru did, but such foresight will be of little use. Like the cities of the north, we have nothing more than a City Watch for our protection, and the handful of guards—such as myself—who protect the caravans on their travels. Many of the caravan guards, I fear, have already left the city, hired to protect travelers on their way to Akazidas'Iteru. Indeed, I have already refused enough *uiqat* for my services to buy this very house."

"Even if they were all here, they wouldn't be a lot of use against an army the size everyone's talking about," Harrier said thoughtfully.

"But you have *walls*," Tiercel said. "Can't you just . . . ?"

"Seal ourselves within them, yes," the Telchi agreed. "And starve, quickly enough, should our enemy have the patience to simply sit outside and wait. The land surrounding us may look barren to northern eyes, but we are in the midst of the orchards and fields which grow the city's food, and provide grazing for our flocks. Bar the gates, and there is less than a fortnight's food within the city. Before that time, I think, the army that attacks us will have cut down the orchards and piled their wood at our gates. Three of them are bare wood. They will burn easily."

"And then the army will be right in here," Harrier said in disgust.

"Yes," the Telchi said. "I believe I underestimated the resourcefulness of the foe you seek to slay, Tiercel. It was foolish of me. The mistake of a novice. I think, perhaps, it is best if the two of you leave the city now. The attack upon Laganda'Iteru came ten days ago, and an army moves more slowly than a few refugees, however ill-provisioned. It is three sennights by caravan between Laganda'Iteru and Tarnatha'Iteru, so perhaps twice that for an army even half the size of the one we are being told of. You will not have all the provisions that I would wish for you, but Latar can guide you to Radnatucca, and if you go now, you will still be able to acquire three *shotor* without too much difficulty."

Tiercel looked at Harrier, and had no difficulty in interpreting his friend's expression. Yes, they could leave now. And probably they *ought* to leave. But from everything they'd learned today, there was an entire Dark-tainted army headed this way with one purpose in mind: to wipe out Tarnatha'Iteru and everyone in it.

He knew it was just one city. He knew there were eleven *Iteru,* and he knew for sure that two had been destroyed and he didn't know how many of them were still left. He knew that there were nine cities in the north as well as a bunch of towns and villages and farms scattered around, and there were nine Elven cities in the Veiled Lands, and villages and farms there too, and probably a lot of other places he hadn't even heard of. And he knew that if the Dark wasn't stopped, and the Endarkened came back, they were all going to be destroyed. And that because of that, the smartest thing for him and Harrier to do would be to leave here right now, while they could still do so safely, and start looking for the Lake of Fire.

And he just couldn't bring himself to do that.

"I think we'll stay," Tiercel said.

"Yes," Harrier said.

Twelve

The Gathering Storm

FOR THE NEXT several sennights, things almost seemed to return to normal in Tarnatha'Iteru. When no army showed up immediately, those who had not fled in the first day or two divided themselves into two factions: those who believed there was no threat at all—or if there was, it was something that could be easily defeated by the city's own resources—and the other group, who believed that the threat was something that certainly must be run from the moment it appeared, but who also believed that they would receive plenty of advance warning of its arrival.

"They're all idiots," Harrier groaned, throwing himself down on one of the cushions in the Telchi's living room.

"Ugh. You stink," Tiercel told him helpfully.

"I've been drilling the new City Militia all morning," Harrier said, pulling himself into a sitting position and reaching for the carafe of cold mint tea that was set out on the table. "You'd stink too. What have *you* been doing?"

"Inventories. Since the Consul took possession of all the food supplies, he's ordered a complete inventory of the warehouses so that—he says—he can properly recompense the merchants for their losses. Really it's so none of it goes, um, *missing* from the warehouses because of the rationing." Tiercel sighed. "Rumor has it that he's going to start searching houses and confiscating stockpiles next."

"Except if you have two or more household members in the City Militia," Harrier said, grinning. "And we have four, just to begin with. Ophare and Latar aren't that good, but at least they're there."

Consul Aldarnas was a wise man. Whether or not he actually believed that an enemy army was coming to attack his city, or that it would be possible to defend against them, he knew that believing there was something they could do to defend themselves against the danger would keep panic from spreading. Before sunset on the day that the news of Laganda'Iteru's destruction had reached him, he'd ordered a City Militia to be formed, to be trained by those who already had some experience with weapons: the City Watch and the Caravan Guards. As one of the Telchi's students, Harrier found himself in the odd position of becoming a teacher when he had barely begun being a student.

"But how'd you get stuck doing that, anyway? Inventory is clerk's work," Harrier added, frowning thoughtfully.

"The Telchi told Consul Aldarnas's Court Chamberlain I could read and write. And I'm not from here, so I'm harder to bribe."

"He didn't tell him about the whole, um . . . ?"

"Me being a High Mage? No. Better off not. And probably just as well that you didn't let him tell anybody you were a Wildmage when we came into the city, you know, because everybody'd be expecting you to *do* something now."

Harrier sighed. "It would be nice to know what. Considering that apparently there are dozens of them down here for every square foot of sand and they didn't do a Light-blessed thing."

"Except disappear," Tiercel said.

"I hope that worries you," Harrier said.

"A lot," Tiercel assured him. "But I don't know what I can do about it."

"Find them?" Harrier suggested.

Tiercel just shrugged. Unfortunately, when they'd found out about the army, he'd taken another careful look at the spells for "seeing at a distance" in his spellbooks just in case he might have missed something the first time and found out that no, he hadn't. They were just about the most useless magic he'd never heard of: either what he looked at needed to be a place he'd been before, or there needed to be some individual there that he already knew, and neither thing was true of any place in the Madiran but here. In fact, Tiercel couldn't see a lot of point for a spell that would only let you see a place you'd already been, but a lot of the High Magick was oddly confusing that way.

The Wild Magic, of course, didn't have the same sort of limitations, and Scrying didn't carry a Mageprice. Harrier pointed out first, that there were no guarantees that it would be *useful,* since the last time the Wild Magic had decided to do something for him, it had involved slaughtering a bandit army and all of the Telchi's men, and next, that according to the spell, the Wildmage would be shown what the Wild Magic felt he needed to see, rather than what *he* felt he needed to see. Last, he pointed out that they didn't have any of the ingredients and couldn't meet any of the proper conditions. But just when Tiercel was about to completely lose his temper and call Harrier a coward, he'd agreed to try.

"Trying" had begun with a visit to the local herbalist, since there weren't any ferns in the Madiran and no possibility of getting any. Harrier had been absolutely certain that something called "desert lily" would work as well, and he didn't look happy about knowing it. Then one morning instead of going off to drill the Militia he'd locked himself into their bedroom with the largest glass bowl Tiercel had ever seen (bought new for the spell) and the bottle of dried desert lily and a jug of date wine and a larger jug of water to fill the bowl.

It was dusk by the time he'd come out. He'd looked shocked and tired and sick, and he'd refused to tell Tiercel what he'd seen, only that it wasn't anything that would do them any good.

Tiercel hadn't asked him to do magic again.

"Are they any good?" Tiercel asked now, returning to the subject of the City Militia.

Harrier sighed, and ran a hand through his hair. It was so wet with sweat that it was nearly black. "No. If they weren't practicing with wooden weapons they'd all have killed each other already. There's worse, though."

Tiercel looked up at the note of disquiet in Harrier's voice. He sounded worried, and Harrier didn't exactly worry most of the time, or at least he hadn't used to. Before all this had started, all the way back in Armethalieh, Harrier had pretty much assumed that no matter what the two of them were doing, it was going to go spectacularly wrong, and had complained accordingly. Tiercel used to think it was funny.

"Caldab and Garam are two men Macenor Telchi knows. Caravan guards, like him. They have families here, so they didn't take jobs the way a lot of the other guards did when everybody was hiring people about a moonturn ago. And . . . when nothing happened after a few days, the Consul decided to send them on a scouting mission to see, I guess, whether or not the stories were true."

"He can't have thought they weren't," Tiercel protested.

"How do *I* know what he thought?" Harrier grumbled. "I know what Niranda said, that Piaca wouldn't have lied, but . . . rich merchants? I can think of a dozen reasons merchants would leave a place and lie their heads off about it. And . . . yes. Twenty or thirty regular people followed them, and they *said* they saw an army, and they *said* they saw the city burn. And I can think of half a dozen ways to fake that. No, I don't think they were lying. But what they said they saw doesn't have to have been true."

"You don't believe that," Tiercel protested.

"Not for a minute," Harrier said. "But if I were the Consul, that would be the way I'd have to think. So he sent scouts to go see if the story was true, three sennights ago. And they haven't come back."

"That's not enough time to . . . you didn't tell me," Tiercel said, feeling oddly betrayed.

"Macenor Telchi only told me an hour ago," Harrier replied. "The Consul swore them to secrecy, and slipped them out of the city by the South Gate in the dead of night so nobody would know. But they told the Telchi, so that he'd take care of their families if they didn't come back. He said the Consul gave them racing *shotors* from his own personal stable, and no matter how ugly those things are, they're fast. They can go for almost a sennight without food and water, longer without food if there's water, and the refugees said the wells along the road were still good."

"So in three sennights, they could have gotten there and back again," Tiercel said, working it out.

"At least one of them," Harrier agreed grimly.

It wasn't anything they hadn't known, or at least hadn't suspected. But being this much more certain was worse somehow.

Harrier poured himself another glass of tea. "Look, Tyr," he said, and his voice was as serious as Tiercel had ever heard it. "We both know that when this Darkspawn army shows up it's going to be up to you and Ancaladar. What are you going to do?"

"Me?" To his vast irritation, Tiercel heard his voice squeak in alarm.

Harrier smiled grimly. "You. Please don't tell me I'm a Knight-Mage. I . . . *know* it." He closed his eyes, as if he were remembering things he wished he'd never known. "I can tell you the walls won't hold. I can tell you they can be scaled, inside and out. I can tell you how to take them down. And—I guess, maybe—I could do a fair job of defending this place. For a while. If anybody would listen to me. They won't, though. I'm not Kellen the Poor Orphan

Boy, and I don't have an army. *Or* a magic sword. And since this is *not* the time to expect me to start figuring out how to cast major Wild Magic spells—just leaving aside the fact that I'd need to get a bunch of people to lend power to any really big spells, which would mean telling them I'm a Wildmage, which could get really ugly really fast— it's up to you."

Unfortunately, even though Tiercel knew that Harrier didn't want to cast spells at all, he also knew that Harrier would do it if he had to. But Harrier was telling the honest truth. He'd barely managed to Heal the Telchi at all. For anything more significant, he'd need a lot of people to share the cost of the spell.

"I don't want to hurt anybody," Tiercel said in a low voice. It was what it all came down to. He'd been thinking about what he might have to do to defend the city ever since the first refugees had arrived in Tarnatha'Iteru, and all he could think of, every time he closed his eyes, was the road outside Windy Meadows, and summoning Fire to burn the Goblins, and how they'd screamed as they'd burned.

"I know," Harrier said, and he didn't sound very happy either. With good reason: *his* Gift didn't really have any other use: High Magick could be used for a lot of different things, but as Harrier had said from the very beginning, there was only one thing a Knight-Mage—or the spells he could cast—was really *for.*

"So I've been thinking," Tiercel said. "We aren't *sure* of why they're after the *Iteru*-cities, but if there's one thing I *do* know from listening to Father talk about the kinds of cases that are heard in the Magistrates Courts, I know that if it's too difficult to get at Tarnatha'Iteru, they'll just go and try something else, somewhere else."

"You think you can scare them off?" Harrier said dubiously.

"Maybe," Tiercel said. "And Akazidas'Iteru has been warned by now, and its Consul will almost certainly send a dispatch rider to the Chief Magistrate. I'm not sure what she can do though, because . . ."

"The Nine Cities don't have an army any more than the *Iteru*-cities do. And the last time anybody tried to call up the Treaty Levies was during the last war, and it didn't work then," Harrier agreed. "Don't stare at me like that: the provisions for the Treaty Levies are still on the books, and the Portmaster of Armethalieh Port is supposed to have ten heavy warships provisioned and ready to launch at all times in support of the King of the Elves. Drives Da half-mad—he's always petitioning to get the law struck, because it was ancient in First Magistrate Cilarnen's time, and we aren't even sure what kind of ships they're supposed to be any more. But First Magistrate Cilarnen decreed that the treaty provisions should stand as long as the City walls did, and First Magistrate Vaunnel says that part of the City wall is still standing so the Treaty and all its provisions does too, so we pretty much ignore it."

Tiercel laughed. "I'm always surprised at the things you know."

"Been listening to you all these years, haven't I?" Harrier got to his feet. "I'm going to go take a bath. Don't know why I bother, since I'm going to be out drilling those lazy idiots as soon as the hot part of the day passes."

"To keep from stinking me out of the house for the next few hours," Tiercel pointed out, "since I'm not going to be back to reckoning up measures of grain and barrels of oil for at least that long."

Harrier laughed. "I guess when the army gets here and sees Ancaladar sitting on the wall, it'll make them think twice, though."

"It would," Tiercel agreed, "but I'm not going to call him."

Harrier had been halfway out of the room; he stopped. "I'm sure you're going to explain that."

"*We* know he's harmless. But he'd scare everybody in the city as much as he'd scare an approaching army. So they'd unbolt the gates and go rushing right out to escape. I don't think that would be a very good idea."

"Maybe not."

* * *

THE NEXT SENNIGHT went very much as the previous
three had gone, with a few small differences.

There was a renewed exodus of people heading northward. Whether it was because rumors of the true reason
for Caldab and Garam's unexplained absence had spread,
or because the fact that the Consul continued to prepare for
misfortune had caused those who were undecided about
leaving to make up their minds, or whether Tiercel's quiet
persistence in insisting that people should leave the city
while they could convinced people, it wasn't really possible to tell. From the very beginning, Tiercel had done his
best to persuade everyone he spoke to that leaving the city
would be the best course of action. In the sennights he'd
spent searching Tarnatha'Iteru for any information that
might reveal the location of the Lake of Fire, he'd made the
acquaintance of a very large number of people, and he
drew upon that familiarity now, urging everyone he knew
even slightly to leave while there was still time. But without having hard facts to present—which he couldn't do—it
was difficult to convince people to leave who weren't of a
mind to leave anyway. And the more time that passed without anything happening, the harder it was to convince
people that there was any real danger at all. To leave the
city, for nearly everyone who lived here, meant to abandon
everything they owned, and few people were willing to do
that except if they were panicking, or if the threat was actually in sight. There were very few who were willing to do
something that would cost them so much on the basis of
warnings they considered vague. If the army had not come
yet—so the common wisdom ran—perhaps it would not
come at all. And the city walls were high.

But some *did* heed the warnings, and just as before, the
Consul did not hinder anyone who wished to leave the city,
though now anyone wishing to leave had to depart at the
times customarily assigned to such departures: between two
hours after sunrise, when the city gates were unbarred for

the day, and one hour before sunset, when the gates were barred for the night. The Telchi told Harrier and Tiercel that he suspected that the Consul had sent more scouts out to see the location and disposition of the enemy army, since by now he must be nearly certain it existed. But if he had, all of them were fairly certain that the scouts hadn't reported back—though none of them had any definite information. There were dozens of different stories making the rounds of the city, none of which made very much sense. Consul Aldarnas had taken to appearing on the balcony of his Palace twice a day, just so that anyone who cared to could see that he had not fled to safety. Even though there was no enemy anywhere in sight, without rationing and fixed prices, half the people in the city would have starved a fortnight ago—anything in the markets that didn't have a price fixed by the Consul was either completely unavailable, or selling for ten times what it had gone for a moonturn ago.

And despite this—despite the fact that the city lived under constantly increasing fear—nearly three-quarters of the inhabitants firmly refused to leave. Tiercel wasn't sure that even the Consul could order them all to leave, and Harrier said there weren't enough men in the City Watch—even if you counted in the Caravan Guards and the new Militia for good measure—to force them to. And it didn't matter one way or the other, really, Harrier added, because there weren't enough supplies, even if they stripped the entire city, to get them all to Akazidas'Iteru safely, because in the north Windrack was a cool month—early spring—but here in the Madiran, it was already brutally hot. Some of the people in Tarnatha'Iteru could still leave—but not all of them.

And in a few moonturns, Tiercel realized, it would be an entire year since he'd left home.

Meanwhile, Harrier continued to try to convince Tiercel to rouse Ancaladar from hibernation. He'd agreed that probably bringing Ancaladar to the city wouldn't be a good idea, but he didn't see why Tiercel shouldn't wake Ancaladar up and just *hide* him somewhere. Tiercel hadn't even bothered to point out that *hiding* someone about the size of one of those heavy warships Harrier's Da didn't keep around the Port would be difficult at the best of times, much less with Ancaladar waking up hungry and needing to hunt. He didn't want to think about the fact that what Harrier kept referring to with ghoulish good humor as "the Darkspawn army" was probably something that might actually be capable of hurting Ancaladar, and that they didn't really know where it was. For all they knew, it had decided to bypass Tarnatha'Iteru completely and head straight for Akazidas'Iteru.

One of the things the three of them had discussed in one of their private councils of war was going to the Consul and revealing who they were—or who Tiercel and Harrier were, anyway. Harrier could prove he was a Wildmage simply by showing that he held the Three Books, if he had to—and Tiercel knew enough spells to impress most people. They hadn't suggested the idea because they thought it was a good one, but simply because every idea had to be suggested.

The Telchi had hesitated for a long moment, regarding them both somberly.

"Did I think that it would be . . . entirely useful . . . I would say that this would be a thing worth doing," he said at last. "Harrier's skills would be of great worth did he have the support of the Consul behind him, so that his advice could be followed. And you, Tiercel. Your power is great, and if you did not have to work in secret, perhaps there would be less apprehension among the people."

"But?" Harrier said.

"But there would be a great temptation, I think, either to ask of you what you could not do, or to blame you for that which is not of your doing."

"HE THINKS CONSUL Aldarnas would blame us for the existence of the people who are destroying the *Iteru*-cities?" Tiercel asked later.

"Well, once you finished explaining to him about how they were all Dark-tainted, and about your visions of the Lake of Fire, *yes*," Harrier said. "Now tell me that explanation wouldn't come into things somewhere along the way."

Tiercel didn't answer, mostly because he couldn't imagine any explanation of their presence in the city—and his abilities—that *didn't* involve his visions and the rebirth of the Endarkened. And Harrier and the Telchi were right: he really couldn't see that going over well. "What do you think he'd do?" Tiercel asked.

"Depends on how fast you could get Ancaladar here. So why don't we just skip the whole thing?" Harrier said. "And why don't you come up with a nice plan that *doesn't* involve us having to explain anything to the Consul—or me actually having to turn the Militia into anything like an army?"

Tiercel picked up the nearest object—a pillow—and tossed it at Harrier, who caught it easily. At least—based on the maps Tiercel had studied, and all of their best guesses at the size of the enemy army—they had at least another fortnight to get as many people as possible to leave the city and to try to come up with a definite idea of how to defend it. And at least they'd have a little warning when the enemy approached.

BUT THEY WOULD have had no advance notice at all if not for the flocks that sheltered within sight of the city walls by night, for when the Isvaieni army approached Tarnatha'Iteru, it did not beat drums to announce itself. And it came by night, not by day.

The first indication Tiercel had that anything was happening was when he found himself being roughly shaken awake from a sound sleep.

"Get up," Harrier said urgently. "Get dressed."

Tiercel barely managed to get his eyes open, but the sight of Harrier in full armor, wearing swords crossed on his back, jolted him fully awake. He knew that the Telchi had given Harrier his own set of swords recently, but he'd never seen Harrier actually *wear* them. In the distance— now that he was awake—he could hear the sound of horns blowing—the same horns that blew at dawn and sunset when the city gates were opened for the day and closed for the last time. But it was the middle of the night.

"They're here," Harrier said as Tiercel scrambled into his clothes. "Ten minutes ago Caldab heard the flock guards barking—all of them at once. He ordered the torches lit along the wall, and the herders ran out and lit the northern emergency beacons that we set up. The army's a couple of miles out."

"Come on," Tiercel said.

The two of them shoved their way through the crowds milling about on the streets. From the snatches of conversation Tiercel overheard, no one was quite certain of what was going on. Some thought it was a fire, others that they were being warned of the approach of a Sandwind. A few moments later, the horns fell silent, and the silence seemed as ominous as the sound had. Soon he saw Militia members, easily distinguished by their green armbands and green sashes, going along the streets ordering people to go back inside. Some of them did as they were told, some of them argued.

When Tiercel and Harrier arrived at the South Gate, a work party was already bringing wagons full of bricks to block it. Not the small three-wheeled carts that Tiercel was used to seeing, but full-sized wagons that took a dozen men to shift.

"The gate's been barred, and it opens in anyway," Harrier said as they climbed the staircase. "Once the cart's in place, they'll pull the axel-pins. The East and West Gates are being blocked the same way. Nobody's going to be able to open them."

"Don't you think that's a little . . . ?" Tiercel began, but Harrier simply pointed toward the wall. The top of the wall could only be reached by steep narrow staircases that ran beside the gates. Access to the steps was guarded by several men, some of whom wore Militia green, others of whom wore the familiar armor of the City Guards. They allowed Tiercel and Harrier to pass without challenge, though several of them gave Tiercel questioning looks.

The steps were narrow and worn with age, since the steps over the lesser gates were rarely used, and consequently not kept in good repair. When Tiercel got to the top, he glanced back across the city. Parts of it were still dark, but most of it was brightly lit, and the Consul's Palace was ablaze with light. This was the first time he'd actually been up on the city walls, and he was surprised at how far he could see.

Harrier tugged at his sleeve, and he turned away from the city and walked toward the edge of the wall. There were several Guardsmen standing there, gazing out into the darkness, and to Tiercel's faint surprise, the Telchi was there with them. They moved aside as Tiercel and Harrier approached, making room for them, and Tiercel got his first sight of the enemy.

"Don't you think that's a little stupid?" he'd been about to say to Harrier before they'd come up here, meaning the idea of blocking every exit from the city but one. But now, looking out over the plain below, he understood. The walls were their only defense, and they would only be a defense as long as the gates could be kept closed. The City Guards could be trusted to follow orders where City Militia could not, so for all their sakes, having only one set of gates to defend against panicked citizens was probably one of the smartest choices anyone could make. He wondered if the decision had been Harrier's.

He stared out at the approaching enemy. Harrier had said that the presence of the enemy had only been discovered by the barking of the dogs. In that case, they must have approached in total darkness, but now that they'd been discovered, there was no more need for concealment. Torches sparkled among their ranks. Between the torches they carried, and the row of warning beacons burning on the ground about a mile away, Tiercel could see them clearly.

They were mounted on *shotors*. The animals moved forward at a slow walk. They didn't advance in columns, nor did they beat drums and shout, as the refugees from Laganda'Iteru had said they did. There were far too many of them to count—so many that the line of silent marchers stretched so far into the distance that the flames of their torches were barely visible sparks.

"It is very odd," the Telchi said quietly. "I see Adanate Isvaieni, and Lanzanur, and Fadaryama, and Hinturi, and Kadyastar all here together. Yet the tribes do not band together for any reason. And many of those tribes do not approach the *Iteru*-cities at all."

"We cannot possibly hold the city," Harrier said.

He didn't sound either happy or upset about it, Tiercel realized. He sounded as if he was stating a fact that was so obvious that there was no point in having feelings about it. *"The sun is going to rise today,"* or *"it's raining and you're going to get wet if you go outside,"* or *"if you drop that dish it's going to break."*

"We cannot possibly hold the city."

When Tiercel stopped staring out at the approaching army, awareness of the world around him rushed in like the ocean rushing in at high tide. He could hear the shouts and screams from the streets below as the city awoke to its peril; feel the rising wind that told him—after so many moonturns spent on the road—that it was an hour or so before dawn.

"I need to go out and talk to them," Tiercel said, turning away from the wall.

Harrier grabbed for him and he dodged, evading his friend's lunge with years of practice. The fastest way to the only gate that still opened was along the top of the wall. Tiercel ran.

The top of the city wall was as wide as the widest city street below, and the guards along the top of the wall were gathered near the outer edge, hands braced on the low wall that edged the top, peering out into the darkness. There was plenty of room for Tiercel to run, and he did. He could hear Harrier's footsteps pounding along behind him, but he'd always been faster than Harrier was, even now. Harrier was gaining on him, but he hadn't caught up.

The steps down to the ground from the North Gate were wider than the others, wide enough to take at a run. There were City Guards standing around at the bottom, and Tiercel was moving too fast to dodge all of them. A couple of them grabbed him—startled and worried and frightened—and by then Harrier had jumped down the last five steps and pounced on him.

"Wait—wait—wait—" Harrier gasped. "If we're going to do this incredibly stupid thing, we'll need horses."

"You're going with me?" Tiercel asked in disbelief.

Harrier simply smacked him.

A FEW MINUTES later they rode out through the gates on a pair of horses from the Consul's private stables. They hadn't had to go far at all to get them; half-a-dozen horses and the same number of *shotors* were being held right at the gate, standing saddled and bridled and ready to go behind a line of City Guard. Tiercel wasn't sure what their purpose was: last-minute escape? Bribes for the enemy army? He didn't think they'd work for either purpose. Despite that, he wasn't quite sure how Harrier had managed to talk the Captain of the City Guard into giving them two of the horses and opening the gate. Saying "my friend has something he wants to try," really didn't seem to Tiercel as if it was a really persuasive argument.

"I don't quite see . . ." he said, as they rode out through the gate.

"Oh, come on, Tyr. You remember Batho."

"No."

"He was on the wall the day we came. He wasn't the Captain of the Guard then, but Gurilas deserted when the refugees arrived, and he was promoted."

"Clear as mud."

"So, he's a friend of the Telchi's, and I've been training beside him for almost a month, and he knows I'm the Telchi's apprentice, and he probably actually thinks we want to make a run for it, and won't he be surprised?"

Tiercel would have laughed—Harrier's bizarre sense of humor surfaced at the oddest moments—but he happened to glance up. Even on the northern side of the city, they could still see the column of the advancing army. It was getting close. "Come on," he said. "We need to hurry."

They spurred their horses into a gallop.

IF THE ADVANCING Isvaieni were surprised to see their path barred by two lone riders, their leaders gave no sign of it. To Harrier's ill-concealed astonishment (he did his best not to show how stunned he was, but the Telchi had said that every thought he had was displayed on his face for the world to see, and Harrier had no reason to doubt it), when they brought their horses to the front of the advancing horde (calling them "the Darkspawn army," accurate or not, had seemed a lot funnier when he couldn't see them), the line of *shotors* slowed, then stopped. If they hadn't been moving at the slowest of slow walks, they all would have started banging into each other immediately, but all that happened was that a sort of *ripple* of stillness spread through the army, as rider after rider brought his *shotor* to a halt.

One of the many lessons the Telchi had been teaching him that wasn't immediately involved with hitting someone or avoiding being hit was in learning to estimate, at a glance and at a distance, the number of people in a group. Harrier hadn't quite been sure what purpose learning something that arcane could have. Now he knew. It was so that he knew that there were between four and five thousand people out here. Nearly as many as there were still inside the city. And all of these were prepared to fight.

"We want to talk," Tiercel said quickly, before the other man could say anything. "My name is Tiercel Rolfort. I'm from Armethalieh. It's a city in the north. I want to know . . . what you want."

The leader of the army stared at Tiercel for a long moment. A *shotor* was a good bit taller than a horse, so he was looking down. Harrier had a desperate urge to reach for his swords, but the man was armed, and so were the men on both sides of him. Harrier wasn't sure how quickly Tiercel could cast a spell, but he wasn't sure it was fast enough to keep them from getting killed if Harrier did something that blatantly provocative.

"Once Golden Armethalieh was the last defense against the Darkness," the man said slowly. "I, Zanattar of the Lanzanur Isvaieni, say this. Now Armethalieh is a crucible of error and Taint, just as the *Iteru*-cities are. Its day for Cleansing will come."

"You're wrong," Tiercel said firmly. "Armethalieh isn't Tainted. And neither is Tarnatha'Iteru. But—"

"You follow the False Balance. Since the time of the Great Flowering, the Balance of the World has been out of true, for the Light destroyed the great evil that beset the world in that time—as was only right—but those who kept the Light in those days did not stop where they should have, and so ever since that day, the Great Balance has been tipping more and more away from what the Wild Magic means it to be. Generation after generation has followed this False Balance, upholding it for their own purposes. They have taught that Light is always good. But the children of the desert know better. Light scours. Light blinds. Light kills. It is Darkness that is the friend and ally of the desertborn, and the True Balance contains both Darkness and Light. This is the Balance as it was kept in ancient times, the Balance that will be restored to the land."

You've got to be joking. Harrier didn't need to see Tiercel's face to know he was as stunned as Harrier was. You didn't need to be a Wildmage to know that this was crazy talk. Anybody who'd ever gone to Light-Day services knew it.

"No," Tiercel said urgently. "Zanattar, you have to listen to me. The Light sent me here because—"

He didn't get a chance to finish. Harrier saw Zanattar reach for his sword, and he cried out and spurred his horse forward, reaching back to draw his swords, and Tiercel raised his hands, and a wall of purple light appeared between him and the Isvaieni army.

Fortunately Harrier hadn't drawn his swords before Tiercel cast MageShield, because the sudden appearance of the glowing wall of light made his mount plunge and rear, and he needed both hands to control it. Tiercel was having the same problem.

It took the two of them several minutes to calm the animals. The horses would have been happy to simply bolt, but in one direction there was the wall of Mageshield, and in the other there was the wall of the city. Frankly, Harrier would have been happy to simply get off and walk, if his mount would cooperate by holding still for long enough.

When it finally did, he looked up to see that the wall of MageShield extended as far as he could see. He looked up. It went as high as he could see, too, arcing over the city.

"Tiercel?" he said.

"The Light sent me here because there's Darkness somewhere out there in the desert," Tiercel said quietly. After a moment, Harrier realized he was finishing the sentence Zanattar hadn't let him say.

"You've cast MageShield all around the city," Harrier said.

"I had to," Tiercel said. "Anything less, and they'd just have come around it."

Like the flames of a fire, the shield wasn't quite opaque. Through the barrier, Harrier could see—dimly—the Isvaieni army. They weren't approaching closely—in fact, they'd retreated—but they were spreading out all along the front of it in an ominous mass.

MageShield didn't block sound at all. He could hear the sounds of shouting, voices mingled and blending until the only thing he could really make out was that they were all angry. It was a bone-chilling sound.

"We need to get back inside," Harrier said. *If they'll let us in.* He turned his sweating, trembling mount and forced himself to look up at the city walls. The entire wall above them was crowded with bodies. Everyone looking down at them was white-faced and silent, but Harrier could already hear the sound of screams and wailing from within the city.

"WHO TOLD HIM that, do you think?" Tiercel asked. "About the Light, and the Balance?" They were riding slowly back toward the gate, and Tiercel sounded as if he'd suddenly decided that knowing the source of Zanattar's ravings was of vital importance.

The wall of MageShield fire gave everything an eerie brightness—far brighter than even the full moon, bright enough to cast their shadows on the wall beside them, dark purple against bright purple. In this strange light—bright yet unclear—Tiercel's hair was vivid pale purple, his skin a darker unnatural shade of violet, their chestnut horses indistinct black blobs.

"I don't know. Maybe he made it up," Harrier said. "Maybe he's been talking to your Fire Woman. Do you think it matters? It's not like he's going to tell you now."

"No. But I'd still like to know . . ." Tiercel stopped.

"Why they told him that? Oh, come *on,* Tyr. So he'd come here with all his friends and destroy the *Iteru*-cities, why else?"

"Okay," Tiercel answered. "Why did they want him to do that?"

"Supply," Harrier answered. It hadn't occurred to him until Tiercel asked, but suddenly it made sense to him, unfolding in his mind as if someone had unfurled a map upon a table. He saw Armethalieh and Sentarshadeen, the closest northern cities to the Madiran, saw the Armen Plain and the Trade Road. "If anybody wants to enter the Madiran—for trade or any other purpose—they need to supply at the *Iteru*-cities before they head farther south. I bet they've destroyed the wells when they've destroyed the cities, too. They can retreat into the desert, and nobody can follow them. It makes sense."

"I don't like it," Tiercel said stubbornly.

Harrier just snorted. "There are so many things about this that I don't like. How long can you hold that shield in place, anyway?"

"As long as I have to," Tiercel answered quietly.

Harrier deliberately didn't look at his friend as the words struck through him. When he'd asked the question, he'd only been thinking of the Isvaieni, and how long it might take them to give up and *leave*. But now he realized they had another problem—and a greater one.

What if they didn't?

Tiercel drew on Ancaladar's power to cast his spells, and Ancaladar's power was as close to infinite as made no difference. There wasn't any way for Tiercel to use it up.

But Tiercel could use *himself* up. Harrier'd listened to him talk about the High Magick for long enough to know that there were pretty much two kinds of spells. One kind you cast and they were over and done with, like Fire or MageLight (Tiercel's MageLight, anyway), for example. The other kind needed to be held in place by the will of the Mage.

Like MageShield.

Ancaladar's power was infinite.

Tiercel's endurance wasn't.

Thirteen

❧

The Wind that Shakes the Stars

ZANATTAR OF THE Lanzanur Isvaieni had set out with all
the other young hunters of the tribes in search of the Nalzindar. They had gone forth from the plains of Telinchechitl
in groups that each numbered as many as a man had fingers and toes, swiftly crossing the Barahileth. Where once
there had been nothing but an arid waste of sand and salt
and the *ishnain*-pans whose white dust could blind the un-
wary and raise sores upon the skin, now Bisochim's magic
had hidden deep wells of sweet water so that his pledged
Faithful could make their way in safety. They reached Kannanatha Well, and the edge of the Isvai itself, and set off in
search of their lost brethren.

For days they searched. Had anyone but another Isvaieni
viewed their progress, it would have seemed that they wandered aimlessly, but Zanattar and his comrades followed
the ancient paths that all the tribes, from Adanate to Zarungad, followed between the wells and oases that were life itself in the desert. The Nalzindar followed them as well, for
to turn your back upon water between Sand and Star was to
turn your back upon Life.

They found nothing.

The very sand itself had been scrubbed clean, as if by
Sandwinds so powerful that Zanattar could not imagine
their force. The *sheshu* and the *fenec* cowered in their bur-
rows, just as if there had truly been a great storm, and the
desert antelope were scarce and skittish, driven far from
their normal grazing. At first, Zanattar and his followers
struggled even to feed themselves, for the hunting was
poor, and they had not thought to bring food beyond what
they would need to cross the Barahileth, for the Isvaieni

had always fed themselves upon what the Isvai would give them.

At the end of a fortnight, there was talk of turning back, for the same thought was in every mind: there was nothing here to find. Kazat and Larazir, brothers and members of the Thanduli Isvaieni, said aloud what all were thinking, one night as they sat before the tents, drinking *kaffeyah* and listening to the *shotors* grind their teeth as they chewed their cuds. Perhaps, Kazat said, Shaiara had taken her people and found sanctuary in the *Iteru*-cities.

"Perhaps she has taken them north into the Great Cold," Zanattar answered contemptuously. He knew only as much as anyone knew of the Nalzindar, but it was enough to tell him that they would never go willingly to the desert's edge. But he led this small party by courtesy, not by right, and though they had all pledged oaths of blood-fellowship to each other and to Bisochim's holy cause back in Telinchechitl, Zanattar was not foolish enough to test those pledges by ordering the others to do something they truly did not wish to do.

So matters stood, and all but Zanattar were agreed that they must return to Telinchechitl to confess their failure. In their travels, the party had sometimes seen the signs of other searchers: the spark of a campfire miles away in the night; the scent of smoke carried on the wind. Sometimes they had seen the signs of recent grazing at an oasis, telling them that another group of searchers had stopped there recently. But just as Zanattar's searchers had been the first group to depart the Barahileth, they would be the first to return and confess the truth of their shameful failure. They were returning to Kannanatha Well by a route they had not yet taken, and they would have crossed into the Barahileth within the next fortnight, had Luranda not found the body.

Luranda was of the Adanate, of Bisochim's own tribe, though he had donned the Blue Robe and left their tents many years before she had been born, and she knew as little of him as anyone among them. Even so, she might have claimed pride of place in their company had she chosen to, for all knew that the Adanate were favored by the Wild Magic because of Bisochim, but she did not. Zanattar had never seen her claim praise for anything save her own skills, and he had already had cause to note her ability as a tracker. Now he had cause to admire it.

As was only prudent in the desert, they had set their tents as the sun climbed toward midheaven, for unless need was dire, no one traveled during the hottest part of the day. As the sun slanted westward, they struck the tents again, and packed up their camp, and proceeded southward once more as the shadows stretched long across the sand. In a few hours, when twilight came, they would pause again to hunt and to eat—fresh game if they had been fortunate, supplies from their stores if they had not. The Isvaieni followed the rhythms of the desert, and the desert did not wake to hunt and feed until evening cooled the air. But they had barely gotten underway when Luranda signaled a halt.

"Something," she said softly. "Something is there."

Zanattar and the others peered into the distance where she pointed, but none of them could see anything, only the softly rolling line of dunes. No tracks, not even circling birds. Yet they followed at a respectful distance when she tapped at her *shotor*'s shoulder to make it kneel, dismounted, and walked slowly up over the top of the dune. At the top she dropped to her knees and began to dig. The sand was as fine as the finest driest flour, and it spilled away from her hands, cascading down the far side of the dune with a dangerous hissing sound.

Zanattar and the others stood well back from the edge, for all the desertborn knew that such soft loose sand was a danger—a man might lose his balance at the top of a dune and fall, going to his death, buried and smothered by the shifting sand. But Luranda was careful, deft, and quick.

The first thing she uncovered was a sight familiar to all, though none of them had looked to see it here: the skeleton of a *shotor*. As she dug further, sand spilling away from her cautious clever fingers, more of the skeleton was revealed.

"It wears a saddle," Zanattar said in surprise.

"We all knew that the Sandwind had scoured the Isvai since we were borne away to safety," Luranda said quietly. "And—see? No other dune in this line is so high. I thought it might have built itself upon something."

Zanattar nodded, and knelt beside her to dig. Soon the others joined him. With the added help, the top of the dune was quickly dug away, and as it was, its terrible secret was exposed.

The skeletons of three *shotors,* their bones scoured in a fashion familiar to all who had ever faced the Sandwind's fury. The terrible desert wind did not stop with killing, but—did it go on long enough—could flense flesh from bones and leave them polished as cleanly as if they had lain in the desert for many seasons. The wooden remains of its saddle still clung to one of the *shotors,* and scraps of the light wooden pack-saddles lay tangled with the bones of the other two. And beneath the bodies of the *shotors,* their owner.

Kazat drew back with a cry when the figure was exposed, and Zanattar gripped the hilt of his *awardan* tightly. Luranda turned away, wrapping her sand-veil securely around her face, as if by doing so, she could unsee what she had seen.

The body beneath the *shotors* was as skeletal as they, but it had been sheltered enough so that some scraps of its clothing still clung to the scoured bones. Though faded by sun, they were still recognizably blue.

"So the False Balance claims its first victims," Zanattar said harshly.

"What are you saying?" Larazir asked slowly.

"You have lived between Sand and Star all your life, Larazir, as have I. When the Blue Robes come to us, it is to turn aside the Sandwind, not to die in it," Zanattar answered gruffly. A knowledge that had been growing in him ever since he had heard Bisochim speak was taking form upon his tongue at last. It was not enough to search for the Nalzindar. If they had not been found—if they had not heeded Bisochim's call to join him in sanctuary—surely they no longer existed at all. Or if they did, they had rejected their part in the Isvaieni's great birthright. They had become as Tainted as the city-dwellers and the people of the north. "You see before you, not the proof we did not need that Bisochim has spoken nothing but truth—as if any Wildmage could do otherwise—but proof that the war has begun. Our enemies have begun by reaching out to strip our defenders from us, those who would help us to protect the True Balance. Shall we now go crawling back to safety as if we were *ikulas* too timid to course prey and beg Bisochim to protect us as if we were not bold hunters, but children too young to tend goats?"

"How do we fight magic with *awardan* and spears, Zanattar?" Kazat asked.

"We do not." Zanattar spat onto the sand in contempt. "It is plain that magic seeks out magic—how else would it be that it has slain the Blue Robes, yet allowed us to move across the face of the Isvai this past fortnight untouched? I admit, I wondered at the absence of the Blue Robes from our camp in the Barahileth, but now I understand. They were slain as they rode to join us and unite their power with Bisochim's. Perhaps that which killed them would have slain us as well had we been here, but through Bisochim's foresight we were saved, and now it has obviously withdrawn itself once more to prepare its great armies for the final battle. And we must do all we can to aid him before that day comes."

"What is your plan?" Luranda asked. Her eyes burned with dark fire at the terrible crime she had uncovered. No one here doubted that having discovered one dead Wildmage proved that all were dead, for Zanattar was right in both the things he'd said to them: no Wildmage could be slain by an ordinary Sandwind, for their magic would easily protect them, and if the Wildmages of the Isvai had not been slain by unseen forces of greater power than they possessed, they would surely have joined the tribes in the great gathering in the depths of the Barahileth.

"The soft dwellers in the *Iteru*-cities have forgotten the lessons of the Isvai, if ever they knew them," Zanattar said. His teeth flashed white in his beard as he smiled a terrible smile. "The desert does not belong to them, but to us. We shall reclaim it, in Bisochim's name, and cleanse it in the name of the True Balance."

IT WAS THE work of only scant days to gather together several of the other roving bands of Isvaieni. They carried the bones of the dead Wildmage with them, so that all could see and know the truth. Once several of the bands of scouts had been gathered together, it became a simple thing to gather still more: they gathered at Sapthiruk Oasis and lit signal-fires at night. Such fires could be seen for miles across the desert, and all the roads that led through the Isvai crossed at Sapthiruk Oasis.

Kazat and Larazir went to Zanattar when he began his Ingathering, to ask him if word should be sent to Bisochim of this plan. Nor did Zanattar begrudge them their bold speaking, for it was only a coward or a fool who would not listen to all the voices in a council.

"You may go if you wish," he said to them, nodding. "And I will not hold any here who wish to ride with you. But I say this: surely a Wildmage who commands a dragon must know already of what we plan? The Wild Magic has always sent the Blue Robes where they are most needed by the Isvaieni, for they have the art of seeing and knowing at a distance. Yet has Bisochim come among us to turn us from this course? The Lanzanur were among the first to pledge to his cause, and we know his sight is long and that the fire in his heart is pure. Were we in need of his warning to turn us from an evil course, I know well he would come to us. And never would I wish to make you act against your own hearts' guidance, yet I say one thing more: those who worship at the shrine of the False Balance are many, and we, even in our numbers, are few."

Kazat and Larazir regarded each other silently, and Zanattar saw them take counsel of one another with their eyes. "Indeed, your words are wise," Kazat said at last, and Larazir said: "It is as you say. Surely Bisochim knows of this already, and every *awardan* will be needed in aid of this holy task."

Zanattar compelled no one to follow the course he was determined to follow himself, but all who had come to the Isvai upon the search for the Nalzindar were the young hunters of the tribe, men and women who had come seeking lost brethren or the enemy who had slain them. Now that they had discovered a greater enemy, and that the war that Bisochim had promised them all was already upon them, not one of them wished to turn aside from it, lest his or hers be the sword or the spear needed to claim the victory for the True Balance and avenge the death of the Blue Robes.

To hasten the ingathering, Zanattar sent out small swift parties to the other oases, bearing a simple message: *come*. If no one was there, it was easy enough to leave the message in desertsign, so that the next Isvaieni who saw it would see and heed.

First tens, then hundreds, of Isvaieni came to Sapthiruk to hear the words of Zanattar and Luranda, and to see the terrible relic, and when the band was already as large as the largest tribe, they began to march, knowing that others would find them as they rode, drawn by the sight of dozens of tents and cookfires in the night.

Their destination was Orinaisal'Iteru.

The String of Pearls formed a ragged crescent around the north and east of the Madiran, from Akazidas'Iteru, at the mouth of the Trade Road, to Orinaisal'Iteru, a city only by courtesy. Orinaisal'Iteru did not even have its own Consul, being governed from Ilukhan'Iteru, its nearest neighbor. But its *Iteru* was deep and pure, and it supplied the caravans that went into the deep desert to mine salt and *ishnain* and harvest desert plum and spicebark and oilbush.

At Orinaisal'Iteru, Zanattar simply stood outside the gate and demanded that they open them, and though he stood at the head of two thousand Isvaieni, they did. He cut the throats of both the men on the gate before they could question him, and so he never had the opportunity to ask them why they had been so foolish.

In his wake, his new army poured into the town. They slaughtered everything that lived: man, woman, and child.

The Isvaieni were no strangers to death, and the people of Orinaisal'Iteru were neither of their many tribes, nor even Isvaieni. What was far worse, they were people who were already tainted by the False Balance, in league with those who had murdered the Wildmages who had protected the Isvaieni for generations. If they had not already taken up weapons to attack the Isvaieni, that day would soon come, and for that reason, it was far better for them to die now before they could become a true threat. Only a fool let the scorpion's clutch hatch when he might grind the eggs underfoot.

The Isvaieni ran through the town on foot, for though the ancient story-songs spoke of battle-trained mounts who were as much warriors as their riders, the *shotors* of the Isvaieni were not such creatures. *Geschaks* and *awardan* ran red with the blood of those who had rejected the True Balance, and in the midst of the fray Zanattar saw Luranda, her eyes wild with rage, brandishing the severed head of an enemy.

When the slaughter was done, the Isvaieni searched what remained and took away anything that looked as if it might be useful. An army needed food and additional pack animals, and if the city-bred *shotors* were inferior to the desert-bred stock, they would serve.

When they had taken everything useful from Orinaisal'Iteru, there were two tasks remaining.

In the desert, water was a sacred thing. A man might meet his greatest enemy at an oasis, and he would not keep him from drinking, nor slay him within the bounds of the oasis. And though there was no charity given among the desertfolk, no gifts of shelter or food or clothing, water was freely given. Even to a stranger. Even to an enemy.

So when Zanattar proposed to destroy the *Iteru*—the deep desert well from which Orinaisal'Iteru took its name and its life—it was a matter all must discuss.

For three days the Isvaieni considered the matter. Zanattar did not hurry them. He simply went from tent to tent, speaking the truth that was in his heart: if the *iteru* remained, it would be as if the city were never destroyed, for when the armies came down from the north seeking to slay them all, they would find sweet water in abundance here at the edge of the Madiran—enough, perhaps, to allow them to enter the Isvai.

In the end, his counsel was followed. The army drank deep from the *iteru* of Orinaisal'Iteru, and then they levered the great cover-stone off the cistern and packed the well with rotting bodies. When that was done, they set fire to all that remained. Much of the city was cloth and dry wood. It burned well.

Ilukhan'Iteru was only five days' march away, but by the time they reached it, Zanattar's army had nearly doubled in size. So many Isvaieni left a clear trail, one that any of the desertborn could follow, and at Orinaisal'Iteru Zanattar had made certain to leave a clear record of his purpose in desertsign that any Isvaieni could read. He had no doubt that all who had sworn the blood-oath to consider all Isvaieni as one tribe united under Bisochim would see, and follow.

At the gates of Ilukhan'Iteru, the guards were more prudent. They saw thousands of Isvaieni gathered outside their gates, and would not open them. The master of their city came and ordered Zanattar's people to leave, and when they would not, ordered his men to loose arrows down upon them. But the guardsmen had to go and fetch their weapons, and so many minutes passed between the command and the moment when the guardsmen returned, that Zanattar, barely believing they could be so foolish, had sufficient time to order his army to retreat out of arrow-range—save for a few archers, who shot every guard on the wall dead as he appeared.

Then, when the wall was clear, the Isvaieni took oil and rags and fire, and shot flaming arrows over the walls into the city until they tired of the game.

And then they waited for night.

As they waited, they swept through the surrounding countryside. There were fat flocks set out to graze, and they slaughtered every single animal. Soon the luscious scent of roast meat wafted up into the city—along with the screams of the unfortunate herdsmen, though the screaming did not go on for long.

There were also orchards surrounding Ilukhan'Iteru. When the Isvaieni had finished their feasting, they stripped the trees of their fruit, then cut them all down, for on the march toward Ilukhan'Iteru, Zanattar had pondered the question of how he might gain entrance to the city if its rulers should prove wiser than those who had overseen Orinaisal'Iteru had been. He knew nothing of cities, but there were many in his army who had actually walked the streets of an *Iteru*-city, and so Zanattar knew that each of the *Iteru*-cities had four gates, and that the gates opened inward, and his own eyes told him that three of the gates were made of wood, and any fool knew that wood burned. Zanattar directed his army to pile the wood at three of the four gates leading into the city. It was quite safe for them to do so, as his archers shot anyone who appeared upon the walls.

When night fell, they set fire to the pyres they had built against the gates. Once the smell of the smoke reached the city-dwellers, men rushed to the walls again, but the Isvaieni had a great supply of arrows. No one was able to pour water down upon the pyres from above, nor to drop heavy stones upon the blaze to scatter the wood, nor succeed in doing any other thing to quench the burning. Soon, even over the sound of the blaze, Zanattar could hear the sound of the soft city-dwellers shouting and quarreling with each other, and he smiled.

On three sides of the city, his army stood visible in the light of the burning pyres. Some held torches, and others fired upon the guards upon the walls. On the fourth side, the side where the Great Gate stood, all was darkness and silence.

And soon enough, the great metal gates swung inward as people attempted to flee the city.

Then the warriors that Zanattar had concealed there when darkness fell, rushed upon those who fled, and slit their throats with sharp *geschaks,* and rushed into the city, howling a cry of victory.

It took them much longer to kill everyone here, for this city was much larger than the last, but in the end they were victorious. A few Isvaieni died in the fighting, but only a few. Despite which, Zanattar felt each death keenly.

This time, there was no dispute as to whether the *Iteru* should be poisoned. As soon as the killing was done, and their own water supply replenished, and each *shotor* had drunk its fill, it became a game to find the deadliest poisons with which to taint the water. They found a storehouse of *ishnain,* and slit bag after bag of the choking white powder, throwing it into the cistern below until the water turned white. Salt, too, so much that the *Iteru* would never run sweet again, and several sacks of dust that Baralda found in one of the shops and said was a metal-poison that his people traded: it turned the water blue as the *jashyna*-stone, or the sky at sunset.

Then they filled the well with bodies, and tore down the remains of the gates. This time Zanattar decreed that all that could be burned should be heaped around the walls before they set fire to the town, for the walls were high, and thick, and he did not know how else they might be brought down.

They stayed to watch the city burn, hoping for a sign from the Wild Magic that they were doing that which it asked of them. Zanattar hoped most of all, for in his heart, despite his brave words to Kazat and Larazir, he hoped for true guidance and certainty. He was the son of Kataduk, who had raised him to succeed her as the leader of the Lanzanur Isvaieni, but never had he thought to lead so many to do so much. Nor had he thought to ask such things of the people he led, for in ordinary times the leader of a tribe settled small disputes, set dowries, helped his people to keep the Balance, led them in matters of hunting and trade.

But these were not ordinary times, and now the Balance— the True Balance—had called Zanattar to lead a greater tribe than any he had ever imagined to keep a greater Balance than any he had ever suspected. And there was no storyteller or song-weaver beside him, no Wildmage to come out of the desert at the time of greatest need. Nor could he rely on the ancient desert custom that his enemy would stop with harsh words and blows and perhaps the raiding of flocks. No, this enemy sought his life-blood and that of all Isvaieni. And so, though he told himself that Bisochim would come to them if this course were not what the Wild Magic willed, now Isvaieni blood had been spilled, and Zanattar knew in his heart that he must seek a sign from the Wild Magic itself if he was to lead his people onward. And so he watched Ilukhan'Iteru as it burned, and waited.

And to his joy, and to that of all who followed him, they saw great cracks appear in the walls, and the section over the Great Gate collapsed entirely. It was not as glorious a sign as if the earth had opened and swallowed the city whole, but they were not children, who needed to be taken by the hand and shown wonders. It was a sign. It was enough.

They continued onward.

There were times when they must wait outside a city for a sennight and more before it fell to them, and times when the city's defenders rushed out at the first sight of them to do battle. The road between the *Iteru*-cities was a hard one, for the small traveler's wells had never been meant to provision an army in its thousands, and with each day that passed, more Isvaieni came to them from out of the desert, until all who had ridden out of Telinchechitl had joined them. Zanattar thought bleakly that did the fat city-dwellers know how exhausted and thirsty the army that stood outside their gates was, they would not be so afraid. Often, only sheer numbers saved the Isvaieni from destruction—Zanattar could not count the number of times he had yanked one of his exhausted brethren from the path of a killing blow.

They spent longer in each *Iteru*-city recovering after each battle, and did all that they could to find ways to carry sufficient water with them. And every one of them knew that there was no possible way that it could be done—not if there were ten pack-*shotors* for every Isvaieni here. And there were not.

Food was no difficulty. There was food in abundance in each *Iteru*-city that fell to them, theirs for the taking. And here in the Madiran, game was plentiful. It was water that they lacked. Water for their *shotors*. Water for themselves.

But never, no matter the cost to them, did they fail to destroy the *Iteru* at the heart of each city that they burned. Every Isvaieni believed the truth of what Zanattar had said: to destroy the wells from which the *Iteru*-cities drew their life was to destroy the ability of the enemy to rebuild the cities themselves.

Perhaps eight thousand Isvaieni had ridden out of the Barahileth to search for the Nalzindar. They were the future of the tribes, for all that remained behind were old men and women, and children too young to go. Of that number, something over six thousand remained when Zanattar approached the walls of Tarnatha'Iteru. Of the dead, some had fallen to enemy blades and arrows, some to weakness upon the march. The names of all would be remembered as heroes, valiant warriors in the first battles that the Isvaieni had fought against the Darkness that sought to claim them all.

The road north from Laganda'Iteru was harder than many before it, for the Wild Magic seemed to have turned its face from them from the moment they reached its gates.

The city was roused to its danger long before they drew near. They drummed and chanted as they always did, but never before had the city-dwellers seemed to be aware of their peril. Here the walls were ringed with torches immediately, and the arrows of the city-dwellers blackened the sky.

Zanattar's people could not shoot back—they had exhausted the last of their arrows sennights ago, and they could scavenge no replacements. The bows of the city-dwellers used a longer shaft; it would not fit the short desert bows of the Isvaieni. But by now his people well knew the distance an arrow fired by one of the City Guard could travel. They drew back and waited, as always, slaking their hunger on the city's flocks. This time they could not build pyres against the gates, for they could not approach the city walls in safety, and Zanattar would not spend the lives of hundreds of his people to set fires their enemies would quickly quench. Instead, they burned the trees where they stood, for the wind was with them, and the thick black smoke rolled over the city. And Zanattar waited, hoping for a sign that their great enemy had not turned his attention to the Madiran once more, hoping he had not led his people to their deaths out of carelessness and pride.

He nearly despaired, but at last he knew that the True Balance had not forsaken them, for in the depths of the night, the gates of the city opened—not one gate, but three, and Zanattar was not slow to take advantage of this gift, though it was a two-handed gift, giving and taking away in equal measure, for the people of the city fled into the night, and the Isvaieni dared not follow. Zanattar heard the fleeing hoofbeats, but his warriors were on foot—rushing toward the open gate before it should be closed again, before the guards should think to look outside the wall instead of in. Half his army, moving stealthily through the night, the other half to guard their tents and *shotors* against unforeseen attack—for to lose those was to lose all—and to pretend to any who watched that they were the whole of the Isvaieni army, waiting in plain sight.

But Zanattar's chosen Faithful took the gates. They held the gates, and ran up the stairs, and took the walls, and flung the men upon them to their deaths, and Zanattar and Luranda's men and women filled the city.

But this time, as they killed, the city burned around them, for those who had fled had set fires to cover their tracks, and the fires spread. The Isvaieni were forced from the city by the flames before their work was done. They killed everyone who tried to follow them, but when the work was done and the cost of the battle was reckoned, there was wailing and lamentation among the tents of the Isvaieni, for many who had entered the city in Bisochim's name did not come forth again.

It was three days before the fires died and the army could enter Laganda'Iteru again. When they did, the Isvaieni discovered that the mechanisms that could be used to draw water up out of the *Iteru* had been burned away. Zanattar searched for Luranda's body everywhere, but he did not find it. *Everything* had been burned away—what had been city was now charred waste—there were pieces of what had once been city-dweller houses, and piles of broken stone, and the air swirled with choking gray dust. They had saved the bodies of those that they had killed outside the walls to defile it, and were grateful now that they had, for within the city itself there were no bodies left with which to poison it. With the pumping mechanisms gone, it was the work of a full day to provide the army with even the bare minimum of water, and what they drew up tasted of charcoal and ash. In those long hours, Zanattar came to know that the Wild Magic had not turned its face from him—but he also knew that the face that the Isvai showed to her children was often unforgiving and merciless.

"We are being tested," he said when they left the city. His chosen *chaharums,* the trusted men and women who did all just as he would do it, carrying his words among the great army—for Zanattar himself could not be everywhere among so many—gathered around him. They would hear his words and pass them to the people, so that his words could be known by all. "As a father tests a son, or a master hunter tests one who comes to him for teaching. To cleanse this city has been hard. We have all lost friends and comrades. I say to you: our road shall become harder yet. I will think badly of no Isvaieni who wishes to return to Bisochim now. You have all won many victories. He will welcome you. Give me no answer now, but carry my words to all the people."

The *chaharums* did as Zanattar had bid them, and he waited a full day and a night, and not one of the Isvaieni chose to leave.

WHEN THEY REACHED the gates of Tarnatha'Iteru, Zanattar knew he had been right to fear the Wild Magic's harsh testing. They approached by night, and in stealth, but guard-dogs alerted the city, and warning-beacons were lit, and the wall was ringed with torches. His people were weary with the long journey here, and there had been little food and less water on the long days of the journey. They must take the city, and take it soon, if they were to survive.

It was for this reason that when the two children—bold and unafraid—rode out to face his army, Zanattar did not slay them immediately. Such foolishness, such madness, must be another sign, and he wished to interpret it before he acted.

One boy had hair the color of a newborn *shotor*'s coat, and eyes the color of the desert sky. The other had hair the color of embers, and he bore twin swords upon his back, and gazed at Zanattar as if he wished him to die. Yet it was the sky-eyed one who spoke, offering bold words of question and challenge, and Zanattar answered him fairly, even though he said—plainly—that he served the False Balance.

Zanattar wondered if this—*this*—was what all the tests and ordeals he and his people had been sent by the Wild Magic had been for. If, perhaps, Zanattar had been given the power through his passion and his sacrifice to convince those who followed the False Balance to turn from their error. For surely, if he could turn strangers from Armethalieh Itself to the way of the True Balance, then perhaps it would be time to follow a new way, a way of words and persuasion? He spoke long and carefully, bringing forth all the words he had kept in his heart, all the words he had heard Bisochim say, all the words he knew to be true and good.

And the child rejected them all.

Zanattar knew, then, that they must be the first to die, as a sign to all who remained within the city. Perhaps this was why they had been sent forth: so that the people of Tarnatha'Iteru, seeing them die, would allow their own deaths to be quick. He reached for his *awardan*—

—and a sudden wall of light, bright and shocking, appeared between him and the children. He shouted in surprise at the unnatural thing, and his *shotor* bawled in terror, and all around him, the people were cast into confusion and terror.

By the time he could force his beast to kneel and return to the purple light, the city was gone. All that remained was the light, covering it like a great upturned bowl. He drew his *awardan* and struck it, but the steel only rang off the light, as if he had struck stone. And then Zanattar knew the true reason why they had been tested so long and so hard, given so many chances to turn aside from their path. Their great enemy had already returned to the Madiran. He had come in the form of children—did not all the ancient story-songs teach that the Endarkened could take on many forms that were fair and pleasing?

The story-songs also taught that the power of Darkness was weak at first, requiring allies and sacrifices. They must have come seeking both. But if his people were strong enough, and strong in their devotion to the Wild Magic, they could yet prevail. And victory would be won for the True Balance here.

Fourteen

City Under Siege

HARRIER AND TIERCEL rode back to the Main Gate. The wall of MageShield was closer here than it was between the south wall of the city and the Isvaieni army, forming a corridor about twenty yards wide. Their horses kept shying, both from the sight of their own shadows on the city wall, and then from the glowing wall of MageShield. While the shape of the shield was firm and immobile, and it wasn't at all warm, the light of its surface rippled and shifted like flames, and the horses didn't like that at all.

After a few minutes, the noise began.

It had never really been quiet, because the city had been filled with shouting even when they left. But now everyone in the city had seen the sky turn bright glowing purple—even if they couldn't see the fact that the city was surrounded by walls of purple fire—and it sounded as if there were riots going on in the city. Harrier only hoped the Militia was actually being of some use and keeping order, because if they weren't, people were going to be killing each other soon.

It wasn't just the city making noise now, either. The refugees from Laganda'Iteru had all said that the Isvaieni army had approached their walls making a lot of noise. They'd approached Tarnatha'Iteru in silence, but they weren't silent now. They were shouting, and it sounded like chanting, and there were a lot of them. Too many to make out anything like words—it just sounded like the worst kind of winter storm back home—wind and rain and the ocean beating against the docks. Every once in a while Harrier would glance up at the top of the wall. Guardsmen stood all along the top, looking down at them, but they were all wearing their helmets, and Harrier couldn't see any of their expressions.

It seemed as if something like their return to the city ought to take place in eerie and utter silence, but it didn't. There was so much noise he could barely hear himself think. He couldn't tell what was coming from within the city, and what was coming from outside of it, and all that noise wasn't making the horses any calmer, either. The ride back to the Main Gate seemed like the longest journey he thought he'd ever taken, and even if the inside of the city was probably just about as bad as the middle of the Isvaieni army right now, Harrier couldn't wait to get inside, and, looking at Tiercel, he was pretty sure he felt the same way. When they got to the Main Gate, Harrier shouted up to Batho to open them up and let them in.

And Batho refused.

"Who are you?" he shouted down. He had to shout, because between the noise from the city behind him and the noise from the Isvaieni army outside of it, it was rapidly becoming impossible to hear yourself think.

Harrier swore and vaulted down off his horse. The animal promptly galloped off, but there wasn't much of any place for it to go. It didn't seem to care, though—it galloped off around the corner of the city and vanished from view.

"We're the same people who left an hour ago! And now you've got a spell-shield around your city that the army can't get through! And you ought to be happy about it!"

Batho withdrew from sight without answering.

Harrier went over to Tiercel's horse. It was jerking its head skyward fretfully, but he grabbed its reins and held it steady long enough for Tiercel to dismount. As soon as he had, it trotted off after the other one, kicking up its heels as it went.

"I think he'd like it better if he knew why the shield was there," Tiercel said quietly.

Harrier looked up at the wall. No one was in sight. "Hard to explain that to a wall," he said.

As they stood there, the sky began to lighten. It was only possible to tell because the MageShield seemed to change color and intensity as the light outside it grew. Every few minutes, someone would glance over the edge of the wall to see if they were still there, then withdraw.

"Where do they think we're going to go?" Harrier muttered. Tiercel only sighed.

Harrier was starting to wonder what they were going to do. They didn't have any shelter—MageShield wouldn't protect them from the sun—and the watering-troughs for the flocks, though outside the city and inside the shield, were fed from the city wells. Water had to be pumped into them by hand. He wasn't sure that anyone within the city would do that for them. And if Tiercel *did* drop the shield so they could go off in search of one of the other springs, well . . . he didn't think they'd reach it before the Isvaieni reached *them.* "I don't suppose you'd consider calling Ancaladar *now?*" Harrier asked in long-suffering tones.

Just then there was movement on the top of the wall once again. Harrier looked up. "Light defend us," he said softly. Batho was back, and standing with him was the Telchi, Consul Aldarnas, and someone Harrier recognized after a few moments' study as the Chief Light-Priest of the Main Temple, Preceptor Larimac.

"Do you swear by the Light that you mean us no harm?" Batho shouted down.

"Oh, for the love of—Batho, if Tiercel hadn't cast that spell, this damned city would be *on fire* right now and you know it!" Harrier bellowed back.

"We mean you no harm!" Tiercel called up. "I swear it by the Light!"

There was another long pause. The party on the top of the wall retreated.

"Do you really think *yelling* at them is going to do any good?" Tiercel demanded.

"Oh, sorry. I'm afraid I was thinking about how much fun it would be to *die* here outside the gates because they wouldn't let us come back inside after you'd saved their city."

"Look, if you'd just let me—"

"Shut up," Harrier said, because he'd heard the sound of the bars of the gates being lifted. A moment later they began to swing inward. And a moment after that, people began to emerge from the city.

First came a dozen Guardsmen, all fully armored, all with swords drawn. Next came Consul Aldarnas, surrounded by members of his personal guard, with a couple of nobles and the Telchi in attendance. Next came Preceptor Larimac and four sub-Preceptors, followed by another dozen Guardsmen. ("I wonder if there's anyone left guarding the city?" Harrier muttered.) The Telchi must have spoken for them; it had to be why he was here, because there was no other reason for him to be in the Consul's party.

Consul Aldarnas was a robust man old enough to have grown children. They and their families—along with his wife—had been quietly sent north sennights ago, while he had stayed behind to keep order in his city. Now he pushed forward through the mass of guards and advisors that surrounded him (none of them really wanted to get too close to the wall of MageShield except the Telchi) and walked forward until he came to a stop in front of Tiercel and Harrier.

"You are the one who has cast this spell?" he asked Tiercel.

"Yes, sir," Tiercel answered.

"I have known many Blue Robes—you have always been welcome in my city and at my court—yet never have I known you to have such spells in your keeping," the Consul said.

Tiercel glanced toward him, and Harrier knew that he ought to speak up, and say that *he* was the Wildmage, not Tiercel. But he remembered what the Telchi had said before, and didn't. For all they knew, Tiercel was about to be arrested. And even if he wasn't, there were a lot of other people here, and any one of them might take it into their heads to blame one or the other of them—or both of them—for that army out there. He needed to be free in order to rescue Tiercel. If Tiercel needed to be rescued.

"I'm not a Wildmage," Tiercel answered. "Once, a long time ago, there was another kind of magic, called High Magick, that those born with something called the Magegift can learn. When I discovered I'd been born with the Magegift, I studied the ancient spellbooks. There are many books about the High Magick in the Great Library at Armethalieh."

Harrier was impressed. Nothing Tiercel had said was a lie, but the statements, taken together, provided a very different picture of things than the actual truth.

"Why have you come here?" the Consul demanded bluntly.

"The magic sent me visions of danger," Tiercel answered simply. "I needed to know where they came from. You know, I imagine, that I have been asking if anyone in the city knows of a Lake of Fire anywhere in the desert. My vision has shown me this place. But I don't know where it is."

The Consul's mouth tightened; whether it was in rueful acceptance of Tiercel's honesty, or in irritation at the situation, Harrier wasn't quite sure. "You're only a boy," he said. "If you were having visions of danger, surely there was someone you could have told? Your parents?"

"It took me a long time to learn my spells," Tiercel said quietly. "Until I did, I couldn't prove anything to anyone. Even afterward—all I could prove was that I could do magic. I couldn't prove there was any danger. I can't even prove it now. I think the Lake of Fire is somewhere in the desert. I think that whatever's there, it's convinced the Isvaieni to band together to attack you. The spell I've cast around your city is called MageShield. I'll hold it in place as long as I can."

If it had been up to Harrier, he would have left out the part about Tiercel needing to hold the shield in place and possibly not being able to do it forever, but it must have been the right thing to say, because the Consul nodded. "If you and your friend will swear before the priest that you mean no harm, you may come back into the city," he said.

It was oddly disturbing to be called upon to do something like that. Everyone knew that an oath was sacred, and an oath sworn before a Light-Priest was doubly so, but except in the cases of Nobles who married (since a marriage between Nobles could not be set aside once it was made, and so a Noble-class marriage was an oathbound matter) a person might go his or her entire life without making such an oath. Certainly Harrier had never expected to take one, unless he became the next Portmaster and married the sea just as Da had done.

But it had to be done, so both Tiercel and Harrier put their hands over the Light-Priest's and swore an oath in the name of the Eternal Light—and in the names of the Blessed Saint Idalia and Kellen the Poor Orphan Boy (which Harrier found more than a little disturbing, knowing that he'd now met Idalia *in person*) that they meant no harm to anyone within the city walls. It was only the truth. And after that, the Consul was satisfied, or at least satisfied enough that they were beckoned to his side.

"I feared, watching, that I would need to seek out a new apprentice," the Telchi said quietly.

"I'd been thinking the same thing," Harrier answered somberly.

Now that the oath had been sworn, the party marched back into the city once more. It was too much to hope for that the three of them would be allowed to simply go home after that, and they weren't.

The plaza outside the entrance to the gate was weirdly empty—guardsmen stood blocking off every entrance to it, and the ends of most of the streets were blocked off even further with makeshift barricades of carts and rubble, though people crowded the streets beyond—and they tramped across it until they came to the entrance to the

Consul's Palace. The colonnade of pale stone glowed weirdly in the combination of dawn light and MageShield, as if the stones were lit from within.

At the steps, Harrier abandoned his last hope that Tiercel would simply be thanked and dismissed. The Consul gestured, obviously expecting all three of them to follow him up the broad steps. Since they still had half-a-dozen soldiers behind them, there was little doubt that they would.

Harrier had never been inside the Consul's Palace. Tiercel had been here several times, since a number of the maps and records he'd consulted in the past sennights were located here, but Harrier had never gone. He'd gotten the impression, though, from everything that Tiercel'd said, that the place was kind of . . . spacious.

If it was, there was no way to tell right now, because it was as jammed full of people as the main marketplace at the height of selling time. Every noble and rich merchant in the entire city—and probably every member of their families, and most of their servants—were here, jammed into the outer courts of the Palace, and all of them were talking at once. The Consul's personal guard shoved through them ruthlessly—Harrier had to admire their efficiency, even while something inside him cringed every time someone went sprawling because of a too-enthusiastic shove. Their methods worked, though. Soon enough the Consul's party had worked its way through several sets of rooms—each set less crowded than the last, though there were people in all of them—until finally they were in rooms that were—nearly—empty.

At least they were empty of *people*. They were furnished with a degree of opulence that would have made Harrier blink if he hadn't been a guest in an Elven household where the plates laid out on the table for dinner each evening were probably worth more than the contents of this entire palace.

"I thought you would be more comfortable here," the Consul said, turning to them.

Than in our own home? Harrier wondered. *Yeah, right.*

"Are we prisoners?" Tiercel asked, looking around. A footman stood quietly just inside the door. The Consul's personal guard waited outside in the corridor. The Light-Priest and his retinue—and the City Guards—had left them at the last set of rooms. It was just them now—Tiercel and the Telchi and Consul Aldarnas and him—and it should have been reassuring, but somehow, Harrier had felt less nervous when there'd been more guards.

"Could I hold you prisoner if you did not wish to be held?" the Consul asked.

"No," Tiercel answered simply. "Please believe me. I only want to help."

"Of course," the Consul said, and Harrier felt faintly uneasy. "But I must ask you, with this great power that you possess, why did you not come forward sooner? Why conceal yourself among my citizens?"

He did not even glance toward the Telchi, but Harrier knew that Consul Aldarnas was perfectly aware that the Telchi had brought them to Tarnatha'Iteru and sheltered them and he probably suspected that the Telchi knew far more than he'd told.

"What difference would it have made?" Tiercel answered. "Either you'd think I was crazy, or—maybe—you'd think I was the reason the army was coming here in the first place. Which doesn't make much sense if they've been destroying cities for at least four moonturns and I only got here a moonturn and a half ago."

"If you aren't allied with them, how do you know how long they've been attacking the *Iteru*-cities for?" the Consul asked.

"Because they're Isvaieni," Harrier said, taking half a step forward. "And when we arrived, people were saying that nobody had seen any Isvaieni since Snows—if not longer."

The Consul turned and looked at him, and Harrier saw in his eyes the knowledge that Harrier wasn't telling everything he knew. He had a sudden mad impulse to confess, to tell the Consul that no, he wasn't a High Mage, but he *was* a Wildmage. A moment later he realized with a feeling almost of panic that his Three Books were back at the Telchi's, and he probably wasn't going to be able to go and get them, or even send the Telchi to get them, because the Telchi was certainly under as much suspicion now as he and Tiercel were, and there was no one else he could possibly send. But he kept silent with an effort, and after a moment, the Consul merely nodded.

"The city is . . . unsettled," he said. "I shall tell my people there is nothing to fear, and that the light they see in the sky will defend them." He paused, regarding Tiercel. "It is said that the High Mages of old had many other spells at their command. Is there more you can do to save this city?"

Tiercel hesitated for a long moment. "I know what you're thinking," he said finally. "I've read those stories too. The old High Mages slew the Endarkened, and called down lightning out of the sky. Those aren't spells I know. I'm sorry. If I did know them, I might be able to use them. I'll try to think of something that will help."

"I hope—for all our sakes—that you can," the Consul said. He nodded to both of them, and walked from the room.

Tiercel looked at the Telchi. "You could . . ." he began, and the Telchi smiled. "Yeah, I guess not," Tiercel said, sighing. "Wait outside," he said to the footman. The servant bowed and withdrew, and Tiercel walked over and closed the door.

The Telchi was in motion, walking through the inner rooms, opening the shutters and peering out, closing them again. "We are alone," he announced, returning.

Harrier sat down on the nearest chair, feeling suddenly exhausted. "Are you all right?" he asked, looking at Tiercel.

Tiercel shrugged, sitting down as well. "Sure. It isn't hard to hold the spell, not with Ancaladar's power to draw on. I just have to be . . . awake." His voice flattened on the last word, and Harrier glanced at the Telchi. The man's face was grim, and Harrier knew they were both thinking the same thing: that Tiercel had bought the city a little time, but not very much.

"I do not think this spell will drive them off," the Telchi said quietly.

"Not since they seem to think we're the Darkspawn," Tiercel said in frustration. "I don't know where they could have gotten such a stupid idea."

"From the Endarkened, where else?" Harrier said irritably. He didn't want to be angry at Tiercel, but he didn't think he'd ever been so frightened in his life—not even when they'd been facing the Goblins and he'd been certain he was going to die within the next few minutes. "Think about it, Tyr. You don't even have to subvert them if you can just convince them that the people you want them to destroy are evil. They'll go out and do it thinking they're doing good."

Tiercel laughed raggedly. "Oh, that's just great! Even if I *did* know how to call down lightning—which, fortunately, I don't—how could I possibly use it against a bunch of innocent people?"

"The inhabitants of Kabipha'Iteru and Laganda'Iteru would perhaps disagree with you as to the innocence of this army," the Telchi said. "Were any of them still alive. And if this army is not stopped, the people of Tarnatha'Iteru will join their fellows in death. And so will we."

Tiercel looked from one to the other of them, wild-eyed. "What do you want me to do?" he asked desperately. "What do you want me to *do*?"

"We will think, together, calmly, of what you may do," the Telchi said. "And then we will plan."

But as it turned out, there wasn't a very great deal that Tiercel *could* do in defense of the city beyond what he was doing now. Ancaladar and Tiercel had been working—very hard—at the High Magick ever since they had Bonded. And nearly all of their work had been on shields.

"And wards," Tiercel said, with the air of one who knew it wasn't very helpful. "Which means if we were to be attacked by a High Mage, an Elven Mage, or certain sorts of Otherfolk, I'd be all set."

"And why was he having you learn something that . . . useless?" Harrier demanded.

"Because the Endarkened are classified as Otherfolk, Har," Tiercel said, sounding defeated. "He was teaching me to protect myself against the Endarkened."

"Do not apologize for being prepared to do battle, even if you are not prepared for the battle that has been offered," the Telchi said.

"Well, you weren't just casting a bunch of wards and shields at Blackrowan Farm," Harrier said.

"Transmutation," Tiercel said. He smiled painfully. "If we were the attacking army, that would actually be useful. I could turn the walls to water. As it is, no."

"Can this spell be used on living flesh?" the Telchi asked.

"No!" Tiercel said in horror. Then: "No," more quietly. "It can't. And even if it could . . . it would kill them."

"Sometimes some must die so that others may live," the Telchi said.

"You aren't talking about 'some,'" Harrier said grimly. "Unless they're all killed, whichever ones aren't dead will just go on with their attack. So you're talking about killing almost five thousand people."

"There are nearly that number within this city," the Telchi said remorselessly. "It seems a choice must be made."

"Not by me," Tiercel said. He got to his feet and strode away.

Harrier wasn't sure what to do, not really. He'd hoped, when he'd first heard the word "army," that it would be, well, *smaller*—if there was one thing he'd learned growing up on the docks of Armethalieh, it was how much a tale grew in the telling. He'd hoped, too, that no matter what size this army was, it would be something that Tiercel could frighten away. Because that had been a *good* plan: to convince the enemy that Tarnatha'Iteru was a place that just wasn't worth their trouble.

But now that he'd seen the army and listened to Zanattar, he just didn't think that it was going to work. And it wasn't . . . fair . . . that Tiercel should have to make decisions like this (because the final decision was Tiercel's, Harrier knew; nobody could force him to cast a spell). The trouble was both Tiercel and the Telchi were right. In one sense, it didn't matter how many people the Isvaieni outside the gates had killed. They'd been tricked into doing it, so killing them just because you could was wrong. They deserved a trial, a sentence, the same protection of law that anyone else living in the lands ruled by the High Magistrate got. And in another sense, if they *weren't* killed immediately, by anyone who could (and the only one who might be able to was Tiercel, Harrier knew that perfectly well), they'd kill everyone in Tarnatha'Iteru as soon as they could. And they weren't going to just go away.

"I'm hungry," he said, because he realized he was. It might be ridiculous to think about breakfast at a time like this, but he'd already been up for hours, and his stomach didn't care whether there was an army outside the city or not.

"I do not think the Consul means to starve us," the Telchi said. "I shall go and see what may be arranged."

When the Telchi was gone, Harrier went and found Tiercel. He was in one of the inner rooms, staring out the window through the closed lattice. The room was set up for sleeping; the coverlet on the single low bed was heavy silk—the most expensive sort there was, the kind that shifted between colors depending on how the light hit it. Most silk of this kind only showed one other color: this silk showed three—there were gold and blue and even pink highlights in the green, and it was another slightly-unwelcome reminder of how rich and powerful the man was who currently had them as so-called guests beneath his roof.

"Hey," Harrier said, sitting down on the bed. His clothes

were dusty and smelled of horse, and he realized it didn't really matter if he ruined the expensive silk or not. One way or another, nobody was going to care.

"What?" Tiercel said sullenly.

"Breakfast's coming," Harrier said. "And . . . I figured you were going to explain to me, oh, why you didn't want to call up Ancaladar to chase those guys off."

"It wouldn't work," Tiercel said, flopping into a chair. It creaked alarmingly, but he didn't even wince.

"You could try."

"If MageShield didn't scare them off, what in the name of the Light *will*? They might scatter for a day or so, but they'll regroup and come back. And they have javelins. I've read about the Isvaieni. In the desert, they hunt using spears and arrows and a kind of heavy curved sword called an *awardan*. They throw their spears."

"Ancaladar has scales."

"He has wings, too. And if he flies low enough to scare them at all, he flies within javelin range. If his wings are badly damaged enough, he can't fly."

"So—really—you're saying there's pretty much no point because he wouldn't really scare them anyway," Harrier said. Tiercel flashed him a grateful smile, then turned back to the window.

"Tyr," Harrier said, hating himself. "The Telchi won't think of it because he wasn't there—at Windy Meadows—but . . . you could cast Fire." He knew Tiercel didn't want to think of it. He didn't want to think of it either. But the words had to be said.

"No," Tiercel said.

"*Tyr—*" Harrier said desperately.

Tiercel turned away from the window again. "They won't leave! You know they won't! And you said it yourself—unless they're all *dead,* the survivors will attack the city! I'd have to set five thousand people on fire," he finished quietly. "I can't. I'm sorry." He gazed at Harrier, and his expression was suddenly more bitter and angry than Harrier had ever seen. "Could you?"

"Me?" Harrier asked in shock.

Tiercel smiled coldly. "Fire. The first spell. The simplest spell. Of the High Magick and the Wild Magic both. If I can set the Isvaieni army on fire, Har, so can you. You're already pretty good at Fire. Still, you might need to practice for a day or two, on little things. Stray dogs, maybe, or horses—"

"Stop it."

"Why? Easy enough for you to ask me to do. Do you think they wouldn't scream as they died? The Goblins did."

"They killed Simera!"

"*I know! I* know," Tiercel said again, more quietly. "If I could have—if I'd thought, if I'd known—I would have killed them sooner. But I can't stop hearing their screams." He turned away, back to the window, and Harrier saw him bring his hands up to rub his eyes.

Tiercel would have killed the Goblins. If Harrier had possessed the Three Books—and the power—back at Windy Meadows, he would have done it too. But this was different. This was five thousand *people,* and Tiercel was right. They'd been tricked into doing this.

And Tiercel was wrong. Harrier could no more cast Fire as a spell to burn several thousand people to death—people who were not Tainted—than he could run through the streets of Tarnatha'Iteru and slit throats with his swords. He thought of his disastrous attempt at Scrying, of the vision he'd refused to confide to Tiercel or to anyone else.

The day was bright and the sky was clear, and he stood on a plain, in the midst of a lake, not a lake of fire, but a lake of water, and a quiet sad voice—it came from outside, but somehow it was his—spoke, saying: "This is Tarnatha'Iteru. This is all that remains," and he didn't know if Tiercel was alive, if he was alive, what had happened to the people who lived there, or to the army that was coming to attack them (then), or even when *he was seeing. And he'd done the spell three times, and he'd never seen anything different.*

"We'll think of something else," Harrier said. "Maybe

there's something in one of your High Magick books. Something you haven't studied yet."

"Maybe," Tiercel said wearily.

WHEN THE TELCHI returned with servants bearing trays of food, both boys were grateful for his arrival. Their own company didn't seem to be leading to much of anything but fighting right now, and Harrier didn't really want to fight with Tiercel.

The Telchi had brought a large pot of *kaffeyah* along with the meal, and insisted that Tiercel drink several cups. He said it was known in the south to be a strong stimulant which promoted wakefulness and alertness, and that Tiercel would need both in the coming days.

Harrier picked up a *naranje* from the tray and tossed it into the air. "Haven't seen one of these in a while," he said, catching it and starting to peel it. *Naranjes* and most other delicacies had vanished from the marketplace at the first hint of danger, vanishing into a network of secret— outrageously priced—transactions.

"It is perhaps one of the advantages of being the Consul," the Telchi said blandly.

"I hope there are others," Harrier said. "Tiercel needs his books. All of them."

"I don't—" Tiercel began.

"You want to look for something that will *work*," Harrier said. "For all you know, there's some spell in there that will just convince them all to pack up and *leave*. You'd feel pretty dumb if you didn't look for it, right?"

"I guess I would," Tiercel said reluctantly.

THEY COULD OPEN the shutters on the windows, but there wasn't much to see. From the bedrooms, all they could see was a private garden thirty feet below. There was no balcony, and no way to climb down the wall, and even if they had, there was no gate leading out of the garden that either

of them could see. And where could they go if they got
out? Tiercel had sealed the city, and they were inside the
shield. From the windows in the sitting room, they could
see out toward the city wall, though it was some distance
away. They were almost level with the top of it—only a few
feet below it—and they could see the guards patrolling
along its top. If they looked straight down, they could
see a sort of back-courtyard, a private space between the
palace and the wall. Because (Harrier supposed) it was
private and protected, it was where the Nobles went to get
some fresh air. Not that there was really any actual fresh
air in the city right now. Everything was sealed beneath
the MageShield.

Harrier was getting very tired of purple.

IT WAS LATE in the day before Tiercel's books arrived, and
by then both boys had become very tired of their suite of
rooms. Its lavishness didn't impress either of them, there
was no point in bathing when neither of them had clean
clothes, and they couldn't leave. There were guards on the
door—very polite, but guards nonetheless.

When the men came bringing what they said were Tiercel's books, Harrier expected to see one or two men carrying parcels. Instead, two dozen palace servants, and a dozen
City Guards, and several attendants, came bustling in. The
servants were carrying six enormous brass-bound leather
chests on poles—from their size and weight, they must
have brought, not just Tiercel's books, but *everything*: the
entire contents of their room.

Accompanying the procession of chests and servants
and guards—an additional surprise, though they were both
amazed already by the arrival of their luggage—was Preceptor Larimac. He had two men with him that he introduced as Sub-Preceptor Daspuc and Sub-Preceptor Rial.
Both young men looked nervous.

"I thought perhaps they could assist you in your work,"
Larimac said.

"Ah," Tiercel said. "No."

Larimac raised his well-manicured brows. "They are very well schooled, young man."

"They are not High Mages," Tiercel answered, sounding faintly irritable. "Or if they are, sir, I'll be very surprised. And if you please, the proper form of address is 'my lord.' My father is Lord Rolfort of Armethalieh; I am his eldest son."

Harrier stared fixedly at the carpet so that nobody there would see his shock. Tiercel never used his title. *Never.*

Of course Harrier knew that Tiercel was really "Lord Tiercel" just as he knew that Tiercel's parents were Lord and Lady Rolfort, but Tiercel never used his title. Nobody was allowed to use their titles in school of course (even if they had any), but Tiercel thought it was foolish to use his at all; it wasn't as if the Rolforts were anything but the most minor nobility.

"I beg your pardon, Lord Tiercel," Preceptor Larimac said stiffly. "I had not been informed."

Tiercel shook his head. It wasn't quite an apology, Harrier knew. "I've been traveling anonymously," Tiercel said. "But the time for anonymity is past. I don't object to your people staying, if that's what you want. But the High Magick is something that takes a long time to learn, and one must be born with the ability. If they had been, you'd already know."

"I see," Larimac said, and Harrier was grateful that he didn't ask Tiercel what the signs were that someone was born with the Magegift. The two of them were both fairly sure by now that without the intervention of the Wildmage who had tended Tiercel as a child, the appearance of his Magegift last year would have simply killed him.

He glanced at Daspuc and Rial, and if they'd looked nervous before, they looked practically terrified now. "Perhaps they can be of some use to you nonetheless," Larimac said.

"They can certainly help me unpack, if they're willing

to do that," Tiercel said, relenting. "I'm not really sure where I'm going to put all of this."

Preceptor Larimac looked faintly surprised. "You have but to ask for anything you need," he said. He bowed, and withdrew. The guards left, and all of the servants who'd brought the chests left as well, taking the carry-poles with them. Harrier supposed that if they actually got the chests emptied, they could call the servants all back, and they'd bring their poles and take the chests away again.

"The first thing you should ask for is a bookcase," he told Tiercel, flipping the catch up on the nearest chest and lifting the lid. "Hey, they brought our clothes."

"I wonder where the Telchi is?" Tiercel said.

The Telchi had gone to the door about half an hour after they'd finished eating. The guards had let him leave, and when they had, Harrier had suspected that they'd let *him* leave as well—he was, after all, a member of the City Militia. But he wasn't about to leave Tiercel alone here.

"He sees to the defense of the city, Lord Tiercel," Rial said, swallowing hard. He glanced at Harrier, obviously wondering if Harrier was "Lord" anything, and Harrier had no intention of telling him that he was. He had no intention of telling him he was the son of the Harbormaster of Armethalieh, either, although it wouldn't really make much difference one way or the other. If the information that Tiercel Rolfort, son of Lord Rolfort, was in Tarnatha'Iteru got back to Armethalieh, the Gillains would be pretty sure their son was there, too.

"Is it very bad out there?" Tiercel asked.

"Consul Aldarnas has announced that the light in the sky defends us from our attackers," Rial said. "He has said that it is a spell of the Wild Magic, cast in secret by Wildmages who have come to defend our city."

"But that isn't true!" Tiercel said, aghast.

"What else could he say?" Harrier asked patiently, after he'd thought about it for a moment. "I'm pretty sure the mob in the streets aren't in the mood for long explanations. And at least they've *heard* of Wildmages."

"But . . . ?" Daspuc said, looking from one of them to the other in confusion.

"It was my spell," Tiercel said. "I'm not a Wildmage. I'm a High Mage, like—like they had a long time ago."

"But you will defend us?" Daspuc asked.

"I'll try," Tiercel said grimly.

AS THEY UNPACKED—and Harrier realized that whoever had gone to the Telchi's house to get Tiercel's things had simply brought every single item that wasn't obviously a piece of furniture—he began to worry. What was he going to do if Daspuc or Rial pulled out the Three Books? Everyone here knew what Wildmages were—either of them would be sure to recognize them immediately. And Tiercel had already said *he* wasn't a Wildmage. He wasn't sure what he could do about it, though.

"Lord Tiercel, what do I do with the blank notebooks that were in this bag?"

Harrier's head whipped around. Rial was holding up his traveling bag, and had obviously felt the need to dig through it. Harrier didn't know what Rial'd done with the packets of herbs—possibly thrown them out; they'd had to call for a container into which to toss items that never should have been packed at all—and the little brazier that had been in the traveling bag was sitting on top of one of the empty chests. Harrier restrained himself from slapping the books out of Rial's hands with an effort. *The man is a Preceptor of the Light, you idiot—when did you ever start thinking it was a good idea to* hit *Preceptors of the Light?*

But all Tiercel said was, "Here. I'll take them." Rial passed them to him without comment, and only after Tiercel had set them safely out of the way, did Harrier's brain catch up to his ears.

"Blank notebooks." Rial had called them *"blank notebooks."*

He hadn't seen anything out of the ordinary at all.

* * *

THEY WOULD ALL have been finished sooner if Tiercel hadn't insisted on organizing everything as they went and making friendly conversation. By the time the chests were empty the two of them knew that Rial and Daspuc were only a few years older than they were, that Daspuc's family had left the city when the first warning had come—though Daspuc had remained to serve the Temple—and that Rial's family was all still here.

"It is not so bad, Tiercel," he said (Tiercel had insisted that there was no need to use his title except when Preceptor Larimac was around). "The Temple has been allowed to keep special stores of food, and we are allowed to supply our families even though they draw rations in the Marketplace as well. So they have not suffered."

Except that they might be going to die, Harrier thought, and didn't say.

"Do you need *all* these books to cast your spells?" Daspuc asked curiously.

Tiercel laughed, not happily. "Ten times this number, if I could have carried them with me. And not to cast them. Just to learn them. Look at them if you like. I don't know all the spells written down here. Some I haven't learned yet. Some I can't learn—they take many High Mages to cast, or years of study. Or equipment I don't have."

"It seems very complicated," Rial said hesitantly. "I think the Wild Magic might be simpler."

"It probably is," Tiercel said.

WHEN THEY WERE finished, Rial went to the door to call for the servants to take away the empty chests, and Harrier began taking armloads of clothing into two of the bedrooms. As soon as he could do it without attracting any particular attention, Harrier picked up the three "blank notebooks" and slipped away. Tiercel was getting along just fine with the two Sub-Preceptors (Harrier thought that at least Daspuc had been sent to spy on them, though he wasn't really sure what Larimac thought he'd learn), and Harrier, well . . .

He hated to admit that anyone else was ever right. And he especially hated to admit that Tiercel was right. Not because Tiercel never was (because he was a lot of the time) but because—back in the old days, in Armethalieh—when Harrier told Tiercel he was right about something, at least something they'd argued about, Tiercel would usually take that as a license to go off and do something *really, really stupid*. Like exploring the old sewer system when they'd been kids. Or going off to that abandoned warehouse at night, the one that had turned out not to be abandoned. Or making *umbrastone* up in the attic because he'd found a recipe in an old book—and after they'd both been caught and thoroughly punished—Harrier's middle brother Carault told him that if they'd been stupid enough to get the recipe *just a little different* (but still wrong) they'd have blown up Tiercel's family townhouse.

And here they were, and the stakes were much higher, but he had the same fear: that if he said that Tiercel was right, Tiercel would use it as a justification to do something that had nothing at all to do with common sense. Because he thought it needed to be done, or it was the right thing to do.

And Harrier was afraid of what it might be.

So he turned to the Three Books, hoping there were answers there. Too late now to wish he'd practiced the spell-casting part of being a Wildmage just a little harder, and he still wasn't sure that the Wild Magic was something you *practiced*. But if he'd done a Scrying Spell moonturns ago—the first time Tiercel had asked, long before they'd even heard there was an army—what would it have showed him? *The Book of Moon* said the Scrying Spell showed you what you needed to see, but he didn't understand how he could possibly have needed to see what it had shown him when he'd actually done it. Despite what he'd experienced when he'd Healed the Telchi, incurring

Magedebt and having to become the eyes and hands of the Wild Magic still disturbed him, and at last he realized why. The Wild Magic was good. But what was good wasn't always kind—you could be kind without being good, and good without being kind, and Harrier was honest enough to admit that he was afraid to take that final step. He still wanted to be both.

He didn't find anything that he thought of as useful, but somehow, the more he read, the better he felt about things. When he didn't find anything he could use in *The Book of Moon,* he found himself reading *The Book of Stars*—it was the one he'd only skimmed before, as it had no spells in it at all, just what seemed like advice. How to think. How to act. How to—pretty much—relax and wait for the Wild Magic to show you what to do, and even if Harrier doubted that the Wild Magic was going to fix things in any way he really liked, it was comforting to hope it would. At least, after he'd been reading for a while, he no longer wanted to hit anybody.

After a while he was roused by the sound of a knock on the door. He quickly stuffed the Books under the nearest cushion and got to his feet. But when he opened the door, it was only Tiercel.

"We have a bookcase," Tiercel announced.

"That's . . . nice?" Harrier said. "There's nothing I like better when my city is besieged by crazy people than a nice bookcase."

Tiercel frowned. "Are you drunk? Because—"

"No. I've been reading."

"That explains it then. Daspuc and Rial have gone back to the Temple for evening Liturgy. They'll be back tomorrow. And I had a chance to check a couple of my spellbooks. You won't like what I found. Or maybe you will. I don't know."

"You sound funny," Harrier said.

"So do you. Are you *sure* you haven't been drinking?"

"There isn't any wine in here, just to begin with. So what won't I like?"

"I'd forgotten some things about MageShield. It's . . . it's a shield, you know?"

"Probably why they call it 'MageShield,' Tyr."

"No," Tiercel said seriously. "If it was just that, they'd call it, I don't know, 'Shield,' or something. It's a *MageShield* specifically. I mean, it keeps out spears and arrows and people—and that's good. But it won't let magic through either." He looked at Harrier as if Harrier should understand what that meant, and Harrier didn't, and he knew it was obvious from his expression. "Spells won't pass through it, Harrier," Tiercel said quietly. "Not in, and not out."

"Oh," Harrier said, when he'd thought about it for a moment. "So . . . ?"

"It doesn't matter what spell I find in the spellbooks, really. I'd have to dispel MageShield to cast it."

"The walls will stop them," Harrier said.

Tiercel shrugged. "For a little while."

But when the Telchi returned to share their evening meal, he brought a ray of hope.

"The enemy army is in poor condition," he announced, seating himself at the low dining table and dipping a piece of flatbread into the bowl of stew. The new bookcase towered behind him. It was an enormous item of lacquered and gilded wood, large enough to hold all of Tiercel's books in one place, but it really didn't seem to quite belong in the room.

"That's good?" Tiercel said, puzzled.

"How poor?" Harrier asked.

"I have observed them for most of the day. They have not encircled the city, as any commander would who wished to lay a siege. They have pitched their tents in the orchards and most of them remain within. It is obvious that they seek water and food."

"The orchards are watered by canals," Harrier said.

"Fed from the city's *Iteru*," the Telchi said, nodding. "The water to the canals was shut off the moment the army drew near, and they have already drunk them dry. Now, the only water to be found outside the walls is a spring five miles to the east. It is barely sufficient for a flock of thirsty goats; it will not meet the needs of so vast an army. Radnatucca Oasis is a day's journey into the desert—but it, too, has insufficient water for so many people and *shotors*."

"How long can they survive without water?" Tiercel asked, when no one said anything else.

"The Isvaieni are hardy folk, used to privation," the Telchi said. "Perhaps even a sennight. If they slaughter their beasts and drink their blood to survive, even longer, but if they do, they know they doom themselves, for they cannot cross the desert again on foot, so they will delay doing so as long as possible."

"No," Tiercel said, shaking his head. "Why would they wait—try to hold out—if they don't think the shield is going to come down? And why would they think it will?"

"They don't have anywhere else to go," Harrier said after a moment's thought. "Laganda'Iteru is a moonturn and a half back up the road. Akazidas'Iteru is at least that far to the west. There's not enough water for them along the road either way. There's not enough water out in the desert. They *have* to take the city."

"Can they be convinced that this is possible?" the Telchi asked quietly. "Convinced that the shield Tiercel has cast will fall swiftly?"

"What good does that do us?" Tiercel asked. Harrier stared toward the bookcase. He didn't want to see the hope on Tiercel's face. He didn't want to hope himself.

"If they think the city will fall to them, they will wait. They will give what water there is to their beasts and stint themselves. Each day, each hour, they will weaken. If you can manage to hold them off for a sennight—even for five days, or four—they will be too weak to raise their *awardans* against their attackers. We can ride out from the city—all of us, every man who can hold a weapon—and slay them."

To hold the shield in place meant that Tiercel would have to stay awake. Harrier didn't want to think about what it would take for Tiercel to manage to stay awake for that long. He hoped that somewhere in all those High Magick books of his there was a spell for that.

"I can help," Tiercel said. "When—When it's time, I'll set fire to their tents. Their *shotors* will panic."

"Then this is a good plan," the Telchi said with approval. "And may the Giver of Swords and the Lady of Battles grant that all goes as we wish it to."

Soon Harrier began to yawn, and Tiercel demanded that he *go to bed right now,* because if Tiercel had to be awake for the next sennight, he didn't want Harrier yawning in his face. "And go take a bath first," Tiercel demanded.

"You just want to see if we get hot water here," Harrier gibed, and Tiercel grinned.

Fifteen

The Long Watch

IN THE MORNING, Harrier awoke at his usual hour. Between the too-soft and unfamiliar bed and the strange violet light coming in through the windows, he was disoriented at first, but he soon remembered where he was. He dressed and went out into the main room. Tiercel was sitting at the low table, books spread out all around him, and a pot of *kaffeyah* at his elbow.

"I've decided I really hate this stuff after all," he said conversationally. "It tastes awful."

"You won't have to drink it for too long," Harrier said.

"When this is over, I'm going to sleep for a week, I think." Tiercel waved at a high narrow table by the wall. "They brought breakfast earlier, but I put it over there. I was using the table."

Harrier went over to the other table. It was tall and narrow; he vaguely remembered that some ornamental vases or bowls or something had been on it earlier, and he wondered where they were. It was high enough, too, that he could eat standing up, and did. Before he was quite finished, one of the footmen came in to tell them that they had been summoned to a private audience with Consul Aldarnas. Tiercel quickly got to his feet and put on his long vest and his boots. Harrier went to get his swords, but when he came back carrying them, the footman frowned and told him that no one carried weapons into the Consul's presence. So Harrier reluctantly left them behind and the two of them followed the footman to the Consul's Audience Chamber.

In Armethalieh, they'd both attended the important ceremonial events held on major holidays: the yearly Opening of the Law Courts, the Commemoration of the Sacrifice of Saint Idalia (held in the Main Temple of the Light, but everybody who couldn't fit inside the Temple crowded the square outside just to be there). They'd both seen important people on thrones wearing elaborate costumes before.

But the Chief Magistrate only sat on her Throne of Justice once a year. The rest of the time she sat at her Magistrate's Bench just like any other Magistrate. And the figure on the throne in the Light-Temple was a statue, not a person, and only on a throne at all so everyone could see her (and only on display for that one day every year, anyway).

Apparently in the *Iteru*-cities people sat on thrones all the time, because Consul Aldarnas looked very comfortable there. The Audience Chamber was large. There were about twenty ordinary nobles here and the room still looked empty. Six members of the Consul's personal guard stood around the throne, and Harrier was keenly aware that he wasn't armed. It would be difficult, he thought, but not impossible, to disarm one of the Palace Guards and take his weapon if they were attacked. And he didn't see anyone else carrying so much as a belt-knife.

The throne itself didn't look very comfortable—it seemed to be made of stone. And Harrier wasn't really sure how much *Consuling* Consul Aldarnas could be doing from up there, because there were eight steps up to the throne and all he could possibly see from there would be the tops of people's heads. But he looked fairly happy with the arrangement.

It was a long walk across the room, and everybody stared at them. When they got to the foot of the steps, the foot-man who'd brought them there bowed and backed away, and an important-looking man stepped forward. Harrier had thought until he moved that he was one of the nobles who was just hanging around the Audience Chamber be-cause he could, but then he realized that he'd seen him before, when the Consul had come outside the city, and so he must be one of his servants.

"Lord Tiercel and his attendant," the man announced.

Tiercel looked at Harrier, surprised, but Harrier didn't see any reason to correct them. He'd already gotten the idea that here in the Madiran nobles traveled with large retinues at all times. And certainly with guards. It didn't bother him if they thought that was what he was—and that was *all* he was. At least that way, they probably wouldn't try to split the two of them up.

"I am told that you have a plan for the defense of the city, Lord Tiercel," the Consul said. "I wish to hear it."

At first Harrier was surprised, and then he was angry. It seemed to him that the Telchi had betrayed them by telling Consul Aldarnas that there was a plan at all—and telling him that it was *Tiercel's* plan, when it was more of an idea they'd talked Tiercel into, seemed even more dishonest. But the longer he stood there, the more he understood why the Telchi had done what he had. Certainly he would have been questioned when he'd left their rooms—anybody who thought he wouldn't be was an idiot. Daspuc and Rial probably were, too—and so was everyone who went in and out. And it was much better if the plan seemed to come from

Tiercel—who was not only a noble, but a Mage—than from one of the Consul's own subjects.

Tiercel looked around the room. So did Harrier. Everybody in the room was edging forward, doing their best to do it as inconspicuously as possible.

"Okay," Tiercel said, raising his voice. "Sure. It's pretty simple, really. You see—"

The Consul got to his feet. "Come," he said, interrupting Tiercel. "Walk with me."

He trotted down the steps of his throne and strode off. Tiercel and Harrier followed. Glancing over his shoulder, Harrier saw the Palace Guards move to intercept the others in the room who tried to accompany them.

THE CONSUL LED them to yet another garden-courtyard. Along the way, they collected a couple of members of the Palace Guard. Harrier wondered if the High Magistrate went everywhere with guards. He had no idea, because he never saw her. He didn't think so, though. He was sure Tiercel's father would have mentioned something like that to Tiercel—or Da would have, since both of them saw her often enough.

The air in the garden was moist and inviting. It smelled of *naranjes* and *limuns;* fragrant exotic fruits, and green growing things, and flowers, and water. There was a tiny fountain in one corner, and the jet of water rose straight up and splashed back down upon itself.

"You just wanted to see if I'd do it in there," Tiercel said. "You really shouldn't do things like that. I've been awake for a whole day, and I have to stay awake for almost a sennight, you know."

"Do you have no fear at all?" the Consul asked curiously. He walked to a bench—it was probably white, but it looked purple right now—and sat down.

"Of you? Not really," Tiercel said kindly. "Why would you want to hurt me?"

Harrier could have explained to Consul Aldarnas that Tiercel was like this *all the time,* even when he hadn't been awake for too long and wasn't dealing with having to defend a city from a bunch of crazy Isvaieni, but he didn't really think the man deserved to know. So he just stared at the ground. The floor of the garden was covered in ornate colored tiles, but though they looked a little like the shiny ones he'd seen set into the walls in some places in the city, they weren't at all slippery.

"I have no desire to hurt you, Lord Tiercel," the Consul said, and from the faintly exasperated tone of his voice, Harrier thought he was trying to decide between Tiercel being simple-minded (or crazy) and Tiercel trying to drive *him* crazy, and Harrier wasn't going to help him out there either. Tiercel was just Tiercel.

"Oh, good," Tiercel said. "I suppose you'd like to hear the plan?"

"Yes. If you would find it convenient to enlighten me."

It took Tiercel about ten minutes to begin the explanation of the Telchi's theory that the Isvaieni were already weak from their long journey here, and would get weaker the longer they waited.

"There isn't enough water outside the shield to supply their army," Harrier said, when it became obvious that Tiercel simply couldn't bring himself to get to the point. "They could hold out for longer than Tiercel can maintain the shield if they're willing to sacrifice their *shotors.* If they don't do that, after a few days without water they'll be so weak that your City Guard and our Militia—and everyone in Tarnatha'Iteru who can hold a sword—should be able to go out through the gates and . . . kill them."

It was almost as hard for Harrier to say the words as it was for Tiercel, but he managed. At least it would be weapons against weapons, instead of using spells against people who had none. And even though he knew—both as a Knight-Mage and because the Telchi had said so—that the Isvaieni army didn't have the choice of just leaving, he still wanted to think that they could. If they scattered up and down the Trade Road, spread their army among all the oases and wells within fifty miles, they could find enough water to survive. He knew they wouldn't, but they could.

"I'll convince them the MageShield is going to fall—very soon—by dropping it and putting it back up several times in the next few days. It will look as if it's flickering," Tiercel said, his voice flat with sorrow. "It won't be. The more often it does it, the more convinced they'll be that it's only a matter of time before it vanishes forever."

The Consul thought for a long moment before he nodded. "Yes. If you have no better plan to offer us yet, this is a good one. Where must you be to do your magic?"

"Anywhere, really," Tiercel said. "But . . . it might be useful if I were where I could see them. Then I can put the shield back into place just as they reach it."

"Forcing them to exhaust themselves to no purpose. Yes. It is a good plan. I shall announce to the people that though the shield above them will vanish, it is only temporary, and they must not fear. Then you may do your work."

"No," Harrier said. The Consul gazed at him in surprise. "Sir. Think. If it were really happening, if the shield really failed, what would the people do?"

He hadn't meant to say anything. He hadn't really wanted the Consul's attention at all. He'd had to speak up to help Tiercel explain the plan, but he certainly hadn't expected to do what amounted to *arguing* with Consul Aldarnas.

Only . . . he *knew* this was important. He hadn't even thought about it until the Consul had said he was going to announce to the people that Tiercel would be taking down the MageShield and it was nothing to worry about, but the moment he had, Harrier had realized: if the whole plan was based on *tricking* the Isvaieni into believing the shield was failing . . .

"They would panic," the Consul said slowly. "They know, now, that this MageShield is their defense."

"Then that's what the army will expect to hear," Harrier said grimly. "Panic. So they'll need to hear it."

"There will be injuries," the Consul said. "Damage to the city."

"I'm sorry," Harrier said. "If the Isvaieni think it's a trick, though . . ."

"Yes. I thank the Light that you were sent to me. Both of you. It shall be done just as you have said. Now, perhaps, would be best. There will be fewer people upon the streets."

Tiercel nodded and the Consul got to his feet.

WHEN HARRIER HAD been making plans with the Telchi, with the Militia, and with the City Guard, about what to do when the Isvaieni came, one of the things that had concerned all of them was securing the gates—not as much from the enemy, as from the city's own inhabitants. The lesson of Laganda'Iteru was clear—people terrified by the sight of an approaching army would rush out of the city to their doom, leaving the city gates open and the city vulnerable to assault. The only defense against that was to seal off the gates—as they'd done. And—as Harrier now discovered—to seal off access to the city walls as well.

Though there was little people could do from the top of the wall but either jump to their deaths or—perhaps—climb down the outside of the wall using ropes, desperate men might try, and Tarnatha'Iteru did not possess enough guards to keep watch on all four of the staircases leading to the top of the city wall, and so when Harrier and Tiercel were led up the heavily guarded stairs beside the Main Gate and onto the wall itself, they saw that the other staircases had been smashed to rubble with hammers. It would be impossible to get up to the wall from anywhere but the Main Gate now.

They reached the portion of the wall that was over the South Gate. There the Telchi came to join them—he had been out patrolling the city and the walls, as Harrier would have been under other circumstances. It seemed almost pointless to stand guard over the walls when the city was surrounded by MageShield, but nobody (Harrier supposed) really understood that, and it was just as well to give people something to do.

"Okay," Tiercel said in a low voice. "Here goes."

He didn't raise his hands, or make any elaborate gestures like the Mock-Mages in the Festival-Day plays, and Harrier couldn't remember whether he'd waved his hands around when he'd cast MageShield in the first place. It was just that one moment the city was surrounded by a glowing wall of purple fire that made Harrier's eyes ache to look at it . . .

. . . and the next moment it wasn't.

He blinked. The morning light was sharp and clear and honest, and he could feel the last of the night cool roll in off the desert, and the promise of the baking day's heat to come. The Isvaieni army was almost too far away to see, but when he looked carefully he could see that the groves a few miles distant were filled with black tents. Even in summer the trees were normally in full green leaf, but now the trees were bare. Harrier supposed the *shotors* had eaten the leaves.

The Guardsmen on the wall gazed around themselves in alarm, and then at Tiercel. They started toward him, and Harrier stepped forward to block their paths, knowing the Telchi was doing the same thing on the other side.

"It's all right," he said. "Tiercel has a plan. This is part of it." He felt like an idiot, and all he could hope was that these men would believe him. The Consul had called him and Tiercel "boys," and they were, and that was all that anyone seeing them would see. It was easy to forget that, when Jermayan and Idalia and Ancaladar had all treated them like men.

"He will still defend us?" Simac asked worriedly. The young Guardsman was about Rial's age. He might even be Rial's cousin—Rial had said that his family was still in the city, and Harrier knew that the post of City Guard was one that was coveted in the *Iteru*-cities. It carried a higher status than being a member of the City Watch did back home.

"Yes," Harrier said, because explaining all the details of everything just wouldn't be terribly useful. All anybody really wanted to know was that Tiercel would protect them and Tarnatha'Iteru wouldn't be overrun.

The Isvaieni saw that the shield was down. The sound of their distant shouting began to reach Harrier's ears, and then it was drowned out by the sounds of the people in the city behind him. The noise built slowly, shouts and screams and scraps of sentences. Demands for information. The crash of something falling. The sounds of people shouting at each other until their voices blended into a blur of sound that simply rose in volume. Five minutes passed, and ten, and slowly the distant noise from the Isvaieni army increased until it could be heard over the noise from the city, as the Isvaieni stumbled from their tents, and saddled their *shotors,* and began to move toward the city in a vast wave.

"Don't you think—" Harrier said.

"Wait," Tiercel said, his voice tense.

The ground shook as the *shotors* galloped forward, and the Isvaieni howled in fury; a bone-chilling sound. The army raced closer to the walls, and closer still, and showed no sign of stopping at all. Then Tiercel gestured, spreading both hands as if he were in the middle of an argument with Harrier and was making a point. And the wall of MageShield fire sprang into place once more, only scant feet away from the noses of the lead *shotors.* The Isvaieni had no warning. The first ranks of the army slammed into the barrier at full speed. The *shotors'* riders were flung from their backs by the impact, falling beneath the feet of the animals behind them.

"Light defend them," Tiercel said quietly.

The outer edges of the army, seeing the danger, desperately tried to rein in or turn aside. A few of them could, only to find themselves jammed against the barrier further down by other riders who were also desperately trying to escape the carnage. More of the Isvaieni army was swept into a collision with the MageShield by the momentum of the riders behind them, and the center of the column had no place to go. Riders plowed into each other, crushing those ahead of them against the barrier. Injured and dying *shotors* thrashed and screamed.

The men on the wall cheered at the sight. In the city behind them, the mob-noises slowly turned to cheers when the people saw the shield appear once more.

"I had to," Tiercel said desperately. "I had to."

"It was the right thing to do," Harrier said, even though he felt sick. He knew some people had died down there when Tiercel had flung up the shield right in their path, and he knew Tiercel knew it, too. They could both still hear the bleating of the injured animals—and worse, the cries of injured *people*.

He wasn't going to tell Tiercel that it was okay to have done it because the Isvaieni were going to kill them if they could, because it just wasn't.

"It wasn't right," Tiercel said, his voice agonized.

The rear of the army—about two-thirds of it—had been able to save itself completely. Those people milled about in confusion. Some riders were retreating from the fallen, some riding after fleeing—riderless—*shotors,* others were moving forward to aid the injured.

"You convinced them that your spell failed. That you got it back into place at the last possible minute. You needed to do that, Tyr. They'll expect something like this to happen the next time. They won't rush it again." It wasn't much comfort. But it was all he could give, because Harrier knew that Tiercel wouldn't accept anything less than the truth. So it would have to be enough.

Tiercel turned away from the edge of the wall, staggering blindly. He would have gone right off the inner edge and down a hundred feet to the street if Harrier hadn't grabbed his elbow and dragged him back.

"Is the Mage ill?" Simac asked, sounding worried.

"Tired," Harrier said.

"I shall accompany you," the Telchi said.

"Leave me alone," Tiercel snarled at Harrier.

"Shut up," Harrier said, and the Telchi said: "Not here."

One on each side of Tiercel, they walked back along the wall.

It was a long walk. The Consul's Palace and the Great Gate were at one end of the city, and the South Gate—where they'd been standing—was at the other. It was a distance of several miles, and going out, Harrier and Tiercel had both been glad to stretch their legs. But going back, all the guardsmen on the wall wanted to stop them and congratulate Tiercel on killing so many of the enemy. Harrier could tell that Tiercel found hearing their praise almost unbearable. He knew he should protect Tiercel. Stop them. *Do something.*

But it was all he could do to keep from shouting at them himself, to keep from drawing his swords and simply forcing everyone out of their path. *He killed a bunch of people and you think that's a good thing?* Harrier wanted to shout.

Only he knew it was. Their whole plan was based on being able to kill all of those people out there, and Harrier knew that in a few days he'd be one of the people riding out of here with a sword to do it, and he was angry and terrified and he hated the thought.

And then he thought of everyone in Armethalieh. His ma and da, and his brothers and their wives, and his nieces and nephews, and Tiercel's parents and his sisters and his baby brother, and, oh, pretty much everyone either of them had ever *met*. And if they didn't manage to get out of this city alive and find the Lake of Fire and *do something,* all of those people were going to be in as much trouble as everyone here was in right now, because *the Endarkened were coming back.*

The Telchi stepped forward and said firmly that the Mage needed to rest and meditate after casting his spell. It was a ridiculous notion, but then again, nobody here had any more notion of what a High Mage did than Harrier'd had this time last year. Nonsensical as his words were, they made the guardsmen step back and leave Tiercel alone, and when the three of them reached the foot of the steps at the Main Gate, and the servant from the Audience Chamber approached them to say that the Consul wished to see them, Harrier simply repeated what the Telchi had said, and added that they'd see Consul Aldarnas when his master had refreshed himself.

"YOU *DIDN'T* JUST say 'when my master has refreshed himself,'" Tiercel said in disbelief. The moment Harrier had come in he'd known the rooms were empty—it was a weird feeling—but he'd still wanted to check. He'd been right. There was nobody here but the three of them.

"Hey," Harrier answered, mock-indignantly, "I wasn't the one who decided I was your attendant back in the Audience Chamber." At least Tiercel didn't look quite so much as if he wanted to *hit* somebody now.

"So now you're my servant?"

"Oh, you wish," Harrier said feelingly. He walked over to the side-table. The breakfast dishes were gone, but there was a selection of fruit and pastry set out, a beaker of cold mint tea, and a *kaffeyah* service all set up and ready. Looking at it, Harrier thought that Rial had probably thought the brazier in his bag had been part of a *kaffeyah* set, because it looked very much like the little brazier that went under the pot to heat the water.

"Yeah, well, you didn't exactly argue," Tiercel said.

"It's always been my life's ambition to wait on you hand and foot." Any other time, Harrier would have found this conversation annoying. Now he was just grateful that Tiercel was talking about something—anything—besides what had just happened on top of the wall. He picked up the tray with the *kaffeyah* service and brought it over to the table. He'd prepared *kaffeyah* for the Telchi often enough. "Light that, will you?" he said, when he was done setting up the pot.

"Do it yourself," Tiercel said sulkily.

Harrier laughed. "What am I, your servant?" Sympathy was the last thing that would be good for Tiercel, even if it was what he deserved.

"Hah. Funny." Tiercel pointed a finger at the brazier beneath the pot, and it *whooshed* into life.

"I CAN'T DO that again," Tiercel said a few minutes later.

He'd been staring off at nothing as the *kaffeyah* brewed. Daspuc and Rial had come to the outer room—because they were supposed to be here and do something or other with Tiercel today, if just help him read through all his High Magick books—and Harrier had gone and sent them away, telling them to come back after midday. It felt very odd to him to be giving orders to Sub-Preceptors of the Light, but Tiercel's safety (and comfort) was more important.

At first Harrier thought that Tiercel was talking about hurting people. Every time he closed his eyes, Harrier could see the mass of bodies and hear the screaming. It had to be far worse for Tiercel—he'd caused it to happen.

But to his surprise, Tiercel ran a hand through his hair and said: "I'm tired," and Harrier realized that what he was talking about was walking for miles from one end of the city to the other. He frowned. There wasn't any other way to get to the wall above the South Gate. Not anymore.

"I shall go," the Telchi said. "You may stand upon the wall here, and I shall alert you when it is time to replace the shield again. I shall allow them to approach closely, but not to be trapped within it."

"Don't you need to see where it goes?" Harrier asked curiously.

Tiercel gave him a long-suffering look. "I couldn't see all sides of the city the *first* time, Har. No. Just . . . I don't . . ."

"In any event, it would be imprudent to cause great loss of life among the Isvaieni's *shotors*," the Telchi said reprovingly, before Tiercel could tell him that he didn't want to make anything like what had happened today ever happen again. "Our purpose is to deny them the resources to feed their army."

And the Isvaieni would simply cook and eat the dead animals.

LATER THAT AFTERNOON Tiercel and Harrier went to another audience with the Consul; this time in his private rooms, not the Audience Chamber. The Consul thanked Tiercel for all he was doing to save the city, and promised him that once this was over, Tiercel would have all the help he could provide in locating the Lake of Fire. It was a gracious gesture, though it was hard to imagine what help that would be, unless Consul Aldarnas had information that even the Merchants' Guild lacked.

After they returned to their rooms, the Telchi insisted that Harrier resume his lessons—there was little else for either of them to do, he pointed out, and a shaded garden outside at their disposal. The two of them spent the entire afternoon at sword-work, and Harrier felt much better after resuming his routine.

Tiercel dropped and recast the shield once again late that night. He told Harrier about it when Harrier got up the following morning. By then Tiercel had been awake for two days, and he was beginning to look as bad as he had back in Armethalieh when they'd both thought he was dying of something.

During the day that followed, he dropped and recast the shield another three times. Each time—the Telchi told them—the Isvaieni mounted their *shotors* and rode down toward the city. But by the middle of the second day, only a few hundred would come. The guards on the walls would shoot at them while the shield was down, but only if they came close enough that they could be sure of shooting the riders and not the *shotors*.

By the fourth day, Tiercel didn't bother to search through his books for spells any longer.

"I can't concentrate," he said.

His voice was slurred. He was never left alone now—Haspuc or Rial or Harrier or the Telchi or someone else was always with him to help him stay awake. The Telchi said that by now the Isvaieni were undoubtedly very weak. He also said that they certainly wished to seem weaker than they were, so Tiercel must hold out as long as he could. And he must do it on will alone, and whatever help *kaffeyah* could give him. The city's Healers had drugs to summon sleep—and drugs that would banish it, too. But too much or too little of either could have the opposite effect—and an overdose of either drug could kill. They didn't dare take the chance.

"So don't," Harrier said agreeably. "Just pay attention." Harrier still wasn't completely clear on how the High Magick worked, but Tiercel had said back at the beginning that the MageShield would only be there as long as he was conscious to hold the spell in place, and Harrier had to figure he knew what he was talking about.

"I can't," Tiercel whined.

Reflexively, Harrier glanced through the open doorway to the sleeping room's window. But the light was still purple. The MageShield was still in place.

"It's hot in here," Tiercel sighed. He rubbed his eyes. "I keep saying that, right?"

"You're running a fever," Harrier said. "I guess it's from staying awake."

Certainly Tiercel *looked* as if he was running a fever. His eyes were red-rimmed and glittering, his skin was pale, and his cheeks were flushed. Harrier was starting to wonder if maybe Tiercel ought to be let to try to get a couple of hours of sleep—surely the Isvaieni couldn't get over the wall in a couple of hours. Except maybe a lot of them could. And he didn't think that after four days awake they could wake Tiercel up after an hour or two asleep.

Tiercel nodded jerkily. "Yeah," he said, far too slowly. "I guess . . ." he trailed off and stopped, as if he'd forgotten what he wanted to say right in the middle.

Just then Daspuc walked into the room and bowed. The young Light-priest had lost much of his fear of this peculiar situation in the last four days. *You can get used to anything with enough time,* Harrier thought. "Master Harrier," he said quietly. "It is time."

"Come on, Tyr," Harrier said, taking Tiercel by the elbow and guiding him from the room.

BY NOW HARRIER was pretty familiar with the layout of the Consul's Palace. He led Tiercel through several private corridors and up a flight of stairs that led to the roof. Yesterday Tiercel had been unsteady on the stairs, but today he stumbled so badly on every step that Harrier practically had to drag him.

The roof of the palace was another garden. There were plants in pots—Harrier could identify less than half of them, but all of them smelled nice—and little ornamental wooden buildings where you could sit and look out over the city, and (if the city wasn't covered in MageShield) be cooled by the evening breeze. All Harrier cared about was that it wasn't as far for Tiercel to walk as up to the top of the wall.

"Okay, Tyr," he said. "Drop the shield."

"Okay," Tiercel said docilely.

The shield vanished. Since it had been doing that every once in a while for the past few days and had always come back, nobody in the streets below paid any attention any more.

And by now they weren't bothering with spotters, either. They were just timing it out to the point where Tiercel put it back into place. Five minutes here, ten minutes there, because they knew by now that it would take the army at least half an hour and maybe longer to move its scouts toward the city.

Harrier counted slowly; he knew Tiercel was too. When they got to a hundred, it would be time for Tiercel to cast the spell again. He reached a hundred.

Nothing happened.

"Tiercel?" he said.

Tiercel was staring off into space, weaving slightly back and forth on his feet, his eyes unfocused. Harrier grabbed him by the shoulders and shook him violently. Tiercel gasped and stared at him wildly. "What? What?" he stammered.

"Cast the shield! Cast it now!"

Suddenly the sky over the city bloomed with purple light.

"Did you see him?" Tiercel demanded, sounding frantic. He jerked himself free of Harrier's grip and stumbled away. "The man—the one we saw in Ysterialpoerin! The one I saw on the Plains—the one who couldn't see you! He's here!"

There was so much conviction in Tiercel's voice that Harrier actually looked around. But there was nobody on the roof except them.

"No," Harrier said quietly. "No, Tiercel. I didn't see him."

"He's here," Tiercel said. "I don't know how he got into the city, but he did. He's been following us since we left the Veiled Lands. He didn't want to come near me while Ancaladar was with me, but he came back."

It would have sounded reasonable, except for the fact that it was impossible. Not that they couldn't have been followed—because whatever that *thing* was, Harrier knew it wasn't human. It might even have taken it this long to find them again after they'd vanished through the Magedoor into the Veiled Lands and come back out the other side.

But what he *did* know was that nobody had entered the city since Tiercel had put up his shield, and that there was nobody on the roof.

"C'mon, Tyr," he said gently. "Let's go downstairs."

AFTER THAT, HARRIER was too worried to leave Tiercel alone with anyone else. When the Telchi came to join them a few hours later, Harrier told him what Tiercel had said.

"Who is this man?" the Telchi asked. "What does he look like?"

"I don't think he's a man," Harrier said slowly. "Tiercel thought he was something, well, *not human*. But we were never sure what." He shook his head in frustration. When they'd gone with Ancaladar through the Magedoor, there'd been so many new things to think about all at once—and then, when they'd left Karahelanderialigor, and he'd gotten his Three Books, there'd been *that*—that he'd almost forgotten about the strange red-haired man. When Tiercel's visions had returned outside the Veil, Harrier had worried about their attacks resuming, but as the sennights passed, it had almost become a habit of paranoia rather than that he'd actually expected something to happen.

He described the man—for lack of anything better to call him—as best he could. If he'd been the strange bear that attacked them just north of Sentarshadeen, they'd seen him three times: once there, once on the Plains just before they'd met Roneida, and once—perhaps twice—in Ysteri-alpoerin. And each time, except for the red coloring, he'd looked different.

The Telchi frowned when Harrier was done, weighing his words. "This is troubling news. The Endarkened, it is said, could change their form so."

"Yeah," Harrier said, sighing. "But Tyr said he didn't think it was really *evil*, whatever it was, and whatever it was trying to do. And if it *was* one of the Endarkened, I don't think either of us would be alive right now."

"Very true," the Telchi agreed. "Still. A red-haired man in the city should be simple to find."

Harrier nodded. He and Tiercel stood out here because they were both so fair, and because his hair was red and Tiercel's was blond. The southerners were the descendants of High Reaches folk; Harrier hadn't seen anyone with blue eyes since he'd come to Tarnatha'Iteru, and everyone's hair was some shade of dark brown. There'd been other northerners in the city when they'd arrived, but the last of them had left a moonturn before—whether because they believed in the danger, or simply because they thought the city was unsettled didn't matter: they weren't here now.

"If he's here," he said.

"I saw him."

Though Tiercel was right there in the room while the two of them were having the conversation, he'd simply stared silently off into the distance, and after a few minutes, both of them had almost managed to forget that he was there.

Harrier hesitated. He didn't want to say that Tiercel was probably seeing a lot of things that weren't there right now, but he was thinking it. Tiercel's eyes were sunk into his skull, and he looked more than exhausted: he looked ill. Harrier couldn't imagine how he was managing to stay awake.

"You think I'm crazy," Tiercel said.

"I think you've been awake for four days," Harrier said.

"I saw him," Tiercel repeated stubbornly.

"We will search for this creature Harrier has described," the Telchi said. "If we see it, we will tell you."

Tiercel nodded. "I'm going to . . . stay awake," he said vaguely.

THE MAGESHIELD FLICKERED twice that night, but it wasn't something Tiercel did intentionally. Each time, Tiercel simply lost control of his spell. Fortunately Harrier was sitting up with Tiercel and was able to shake him hard enough to make him set the spell again. But Harrier thought that the time was coming—soon—when that wouldn't work, and Tiercel's shield would fall once and for all. Four days, maybe five, in the baking sun with minimal water— was it enough to weaken the army outside their gates to the point where the men of Tarnatha'Iteru could overwhelm them? He'd only spent one night without sleep, keeping Tiercel company, and his eyes felt as if they were filled with sand. He couldn't imagine what Tiercel felt like by now.

"You have to wake Ancaladar up," he told Tiercel urgently. It was dawn. Five days now.

"No," Tiercel mumbled. "Isn't time."

"It is," Harrier said pleadingly. "It really is. Come on, Tyr. Do you think anybody in the city's going to notice one little dragon at this point? So he's hungry. He can eat all the Isvaieni *shotors*."

"No," Tiercel repeated stubbornly. Harrier wasn't really sure whether Tiercel heard him, or understood him, or was just holding onto the last clear idea he'd had days ago: that Ancaladar would be vulnerable to the spears of the Isvaieni army. He coaxed and argued until Tiercel became terrifyingly hysterical, but he couldn't make him change his mind.

The Telchi entered the room, drawn by the shouting.

"Do not try to reason with him," he said quietly. "He is too tired to see reason. And you will only exhaust him further."

"I *won't!*" Tiercel said—one last refusal of Harrier's arguments. He shambled over to the window and stood gazing out, ignoring both of them.

"I just—" Harrier began, and stopped. This wasn't the time to care about who was right or wrong. "Yeah. I think we need to plan on attacking the Isvaieni soon," he said, lowering his voice although he doubted Tiercel was still paying attention. "I don't think Tiercel's going to be able to hold the shield in place much more than another day. If that long."

"In truth, I am grateful we have been granted this much time," the Telchi said. "The City Guard and the Palace Guard are both well-trained and drilled. The Militia has some training. In the last four days, arrangements have been made to stockpile weapons at the Main Gate, and in a number of places throughout the city, so that when the signal is given that the shield has fallen for the last time, everyone who is willing and able to fight may arm themselves quickly."

"Horses? *Shotors*?" Harrier asked.

"Very few," the Telchi answered. "And not trained for battle. But neither are the mounts of our foes. This battle will be fought on foot."

"They'll need to stay away from the city wall," Harrier said, half in a daze. "You can't let the Isvaieni back them against it and trap them. Out the North Gate, swing wide, straight west, then back. If you're lucky, you can come at them from behind."

"If the Lady of Battles is kind, our fortunes will run just so," the Telchi agreed. "I know you had meant to come with us, Harrier. But I think your place will be here."

"I . . . what? Here?" Harrier said, confused. "No. I—"

"You stay by his side now to keep him awake as long as possible," the Telchi said. "And when we go forth, the gates will be barred behind us, but the enemy may still gain access to the city. Would you leave him defenseless? Worse, what if he should wake again, and, not knowing what he does, cast his spell once more?"

Harrier winced at the image the Telchi evoked. He didn't know what would happen if you were actually in the middle of MageShield when it was cast, and he really didn't want to. He nodded reluctantly.

"Good," the Telchi said, satisfied. "Now, come and eat. And see if you can persuade Tiercel to eat as well."

FOR THE WHOLE of that fifth day, Harrier felt as if he was in a race—a slow terrible nightmarish race where the consequences of losing were too terrible to imagine. Tiercel no longer dared even sit down, for fear of falling asleep; he leaned against the walls, blotting his face and neck with towels dipped in ice water, moving restlessly from place to place to try to stay awake.

The shield kept flickering—gone and back so swiftly

that if Harrier hadn't been watching for it, half-sick with knowing what the instability represented, he wouldn't have noticed what was happening. It would have been a beautiful job of pretending that the shield was about to fail at any moment. If Tiercel had been pretending.

IT WAS THE middle of the night. They'd gone up to the roof garden. Tiercel had insisted, saying it would be cooler there, although no part of the city was very much cooler than any other part with the MageShield in place. He kept walking over to the very edge of the roof and looking down, which was more than enough to keep Harrier wide awake— even in the middle of his second day without sleep— because the roof was flat, and there was no wall or anything at the edge, just a sheer drop. Harrier kept leading him back to the center of the roof, and Tiercel kept wandering away to the edge again.

They weren't alone. Rial was sitting on a bench inside one of the wooden buildings—they were really just roofs and pillars—reading a copy of *The Litany of the Light* by the light of a lantern. Several of the Palace Guard stood near the top of the staircase. They were there to turn away anyone else who tried to come up to the roof rather than to guard Tiercel, and Harrier was grateful for their presence.

"He's out there somewhere, you know, Har," Tiercel said in a dreamy voice. "He's waiting."

"He can't get up here," Harrier said. There was no point in arguing with Tiercel that the Red Man wasn't out there. Tiercel would only get upset.

"He doesn't have to," Tiercel said, still in that frighteningly calm voice. He took a step toward the edge of the roof again, swaying dangerously as he did. "He's crowned in fire. We're all going to burn. I—"

Harrier never found out what Tiercel's next words might have been, because his eyes rolled up in his head and his knees buckled. He fell forward.

And the MageShield above them vanished.

Harrier dropped to his knees beside Tiercel and rolled him onto his back. Tiercel's mouth was bleeding where he'd bitten his lip when he fell. Harrier shook him and slapped him, but no matter what he did, he couldn't rouse him.

"Sound the alarm," he said quietly. "It's time."

It seemed like forever before the guards began to move.

Harrier stared down at Tiercel. He touched his forehead. It was cold and clammy, as if a fever had finally broken.

"Let me help you carry him to his bed," Rial said quietly, coming to kneel beside Harrier.

"You'll need to go home," Harrier said. "To your family."

"My youngest sisters and my young kin go to seek shelter in the Light-Temple," Rial said. "The rest of my family goes to arm themselves. As shall I. Preceptor Larimac has said that the Light does not ask us to seek battle or to avoid it, only to choose it carefully and wisely, doing no more injury than we must. I shall be proud to stand at his side today."

"I could—" Harrier said, torn between knowing he needed to protect Tiercel and needing to do what he thought of as his duty: help to protect the people of Tarnatha'Iteru.

"Your place is with the Mage," Rial said gently. "Come. Help me lift him."

Harrier took Tiercel's shoulders and Rial took his feet, and they carried him over to the stairs and down. When they were halfway down the staircase, Harrier heard the warning horns begin to sound throughout the city.

People were running through the corridors of the Palace, but though everything looked chaotic, Harrier didn't get the sense that anyone was panicking. He wondered if it was because the disaster they'd all anticipated for so long was finally here, or because they all had clear instructions of what to do and were certain of their victory.

They'd only gotten Tiercel part of the way toward their rooms when Harrier pulled them all to a halt. "No," Harrier said. "Wait. Here."

"But—" Rial said.

"I know," Harrier answered. "But it has a view of the Main Gate."

He and Tiercel had been in this room a couple of days ago while they'd been waiting to see the Consul—Harrier wasn't quite sure what the room was *for,* but it had a couch and some tables and a set of enormous windows that opened onto a tiny balcony that overlooked the Gate.

The horns had stopped blowing now. Their warning had been given.

He and Rial carried Tiercel into the room and laid him down on the couch. There was a small lamp burning on one of the tables, barely enough to give the room a little light. Tiercel looked as if he was dead, but he was breathing shallowly.

"Now I leave you," Rial said. "The Light be with you, Harrier, and with Tiercel."

"And with you," Harrier said. "I'll see you again soon."

"I regret what I am about to do," Rial said softly. "I hope those poor people outside our walls will be granted peace by the Light."

"So do I," Harrier said. "Give me—" he said impulsively.

"Of course," Rial answered, and before he left, he called down the blessing of the Light on both Harrier and Tiercel.

WHEN RIAL WAS gone, Harrier took a spill and lit one of the larger lamps in the room. He closed the door, then dragged one of the large tables across it to block it. He wasn't worried about being attacked, but the door had no lock, and he didn't want the two of them to be disturbed.

He went over to the window and folded the shutters back. The Main Gate was distant, but the few buildings between the Consul's Palace and the Gate were low, and Harrier could see it clearly. A crowd filled the entire plaza—visible only by the torches they carried—and as he watched, they began to pass out through the Gate. *Hurry,* Harrier thought, clenching his hands into fists. *Hurry.*

It was strange, after so long behind Tiercel's MageShield, to see the blackness of the sky and feel the cold night wind on his face. The column of marchers moved so slowly, and Harrier was guessing at what was out there as much as seeing it. From the height of some of the torches, some of the people were mounted. Most were not. He could hear a faint distant babble of noise from the moving crowd.

He stepped out onto the balcony, and listened, but he heard no other sounds at all.

He thought he must have stood and watched for almost an hour before the Plaza was dark, and faintly, in the distance, he heard the booming sound of the gates being thrown shut again. The guards on the walls would watch and wait to see when it was time to open them again. He glanced at the sky. The position of the stars told him it was at least an hour, maybe two, until dawn. And no moon tonight. He wasn't sure whether that was good or bad.

Still no sound, and he began to worry. Almost two hours, now, since the shield had failed. His imagination showed him what his eyes could not. The people from the city would have gone out the Main Gate, swinging wide of the wall and heading south—

Oh, Light, no—Harrier thought in horror, just as he heard the first screams.

"Stupid. We were so stupid," he groaned aloud. He pounded his fist on the balcony rail in frustration, wanting to blot out the sounds he heard. And he couldn't. He drew a long shuddering breath. "The horns. It was the horns."

Now—when it was far too late—he realized he'd made a horrible mistake. It hadn't even been his to make—he hadn't been consulted on how the Consul planned to rouse the entire city when it was time for the final attack—and even if he had been, he wasn't entirely sure the man would have taken his advice. Harrier wasn't sure what advice he would have had to give—when the shield fell, the city needed to be alerted *quickly.*

But he might have, Harrier told himself furiously. *You know he might have. He did before. You could have come up with something.*

But he hadn't. He didn't. And the Isvaieni had heard the horns, and known this time was different than the times before. And they'd had the strength to lay an ambush of their own.

It wouldn't have mattered, Harrier told himself. Their plan—their *entire* plan—was based on the Isvaieni being too weak to fight. Whether they were warned or not shouldn't matter. *But it has,* Harrier thought in anguish. *It did.*

The sound of battle grew louder. Human screams, and the shrieks of wounded *shotors,* and an unearthly wailing that was the sound of a mortally wounded horse. The sounds made his blood run cold. And what was worse—far worse—was that he knew to the last man how many men there were in the City Guard and the City Militia. There were—perhaps—a hundred men in the Palace Guard. Add to that everybody in Tarnatha'Iteru able and willing to carry a weapon . . .

. . . and they were still outnumbered by the Isvaieni army two to one. And the Isvaieni were desperate to win. *It won't take their whole army to wipe out everything we can send against them,* Harrier thought. *Where will the rest of them be?*

We have to get out of here.

He went to drag the table away from the door.

Sixteen

Crowned in Fire

HE WASN'T SURE where they should go. All of his instincts told him to help, to *fight,* but Tiercel was helpless, and Harrier needed to protect him. Once the Isvaieni entered the city, the Consul's Palace would probably be one of the first places they'd come.

It was just too bad that Tiercel wasn't conscious right now, too, because since their arrival, Tiercel had gotten to know the city almost as well as they both knew Armethalieh. Tiercel would know where they could hide.

Hiding won't do us much good when they burn the city down around us, Harrier thought grimly. But they didn't have to hide forever. Just until he could wake Tiercel up. Then Tiercel could call Ancaladar, and . . .

"You should have listened to me," Harrier muttered. "Next time, you're going to listen to me if I have to *beat you senseless.*"

He started to hoist Tiercel to his shoulder, and stopped. He was still wearing his swords sheathed on his back. They were so much a part of him by now that he'd forgotten they were there. He let Tiercel slump back to the couch while he unbuckled his harness. After a moment's thought, he unclipped the swords and their sheaths from the leather, rolled the harness and tied it around his waist, and stuffed the swords through it. It was awkward and uncomfortable, but he thought the arrangement would hold. Then he picked Tiercel up and flung him over his shoulder.

The weight made him stagger. He'd done hard physical labor all his life, but Tiercel didn't weigh all that much less than he did. But he didn't have any choice. He walked carefully to the door and dragged it open.

The hallways were clear. Harrier wasn't sure where everyone was—maybe they were all locked in their own rooms. He'd willingly warn anybody that he saw, but whether he warned them or not, soon everybody would know that their army had lost and the city was about to be overrun, and he wasn't sure what possible help or advice he could offer. *Wildmages are supposed to help when things like this happen,* he thought. *I don't know what to do.* And he didn't know where all the other Wildmages were, either. The ones who should know what to do, because they knew how to be Wildmages. He didn't want to think that something had happened to all of them. It was too terrifying.

There was no one on the broad staircase leading to the first floor, and no one at all in the enormous outer courts—spice-seller's court, money-changer's court, lesser lawcourt. He carried Tiercel into the outer plaza, every muscle in his back screaming for rest. The deep blue light of false dawn shone through from the plaza outside. The outer plaza was as empty as the palace itself.

His mind was churning over possible destinations. He thought there had to be lower levels of the palace. Storage areas. Servants' quarters. There had to be some place where the water was coming into the palace and the sewage was going out. If he could find that place, maybe nobody would find them there.

He tried not to think about what he was doing. Saving himself and letting everyone else die. It didn't help that he knew he couldn't save them—that all he could possibly do was die along with them. That he had to save Tiercel because Tiercel might be the one who could save so many other people. All he could think of—because that's what it felt like—was that he was running away and saving himself because he was a coward.

As he stood in the middle of the outer plaza, looking for doors that might lead down, he saw movement outside. A man was walking up the steps into the palace.

He held an *awardan* in one hand, and a bundle in the

other. The front of his robes was black, and just as Harrier was realizing that the reason the *awardan* looked so strange was because it was covered in blood, the man flung away the bundle, and it rolled messily across the ornate marble floor, and Harrier realized it wasn't a bundle, it was a head.

"Fortune favors me," the man said.

"No. No, it doesn't," Harrier answered. He let Tiercel slide down off his shoulder and drew his swords.

He didn't know what was going to happen now, but he knew that if he didn't stop this man, this man would kill Tiercel. That was all he was thinking about. He was exhausted, and so terrified he was actually beyond fear. He couldn't remember a single thing the Telchi had ever told him about fighting, or even a single word he'd read in any of his Three Books. *Please,* he thought. *Please.*

The man stepped forward, raising his weapon.

It seemed to Harrier that the man moved slowly. That his body was telling Harrier where to strike, and when. Harrier knew—though he wasn't thinking in words—that he couldn't catch the man's blade with his own, because the swords he carried were light and flexible, and they could be sheared through and broken by the heavier steel.

He simply wasn't there each time the man struck.

Cut to disable. And a line of blood appeared high on the man's sword-arm. Harrier felt the drag as his blade pulled through the rough fabric of the robe. The man roared in pain and anger, dropping his sword and scrabbling in his belt for a knife. His sword-arm dangled lifelessly, and spreading blood darkened his sleeve.

Cut to disarm. And Harrier's blade flashed down, slicing the knife-hand away at the wrist. He would have stopped in shock, but his body was already moving forward for the final blow.

Cut to kill. And his blade slipped across his attacker's throat as he spun—around, away, back—and the man dropped to his knees, head lolling forward as blood first gushed, then flowed slowly from the terrible wound in his throat. The body slipped sideways to the floor, and Harrier stared down at it in horror.

"Oh, Light, I . . ." He stared down at the swords in his hands. Both the blades were bloody, and he couldn't remember how they'd gotten that way. "I'm sorry," he gasped. He took a step back; the blood was spreading fast.

He wanted to throw his swords away. He didn't know what to *do*. He'd just killed somebody, and all he could think of was that he'd never dare tell Da about this. Never.

He wanted to cry.

Isn't this what you trained to do? Isn't this what a Knight-Mage does?

I don't want to be a Knight-Mage any more. Please.

But the blood was still spreading, and it was going to reach Tiercel in a minute, so Harrier set his swords down carefully on the floor and staggered away from them and dragged Tiercel to a place where the blood wouldn't reach him. He could smell the blood now: hot, and metallic, and a little like spoiled meat, and the smell would have made him want to gag, even if what he'd just done hadn't made him sick already.

He dragged Tiercel all the way over to the pillar by the door—because it was easier to drag him than it was to carry him—then he came back and used his short sword to cut a piece from his tunic so he could wipe both the blades and sheathe them and tuck them back into his belt, because they'd been a gift from the Telchi, and it occurred to Harrier now that the Telchi was probably dead.

He'd gone back to the pillar to where Tiercel was when he heard voices in the plaza outside. People. Laughter. And he knew if their own people had won, there might have been cheers, but not laughter. He flattened himself against the pillar. *Too late,* he thought.

He heard a dog bark in the distance, and abruptly stop. There were screams and shouts, but they seemed so far away. Nobody had expected this. They'd expected victory.

They'd sent out an army. If they'd heard the sounds of the battle, they hadn't understood what they were hearing. They thought they were winning.

He knelt down beside Tiercel. The pillars were huge—they'd hide both of them from anyone in the plaza so long as they didn't come up the stairs, but he didn't dare cross the open space—now—to look for better shelter. He put a hand over Tiercel's mouth and shook him, pinched his ear-lobes, tried every nasty painful trick on Tiercel his brothers had ever tried on him. None of them worked. Tiercel didn't wake.

Suddenly a hand fell hard on Harrier's shoulder. He thrust himself to his feet and spun around, heart hammering, grabbing for his swords.

"It isn't time for that yet, you know," a voice said kindly.

Harrier was staring into the eyes of the Red Man.

Tiercel had said he was some kind of Otherfolk, and Harrier tried to see it, but he couldn't. Not really. The man had pale red hair, and brown eyes that were almost red, but that wasn't enough. Was it?

"You can see me," he said slowly, because if this was the same creature as before, he hadn't been able to see Harrier the last time.

"You have become real," the man said.

Harrier didn't know what he meant, unless it was that he could see Harrier now that he was a Wildmage; Harrier didn't really want to ask. "Look," he said. "I need to hide my friend. They're going to kill everyone in the city."

"Yes," the Red Man said calmly.

"They're going to kill *Tiercel*," Harrier said, trying to make the creature understand. "If you wanted him dead, you had plenty of chances. If he dies—" Harrier swallowed hard. "He's supposed to save everyone."

"The world is a dance of light and fire," the Red Man said. "We are the heirs and the children of stars."

"Look," Harrier said again. "Just . . . you need to leave now. I don't know why you're here, or what you want, but you need to go away."

"No fire dies forever. New stars are born. He must be proven," the Red Man said.

This sounded to Harrier like a combination of crazy talk and a threat. He couldn't step back to gain the space to draw his swords—Tiercel and the pillar were behind him—but he could step to the side. He only hoped the Red Man's attention would stay on him. He slid sideways; the smooth marble beneath his feet made it easy. The swords came free of their sheaths with only a slight scraping. "Leave," he said. His mouth was metallic with fear. He didn't know *what* he was facing, only that it wasn't human.

The Red Man turned toward him. It held out its hands to him, palms open, as if it were showing him that it was harmless. But its palms first glittered as if they'd been covered in gold leaf, then glowed as brightly as if they were white-hot metal. The light was too bright for Harrier to be able to look at it directly.

"Will you die so he can live?" the Red Man asked.

"I . . . Light! *Yes!*"

It was why he was here, Harrier realized. It was why he'd come all this way. It was why he'd accepted the Three Books. He'd never expected to become a Kellen and lead vast armies into battle. He'd just hoped to be able to get Tiercel to where he was going.

"Let me touch you."

"Will you—"

"They will not kill him," the Red Man said. It took a step forward, and Harrier brought his hands down, and spread his arms wide, and closed his eyes.

Even through his closed eyelids Harrier could see the light of the Red Man's glowing hand as it approached his face. The heat was enough to make the skin on his face grow tight, and he clamped his jaw hard, hoping he wouldn't scream.

But at the last minute, all he felt was a breath of cool air against his skin. He opened his eyes in startlement.

He was alone.

But not unseen.

He'd barely begun to understand that the Red Man had vanished as inexplicably as he'd come, that he might have a second chance to get the two of them into hiding, when he heard shouts behind him. The sound of running footsteps.

He suddenly realized that he was standing in full view of the Plaza, and he'd been seen. If the Isvaieni came up the steps into the Palace, they'd see Tiercel. Harrier turned and ran down the steps to meet them.

They were so surprised that he gained precious seconds—time enough to dodge, to run along the broad steps, to lead the band of Isvaieni raiders that had been about to enter the Palace back down into the plaza itself.

The plaza was no longer empty. It was filled with scattered bodies—some dead, some still moving feebly. People ran across the plaza trying to reach the palace, because they thought they'd be safe there, but there wasn't any safety anywhere in the city now. The Isvaieni ran after them, cutting them down with single blows, sometimes killing them, sometimes leaving them wounded and dying. In the instant Harrier could spare to look, he thought: *we were wrong—five days—six days—wasn't enough,* because the attacking Isvaieni didn't look cowed and they didn't look exhausted. They looked as if they had all the strength to do whatever they needed to.

Harrier reached the ground, skidding a bit on a bloody patch of stone as he turned. He brandished his swords threateningly, but even though the screaming of the dying all around him filled his ears, even though he knew he was about to die himself, even though he knew these people had already killed everyone he knew here in the city, he wasn't quite sure he could kill anyone else. The image of the man he'd killed filled his mind. The awful finality of it.

The Isvaieni followed him back down the steps, laughing, slapping each other on the shoulders, shouting taunts, encouraging him to do his worst against them, asking him if he was all the city had left to send against them, telling him that they'd killed his father and his brothers and soon they would kill his mother and his sisters as well.

Harrier didn't listen. He watched their hands.

The first one came at him only with a knife, his attacks wide and sloppy, thinking he could frighten him, wanting to make Harrier run. Harrier kept backing away, hearing the Telchi's voice in his head. About how a battle was like love, like an illicit seduction, how first you convinced your enemy that you were one thing and then you became another.

But when the man attacked at last, Harrier was slow to react, thinking of blood on marble. The Isvaieni sprang back, and all Harrier cut was his robe. The Isvaieni snarled, and drew his *awardan,* but when one of his friends moved forward to help him, he shouted that he needed no help to kill a boy who had never drawn blood.

It was ridiculous for such a little thing to upset him after everything else that had happened tonight, but somehow it was the last straw. Harrier felt his heart hammer with fury, and he couldn't really tell *why* he was angry— that they killed so lightly, that they thought it could be as easy for him as it was for them—all he knew was that when the man came forward again—shuffling, flat-footed (and Harrier thought, wild with grief, that the Telchi would never have allowed any of his students to perform so poorly), Harrier spun into him and cut him down without another thought.

As the body fell to the stones the other Isvaieni shouted in shock and drew their weapons, rushing forward, and Harrier was shouting too, crying out as if he were the one being cut, though he wasn't. He only knew that something had to *stop,* and he didn't know what: the killing, the pain he felt at having killed, having to know that the Telchi was dead, the city was dying, that people were dying all around him and *he couldn't do anything about it.* He moved forward into his attackers.

Blood sprayed into his face and he was blinded, but it

didn't matter. He didn't need to see. He knew where his opponents were. Men were running across the square toward him now; he was surrounded by bodies and his swords left arcs of blood behind them in the air as the blades flickered in the rising sun.

He wasn't here at all. Only his body was here, his body that did what it had been trained to do, what the Wild Magic had told him it must. He thought of birds. Herons flying through the morning mist on the Great Plains. Simera had been with them then. He remembered the sight of their wings in the dawn light, how gracefully they'd flown.

He never felt the blow from the club that brought him down.

IT WAS A long time later before Harrier came back to himself at all, and he wasn't really fully conscious. For some reason he couldn't see, and he couldn't move his hands. Someone was dragging him into a sitting position, and forcing his jaws open, and a tube of hard leather was shoved into his mouth, and liquid was poured into it. The liquid was sweet and thick and burning, and he coughed and choked and gagged, trying not to swallow, but when he struggled, all he got for his troubles was a blow to the head.

If he didn't swallow, he'd choke, so he swallowed. After what seemed like an eternity, the pouring stopped, and the tube was withdrawn. "I—What—Who—" he said. His voice was slurred, and he felt weak and sick.

He didn't get any farther than that. The same hands that had held him up forced a length of rag between his jaws and tied it behind his head. He thought he should try to work it loose as soon as they left him alone, but he didn't remember anything after that.

After that sometimes he'd waver near consciousness—always just before someone came to force more wine down his throat. He knew it was wine, now, just as he knew he was being held prisoner somewhere. His head hurt terribly, and he was painfully thirsty, but the one time he'd asked for water when the gag was removed, whoever'd been there had hit him in the face until he'd tasted blood, and then kicked him until someone else had stopped them. He still hadn't gotten any water. Just more of that nauseating wine—date wine, the same wine he'd used to cast the Scrying spell that had been so useless.

Then—after he didn't know how long—there were sounds loud enough to rouse him from his drugged sleep. Roaring. Screams. The bawling of *shotors*.

"Flee, human vermin! Flee or I will destroy you all!" a deep voice bellowed.

Ancaladar.

There was a sudden strong gust of wind. It raised a choking cloud of dust, making Harrier sneeze and cough, and that wasn't a good idea right now, because he realized he still had a gag in his mouth.

Ancaladar roared again, and there were . . . crunching noises. Harrier rolled over on his stomach, groaning. Whatever he was lying on was dusty, making the intense desire to cough and sneeze even worse, and when he rolled, his legs banged into something hard. His ankles were tied together—and his hands were tied behind him—letting him know just how helpless he was, but the pain helped rouse him further. He rubbed his face against the ground, trying to work the blindfold off so he could see where he was. His face hurt, but every twinge of pain brought him closer to awareness.

"Tiercel!" Ancaladar bellowed, and Harrier realized that the one bright spot in all of this was that if Ancaladar was alive, Tiercel was too. He rubbed harder, ignoring the pain in his bruised face. Suddenly there was brightness— though not because he'd gotten the blindfold off—and he could feel sun on his back. He'd been in a tent all along, Harrier realized groggily.

"Harrier," Ancaladar said. "Hold still."

The sunlight went away—Ancaladar's body was blocking it. Harrier froze where he was, imagining a very large black dragon peering at him. He felt a gust of hot breath as

Ancaladar inspected him. "You are so small," Ancaladar said unhappily.

Harrier wanted to thrash, to somehow explain that Ancaladar needed to *do something right now,* because Tiercel might not even be here where they were. He held still with an effort, and felt the ground shake, and heard things go crunch as Ancaladar shifted around. Finally he felt a long dragon talon laid, with utmost delicacy, in the middle of his back.

"Your hands are tied," Ancaladar explained unnecessarily. "But my claws are very sharp. If you can scrape your bonds against my claw, you can sever them."

It took several minutes for Harrier to work himself free. He didn't know how long his hands had been tied. He couldn't really feel them. Ancaladar kept telling him to be careful, but he didn't want to be careful. He wanted to get loose and go look for Tiercel. Finally whatever was holding his wrists broke. He felt a burning ache in his shoulders as his arms flopped to his sides, and as soon as he could, he rolled onto his back again and dragged the blindfold off.

He immediately wished he hadn't. The sunlight stabbed into his eyes like knives, making his headache flare into a constant drumbeat that made lights flash behind his eyes in time with his heartbeat. He dragged the gag out of his mouth and pressed the heels of his hands over his eyes. "Find Tiercel," he croaked. "I'll come when you find him."

Needles of returning circulation coursed through his hands and all the way to his elbows, as if his hands had been asleep for a very long time. After that they simply settled down to ache as if they were badly bruised, and Harrier thought they must be swollen, because when he tried to flex his fingers, they were so stiff he could hardly move them. But he knew he needed to untie his feet as soon as possible.

Cautiously, he uncovered his eyes. The sunlight still made them ache, and he could barely force them open. They were watering so much that tears were trickling down his face, but if he squinted, he could see. He looked around. The contents of the tent had been reduced to ruin by Ancaladar, but there were several pieces of broken glass in the ruins. Harrier coughed and gagged as he caught the scent of the syrupy date wine that he'd been drugged with for Light knew how long. Better that than killed, though he couldn't imagine why they'd bothered to keep him alive. He picked up a shard of glass—only then noticing that he had several deep scratches along his wrists from Ancaladar's claw—and sawed clumsily through the rags that had been used to tie his ankles together.

His feet were in better shape than his hands were, since he'd still been wearing his boots when they'd tied his ankles, and so the bonds weren't as tight. But he still couldn't quite manage to make it to his feet until he crawled to where one of the tent poles lay on the sand and used it as a makeshift walking stick.

When he dragged himself to his feet, he got a good look at where he was for the first time. It was the orchard outside Tarnatha'Iteru. The canals were filled with water again, and the sight and smell of even muddy irrigation ditch water was enough to make Harrier's mouth and throat ache with thirst. The last time he'd gotten a really good look at the orchard, when Tiercel had dropped the MageShield the first time—it had been filled with hundreds of Isvaieni tents. Now less than a dozen remained—if you included the ones that Ancaladar had obviously torn up by their roots looking for the two of them.

"Here," Ancaladar said, sounding unhappy. "He's in here." The dragon nosed at the opening of one of the tents that was still standing.

"I hope—" Harrier's mouth was so dry he had to start again. "I hope there's water here other than what's in those ditches, because I'm about ready to drink that."

"The goatskins hold water," Ancaladar said gently.

It took Harrier a long time to stagger across the space

between the ruined tent he'd been in and the one Ancaladar was waiting outside of.

"Drink first," Ancaladar said. There was a waterskin hanging outside the tent. "You cannot help Tiercel if you are unconscious. And—Harrier—I cannot help him at all."

"You told me that once. I remember," Harrier whispered hoarsely. He wrestled the goatskin down from its hook. The water was warm and tasted of leather, and nothing in Harrier's life had ever tasted so sweet. He drank until his stomach ached, until he didn't think he could hold another mouthful no matter how much he wanted to, and even though everything still *hurt,* he felt stronger. He went inside the tent. Tiercel was lying on the dusty carpet, blindfolded and bound and gagged just as Harrier had been. His head moved from side to side, and he was thrashing feebly.

"Hang on," Harrier said. "I'll get you loose in just a second."

There was a tray of food—bread and cheese and dates—sitting out on a low metal table, as if somebody had been going to sit in here and have lunch and gloat over Tiercel. There was a knife on the tray—one of the same kind of knives that all the Isvaieni seemed to carry—and Harrier picked it up without thinking and then dropped it with a cry.

He thought of the knife in the hand of the man he'd killed. The *men* he'd killed. He remembered that morning on the steps of the palace, and realized he didn't even know how many men he'd killed that day, and realized it had all been for nothing, because they'd ended up here anyway. His hands began to shake, and he forced them to stop, and he forced himself to pick up the knife again. It was just a knife. A tool. It was what people did with tools that mattered.

He cut the rags around Tiercel's ankles first, then sat him up and cut the ones around his wrists. The center pole of the tent was sturdy enough to lean against; he checked before propping Tiercel against it. Then he cut through the gag and pulled it out.

"Oh, Light deliver us," Tiercel said. His voice was hoarse and slurred and his lips were dry and cracked.

"I'd leave the blindfold on," Harrier said. "Really."

He went back to the door of the tent to get the water-skin, but by the time he came back, Tiercel had pulled off the blindfold and was groaning and wincing at the light from the open side of the tent, bringing his swollen hands up to block as much of it as possible.

"Told you," Harrier said without sympathy. He held up the waterskin for Tiercel to drink, and once Tiercel had drunk his fill, washed his own hands and face to remove as much of the dust as he could and then squirted some of the rest of the water over Tiercel.

"Hey," Tiercel said weakly.

"You could use a bath," Harrier said unsympathetically.

"Well, so could you," Tiercel said. He took a deep breath. "I thought you were dead. I didn't know what had happened. When I came to, I knew I'd been tied up. The first time I could manage to concentrate, I yelled for An-caladar as loud as I could."

"And I came, Bonded," Ancaladar said from the door-way, sounding agitated. "I woke, and came as fast as I could."

"You're here, and we're alive," Harrier said soothingly, because Ancaladar seemed really upset. He went over to the table. Even the smell of the dates was nauseating, but he picked up the bread and the cheese and brought them back to where Tiercel was sitting. "Have some food," he said, sitting down carefully. The floor of the tent was car-peted; he wondered if the carpets had come from the city, or whether the Isvaieni had carried them here with them. "I don't know how long we've been held prisoner, but I know they didn't feed us. Or give us any water." He tore off a piece of the bread and chewed slowly. It was hard and stale, but it only served to make him aware of how hungry he was. After a couple of bites he handed the bread to Tiercel and accepted the cheese in return.

"What happened?" Tiercel asked.

"You passed out," Harrier said, staring over Tiercel's shoulder.

"After that. Harrier, I already know the city fell," Tiercel added, when Harrier didn't say anything.

"Rial and I got you inside—we were on the roof, if you don't remember. Everybody who was going to fight went out. There was an ambush. I guess. I think the Isvaieni heard the horns and knew the shield wasn't going to come back up this time." He shrugged. "It didn't matter. They were supposed to be too weak to fight back. After six days without water, they should have been."

"They weren't, though," Tiercel said.

"No. But you were right," Harrier said, looking for something to distract Tiercel. "You said that the Red Man—you remember, he was following us all the way to Ysterialpoerin? You said he was here, and he was."

Tiercel frowned. "I said that? I don't remember."

"You raved about him for three days."

"Yeah, well I probably said I was an enchanted Silver Eagle, too, I mean—wait. He was here?"

"Yeah. We had a wonderful conversation, and he asked what I'd do—pretty much—to get you out of the city alive, and then I got captured by a bunch of Isvaieni and I guess you did, too."

Tiercel gave him an odd look. "That was all that happened?"

"Does there have to be more? Oh, he said I was *real* now, which I found very, very comforting. Not."

"Because he could see you. And you could talk to him," Tiercel said, guessing.

"Something I'd rather avoid doing ever again," Harrier said, reaching for the waterskin again.

"And then they held us prisoner," Tiercel said.

Harrier groaned in exasperation. "Yes, Tyr. They held us prisoner. And I don't know why. And most of them left, because there are only a few tents out there now. And I don't know why they did that either—but most of their tents are gone, and you'll have to ask Ancaladar for details, because he's the one who saw the camp, and he might even have seen where they went."

He'd forgotten just how *annoying* Tiercel could be when he'd gotten fascinated by something and wanted to discuss it endlessly. It was bad enough when it was just something that bored Harrier. It was much, much worse when it was something where Harrier was afraid that Tiercel's endless questions might uncover information Harrier didn't want him to have.

"There were only twelve tents here when I arrived," Ancaladar said. "Seventy *shotors*. They're all gone now," he said, sounding rather pleased with himself.

"Tell me you didn't eat all of them," Harrier muttered, throwing the block of cheese back at Tiercel. Tiercel tried to catch it, but his hands were still too clumsy; it hit him in the chest and bounced to the ground. Harrier suspected the two of them were done with it anyway. He was exhausted and wanted to sleep, ridiculous as that was after all the time he'd spent wine-drugged into unconsciousness.

"I didn't eat any of them," Ancaladar said, sounding affronted. "Well, only one or two of the *shotors*. And only to encourage the people to flee. The *shotors* were far more sensible. They fled immediately."

"They won't come back, will they?" Tiercel asked. Half curious and half worried, and it had always driven Harrier crazy—even more so now, knowing that Tiercel wasn't ever going to change, not if he lived until the end of the world—that Tiercel could never make up his mind to be one way or the other about anything.

"If they try, I will chase them away again," Ancaladar said grimly.

"Can you see where they are right now?" Harrier asked. "Because . . . I'd like to know they're really gone. And I'd like to know where all the rest of them are. There were thousands of them here . . . before."

"The bodies in the city and on the plain outside it are

less than a sennight dead," Ancaladar said. "Five days. Perhaps six. Even though this is a desert, I have . . . some experience with battlefields."

Harrier winced inwardly. *Yeah, I just bet you have.* Until Ancaladar said something like that, it was easy to forget just how *old* the black dragon was, and how much he'd seen. A war he still wouldn't tell them much at all about: the Great War. The war he'd tell them bits and pieces about: it didn't even have a name in their history books, Harrier realized. They just called it The Great Flowering, as if there hadn't been a war, just a victory.

"But they didn't burn the city," Tiercel said, puzzled. "They didn't, right?"

"We'd have smelled that," Harrier said. "And they didn't. They wanted the water," he said, realizing. "The irrigation canals are full, which means they opened the floodgates in the city. Probably to water their *shotors.* And they wouldn't burn the city until the last minute—until they were ready to go. If they did, they wouldn't be able to get at the *Iteru.*" He ran a hand through his hair. It was filthy, and matted with dust, and the back was clotted with dried blood—his. He winced when his hand touched a sore spot.

"You really look awful," Tiercel said.

Harrier smiled, and felt his bruised lip split open all over again. "I guess you did think you were a Silver Eagle after all back there," he said in retaliation. "You were definitely convinced you could fly."

Tiercel made a face, but Harrier was still thinking. "I have an idea about where the rest of the Isvaieni are, but I'd like Ancaladar to check for me, if he's willing," he said.

"Of course," Ancaladar said sympathetically. "I need to hunt, in any event."

"Be careful," Tiercel said.

"Very," Ancaladar agreed. "What is your idea, Harrier?"

"All along we've known that them traveling in such a large group was a problem for them," Harrier said, speaking slowly because his head hurt, and his eyes hurt, and the better he started to feel, the more he realized that everything *else* hurt, too. "That large a group can't find enough water, or food, or much of anything. So . . . now I think they're going home. I don't think they're going to bother with Akazidas'Iteru, or anything north of here. Maybe we actually hurt them badly enough. Or scared them. So I think they split up into small groups to do that, and left over several days. And left the city intact, because it's their best source of water. The last group was probably going to burn it before they went."

Harrier knew he ought to take comfort from the thought that they'd saved Akazidas'Iteru, because if they hadn't been here, if they hadn't done what they'd done, he knew that after the Isvaieni had destroyed Tarnatha'Iteru they would have gone right on to Akazidas'Iteru.

He rubbed his eyes wearily. Had the Light, the Wild Magic, saved one city at the expense of another? He remembered that someone, once, had told him that the Balance was about all things, not just people: about animals and trees and that the Wild Magic wove its plans on so large a scale that the Wildmages who did its work often didn't understand why they did what they did when they paid their Mageprices. But it hurt to think that the Wild Magic could care so little about the people of Tarnatha'Iteru that it had let them all die. *It does care,* he told himself. *It just cares about something else more.* And he didn't know what that was. He knew it was the Great Balance, but that was just a phrase to him. It was too big for him to really imagine. But he tried, because if he didn't, he'd have to think that Zanattar had been right: there was a False Balance and he was following it.

No. He would never believe that. Never.

"So . . . Follow them, and they'll lead us right back to whoever filled their heads with all this 'False Balance' nonsense," Tiercel said, interrupting his thoughts.

"If your Lake of Fire is here, whoever-it-is is probably

camped out right on the shore," Harrier agreed. "But I don't want anything to happen to Ancaladar."

"And I do not wish anything to happen to Tiercel," Ancaladar said in return. "I can fly so high that no eyes upon the ground can see me. And so I shall. I will go now, and first make certain that no enemies surround you, and then see all that lies on the face of the desert."

The dragon withdrew his head from the tent.

"Oh, good," Tiercel said to nobody in particular. "And I . . . I think I'm going to stand up."

By clinging to the center pole of the tent, Tiercel managed to get to his feet. He winced, sucking air between his teeth and hissing in pain, and wavering back and forth, but he didn't fall over.

"Now that you're standing up, what are you planning to do?" Harrier demanded.

"Explore," Tiercel said simply. "I still feel . . . kind of sick."

"They were keeping us drunk," Harrier said, trying not to sound indignant.

"Why?" Tiercel said. "Me, they knew I was a Mage, okay, but why you? And if they meant to keep us as some kind of hostages, why not send us off with the first group that went back, instead of keeping us with the last?"

"I . . . don't . . . know," Harrier repeated steadily. He dragged himself to his feet as well, because right now, the prospect of drowning Tiercel in one of the irrigation ditches was starting to seem really attractive.

He didn't drown Tiercel, but they both decided that the water in the ditches wasn't *that* dirty, and if it was, it was good clean dirt. They found clean clothes in one of the tents—not pants and tunics and vests like the townsfolk wore, but the ankle-length robes and over-robes of the desert-dwellers. Neither of them cared at the moment, though, because they were clean. They carried them to the edge of the nearest ditch and stripped and used the filthy rags of their clothes to wash themselves. Maybe their own clothes could be salvaged later.

"This has blood all over it," Tiercel said, picking up Harrier's tunic from where he'd dropped it in a sodden lump on the ground. Harrier had started to scrub himself with it, seen how soiled it was, and simply tossed it aside.

"They hit me in the head. I bled," Harrier said. He was holding up a wad of wet cloth to the back of his head. The cold felt good, and maybe he could soak the blood out of his hair eventually.

"In the back," Tiercel said. "Not the front. There's blood on the front of your tunic."

"I said they hit me in the head," Harrier said evenly.

"Why?" Tiercel asked simply, regarding Harrier steadily.

"Because they're murderous Darkspawn. And I was trying to get us somewhere to hide until you could wake up and call Ancaladar."

"You killed one of them," Tiercel said, and it was as if he'd suddenly figured out the answer to a question. "That's why—"

Harrier began to laugh. He didn't know why hearing Tiercel say something that was only the truth hurt so much. "You always think you can do things so much better than I can," he said, hating himself and unable to stop. "How many did you kill when you threw MageShield right up in front of them? Maybe I didn't kill as many as you did, but at least I got my hands dirty! I got my hands dirty," he repeated softly.

"Harrier, no! I didn't mean—" Tiercel blurted out.

Harrier turned away and waded out of the canal. He picked up the bundle of clean clothes and walked back toward the tent.

By the time he reached it he was dry, and he began to dress. There was supposed to be a sash worn with this. And something under it, too, he bet. Probably if he looked around some more he could find them.

He saw a shadow stretch across the rug behind him. "Get out," he said.

"I'm sorry," Tiercel said, but he didn't leave. "I didn't know."

"Now you do," Harrier said evenly.

"Do you think I—" Tiercel stopped. "Do you think I feel any differently about you than I did? You did something—"

"I killed people," Harrier said harshly.

"So did I," Tiercel answered.

Harrier shook his head. He couldn't tell Tiercel that was different. He didn't want to tell Tiercel it was different— *how* it was different. Tiercel had stood on a wall a mile away and cast a spell. And he'd known he was responsible, and he'd seen the people die, and it was horrible, but he hadn't stood inches away from another man with a sword in his hand and been sprayed with his blood and seen the light fade from the man's eyes as he fell.

"I know it was different," Tiercel said, still quietly. "I couldn't have done what you did. Not because I don't know how to fight with a sword. It's not that."

"What, then?" Harrier said, when Tiercel didn't say anything else.

"It must have been horrible. Having to kill somebody like that, and . . . having to keep doing it. You weren't even doing it for yourself. I'm sorry."

"You can shut up now," Harrier said. He wasn't angry any more. He just wished he didn't have to remember what he'd done. "I'm sorry," he said, and he didn't really know who he was saying it to. It didn't seem fair to be sorry for the people he'd killed, when they'd killed so many other people, but he was. "They didn't have any choice," he said slowly.

"No," Tiercel said seriously. "Someone lied to them and told them we were Tainted. And they came to kill us, thinking they were doing the right thing. And when they got here, they *had* to get into the city, or else they'd all die. We tried to save the city. And you tried to save me. And we're both still alive. And maybe we'll never know why." Harrier heard Tiercel take a deep breath. "And I guess we have to think of our being alive as a good thing. Because we still have a chance to find the Lake of Fire."

And maybe a better chance—now—than they would have had if Tarnatha'Iteru hadn't been destroyed, because maybe Ancaladar could follow the retreating Isvaieni back to whoever had sent them. Harrier thought of a Balance so vast and terrible that it could sacrifice a city to show them the way to their goal. And he thought of all the cities—all the *people*—there were in the world, not only here, but beyond Great Ocean. For just a moment he could glimpse the scale of that Balance, but then he realized that wasn't the point. For humans to think that way—to see the world on such a scale—meant that they'd say that anything that happened, anything they chose to do, was okay. And that wasn't right. Only the Wild Magic itself could see the world that way. People had to trust in the Light, and care about each other, and Wildmages . . . well, Harrier guessed that Wildmages had to trust in the Wild Magic and pay their Mageprices.

"Stop talking. Now. Really," he said.

"Okay. I'm done," Tiercel said.

WHEN ANCALADAR RETURNED a couple of hours later, the two of them were sitting in the doorway of one of the tents, roasting meat on a spit. They'd found a basket of freshly killed hares in one of the tents—the skinned and cleaned bodies were packed in oil; the tent was obviously meant to be a larder of sorts—and had put together a meal. All of the loaves were unappetizingly stale, but there was an entire barrel of uncooked dough, and Harrier had found a griddle-stone. They ate hot flatbread, and drank mint tea with honey, and waited for the meat to cook.

Harrier could see the walls of the city in the distance. It looked fine on this side—untouched—except for the fact that there were tiny black specks moving along the top of the wall, and when one of them was jostled off and flapped awkwardly into space he realized that they were birds.

When Ancaladar came back, he made a low pass over the city. As he did, suddenly the sky above it was black with birds, as thousands of them boiled up out of it squalling in fright. Harrier saw a flash of motion along the ground, too, as something came running along the city wall, but it was too far away to see exactly what it was.

Ancaladar kindly landed far enough away so that the dust of his landing wouldn't come anywhere near them and spoil what they were cooking. Harrier wondered how they were going to ride him when they left. Ancaladar's saddle was in the storage room at the Telchi's house, and . . . Harrier decided not to think about that.

"This is *our* dinner," Harrier said, when Ancaladar approached. To be fair, Ancaladar actually lay down quite a distance away and simply stretched out his neck in their direction.

"I have already eaten," Ancaladar said mildly, blinking slowly.

"I hope you ate well?" Tiercel asked politely. He yawned. They were both exhausted, and still hungry despite all the bread they'd eaten, and both felt the aftereffects of so many days of captivity lying bound and half-starved.

"Very well," Ancaladar said smugly.

"Are there any *shotors* left in the whole desert?" Harrier asked. He decided that the meat was done. Or done enough, anyway.

"Antelope," Ancaladar corrected. "And pig. More were required than if I'd eaten *shotor*. However, they were far tastier."

"You're going to burn yourself," Tiercel pointed out.

Harrier snarled, sucking his burned fingers. He waved a leg of the hare around to cool it. "Did you see them?" he mumbled around his fingers.

"Those whom I drove from this place continue to flee. They have managed to regain . . . nearly all of their lost mounts. I think they will seek out their brethren, and gain from them enough resources to be able to finish their journey homeward in safety. So they will see no need to return here."

"Yes," Tiercel said, nodding. "But where are they going?"

"The first of them to leave have been less than a sennight on their journey," Ancaladar said. "I do not yet know."

"So what do we do?" Tiercel asked.

"We wait for them to tell us," Harrier said.

THE SUN SET, and the two of them staggered off to sleep the moment the temperature began to drop. Ancaladar said he would stand guard—they were safe from the Isvaieni, but the ruin of the city had attracted many predators, and some of them would undoubtedly come to the orchard seeking water. Harrier knew that normally the irrigation canals were only filled for a few hours early in the morning, to keep the sun's heat from stealing all the water, but without someone in the city to work the mechanisms, they just kept filling no matter how much water evaporated. He guessed you couldn't really say it was a waste, either.

But in the middle of the night the wind shifted, blowing south from the city. By the time the smell woke them, the stench was thick enough to make them gag.

"Oh, *Light*—" Tiercel's voice held nauseated misery. He sounded as if he was on the verge of asking what that smell was, but he knew better. They both did. Dead bodies, hundreds upon hundreds of them, left unburied for nearly a sennight in the desert sun.

They had to do something.

Harrier staggered to his feet. He'd thought of something that might help. Not that anything could completely.

In the Madiran, they called it *gonduruj*—a pale-yellow resin that was harvested from the trees in the nearby hills. It was one of the ingredients in Light-incense, and also used in medicines and even some recipes. He'd seen a sack of it in the provisions tent. He staggered out of the sleeping tent, holding a fold of his robe over his nose.

"What is wrong?" Ancaladar asked when he came reeling out into the open, and Harrier wanted to ask him if he had no sense of smell at all, but that would have involved talking, and that would have involved breathing, and he was trying not to.

He staggered into the other tent, hoping he remembered where the *gonduruj* was, because he thought he'd pass out from the stench in the time it took to conjure up a ball of Coldfire. He knew the wind shifted every night about this time. In the morning the wind would shift back to blow north again, and after sunrise it would drop, but that didn't help them right now. Fortunately the sack was the first thing his hand fell on—about five pounds of resin, and he didn't want to think about what it would sell for in the Armethalieh markets. He staggered back out of the tent with it and over to their cook fire, still clutching the fold of fabric over his nose with his free hand. He could see the banked glowing coals. Good. He held his breath and wrenched the bag open with both hands, and spilled at least two pounds of the precious resin onto the hot coals.

For a second—two—nothing happened. Then the golden globs of resin began to smoke and melt, and a billowing white cloud of fragrant smoke rose up, carried by the wind directly toward their sleeping tent. It was chokingly dense. But it also didn't smell like anything but *gonduruj.* He leaned over the smoke and inhaled, driving the stench of rotting meat from his senses.

"Are you trying to kill me?" Tiercel demanded, coughing wildly as he came staggering out of his tent. He glared around and summoned up his own—much larger—ball of Coldfire. It turned the wavering cloud of smoke an eerie shade of blue.

"If you'd rather smell *that,* fine," Harrier said. "Because, you know, it doesn't seem to bother Ancaladar much."

"I hadn't realized it would trouble you now," the dragon said apologetically. "It didn't earlier."

"We couldn't smell it earlier," Tiercel said, still coughing.

"Build up the fire," Harrier said. "Not too much. You don't want to burn the *gonduruj,* just melt it."

While Tiercel did that, Harrier went off to get a couple of the pieces of cloth he'd seen—they were too short and sheer to use as sashes; he thought they might be headscarves of some kind. He brought them back with another waterskin—tomorrow they were going to have to go to the watering trough at the base of the city walls to refill them, but at least they wouldn't have to go inside—and the two of them wet the fabric down and tied it around their faces. That blocked the smoke—so it was easier to breathe—and if they ran out of *gonduruj,* it might cut some of the smell, too.

Harrier glanced up at the sky. Quarter moon. He thought the moon had been dark when Tiercel's shield had fallen and the Isvaieni had attacked. So it had been about a sennight since then, just as Ancaladar had said.

"We can't stay here," Tiercel said.

"I've got a whole list of reasons why it's going to be really hard for us to leave. Want to hear them?" Harrier asked without heat. In the distance, he heard something bark and then yowl. It didn't sound like either a dog or a wolf, but he couldn't identify it.

"Oh, sure," Tiercel said, and so Harrier sat beside him and beside the fire, and listed every reason he'd thought of.

They had no way to ride Ancaladar without his saddle. Even with the saddle, they had no way to carry supplies for an extended journey—they had to wait until they knew exactly where they were going, and then go there at once. The same problems applied if they simply wanted to move a little way away from here. This was the only source of water anywhere nearby, and they had no way to move the tents—their only form of shelter—and there was probably enough in the way of food here to last them a sennight or so, by which time they might know where they were going, but they couldn't carry any of it with them.

"*Harrier,*" Tiercel said. "We can't stay here."

"If you've got any idea of how we can leave—and stay alive—and figure out where we're going—I'm all for hearing it. I don't like this any better than you do."

"A spell," Ancaladar said.

"What kind?" Tiercel asked, at the same time Harrier said: "Not MageShield, because—"

"No," Ancaladar said. "The flesh rots in the sun. In a moonturn, at most, insects and animals will have finished the work. You could hurry their work. Then we could stay."

"I know we've talked about that, Ancaladar, but I'm not sure I want to try a spell like that. I'm not an Elven Mage," Tiercel said.

Harrier gave him an odd look, but Tiercel didn't seem to think he'd said anything peculiar. "Or, you know, you could just burn them. They're *dead!*" he said indignantly, when Tiercel turned to stare at him. "And that's what they do with people here when they die! I asked!"

He thought Tiercel was going to get upset, but he didn't. "I could," he said thoughtfully. "I'd want to be able to see what I was doing, though. So I want to wait until the wind changes."

A couple of hours later, Harrier found out what he meant.

Seventeen

Unmade by Magic

IT WAS DAWN, and the plume of smoke from the fire had shifted back in the direction of the city. Even though all either of them could smell was *gonduruj,* neither of them had been able to get back to sleep. When the rising sun began to whiten the sky, Tiercel got to his feet and walked through the orchard until he reached the edge. Harrier followed him, puzzled, because Tiercel hadn't told him what he was going to do.

"Har, do you know where the *Iteru* is?" Tiercel asked.

"Near the south side of the city. The Telchi took me to see it one day. It really doesn't look like much—it's just a big round stone—I mean, it covers the well. If you move the stone, there are steps inside, but nobody ever goes down."

"It's covered. Good."

"Look, I don't know what you're planning to do, but shouldn't you get a little more rest first?"

"Dragon," Tiercel explained, gesturing toward where Ancaladar lay watching them. "I'll sleep when I'm done. We both can."

"Okay," Harrier said dubiously.

Tiercel raised his hands.

And the city wall nearest them . . . dissolved.

It was already pale in the dawn light. Then it began to glitter in the sun, and just as Harrier was trying to make up his mind whether he was seeing what he thought he was, it collapsed with a crash.

It had turned to water.

The day was bright and the sky was clear, and he stood on a plain, in the midst of a lake, not a lake of fire, but a lake of water, and a quiet sad voice—it came from outside, but somehow it was his—spoke, saying: "This is Tarnatha'Iteru. This is all that remains."

With a sudden shock, Harrier realized that this, *this,* was what he had seen in the Scrying Bowl. Not exactly, not as it was, but . . . this.

"I told you Transmutation was easy," Tiercel said.

The wave smashed down in all directions—back into the city, spraying up over the standing walls, foaming out over the earth toward them just as if it were an ocean breaker. The water raced toward them in a spreading fan, soaking into the thirsty soil. The last of it seeped into the ground over a mile away.

"Ah . . . you want to tell me why you did that?" Harrier asked, when he was certain the two of them weren't going to drown in the middle of a desert. He didn't know exactly how many thousands of gallons of water that once-brick wall had become, but . . . a lot.

"I need to see what I'm doing," Tiercel repeated. "And I wanted to do the walls one at a time to make sure I didn't drown us. I think they have the most mass of anything I'll be changing."

"Um, you're going to . . ." Harrier said, and stopped as the east wall turned to water and fell. Again Tiercel waited until the water trickled away.

The city looked strange and naked with two of its walls gone. Harrier could see the top of the Consul's Palace in the distance, but none of the streets ran straight, and they weren't standing in a direct line of sight with the South Gate anyway.

Then the west wall fell. By now Harrier was used to the boom and crash of the water, and he didn't even flinch. The air was moist, and everything smelled like mud, and there was enough water saturating the earth now that trickles were actually reaching them, but all the water did was go into the canals.

"Finished?" Harrier asked, when Tiercel took down the

north wall. He tried not to flinch at what the water swept before it as it spread across the plain—tangles of bone and pieces of sun-blackened bodies, distant, but recognizable. The water had scoured the streets of the city too, washing debris—including bodies—down through them and out into the plain beyond. Not many. The streets were narrow.

"No," Tiercel said. "I need to see what I'm doing," he repeated. He took a deep breath.

"You keep saying that," Harrier said, and the sharpness of his tone was caused as much by worry as by irritation. "What do you *mean*?"

"Burning the bodies is a good idea," Tiercel said. "But I need to see them."

As Harrier watched—too stunned to be either horrified or amazed—Tiercel took down building after building, starting at the south end of the city and working north-ward. Wood and glass and metal and cloth—and the bodies of the dead—remained behind. Harrier wondered why, if Tiercel could turn the walls and the stone and clay of the buildings into water, he couldn't just turn everything. He might ask later, but right now he wasn't sure he wanted to hear any more explanations about High Magick. Ever.

The only area of the city Tiercel was careful not to touch was the space around the *Iteru*.

The more that the city was erased, as if it were being *un*-built, piece by piece, the more horrible a sight the remains of Tarnatha'Iteru became. Harrier was grateful that they were both so far away, but it didn't really blunt the impact of what they were seeing. The successive waves of water created as the buildings dissolved piled the rotting bodies and the household debris up against each other like a horrible shoal. Harrier put his arm around Tiercel's shoulders, because he'd begun to sway a little—with shock as much as with exhaustion.

"We'll sleep for a sennight," he promised, and Tiercel smiled faintly.

At last only the Consul's Palace remained.

"I think you'd better, you know, first, because—" Harrier said.

"Yeah," Tiercel said. The wave of water from the transmutation of the Consul's Palace might be enough to break up the bulwarks of debris and sweep the rest of the bodies all the way down to the orchard, and if that happened, Harrier didn't think he'd ever feel clean again.

By now the sun was fully up, and the wet ground was steaming as if it boiled. It didn't matter how wet everything was. Tiercel stretched out his hand, and the bodies burst into flame.

They didn't burn like meat or wood. There was a white flare of flame, as if some cloudwit had flung an oil-filled lantern into the depths of a raging bonfire, and then the bodies were ash. The heat of their burning had caused some of the things around them to catch fire, and the wood and fabric burned with honest orange flame.

Tiercel looked around. There were other bodies in the city that hadn't been washed into the largest group. They burned as quickly as the others. In seconds, the heat of the fires had baked the earth dry, and the wind began to blow the ash away. Tiercel began to look farther away, searching the plain in the distance, and Harrier saw white flares of fire blossom on the horizon. A cold knot of fear tightened in his chest. He'd known—before—that Tiercel's spells were powerful, and certainly seeing MageShield had been impressive. But until today he'd never really grasped how powerful—and how different—Tiercel's magic was from the Wild Magic. All he'd ever heard was Tiercel saying that he didn't know very much, couldn't learn very much, wasn't very good. But this, *this* was what Tiercel meant by "calling Fire."

If this was what "not very good" was, what in the name of the Light would Tiercel be like when he *was* good?

If he got the chance to get that way.

Harrier tried not to shudder.

"Now the Palace," Tiercel said.

No matter how disturbed Harrier was by seeing Tiercel

truly use the powers of a dragon-Bonded High Mage, it was still fascinating to watch the Palace simply turn to water and collapse. There were no bodies inside it—Harrier was relieved to see—but there were hundreds and hundreds of rugs, vases, and pieces of furniture, all of which suddenly appeared suspended in air and then were swept along on a foaming tide of water. When the wave had passed— quenching the small fires that were burning within the space that had once been the city bounds—the only sign that there had ever been a city there at all was a lot of furniture lying around in the mud and a pair of bronze gates, also lying in the mud. And now that Tiercel could see the battlefield beyond the gates, he burned the few bodies left there, too.

It occurred to Harrier that Tiercel could have left the Palace intact. There weren't that many bodies beyond it— not enough to be a problem. And all their stuff had been in the Palace. It might even have still been there. They might have been able to use it.

But he knew why Tiercel had done what he had. When they left here they still wouldn't be able to carry anything with them, much less six trunks of books. Harrier didn't want to walk back into the Palace any more than Tiercel did. And unmaking it that way seemed like a fitting memorial somehow to all the people who'd died here, no matter who they were and what they'd believed.

"I hope you've got a plan for us getting water out of the *Iteru* now that you've managed to dissolve the watering trough," Harrier said.

"The pump system's still in place," Tiercel said. "I'm pretty sure we don't want to drink out of the irrigation ditches—"

"No," Harrier said firmly. "But we can either go into the—We can go to the pump itself, or, if we have to, dig down to the pipes that feed the canals."

"Or Ancaladar can uncap the *Iteru*," Tiercel said. "Later."

* * *

THE TENT STILL reeked of *gonduruj*, but both of them were too tired to care. They flung themselves back down on their looted sleeping mats.

"You don't mind, do you, Har?" Tiercel asked sleepily.

"What? That you turned a whole city into water? Should have done it sooner. Go to sleep," Harrier said.

WHEN THEY WOKE again, the sky was orange with sunset. The two of them staggered out of the tent, blinking and rubbing their eyes. It was strange, Harrier thought, even though he hadn't seen the city from outside all that much, to look northward and not see it at all. There was nothing there now but a plain of sun-baked mud and a jumble of furniture. Some of the pieces were half-charred. Others were intact, but now just weirdly sitting out in the middle of nowhere.

"We need water," Harrier said. He looked at the sky. "There isn't much light left."

"I can make light," Tiercel said. He looked at Harrier. "So can you."

Harrier sighed, and scratched the back of his head, and hit a lump, and winced. "I know." He wondered where his Books were right now. Maybe buried somewhere out there in the mud. "You're better at it, though."

"Um," Tiercel looked as if he would have preferred that Harrier hadn't mentioned that fact. "I guess I'm going to have to make a new Wand," he said randomly.

"I guess you are," Harrier said. He sighed again. "You light us up. Then we'll eat. Then we'll go get water."

"And now that you have finally awakened, I will hunt," Ancaladar said. "And see where the Isvaieni are."

"Probably only about a day farther along to wherever they're going than they were the last time you looked," Harrier said. He glanced at Ancaladar, then back at Tiercel. "How big *is* this desert, really?"

Tiercel shrugged. "You're the one who knows the coast.

I told you nobody's ever really mapped the desert. For all anybody knows, it goes all the way down to World's End."

"Not down to the Horn," Harrier said. "It's jungle down there. But that's . . . almost half a year's sailing. And you just have to turn back, even if you can get there— nobody's ever been able to round the Horn. The storms are too bad."

"So . . . I don't know," Tiercel said. He frowned. "But it can't be that far—where they're going. Because they were seen—here—half a year ago. Then they disappeared. Then they came back to Tarnatha'Iteru."

"So?" Harrier said.

"So," Tiercel said, "in that time they'd gone away, been told we were evil, come back, and destroyed at least two other cities, and from Laganda'Iteru to Tarnatha'Iteru was between six and eight sennights' journey for them."

"So wherever this place is they're going, it has to be fairly close," Harrier finished.

"Yes," Tiercel said.

BY NOW IT was starting to get dark. Tiercel created several globes of Coldfire, making the campsite as bright as day, and went to build up the fire while Harrier went to find something for dinner. The idea of dates in any form was still revolting, but there were *naranjes,* and cheese, and enough flour and onions and garlic and vegetables that he was even willing to try to make a stew.

As he dug through a basket of something that might be turnips, or potatoes, or even flower bulbs, his fingers encountered something at the bottom of the basket that was definitely neither a turnip nor a flower bulb. He pulled them out and held them up, peering at them in the light of the ball of Coldfire that hovered over his left shoulder.

His Books.

"This is . . . weird," he said aloud. Kareta had said they couldn't be taken away from him, but he hadn't thought that meant they'd show up in the bottom of a basket of turnips. That was just . . .

No weirder than any other piece of magic, I guess.

He tucked them into his sash, folding the fabric carefully over them so they wouldn't fall out, and went back to selecting items for the stew.

Soon the stew had been assembled—it would probably actually be ready to eat tomorrow and not tonight, but it wouldn't even be ready tomorrow if he didn't start cooking it now—and they'd toasted a lot of bread and cheese and eaten it with olives and pickled vegetables from a crock that Harrier had found. Tiercel had gathered together all the waterskins he could find from everywhere in the camp. More of them were full—or half-full—than Harrier had thought, so they could probably go another day without getting water, but he wanted to know what their options were for filling them. If they had to use the water out of the ditches, they'd have to boil it, because it had probably been contaminated by runoff from the city.

There were more than fifty of the waterskins—too many to carry empty, and far too many to carry full. Harrier figured they could carry back two or three each once they'd filled them.

To his relief, filling them wasn't difficult at all. Tiercel had left the entire plaza around the *Iteru* intact: it was the only patch of stone left in what had once been a city with a number of cobblestoned plazas. Standing around the *Iteru* were several troughs, and a pump to fill them. It needed to be worked by hand, but it was still there.

"This will help, too," Tiercel said.

While Harrier was working the pump—it took a while to finally start to spew water—and then filling the waterskins, Tiercel had wandered off as usual. Under other circumstances it would have annoyed him, but right now Harrier was just as glad that Tiercel was acting just like his normal self.

"What?" he said, before he looked up.

"This," Tiercel said, sounding annoyed, and Harrier fi-

nally looked. Tiercel had found one of the little wheeled carts.

It was in good shape, even if it had been soaked down pretty thoroughly and then baked dry. It was wood and metal and leather, and all of those things were intact everywhere in the city, Light knew why. "Yeah," he said. They could probably carry twice as many waterskins back and forth, too. "Go find another one," he said.

Tiercel made an annoyed noise and stomped off, and Harrier finished filling the waterskins.

"Tomorrow we can bring both the carts back and fill more of them," Harrier said as they wheeled the two carts back to the tents.

"Great," Tiercel said. "Then we'll have a lot of goatskins full of water. Warm, yucky, bad-tasting water."

"And what if the pump mechanism fails, idiot? Or the *Iteru* goes dry for Light knows what reason? Or something happens that I can't even think of right now? We'll at least have enough water to be able to think things over for a day or two."

Tiercel looked at the sky. "Maybe I could make it rain," he said thoughtfully.

"Maybe you couldn't," Harrier said firmly. "Because I don't think the desert would like that very much, Tyr. If it was supposed to rain down here, it would."

WHEN ANCALADAR RETURNED much later, Harrier was practicing calling Fire.

Doing magic like this—the kind where he had a *choice* about doing it or not—always left him feeling as if he was trying to put his foot on a step that wasn't there, no matter how many times it worked. He was starting to wonder if maybe the only thing that Wildmages really had to practice was the whole idea of flinging themselves into the Wild Magic, just as if they were jumping over the side of a ship in the midst of Great Ocean, and not caring what happened next because it would be whatever the Wild Magic wanted.

If that was what it took to be a good Wildmage, Harrier thought, he was always going to suck at it.

But after what he'd seen this morning, no matter how much his mind insisted that making something burst into flames just by pointing his finger at it and thinking wasn't *normal,* there was something soothing about seeing sticks of wood blossom into the same honest orange flames he could make with flint and steel, and he hadn't been able to practice any spells at all for the whole time they'd been in Tarnatha'Iteru. Of course, the moment he announced his intention to practice, Tiercel announced *his* intention to go for a walk—somewhere out of range of whatever-it-was that Harrier did that affected him and his power—so Harrier was just as glad when Ancaladar returned so he could stop practicing without having it look as if he was stopping because the idea that what he was doing was hurting Tiercel freaked him out.

When Ancaladar rejoined them, he told them that after hunting and checking on the progress of the Isvaieni, he'd flown down the eastern edge of the Madiran, along what the Madirani called the S*tring of Pearls*—the chain of *Iteru*-cities.

"All are gone," Ancaladar said sadly. "All destroyed, their inhabitants slaughtered, their wells poisoned."

"All of them?" Tiercel asked, sounding dumbfounded.

"They must have been wrong," Harrier said. "About the last time they saw anyone from any of the tribes. There are—what?"

"Eleven cities," Tiercel said.

"And if all but Akazidas'Iteru is gone, that's ten of them gone. I don't know exactly where they are, but I'm pretty sure you couldn't even *get* an army from Orinaisal'Iteru to Tarnatha'Iteru in six moonturns."

"You could," Ancaladar said. "If they moved quickly. The two southernmost cities are very close together."

"And obviously they did," Tiercel said.

"And maybe everybody didn't disappear at the same

time," Harrier said, sighing in frustration. "Any idea where they're going, Ancaladar?"

"They do not travel in a straight line through the desert," the dragon said reprovingly. "They move from water source to water source. We shall not know their ultimate destination for some time."

"Too bad we don't have a map of all the water in the desert," Harrier said unwarily.

"I can't draw a complete map," Tiercel said, sounding surprised. "But I can draw a fairly good one—of the Isvai, at least."

By the time Tiercel was done, Harrier had a confused picture of a large hostile desert with oases just close enough together that a determined traveler with a *shotor* could manage to get from one to the next without dying. To get anywhere in the Isvai involved taking a route that wove like the path of a drunken sailor from one dockside tavern to the next—only not quite as straight.

"It is hotter there than it is here," Ancaladar said helpfully.

"And nobody knows their way around it—or where all the water is—but the Isvaieni," Tiercel said. He didn't say this as if it was something he knew. More as if it was something he was just now figuring out. They'd been supposed to hire Isvaieni guides, Harrier remembered, if they'd thought they were going to need to go into the Isvai on their search. He guessed, in a manner of speaking, they had them now.

"When we *do* follow them," Harrier said, "how are we going to do it? Because we're going to have to ride Ancaladar, and as far as I know, he doesn't have a saddle any more. Unless it's out there somewhere, and you can find it," he added, pointing toward where the city had been.

"I'll think of something," Tiercel said.

"You do that," Harrier answered.

* * *

FOR THE NEXT fortnight, the two of them lived a strange quiet existence on the outskirts of a city that was no longer there. They combed through the Isvaieni camp for things they might be able to use, and so Harrier found not only the swords that had been his gift from the Telchi, but the sword that Roneida had given him. He wasn't really sure what to do with Roneida's sword, but it had been the gift of a Wildmage, so he was determined to find some way to take it with them when they went.

Ancaladar spent his nights hunting, and each morning he would report on the progress of the Isvaieni. The bands of raiders were all moving southward, though none of them was moving in a direct line and few of them were taking the same path.

After the first few days, Tiercel started trying to make a new wand from a branch of one of the *naranje* trees. The first four exploded when he tried to use them, but the fifth one survived. After that, he spent his days wandering through the ruins of the city, picking through the debris. He didn't find Ancaladar's saddle—possibly it was one of the many items that had been smashed and then burned—in fact, after a while, Tiercel and Harrier simply started making piles of furniture and setting fire to them. It was practice on Harrier's part, and, he guessed, boredom on Tiercel's.

But Tiercel did find—in the area where the stables had been—a long roll of leather strap, a small barrel of brass buckles, some rivets, and even a couple of hammers. Everything necessary to mend harness.

"You can't make a saddle out of that," Harrier said, looking at what Tiercel had found.

"No," Tiercel said. "But I can make a—a kind of belt to go around Ancaladar's neck. And I can hold onto that when he flies. And you can hold onto me."

Harrier stared at him in disbelief. "That's *it*? That's your plan? He's going to fly all the way up there and you're going to hold onto a string around his neck and just *hope you don't fall off*?" He stared up at the sky. It looked . . . high.

"He'll catch me if I do," Tiercel said confidently. "He'll catch you, too. It's all I can think of, Har."

Harrier looked at Tiercel, then up at the sky again. "This had better work," he muttered.

"I DO NOT like it, Bonded," Ancaladar said when Tiercel explained. Harrier had made Tiercel do all the explaining—not only was it his plan, it was a stupid plan, and Tiercel was better at making stupid plans sound reasonable. Harrier wasn't sure whether it made things better or not to know that Ancaladar was as unhappy with the idea as he was—but as Tiercel pointed out, if they were going to ride him, they needed some way to hold on, and the saddle was gone.

"I don't like it either," Harrier said helpfully.

"If either of you has a better idea, I'm open to suggestions," Tiercel said stubbornly.

Harrier was the one who made the leather strap. At least that way—so he said—he could be sure that the rivets wouldn't pop free at a critical moment. He made a belt for Tiercel, too. At least that way he'd have something to hold on to. After some consideration, he made one for himself, as well. It would help hold his sword-harness in place as they flew, and give him some place to put Roneida's sword.

A few days later, Ancaladar came and told them that the first group of Isvaieni were now heading directly south.

"And I think they follow a trail, for the land they now pass through is so barren as to make the Isvai look like a garden—and the starkness of the Isvai makes the place where you now stand look verdant. Further, they follow a track beaten into the earth by the passage of many feet. I do not think that this is a place that they would ordinarily go."

"Is it time to go, then?" Tiercel said.

He actually managed to sound hopeful, Harrier thought. All the time they'd been waiting here, they hadn't talked about what they were waiting for, or what was going to happen when the waiting was over. He'd almost managed to forget about it.

"Another day," Ancaladar said. "So I may be sure."

THE LAST DAY—and night—of waiting was the hardest. Harrier couldn't think of anything to say. If they actually found the Lake of Fire after they'd searched for it for so long, what then? They'd be facing the Endarkened, in whatever form they were appearing now, and he wasn't sure what Tiercel was supposed to be able to do about it. He didn't know if Tiercel *could* set them on fire, although he guessed he probably *would* if he could. Harrier only hoped he could be of some help, but now that he was actually studying the spells of the Wild Magic as hard as he could, he wasn't sure how. One person couldn't defeat an army, and from what Ancaladar had said, anybody they could possibly have looked to as allies was dead.

He didn't say any of this to Tiercel. There wasn't any point. They couldn't go back. They had to go on. If Tiercel hadn't thought of these things, he didn't need to be told them now. And all Harrier could do was what he'd done from the very beginning: follow Tiercel. Whether he was trusting the Wild Magic to help him make everything right, or just trying to be there to do whatever he could the way he always had, it didn't matter. The result was the same.

They managed to sleep that night, though not very well.

IN THE MORNING when Ancaladar landed he said that the Isvaieni were continuing directly south along the well-marked path.

"There are wells at the side of the road they follow. They are unnatural—for they are spaced exactly a day's journey apart—and new, for they exactly parallel the path that has been beaten into the desert, and I think, from the markings on the ground, that they were made after it, not before."

"We can follow them right to where we need to go," Tiercel said excitedly.

"Yes," Ancaladar said. "It is time to leave, Bonded."

"Get water," Harrier said. "And pack up a bag of food. And don't tell me we aren't going to need it. Something always happens."

Tiercel smiled at him—the same expression he always wore when he was indulging one of Harrier's stupid ideas—and went off to the provision tent.

"You fear to die," Ancaladar said when Tiercel was out of earshot. There wasn't any judgment in his voice. Not even, really, a question.

Harrier laughed, a little startled, because Ancaladar had it so wrong. He'd already been afraid to die, and he hadn't died, and he didn't think he could ever have been that afraid again. He shook his head. "I'm afraid to fail," he said. "You were there. You saw."

Ancaladar had been there when the Endarkened had nearly won. That was more terrifying than anything else could ever possibly be.

"Yes," the black dragon said, and now there was something like approval in its voice.

WHEN THEY WERE both settled on Ancaladar's back, Harrier had a bag of food slung across one shoulder and a waterskin slung across the other, and Roneida's sword carefully tucked through his belt in front. Tiercel complained that it dug into his back, and Harrier pointed out that he had no intention of falling off just to make Tiercel more comfortable.

Then Ancaladar took off.

In the last several moonturns, Harrier had seen Ancaladar take off and land so many times he'd lost count. In the last fortnight, he'd seen him take off and land from the plain outside the orchard twice a day.

It was different when you were sitting on his back.

In the first place, he ran. Fast. And there were no stirrups, and no real way to hold on. They were both straddling Ancaladar's neck, and his scales were slippery, and Tiercel was clutching at the neck-strap, and Harrier was holding on to Tiercel as hard as he could as the landscape blurred past.

Then suddenly Ancaladar snapped his wings open, and *lunged* upward, like a cat after a butterfly, and then he was beating his wings frantically and Harrier had his eyes tightly shut and Tiercel was complaining that he *couldn't breathe* and Harrier had a terrifying sense of gliding and falling and he could feel the hot wind rushing against his face.

Then after a long time—minutes—nothing happened. Harrier opened his eyes warily.

For long moments he couldn't tell what he was seeing at all. Ahead of him was Ancaladar's neck, stretched out as straight as the neck of a swan in flight and gleaming iridescently in the sunlight. Below there was nothing but a vast expanse of dun. He couldn't actually tell how far away the ground was; there were no landmarks to set anything into perspective. It was like every story he'd ever heard the mariners tell about being out in the middle of Great Ocean, with nothing in any direction but water. Except they, at least, had a ship under them and knew where "up" and "down" were.

Then he looked westward, and he could see a sparkle of light; the sun on the sea.

When he saw that, Harrier suddenly realized exactly how high up they had to be, and he clutched Tiercel tightly again.

"Stop that," Tiercel complained. He shifted around, turning sideways, and Harrier gripped Ancaladar's neck with his thighs until the muscles ached. "Isn't this great?" he said.

"Terrific," Harrier said. He remembered the days when Tiercel hadn't even been willing to climb a tree that was barely twenty feet high—let alone up into the rigging of a ship to look out over the docks and the harbor—and suddenly longed for those days passionately. "Will you hold still?"

"Relax," Tiercel said. "We aren't going to fall off."

Harrier wasn't at all sure about that. He also thought, given Tiercel's apparent newfound idiotic and suicidal recklessness, that *he* should have been the one sitting in front and holding on to the neck-strap.

But after a few minutes of level flight he settled down and stopped worrying, because they weren't falling off. And there was a lot to see.

He wasn't quite brave enough to turn around and look behind them, but what he could see ahead and to the sides was fascinating enough. They were so high in the sky that he could see for hundreds of miles, he thought. There was little to see on the ground—Ancaladar's shadow provided most of the definition to what he was seeing, flickering over piled up hills of sand, stretching out flat and long and dark across hard plains of baked clay. Sometimes there'd be a red or gray outcropping of rock, or a little vegetation— darker patches against the gold—but mostly it was just . . . sand.

When they passed over the first group of Isvaieni, it was a shock. They were something he knew the size of. And the men and *shotors* were barely a trail of specks on the land below, there and gone in a matter of heartbeats as Ancaladar swept past overhead.

"What if somebody looks up and sees us?" Harrier finally thought to ask. He knew there wasn't anything the people on the ground could possibly do about them, but he still had the feeling that they shouldn't be seen.

"They won't," Tiercel said confidently. "They just . . . won't think to."

Harrier decided he didn't know what bothered him more: knowing that Tiercel could cast spells this easily, knowing he hadn't noticed that Tiercel had cast one at all, or the fact that they were both probably going to be dead by sundown. He thought it would probably be best if he didn't think about any of those things for as long as he possibly could.

"Now we enter the Desolation," Ancaladar said about an hour later. "We should soon reach our destination."

Looking down, Harrier could see what he meant. They'd just passed another group of Isvaieni on the desert below—even when Ancaladar's shadow passed directly over them they didn't look up, so he guessed Tiercel's spell was working—and even Harrier could see that this part of the desert was somehow . . . bleaker . . . than the part they'd been flying over before. The ground was a paler color, and it seemed to be more of the flat baked terrain and less of the rolling sand.

He also saw why Ancaladar was so confident that he knew where they were going, and no longer needed to wait for them to lead him there. Harrier could see a white scar across the face of the desert below. It ran as straight and true as an arrowshot, and after everything he'd heard from both Tiercel and Ancaladar about desert oases and Isvaieni methods of travel in the past fortnight, he had to agree: somebody had made this, and he was betting on recently.

He forced himself to breathe evenly and not let Tiercel know how nervous he was. They were getting close now.

But when they'd flown for another hour—covering hundreds of miles, they had to be, because it had taken Ancaladar less than two hours to cover the same distance that the Isvaieni had traversed in three sennights of travel—they began to realize that reaching their destination would be no simple matter.

"Hey," Tiercel said in an odd voice. "Is that a second group?"

"It is not," Ancaladar answered, sounding equally distressed.

Harrier looked down. The Isvaieni caravan was below

them again. "But you've been flying straight south the whole time," he said.

"So I had thought," Ancaladar said grimly. He flew on.

An hour later, they encountered the same group again.

"This isn't working," Tiercel said.

"What isn't?" Harrier said. "What's happening?"

"Ancaladar's turning," Tiercel said. "He's got to be. And none of us is noticing until we get back here."

"Okay," Harrier said. "It's magic. You know a lot of . . . defenses."

"I'll try that," Tiercel said unhappily. "But I don't think it will work."

While they flew south—again—Tiercel explained that while a spell-shield might have some effect, what was keeping them away from their destination was probably another spell-shield.

"In which case it won't help?" Harrier said, guessing.

"Right," Tiercel answered.

And it didn't, because soon enough they were back where they'd started from again.

Ancaladar tried everything any of them could think of— flying east and circling around, flying west and doing the same, everything he could think of to somehow go *around* whatever it was that blocked them, but nothing worked. The sun was climbing toward midheaven by now, and even though they were high above the desert heat, they were still hungry and thirsty. And both Harrier and Tiercel were worn down with the constant tension of waiting for something to happen. It was small consolation to know that they'd finally found the place Tiercel needed to go if they couldn't get there.

At last Ancaladar simply climbed high into the cool air and circled while Harrier, holding tightly to Tiercel's belt with one hand, cautiously untangled the waterskin with the other so they could both drink. He thought Tiercel was far too casual about his precarious perch on Ancaladar's back. It was all very well to say that Ancaladar would catch them if they fell. There was the problem of *falling* first.

"We could probably be home in time for tea if we hurried," he said, as one of Ancaladar's wide sweeps over the Isvai let him look briefly northward. He couldn't see Armethalieh, but he could imagine it.

He wondered, suddenly, if that was actually the right thing to do. They'd have to believe Tiercel if he came home with Ancaladar beside him. High Magistrate Vaunnel could gather an army, and—

And how long would that take? A year? At least. And suppose they came. There's no water anywhere in this desert south of Tarnatha'Iteru for sure—and our army would have the same problem the Isvaieni army did: supply.

They could fly back to Karahelanderialigor and ask the Elven Mages to come and help, but Harrier wasn't sure they would. They'd sent Tiercel off alone in the first place, after all.

"We could," Tiercel said. He sounded wistful. "I don't think it's the right thing to do."

"Probably not." Harrier wished it were. He'd like it to be. But if all those Isvaieni had been convinced there was a True Balance and a False Balance . . . who else had been convinced? In ancient times, Anigrel the Black had first convinced everyone in Armethalieh to banish all the Wildmages from the City, and then had spent moonturns telling the citizens that there was no Endarkened threat and no war until it was nearly too late for them to rally their forces and turn its tide. What if someone was doing something like that now? What if—if they went home—all that happened was that Magistrate Vaunnel tried to have them both locked up? Ancaladar could rescue them, he was sure, but . . .

Suddenly Harrier had a horrible blasphemous thought. He knew that the Blessed Saint Idalia had died to destroy the Queen of the Endarkened. He wondered if that was going to happen to Tiercel—if that was what was *supposed* to happen to Tiercel—and if Tiercel was going to be reborn as an Elf and grow up and become an Elven Mage and *then* solve the problem. He bit his lip very hard to keep from breaking into nervous laughter.

"But what *do* we do?" he asked, when he thought he could manage to talk without sounding like a lunatic. "Fun as this is, we can't just fly around up here forever. There has to be some way to get there. Otherwise all those Isvaieni couldn't just be going home again, could they?"

"They are not creatures of magic," Ancaladar said, sounding about as irritated as Harrier had ever heard him sound.

Ancaladar's explanation—when he made it—sounded just about ridiculous enough to make sense to Harrier. Ancaladar said that the magical defense of what was might very well be the Lake of Fire would keep him away from it forever. If Tiercel tried to find it by magic—without Ancaladar—Tiercel wouldn't be able to locate it either. But if Harrier and Tiercel simply walked along the road scarred into the desert down there and followed it to its end, nothing—nothing *magical,* at any rate—ought to stop them from making their way to its end.

"That's stupid," Harrier said. But the more outrageous the explanation for something magical was, the more likely it was to be the truth. In the last year, Harrier had found out more about magic than he'd ever expected or wanted to, and he'd decided that all of it, even—Light forgive him, the Wild Magic—seemed to be pretty unlikely.

"I am sorry, Harrier," Ancaladar said. He sounded exasperated—whether with the circumstances or with him, Harrier wasn't entirely sure. "I do not see how you could possibly do it, in any event."

"Yeah," Harrier sighed. "We're missing a few necessary things: food, tents, *shotors*—and there's the fact that the Isvaieni would be sure to object if they saw us."

"Steal them," Tiercel said.

"Have you lost your mind?" Harrier asked politely,

once he'd decided that Tiercel was talking about stealing *shotors*.

"Ha. No. We know where we can get a tent and food. All we'd need to do is steal a couple of *shotors*. And we can conceal ourselves—I've got spells for that—and we can—sort of—sneak in behind them."

"'All,'" Harrier said, ignoring the second half of Tiercel's idiotic idea.

"Look, I know it won't be easy. But we don't need saddles, because there are saddles back at the camp. And Ancaladar can steal the *shotors* for us."

"I can," Ancaladar said, sounding pleased. "I can swoop down upon them and carry them off."

"Oh," Harrier said. *Are you both out of your minds?* "No swooping. Not while I'm here."

"Indeed not," Ancaladar said firmly. "I shall first locate a suitable place for you to wait. Then I shall acquire some *shotors*."

IT DIDN'T MAKE sense for them to go all the way back to Tarnatha'Iteru and start again from there—for one thing, it would add nearly a moonturn to their travel time, and there wasn't that much food at the camp. For another, it would increase their chances of running into one of the bands of Isvaieni if they had to cross the entire desert. Ancaladar was looking for someplace near the Scar Road where they could wait. He would go and raid a couple of different Isvaieni camps—picking ones a long way away—for *shotors*. (He and Tiercel both agreed that four was a good number; Harrier was too disgusted by the entire plan to comment.) Once he'd brought them back, one of them would stay with the animals to keep them from wandering off while the other flew back with Ancaladar to Tarnatha'Iteru to make up a bundle of supplies and tents (which Ancaladar would carry in his claws) and then return.

"I well recall the days when I refused to be used as a beast of burden," Ancaladar said mournfully.

"It's only once," Tiercel said comfortingly.

"It is always 'only once,'" Ancaladar answered reproachfully.

"There don't exactly look like a lot of *places* down there," Harrier said, leaning over Tiercel's shoulder and peering at the ground. "No, wait. What's that?"

"The place that I saw earlier," Ancaladar said smugly. "There is even water."

"IT'S A CITY!" Tiercel said excitedly, as Ancaladar made a long low circle over it coming in for a landing. Harrier only hoped that Tiercel would bear in mind that he *couldn't fly,* and stay where he was until they were down on the ground again.

"Not for a long time," Harrier answered, looking down.

The bits and pieces and scraps of broken stone and chunks of road going nowhere covered an area he thought might even be as large as Armethalieh. It was impossible to tell whether this city had ever had a wall, but somehow Harrier got the impression that it hadn't. He thought everything would have been more bunched up if it had. All the bits of ruin he could see seemed to be laid out on a grid, as if the whole city had been built—or at least planned—all at once.

Ancaladar landed, and as soon as he did, the heat radiating up from the sand struck Harrier like a blow. *"Hot,"* he said comprehensively. He thought he'd gotten used to desert heat in the last several sennights, but this was like standing inside a bake-oven. He began to sweat immediately, and rubbed at his face, trying to keep the trickles of moisture out of his eyes.

"Yes," Ancaladar said apologetically. He stretched out his neck so that they could both slide off. It was even hotter standing on the ground; Harrier could feel the heat soaking up through his boot soles. Now his skin was only prickling, as the sweat dried on his skin immediately, leaving behind a flaking crust of salt. It itched, and he rubbed at his face distractedly.

"There is water there. And shelter, I believe. I shall return as quickly as I can." Ancaladar swung his head in the direction of something Harrier had glimpsed as they'd been coming in for their landing: it looked like an open basement. The air above it shimmered faintly—if there was an uncovered well here, the sun was probably doing its best to suck it dry of moisture.

"Come on," Harrier said to Tiercel. "If we stay out here, we'll fry."

THERE WAS A well. It was down at the bottom of a flight of stairs, and it was open to the sky. The air directly around the well was a little cooler than it was everywhere else here—probably because the sun was sucking water into the air, but even so, the stone of the basement was too hot to kneel on until they splashed water from the waterskin Harrier carried on it. The stone didn't quite sizzle, but the water dried almost immediately, and as soon as it did, the stone heated up again. Everything in direct sunlight was hot enough to cook on. Harrier took the precaution of refilling the waterskin he carried, even though they both drank directly from the well itself.

It was just as well that Ancaladar had been right about there being shelter here, too, because unless they climbed directly into the well itself, Harrier didn't think they could survive here at all for very long, and even if they did, they'd be badly burned. But a sort of tunnel led off from the basement, and while neither of them was in any mood to go exploring, once they'd gone a few feet along it, they were out of the sun. Even that much shelter was enough to make them feel cooler, after a few minutes' exposure to the sun of the Desolation.

They settled down to wait.

Eighteen

∼⨳∼

Forged in Fire

IT WAS A small matter to shape wood or stone or metal or a dozen other substances in the semblance of living things. Men and women did it daily, and called it art.

It was a greater task to take such semblances and give them the seeming of life. That required magic, and a greater magic than had been seen in the world of Men in a thousand years. Yet it could be done, with time and skill and patience.

One might even, with utmost skill in magic, take the inanimate semblance of a living thing and make it a housing for a thing that lived but had no physical body of its own. To conjure the very Elemental Forces that gave the land itself life, to capture and tame a portion of their vast and nearly boundless essence to animate an object of one's own creation, was a dangerous and delicate task.

Bisochim had done it, merely to see if he could. He was not interested in an unhappy or an unwilling servant, however, so he had released the creature immediately. His ambitions reached far higher.

He intended to create—by magic—what others—what he himself—had only crafted in stone and wood and metal. A human seeming. Living, breathing, *real*. And then he would conjure up the elemental spirit to inhabit it and give it life.

Not an unwilling captive this time. A willing—even eager—tenant.

And once she was bound within her prison of flesh, once she had granted him the immortality that was his payment, the immortality that would free Saravasse from death forever, he would bind her with spells, trapping her eternally both in flesh and rock. Darkness, returned to the world to set the Balance right, yet imprisoned where it could do no harm. Then his task would be complete. The Balance would have been restored. And his people would be safe.

His task was a slow and laborious one—both learning what he must to craft the crucible into which he would pour the alien spirit, and in conjuring that spirit back into the world. When he had begun, so many years before, the alien spirit had been no more than the weakest of whispers against his thoughts; barely more than a desperate hope that what he had longed for so desperately for so many seasons could find a way to come true. He had carefully nurtured the guttering flame, learning all that it could teach, working toward the day when he could set the last of the elaborate complex spell to work and gain his heart's desire.

In the beginning, the ancient power had hungered to possess him, he suspected. He had withstood those tentative assaults, and they had stopped. Once it had understood his strength, his work had proceeded more quickly. As the years passed, he had learned so much. And now the work was nearly done.

But if there was no True Balance left in the world, the teachings of the Balance remained, so Bisochim well knew that each act he performed called up a response from the False Balance that sought to remain unchanged by his actions. The closer he came to the completion of his work, the greater became the efforts of the False Balance to stop him. Knowing the Isvaieni would be but pawns in the war that the False Balance would not hesitate to begin, he had brought them into the Barahileth, to the garden his magic had created—but the Nalzindar had not been among them, and the Isvaieni had not been made to live a life of idleness and plenty. Desiring to cool hot tempers and restless spirits, Bisochim had sent the young warriors of all the tribes upon a fool's errand—to seek out the Nalzindar that he already knew they would not find. In their absence, the gardens of Telinchechitl were peaceful, and Bisochim returned to his work, certain that when the young Isvaieni tired of their futile quest, they would return.

He gave them no more thought than that.

KAZAT SON OF Gatulas of the Thanduli Isvaieni had been born in one birth with his twin brother Larazir eighteen turns of the Wheel of Heaven ago, and in each day of all those years, Kazat and Larazir had been as inseparable as the fingers of a hand, for where Kazat was, there was Larazir, and where Larazir was, there was Kazat.

No longer.

Larazir had always been first into every battle, rejoicing in their most hard-won victories, even those that must be bought with sorrow, such as the battle to win Laganda'Iteru from the Shadow-Touched. And so it was that he had been among the first to mount his *shotor* that day, and first to ride against the walls of Tarnatha'Iteru when—so they had believed—the Demon-child's spell had failed. And it had been a coward's trick, and Larazir had died beneath the hooves of his *shotor*, his body crushed to a bloody ruin against a Demon's magic.

But Kazat did not grieve for him. The loss of his twin had been repaid, the cowardice and treachery of the city-dwellers washed clean in blood. The fire would follow, when the last of the Isvaieni had left that place, but that time was not yet.

In this battle, unlike all the others, they had taken captives, at Zanattar's decree. By the power of the Wild Magic, the Demon-child had been bound into unconsciousness, and though many warriors of the Isvaieni had died in subduing his servant, it had been done at last, and Zanattar had said that these two should be taken before Bisochim so that he might discover the Great Enemy's plans and purpose. Though some had argued against this plan, saying it would be safer to kill them at once, Zanattar had said that they could not be sure that even the child-warrior was human, for what human boy could kill a score of Isvaieni warriors as he had done? And so to slit their throats might be only to free their spirits to enter the bodies of any of the Faithful who now stood as sworn brethren, so that no man or woman might know the face of their true enemy. These were prudent words, and when Zanattar's *chaharums* had set these words before all the people, everyone agreed they were wise words indeed. So the Darkspawn were taken to the tents of the people, bound and hoodwinked and drugged upon sweet wine so they could not wake. In this fashion, Zanattar said, they might be brought safely even to the plains of Telinchechitl themselves, where Bishochim, surely, would know how they might be let out of life without harm to any.

But though he would risk carrying such powerful captives to Telinchechitl, Zanattar was not so rash as to think he might safely bear them farther upon the war-road, and so he sent further word among the *chaharums* that Akazidas'Iteru would be spared the cleansing fire of the Faithful. Let the armies of the north come so far and no farther, and rage in impotent despair, for with the String of Pearls shattered beyond reclamation, they could not provision their great armies to cross the Isvai.

And so it was that the great army that Zanattar had gathered together flowed away from the walls of Tarnatha'Iteru as water flows from a cracked jug, slipping off into the desert in their handfuls, their *shotors* fat with grain and water from the *Iteru*-city they had cleansed of evil, their bellies full with bread and meat from its storehouses. First among those who departed rode Kazat son of Gatulas of the Thanduli Isvaieni, for he was one of Zanattar's most trusted *chaharums,* who had been with him since the moment Luranda had uncovered the bones of the slain Wildmage in the desert, and Zanattar knew that Kazat would say to Bisochim all that he would say himself. It was Zanattar's place to remain, as a good leader must, until the last of the people had departed from Tarnatha'Iteru, and to take upon himself and those who would accept such danger the burden of bearing the Demons across the Barahileth to their judgment.

It was both comfort and relief, after so many moonturns upon the War Road, crowded into the company of thousands of his brethren and coursing the very edge of the Madiran, for Kazat to return to the Isvai once more in the company of no more than a handful of his fellows. It was true that they were not Thanduli, but Zanattar had told him thoughtfully over a cookfire one evening that the Time of tribes was broken. Before they had set out to search for the Nalzindar, all of the young warriors had sworn a blood-oath to consider every other Isvaieni as much kin as if they had been born within the same tent, and Zanattar did not think this oath would have its end simply because their search was over. If Gatulas was Thanduli, Kazat was not: he was more. There must be a new name for the tribe that they all shared. Perhaps they would be known now simply as Isvaieni.

But if Kazat was no longer Thanduli, he was still a child of the desert, and welcomed his return to its clean open spaces, its silence and its vastness. In his heart, he regretted the need that would bring him, far too soon, back to the crowded tents and strange foreign lushness of Telinchechitl, for even the desert waste beyond it was unfamiliar—too harsh, too barren, not home.

It was not his choice, not Bisochim's choice, not the choice of any Isvaieni, that had exiled them to that strange place, he reminded himself. It was the act of the False Balance, that Great Enemy which had slain the Blue Robes, which had sent Demons to defend Tarnatha'Iteru. They would endure it just as they had endured the harshness of the Isvai itself, until the time came to reclaim their true home.

ON THE DAY when Kazat returned to Telinchechitl, Bisochim was sitting in the highest and farthest of the upper gardens of his fortress, taking a rare rest from his labors because Saravasse had come back. She never sought his company anymore—preferring to sleep upon the upper air, descending to earth only to drink and to hunt, or of course, when he summoned her. But she had come today, and at first Bisochim had hoped that the day he had long dreamed of had come, when he would receive her forgiveness and be able to speak to her of his hopes and dreams once more.

But it did not matter what he said to her—how carefully, how patiently he spoke of what was to come, and how necessary it was, not only for the good of all who lived beneath the sky, but to save her life. She still would not speak.

He spoke for hours, using all the most persuasive words he knew—words that had swayed clever and cautious men. He told her everything, holding nothing back from her—every truth, every hope, every fear that he held within his heart, while she watched him with expressionless golden eyes and said nothing.

He made promises to her that he would have made to no other between Sand and Star. He swore that once his work was done, that he would do anything that she bid him to do. They would journey to the Veiled Lands, or beyond Great Ocean, or to any place she chose. Any task she set, he would perform. She had but to name it. Once his task here was complete.

She spoke not a single word in reply.

"Master, you must come. It is urgent."

At the summons, Bisochim flung himself to his feet with a snarl. He glared at Zinaneg's expressionless stone face. The creature had been one of his earliest experiments in fully animating stone: to give stone a voice as well as sentience and movement was still such a delicate task that he didn't see the need to waste the work on his other servants. But to have one among his servants who could carry messages—and speak them—was a thing he had sometimes found useful, though at this moment he was sorely tempted to summon Lightning from the sky and blast it back to the lifeless stone from which he had once summoned it.

"What can be urgent now?" Bisochim demanded with ill-grace.

"Kazat son of Gatulas of the Thanduli Isvaieni has returned from the Isvai. He says that their losses were heavy, but they have been successful: the murders of the Blue Robes have been avenged and the *Iteru*-cities are no more." Zinaneg's voice was as expressionless as its face: the stone homunculus spoke of triumph or disaster in the same even monotone.

But at its words, Saravasse threw back her head and began to laugh.

BY THE TIME Bisochim arrived among the tents to seek out Kazat, Hargul of the Fadaryama Isvaieni was bringing her own band of warriors into the camp as well. On the bodies of those who followed her, Bisochim saw half-healed scars where no scars should be, and both Isvaieni and *shotors* bore the stamp of long privation.

"They are avenged!" she cried, when she saw him. "The Nalzindar and the Wildmages! The Isvai is purified!" The Isvaieni riding with her cheered, brandishing their *awardans*.

All around him, he saw preparations being made for a lavish feast of welcome. *Kaffeyah* simmered in open pans, pots of stew bubbled over open fires, sheep and goats roasted upon the spit, and the smell of baking filled the air—not merely the customary flatcakes that were eaten with nearly every meal, but the strong sweetness of the honey-cake reserved for only the most special occasions.

As he walked through the encampment, congratulating the young hunters upon their safe return, Bisochim's heart was as heavy as his tongue was burdened with questions he dared not voice—for all believed he had sent them forth to seek out the Nalzindar, and he dared not let them suspect that he had never expected them to find them. But there was little need for him to ask anything at all, for everyone he met was eager to relate their triumphs to him, and long before the feast of welcome was set out upon the carpets, Bisochim had the whole of the tale from Kazat himself.

For several sennights the various roving bands of Isvaieni had searched for the missing Nalzindar without success, just as Bisochim had intended. Just as they had been about to give up and turn back, Kazat's band, led by Zanattar of the Lanzanur Isvaieni, and counting as its chief tracker Luranda of the Adanate Isvaieni, had discovered the half-buried bones of a dead Wildmage.

And seeing them, they had declared war upon the *Iteru*-cities.

"She knew no Blue Robe could have died in an ordinary Sandwind," Kazat explained simply. "We all knew, once they explained it to us. Do not the Blue Robes command the Sandwinds to turn aside from us? How could they be killed by one unless it was sent by the False Balance? Luranda and Zanattar told us that soon the False Balance would send, not spells, but armies of men, and we must deny them the aid that the *Iteru*-cities would give them."

And so they had. While Bisochim had labored in the depths beneath his palace, thinking there was no need to do a spell of Farseeing to look upon the bands of roving Isvaieni (for he had inspected the desert closely in his own search for the missing Nalzindar, and had been certain that they could come to no harm in the Isvai), Zanattar had come to a similar conclusion—that Bisochim would come to him if the course he, Zanattar, intended to follow now were wrong. And Bisochim had not. So Zanattar had gathered together all the roving bands of Isvaieni, and together they had destroyed every single one of the *Iteru*-cities—all but Akazidas'Iteru.

"At Tarnatha'Iteru there was an evil sorcerer from the north," Kazat said, bringing his tale to a close. "The road north from Laganda'Iteru was a hard one. There was little water. Zanattar knew we must take Tarnatha'Iteru quickly.

But a monster with the face of a child rode out from its
gates to mock him, and then to wrap himself and the city
in a wall of light. It endured for many days, but by the
virtue of the True Balance it fell at last. They sent forth
their great army, thinking to slay us as we lay helpless, but
we had feigned weakness. We fell upon them like the *pakh*
upon the *sheshu*. Soon the city was ours, and the Demon-
child and his creature became our prisoners."

"You captured them?" Bisochim asked, suddenly alert
and wary.

The Isvaieni lived their life in service to the Balance,
and by the guidance of Wildmages, but they were neither
credulous nor superstitious folk. If Kazat said they had
captured Demons, he had good reason for his belief.

Bisochim knew that whatever the Isvaieni had captured,
they had not captured Demons. In the days when he had
first Bonded to Saravasse and begun to study how to set the
Balance to rights, he had walked long in the land of dreams
that showed the world as it had once been, and there he
had seen the Ancient World and its creatures, and the monsters known as the Endarkened. He knew that whoever or
whatever it was that Zanattar had captured, it was not Endarkened, no matter how much Kazat named it "Demon"
and "monster." The problem with the world as it was wasn't
too much Darkness, but too much Light. Nor—despite
what he had heard—did he think that what Zanattar had
captured were any sort of Otherfolk. Mages, certainly—
enemies and tools of the Light. But Mages could bleed and
die. Bisochim had proved that himself, when he had slain
the Wildmages of the Isvai.

Kazat nodded. "Zanattar felt that you would know best
how to kill them. He said that if we kept them blindfolded
and drugged upon sweet wine they could do us no harm."

"He has done well," Bisochim forced himself to say.

It was many hours before Bisochim could leave the feast
of welcome, for it would have seemed strange indeed did
he not stay to welcome Kazat's band and Hargul's band
and those who had fought beside them in the name of the

True Balance. Many were the stories told, there among the tents, of young warriors—hundreds of them—whose bones now lay upon the sand, of their bravery and sacrifice and fierce courage. More of the young warriors arrived during the feast—for there were many paths to the edge of the Barahileth, but only one road through it—and so places must be made for them upon the carpets and the tales must all be told again, from the first foolishness of the city-dwellers at Orinaisal'Iteru to the hard-won victory over Demon-magic at Tarnatha'Iteru.

When Bisochim at last was able to leave the feast and return to his fortress, Saravasse was gone. He wondered if she'd only come to gloat over his disaster. Surely, in her restless flights over the desert, she had seen all that had occurred. Once she would have hastened to his side with the news the moment she had seen the first attack on the first city, so that the two of them could have ridden forth and stopped it.

Once.

It is all for you, my lady, Bisochim thought desperately, *all that I do. It is for you.* Though even as he thought the words, hoping she would hear them, he knew that they were only a part of the truth. Since he had first taken up his Three Books as a child, Bisochim had known there was some great work set out for him, a work that only he could accomplish. Long before he had met Saravasse he had known the Balance was out of true. It was her power that had given him the strength to do something about it— and their Bond that had given him the need and the will to go on working through the endless years of disappointment and frustration.

And so he prepared his strongest wards to hold the captives Zanattar would bring to him. He did not risk a spell to see where Zanattar was, or to discover the nature of his captives. The wards around the Lake of Fire were impenetrable . . . unless magic was worked through them. Then the spell itself could serve as a conduit back to its caster. If whoever had sent these Mages was seeking them, they would certainly notice his magic. He would not risk revealing the sanctuary of his people. And so, knowing that the Enemy had already reached the Isvai, he could do nothing as he waited for Zanattar's arrival but attempt to master his unruly spirit. So many of his people lost and dead! And in battles that need never have been fought— for surely, surely, once the Balance had been restored, everyone would see there was no need to fight at all? Why fight a battle that was already lost—or won?

He could show nothing of this anguish to his people. They thought they had triumphed. They thought they had done precisely as he had wished them to do. He had told them, after all, that they were surrounded by enemies that wished them harm. He had promised them wars and great battles. The fact that it had been a trick, a lie told out of love to save them from the terrible future his visions foretold him, was a bitter taste in his mouth.

Nineteen

Strangers from the Sky

THE MOON HAD waxed and waned six times when danger came to trouble the Nalzindar's existence in Abi'Abadshar. In that time Shaiara's people had never succumbed to the foolishness of thinking themselves safe, for there was a saying among the Isvaieni: *One is only safe when they are dead, or when they are yet unborn.* And no people between Sand and Star took these words to heart more than the Nalzindar.

Three moonturns ago Shaiara had at last taken the terrible risk of sending a few of her people into the Barahileth, for with all the bounty that Abi'Abadshar granted them, there was one thing it did not supply: salt. She had feared for all her people every moment that the salt-gatherers were gone. In ordinary times, she would never have thought that any of her people would betray the tribe, no matter what torture they were put to, but she had seen how Bisochim could bend the minds of strong men with nothing more than simple words, and she did not believe that anyone could withstand him. Had she been his prey that day at Sapthiruk Oasis, and not the minds and hearts of others, she would not be here now, strong-willed though she was.

But her people had returned safely, their *shotors* laden down with enough salt so that it would be another year, with care, before such a journey must be risked again. It was only then, listening to her heart, that Shaiara came close to despair, for she realized then that she did not believe that one wheel of the year would be enough to set the world to rights. The thought that they would have to spend a year, two years, even three, moored to this one place left Shaiara feeling as if she were trapped in the Third Descent without light, shivering in the suffocating blackness. The Nalzindar were used to going where they wished across the sands of the wide Isvai. It was true that Abi'Abadshar held bounty beyond their dreams. But it was not freedom.

Marap, Narkil, and Turan had harvested with care, disguising their work so that the scars they had left upon the desert would not resemble the work of human hands. They led the salt-burdened *shotors* down into the passage to divest them of their burdens, and Shaiara could see that the *shotors* were not the only thing that must be unburdened, for Marap's face plainly showed that the Nalzindar herb-woman was the bearer of evil news. Such news properly belonged to all the tribe, but it was Shaiara's right to hear it first, and alone. When the *shotors* had been unloaded and turned free to graze, Shaiara took Marap aside to hear words she already knew they both wished could remain unsaid.

"There is a road across the Barahileth, Shaiara," Marap said grimly. "It runs as straight as the flight of doves fleeing the hunting falcon. Worse. There is water. Wells."

Shaiara did her best to school her features to smoothness so that Marap would not see her dismay. Marap well knew this was grim news; Shaiara would not allow her own reaction to make the burden of the telling heavier. But when the time came to share this information with the tribe, it would be impossible to render the bitter words sweet, even if such had been the custom among the Nalzindar. As well to say there were unicorns in the Barahileth as water! Save that a unicorn *could* come to the Barahileth, so the storysingers said, and every child of the desert knew that there was no water here.

"The Shadow-Touched has made them," Shaiara said slowly.

Marap nodded. "We did not disturb them."

Shaiara nodded in approval. Who knew what spells the Shadow-Touched might have set upon his wells? A man who could go against every teaching of the Three Books might well go so far as to poison water.

When the time came to share it, the people took the news of the road through the Barahileth calmly. The Wild Magic had led them to this refuge. It would continue to protect them, or it would not. One could not drink the *kaffeyah* before it was brewed; the trouble of the Shadow-Touched's making was so strange a thing that its manifestation was impossible to predict. They would face it upon the day, and before the day, they would not fret over what they could not control.

Later, when the camp had become quiet, Shaiara questioned Marap carefully on all the details of her journey, settling them in her own head until she knew exactly where this strange dove-road was in relation to Abi'Abadshar. She was relieved to hear it was nearly eight days' journey to the east; in the Barahileth, where one day's travel must be counted as four, none of those who now followed the Shadow-Touched would stumble across the Nalzindars' refuge by accident, and even if they did so, her people were well-hidden.

But it troubled her that she had taken her people, even

unwittingly, not away from Bisochim, but *toward* him. Yet what else could she have done? Abi'Abadshar was the only place of safety she had been able to imagine. And the more she thought about it, the more she thought that remaining in the Isvai, vast as it was, would not have saved them. A road—with wells along its path—must exist for a purpose. Bisochim had not merely taken the rest of the Isvaieni into the Barahileth to remain there as her people remained within Abi'Abadshar. They must travel in and out of it. To what purpose?

At Sapthiruk Oasis, Bisochim had promised the tribes that he would lead them to war. It was a thing too terrible for Shaiara to imagine, but one thing she *did* know: if her tribe had remained in the Isvai, surely they would be lost now.

THREE SENNIGHTS AFTER Marap and the others had returned from the salt-gathering expedition, Shaiara sat in a patch of sunlight in the garden, a basket of *shotor*-wool by her side, and a carved wooden spindle in her hands. She would far rather be anywhere but here and doing anything but this—and if the thread snapped yet again, she would lose her patience as she had not done with any task since she had been a young child. It was why she had come away from the tent, so that she might practice in private—she was not ashamed to fail at a thing before her people, but she was ashamed to lose her temper at her failure. And spinning was a skill that did not come easily to her, but Singi had built what he said was a loom, and if they were to have cloth, there must be yarn, and if there was to be yarn, the Nalzindar must spin it, for there was no one—now—to trade with. In the past, Shaiara had left the spinning to others—the Nalzindar spun the wool of their *shotors,* but only for trade, or to braid into small items. Not to weave.

But now their cloth must be of their own weaving. Much yarn would be needed, and all must spin. And Shaiara feared, just a little, that here in this land of boundless plenty the Nalzindar might succumb to indolence. It might well be hard for them to leave such a pleasant place. *If we ever do,* she thought bleakly. Just as well, against such an unfortunate possibility, that they all still have hard tasks to occupy them now. And how could she ask them to do what she would not? So it would be just as well if she could spin, if not well, then at least not hissing and spitting with frustration like an infuriated fur-mouse.

And so it was with as much irritation as relief that she marked the sound of footsteps running toward her refuge. She quickly set aside the basket of combings that she was attempting to tease into a yarn fine enough for weaving and rose to her feet, sacrificing her concealment behind the scrim of sweet-smelling bushes.

Ciniran bounced to a stop on the soft ground when she saw Shaiara appear.

"I am grateful to find you so swiftly." Though her tone was urgent, her voice was soft, as if someone might over-hear.

"For what cause?"

"There are strangers in Abi'Abadshar."

"Tell me of them. How came they here?" Shaiara willed herself to calm. Neither anger nor fear would help them now.

"There are only two." Ciniran sounded both puzzled and worried. "And they are not Isvaieni. They speak in loud foolish voices and behave as children, yet they have the shape of men. I know not how they came."

Ciniran's tale was simple and troubling. She and Raffa had been searching for new routes to the surface, a constant task of the hunters. They had found one—a slanted open-ing that would only allow a single body to move through it at a time, but it was possessed of the advantage that it did not require the scaling of walls. They had both climbed up it in order to see where it came out, for distance was a deceptive thing here in the underground world. When they reached the surface, they found themselves nearly a mile from the *Iteru*-chamber.

"And then we heard voices—loud voices—complaining of the heat. We went to see where they came from, and there, in the *Iteru*-chamber, we saw them. But there were no tracks of *shotors* upon the sand—nor any *shotors*. And their own footprints began suddenly, as if they had swept them away, and then grown tired of sweeping. Raffa and I watched them for many minutes, but all they do is sit in the passageway and complain of the heat."

They could not have come to Abi'Abadshar without *shotors*. And while the Nalzindar did not keep a constant watch upon the desert—for nothing could approach the ancient city without being visible hours, even days, in advance of its arrival—they *did* keep watch. Unless the strangers had simply dropped down out of the sky, they could not have approached the city unseen between one period of scrutiny from the cautious Nalzindar and the next. And it was unheard-of for non-Isvaieni to venture into the deep desert at all, much less into the Barahileth.

If they had been sent by Bisochim, the Nalzindar were already doomed: whether the strangers vanished here and now with no trace to mark their passing, or returned to their master and told him of a vast ruined city in the desert, the result was the same. Abi'Abadshar could no longer serve as a safe haven for the Nalzindar, and there was no other refuge anywhere between Sand and Star that could hide them.

"Gather the people together," Shaiara said to Ciniran. "If this is a trap, we shall lay a trap of our own."

TIERCEL LEANED AGAINST the wall and watched Harrier jitter. He could think of a lot of consoling things to say. The trouble was, they'd all make Harrier hit him, and if Harrier missed, he'd hit the wall, and then he'd be even more irritated than he was right now. It was funny, Tiercel mused. He'd always used to think that Wildmages were wise and serene all the time. Even meeting Roneida hadn't completely convinced him otherwise, because she'd seemed pretty wise and at least moderately serene. But he'd known Harrier all of both of their lives, and there were three things Tiercel knew for sure right now: one, that Harrier was a Wildmage (or a Knight-Mage, to be precise), two, that Harrier was about as wise as a rock, and three, that Harrier was exactly as serene as a windstorm.

So much for the things "everybody knew" about Wildmages, and telling Harrier that at least they hadn't managed to get to the Lake of Fire so that they were both dead now probably wouldn't be a really helpful thing to say, either. There were times that Tiercel thought that the Wild Magic had a far greater sense of humor than the Light-Priests had ever spoken of, considering that to help him oppose the forces of Darkness, it had made Harrier Gillain a Wildmage.

Even though Tiercel didn't want to die—he hadn't wanted to a year ago and he still didn't—he'd gotten closer to accepting that there wasn't any alternative, especially after he'd visited the Veiled Lands. It was daunting to think something like that, especially now that he was linked to Ancaladar, but it was precisely *because* he was Bonded to Ancaladar that Tiercel had slowly come to believe that the part he'd been given to play in all of this wasn't to win, but merely to *try*. Even Bonded to Ancaladar Star-Crowned, he couldn't master all the contents of the spellbooks of First Magistrate Cilarnen in a few months. And First Magistrate Cilarnen hadn't defeated the Endarkened alone.

The study of the High Magick taught you discipline. Tiercel's love of knowledge had always let study come easily to him; what he'd needed to learn in order to master what little he had of the High Magick had built upon that foundation, teaching him a discipline he'd come to be grateful for later, when he'd realized the sheer *cost* of the course of action he'd committed himself to. He supposed the Elves were right to have told him so little. If he'd known everything before he'd left Armethalieh, he wouldn't have come. He wouldn't have let Harrier come. He wouldn't have accepted Ancaladar's Bond. He wouldn't have come to the Madiran.

He thought of the screams of the dying outside the walls of Tarnatha'Iteru, on one of the last days of the siege he remembered clearly. He thought of Harrier's blood-covered clothes in the orchard outside the city afterward, how Harrier had stood in the ditch and scrubbed himself until his skin was red, and sworn—at first—that all the blood was his. Had the Isvaieni spared their lives because Harrier had killed so many of them? There was no way to know.

It wasn't something the two of them were ever going to talk about.

And all the death and the sacrifice and the killing had done—because one of the two of them had to see things clearly, and Tiercel thought it was going to have to be him—was allow them to survive to get here. Closer to where the three of them were going to die. Because Tiercel couldn't imagine any spell that he possessed that was strong enough to destroy one of the Endarkened.

"What if we went back to Armethalieh?" he said. At least Harrier would be safe there.

"What if we didn't?" Harrier said, sounding a combination of bored and irritated. "How do you know that there aren't already people there going on about the False Balance? I'd rather stay here."

"It's hot here."

"It's summer. It's hot there, too."

"It's not *as* hot," Tiercel pointed out reasonably—and accurately. They were in shadow, but even so, the rock beneath his hand was warm. And in direct sunlight, the rock was hot enough to burn. It was so hot here that Harrier—for a wonder—hadn't complained once about being hungry, though they'd both been too nervous to eat breakfast, and it was well into afternoon now.

"It's still hot," Harrier said, in the tones of one determined to win the argument. "There. Do you think Ancaladar will be back soon?"

Tiercel looked up at the sun. "Maybe. The desertfolk don't like to travel by day. So they'll be in camps right now. *Shotors* should be easy to steal."

"If *I* was a *shotor* and got grabbed by a dragon, I'd bolt as soon as my feet touched the ground again."

"Well, that's why I'll—" *cast MageShield around Ancaladar as soon as he lands,* Tiercel had been about to say, but in the middle of his sentence Harrier got fluidly to his feet.

He flipped Roneida's sword out of his belt toward Tiercel—it landed in Tiercel's lap with a stinging thump— and drew both his swords. "Come out," Harrier said harshly, his back to the wall. "I can't see you, but I know you're there."

SHAIARA WAS PRUDENT. Even though it was the hottest part of the day, because the quality of the intruders remained unknown, she sent a group of hunters out through one of the escape passages and over the sand to come at the *Iteru*-courtyard from the terraces while she led a second band through the passage. She did not mean for the intruders to escape. Nor, if by any chance there were others with them that Raffa and Ciniran had not seen, would knowledge of their presence escape the Nalzindar. Her people would not be able to escape their fate at Bisochim's hands if their sanctuary here had been discovered, but they would at least be able to make their peace with Sand and Star before the end.

She knew from her own experience how long it would take the others to cross the miles of sand that lay between the escape route and the courtyard, and timed her own group's stealthy procession toward the mouth of the passage accordingly, for there was no real cover between the entrance to the garden-chambers and the exit to the outside. The only concealment was distance and darkness.

But even that failed her, for when Shaiara's band were still so far down the passage that the two intruders were no more than faint specks against the brightness, one of them sprang to his feet, and Shaiara saw the glitter of steel in his hands.

"Come out," she heard him say. "I can't see you, but I know you're there."

His companion scrambled to his feet far less gracefully, and though the weapon the first intruder had thrown to him clattered to the stone, he did not stoop to retrieve it.

"Harrier? What?" she heard the second intruder say. When she heard his voice she realized that neither of them was a man grown, as she had first thought. Both boys, but she would not make the mistake of thinking them less dangerous for their youth.

"This place is not deserted," the one called Harrier said in tones of disgust.

Hearing that, Shaiara allowed herself a tiny spark of hope. If they had not come seeking her people, if they, like the Nalzindar, had come in search of a deserted refuge . . .

What still mattered most at this moment was *how* such innocents had come so far into the Barahileth, as much as *who* they were. She saw no bows or stone-throwers in their hands, merely swords, and her people were armed with many of both, as well as hunting spears such as she herself carried, so she motioned to Kamar to nock an arrow and continued forward.

"Are you sure?" Harrier's companion said. "Because—"

"Light and Darkness, Tyr! There are people out there, okay! Pick up the damned sword!"

"Um . . ."

The one Harrier called "Tyr" did not reach for a weapon that Shaiara saw. But he gestured, and suddenly the passage was blocked with purple light.

No one knew what to do. But the purple light did not move, and so Shaiara ran down the passageway toward it until she was within range, and flung the spear in her hand with all the strength she possessed. To her anger and despair, it struck the light and bounced away just as if she had thrown it against stone.

"Hello?" she heard from the other side of the light. "Hello? We don't want to hurt you. We didn't know anybody was here. I'm Tiercel and this is my friend Harrier, and—"

"Oh, for the Light's sake, Tyr, they're probably more of those people who burned down Tarnatha'Iteru! Do you think they're going to listen to you?"

"We have burned nothing," Shaiara called, taking another cautious step toward the glowing wall.

"Shaiara!" Kamar said urgently from behind her. She raised a hand to silence him. The wall was not moving, and they must learn as much as they could about this new enemy. She had little doubt now that they were enemies. Only the Endarkened or their creatures could wield such unnatural power, and all knew that the mouths of the Endarkened were stuffed with lies.

"Well someone did," the one called Harrier responded. She wondered how he could be a warrior skillful enough to sense the approach of a Nalzindar hunting party and still bawl as loudly as a *shotor* that did not wish to be loaded. Surely his enemies must hear him coming for miles away.

"And you have come here to blame us?" Shaiara demanded scornfully.

"We have come here to—"

"Harrier!"

"Tiercel!"

"All I was going to—"

"Shut up."

Were the situation not so grim, Shaiara would have been moved either to disbelief or to mirth. She hardly knew what to think. They wielded the weapons of the Endarkened. But they argued like *children*.

"Hello?" It was the one Harrier had called both "Tyr" and "Tiercel."

"I am still here," Shaiara said stiffly.

"Oh. Good. I can hear you, but I can't see you. It's dark in the tunnel, and the MageShield isn't completely transparent. It won't hurt you. It's just a spell of the High Magick."

"Oh, yeah, great, Tyr, tell them everything."

"Well, Har, unless they're Endarkened, there isn't much they can do with the information. And if they *are* Endarkened, they already know. And—oh, yes. We'd both already be dead."

"We are not Endarkened," Shaiara said stiffly, coming closer.

"No, no, no. I wasn't saying you were. I don't think you are. I mean, I really hope you aren't," the one called Tiercel said. His stumbling copious words were those of a child, and he spoke as if without wisdom, but the more she pondered, the less Shaiara thought it could be true. No foolish child could wield such power as he had already displayed.

"I hope you are not as well," Shaiara said politely. Unwise as it might seem to be so trusting, she found it unlikely that Endarkened wouldn't simply have killed them already. Instead of—as these two seemed to wish—attempting to drive them mad.

"Oh, we're not. We're not. I mean, we'd say we weren't, even if we were—"

"Tiercel!"

"—but we really aren't. Besides, I don't think MageShield is an Endarkened spell. No, I'm pretty sure it isn't. Anyway, we're here to destroy the Endarkened. Well, not here. But, um, *near* here."

"Oh, fine, fine." That was the one called Harrier again. Shaiara was beginning to have some sympathy for him.

There was a silence from the other side of the cold purple fire. Shaiara was close enough to it now that if it had given off heat she would have felt it, and it did not. "What is the High Magick?" she asked cautiously, when she heard the two of them say nothing else.

"A very old kind of—good—magic that was used to fight the Endarkened during the Last War," the one called Tiercel said. "Oh, and Harrier wants me to tell you that I've put up MageShield at the other end of the tunnel, too, so the people you sent around the other way can't get at us either. So don't bother."

Shaiara turned back to the other Nalzindar. She could not see if the strangers' words were truth, but if they were, she would not leave her people out in the afternoon sun if they did not need to be. All had heard the one called Tiercel's words; she flicked her fingers at Natha, and he began running, light-footed as an *ikulas* on the hunt, toward the nearest exit to the surface. He would find Ciniran and the others, and tell them that if they saw purple fire at the entrance to the passageway, they should choose one among them to remain on watch and the rest should return to the safety of their secret underground lair.

"It's okay, though," the one called Tiercel continued. "I know you don't want to trust us. I guess you're probably hiding here. Maybe you're hiding from the other Isvaieni? The ones who burned the *Iteru*-cities? We, um, really aren't sure exactly why they did that. . . ."

"Because the Shadow-Touched has corrupted them," Shaiara said brusquely. Burned the *Iteru*-cities? She hoped with all her heart that it wasn't true, but it made a terrible sense. Bisochim had said that all the peoples of the world save the Isvaieni rejected the True Balance and would seek to kill all those who walked in the true ways only Bisochim and his followers now saw. If that were true, then the logical thing to do was to carry the war to the enemy. First.

"Oh, good," Harrier said. "I was hoping there was a reasonable explanation, after hearing Zanattar go on about False Balances and True Balances and how we were all evil before he and his friends came and *killed several thousand people.*"

"Zanattar?" Shaiara asked sharply. "Zanattar of the Lanzanur Isvaieni?"

"Um . . . we really aren't—" Tiercel began.

"Yes," Harrier said, and his voice was hard. "That's who he said he was."

"But"—and in all the years since she had come to lead the Nalzindar, Shaiara had never felt so lost and bewildered— "how could the Lanzanur destroy one of the *Iteru*? They are not a numerous tribe."

"All the tribes banded together," the one called Harrier said, and now his voice was no longer that of a boy, but that of a warrior, filled with the darkness and quiet of one who held the lives of men in his hands to do with as he chose. "All of them. Except yours. If you're Isvaieni. Which I guess you've got to be, if you're out here in the middle of the Isvai. It would be kind of nice to know how you escaped getting 'Shadow-Touched.' "

"We fled," Shaiara answered, and her voice was as hard as his. "The Shadow-Touched came to Sapthiruk preaching his new doctrine of a False Balance and a True. At first I could not believe what my eyes told me: that the greatest of the Wildmages should have fallen to the Shadow, or that he would use the Wild Magic to bend the minds of others so. But I saw the light of reason leached from the eyes of the leaders of a dozen tribes that day as Bisochim spoke of war. And before I or my people could fall under his spell as well, we came here."

"It's a great story," the one called Harrier answered. "And I'd be more likely to believe it if the road to his fortress didn't go right past your front door."

"Nor do I believe whatever story you will eventually choose to tell," Shaiara answered steadily.

"Now, see? That's the great thing about being a High Mage," the one called Tiercel said. "We don't actually have to wait around here for anybody to believe anybody."

Suddenly Shaiara heard shouts of dismay—audible even through the barrier of purple fire—from the surface outside.

"It's all right! It's all right!" she heard the one called Tiercel shout. "It's just Ancaladar!"

LESS THAN AN hour later, the Nalzindars' tent had been brought up and pitched on the sand in front of the *Iteru*-courtyard. Their new mats of woven grass had been brought up and laid upon the sand—for Shaiara was determined to do all honor to their guests—and a *kaffeyah* service had been brought. They did not have much *kaffeyah* left—and no way to get more—but Shaiara was grateful that they had husbanded their meager supplies in order to be able to offer it now.

It was not possible to argue with the reality of what her own eyes showed her—to dispute truth was not something the Nalzindar did. And what her eyes showed her was the presence of Ancaladar Star-Crowned, who had ridden the winds before the Isvaieni had come to the sands of the south, and who had helped to cast Darkness into oblivion so very long ago.

Tiercel and Harrier were not well-versed in the proper way of telling a tale. They came from far away in the Great Cold, and Tiercel said that there everything was written down in *books,* which must be (Shaiara supposed) why they spoke so badly—and perhaps why they spoke so loudly as well. But she was patient, and soon enough she had the whole of the tale. It meshed with hers like the fingers of two hands. To know with certainty that Bisochim's intention was to call back the Endarkened filled Shaiara with despair.

"Why?" she said.

"Because they're evil?" Harrier said.

It had taken him far longer to trust her and her people than it had taken the Nalzindar to extend their own trust. The tale they brought explained much of that. But Tiercel simply insisted that they *must* be allies, for no better reason than because Shaiara's people had not attempted to kill them yet.

"No," Tiercel said. "Why would this Bisochim do what the Endarkened want, if he's a Wildmage? *You* wouldn't."

Shaiara looked at Harrier in surprise. He shrugged, but did not deny what Tiercel implied. She would require him to state it plainly later, however—she was not entirely certain she trusted the peculiar speech of the North. "Maybe they—I don't know—*lied* to him," Harrier said.

Tiercel frowned. "Somebody told him he needed to fix the Balance."

Shaiara saw him glance at Harrier, and saw Harrier shrug. "There's nothing wrong with it that *I* know of," he said slowly. He hesitated. "It's a good story, though."

"An excellent one," Shaiara said bitterly, "since it has called my brethren to war."

Harrier sighed and ran a hand through his hair. "So he's going to fix the Balance—which isn't broken, by the way—by *killing* everybody?"

"No," Tiercel said, and he sounded certain of this. "He's going to do it by bringing back the Endarkened. *Think,* Har. What did Zanattar *say*?"

Shaiara saw Harrier's brow furrow in concentration. Were he one of her own people, she could be certain Zanattar's words would be rendered exactly. Now, she could not be sure. But when he spoke, she heard the echo of the Isvaieni in his words.

" 'Since the time of the Great Flowering, the Balance of the World has been out of true, for the Light destroyed the great evil that beset the world in that time—as was only right—but those who kept the Light in those days did not stop where they should have, and so ever since that day, the Great Balance has been tipping more and more away from what the Wild Magic means it to be. Generation after generation has followed this False Balance, upholding it for their own purposes—' "

He went on to the end of the words Zanattar had spoken to him. They were not Zanattar's words, though, Shaiara knew. They were Bisochim's.

"So he must think—or have been convinced—that because the Endarkened have been destroyed, there's something wrong with the Wild Magic now, and the only way to fix it is to . . . bring the Endarkened back," Tiercel said. His voice wavered with a disbelief Shaiara understood all-too-well.

"I'm not even going to mention how stupid it is to decide to fix the Wild Magic, considering he's been corrupted by Endarkened," Harrier said in disgust. "The only question now is, what do we do about it?"

"You?" Shaiara asked, and though she did her best to school her voice, she knew her tone conveyed her disbelief.

Tiercel smiled shyly at her. "The, um, the Elves . . ."

"Wanted *Tiercel* to come up with an idea to solve this whole problem," Harrier said bitterly.

"Could you do better?" Shaiara asked sharply.

"No!" Harrier blurted. "That isn't the point! This is the *Endarkened* we're talking about, Noble'dy. Yes, Tyr is the first High Mage born since the Great Flowering—okay, *almost,* Tyr. That doesn't mean he has a better idea of how to destroy the Endarkened than the Elves do. And they aren't doing anything."

"They just don't want to tell me what to do because—"

"—they think they're going to make the same mistakes they made with Kellen the Poor Orphan Boy, and frankly, I don't think that—"

"Enough!" Shaiara said. Both of them regarded her in surprise. "It does not matter *why* the Elder Brethren will not help, if they will not," she finished, more mildly.

"Yes it does," Tiercel said. "You see—"

"Shut *up,* Tyr," Harrier said. "Okay, there's a long really boring explanation that doesn't make any sense, Noble'dy. But it's pretty much that they're afraid to make things worse. And . . . I guess *we're* afraid to ask anybody else for help, too. In case they believe in this 'False Balance' thing."

Shaiara nodded. That much made sense to her, who had seen her fellow Isvaieni throw aside all that she had once thought they knew of truth and sense between Sand and Star to do that which she would have believed they would have died rather than do. "It does not explain how it is that you will accomplish the task which the Elder Brethren have set you."

"Perhaps the answer is here," Ancaladar said. "This place is far older than I. Yet I recognize its like."

"A city of Demons?" Shaiara asked in disbelief, using the oldest name for the Endarkened.

The Star-Crowned blinked slowly. "Not Demons, Shaiara. They do not build cities, nor do their creatures build cities in the light. This was once a place of Elves. And—if I am correct—of my kind as well."

"It must have been a really long time ago," Tiercel said, looking around.

"Elves and dragons together, and Ancaladar doesn't remember it?" Harrier frowned. "That would be, um . . ."

"From the time of Great Queen Vieliessar Farcarinon," the Star-Crowned answered. "And thus, from a time long before there were truly Men at all."

"Elven Mages," Harrier said, as if he'd solved the answer to a riddle.

"Yes," the Star-Crowned said, sounding pleased. "In that age, the Elves held all the world. Then He Who Is came, intending to make it his, and his children's, and Vieliessar Farcarinon made the Great Bargain, to win our aid for her battle."

"But, um," Tiercel said, looking puzzled.

"And then, yes, the Endarkened were cast down, and Vieliessar Farcarinon paid the second half of her Price. She renounced magic on behalf of the Elves forever."

"It can't have been forever, though," Harrier said logically. "Because there have been Elven Mages ever since the Great Flowering, right?"

The Star-Crowned seemed to sigh. "Yes, Harrier. But that is how the legend goes. I do not know why it is that it isn't true."

"The point is that the Demons were cast down," Shaiara said firmly. In even so short an acquaintance with these travelers she had already learned that if she did not steer conversations with them firmly, they would degenerate into long and meaningless arguments. "And that what was done once may be done again. And perhaps—somewhere here within Abi'Abadshar—there is some record of that time? Many things from those days remain."

"Here?" Harrier asked in disbelief, looking around.

Shaiara smiled. "There is more to Abi'Abadshar than sand and weathered stones. Do you think the Nalzindar could survive here if there were not?"

Tiercel and Harrier looked at each other and shrugged.

"There is a city beneath the surface," Shaiara said. "I will show it to you. But I warn you, it is dark."

Harrier grinned. "It won't be for long. Tiercel can fix that." Tiercel kicked him. "Um, yeah. So can I."

Shaiara rose to her feet. The thought that the Wild Magic had chosen these boys to destroy the Shadow-Touched, and meant the Nalzindar to aid them, was a disturbing one, but what else could she believe? All that they had said was both true and logical: there was no one else for any of them to trust.

"What about Ancaladar?" Harrier asked.

"If this place was once meant for my kind, as I believe, then it will be possible for me to enter it," Ancaladar said. "All that will be necessary is some . . . excavation."

"We must leave no trace on the surface for the Shadow-Touched to see, should his gaze fall upon Abi'Abadshar," Shaiara warned.

"Tiercel has a spell," Harrier said.

Twenty

The World Beneath the World

HARRIER SPENT THE next several days getting used to the idea that not only was he not going to be dead immediately, there was a chance he might not end up being dead at all. He'd also made up his mind that the way that the Wild Magic worked *offended* him in a way he really couldn't articulate. He also wasn't going to try now that he and Tiercel were living with the Nalzindar, because they felt about the Wild Magic the way that the people of the Nine Cities felt about the Light Itself. So it wasn't exactly something Harrier was going to make fun of.

And it wasn't—really—that he wanted to make fun of it. And he certainly wasn't going to say anything—anything at all—that would sound even remotely to anybody like this Bisochim's doctrine of a "False Balance." It was just that the Wild Magic's way of tossing people around like ships in a gale, and hoping—or maybe not even caring—whether they came into their home ports with their sails intact . . .

Well, actually, Harrier was pretty sure that the Wild Magic had meant him and Tiercel to end up at Abi'Abad-shar all along. And half of him was annoyed at the method it had used to arrange that, while the other half of him felt a little guilty, because maybe there'd been something he could have done to get the two of them here faster and easier. Only—and his mind kept circling back around to this, no matter how hard Harrier tried not to think about it—if he'd done anything different, surely Zanattar's Isvaieni would have done exactly the same things *they'd* done, except they'd have gone on to destroy Akazidas'Iteru next, and then maybe kept going north. So try as he might, Harrier couldn't come up with any neat and simple answers. Which meant that the Wild Magic wasn't neat and simple either. And that *offended* him. Even though it had brought him and Tiercel to a place where they might actually find something that would *help*.

The first thing they'd found was information, of course. It wasn't that Harrier didn't trust and believe in Tiercel's visions, but even Tiercel didn't know exactly what they meant. Shaiara's information made a little more sense to Harrier: it was made up of what she'd seen, and what she'd done, and what she knew, and what she thought about all of it. Harrier was able to prove to the Nalzindar that he was a Wildmage as simply as by lighting the evening's cookfire, after which they trusted him implicitly.

They were grateful for his presence, since he was the first Wildmage they'd seen in more than half a year (even if, in Harrier's own opinion, he wasn't that much of one).

The Nalzindar had no more idea than anyone else Tiercel had talked to of where the rest of the Wildmages had gone, but considering everything Harrier and Tiercel now knew about what was going on in the Madiran, the Isvai, and the Barahileth, it probably wasn't anywhere good.

In his own way, Tiercel was always logical. Harrier admitted that, even while—half the time, more than half—he wanted to strangle his friend while he was *being* logical. It was Tiercel who'd listened to everything Shaiara told them, and then figured out that whatever *Bisochim* thought his plan was, it wasn't the same plan as the Endarkened's. Their plan was undoubtedly the same as it had been for as long as any race that walked beneath the Light could remember: destroy all that lived.

But to do that, the Endarkened had to regain the foothold that the Blessed Saint Idalia had destroyed so completely, and somehow manage to return to the world—or at least *communicate* with it. And that was more difficult than it seemed, just offhand: if the Endarkened could talk to just anybody, they would have done so centuries ago. And if they could corrupt just any Wildmage, they would have done that, too.

"So you're saying this Bisochim guy is the first Wildmage in a thousand years that the Endarkened could Taint?" Harrier asked.

It was the evening of their third day in Abi'Abadshar. They sat on one of the overturned stone pillars that lay a few dozen yards from the entrance to the subterranean city, waiting for Ancaladar to return from his evening's hunt. Though the temperature dropped even more abruptly between day and night in the Barahileth than it did in the Isvai, the stones of the ruins stored the heat of the sun and radiated it back for hours. Tiercel had assured Shaiara that he had spells in plenty to keep either of them from being seen, should anyone be looking for them, and the Nalzindars' underground home was odd enough that both of them wanted a little time out in the open air. And both of them had the sense that this was the sort of conversation that was better conducted where the Nalzindar couldn't hear it, because they still weren't quite sure how the desertfolk felt about the whole idea that the Endarkened had managed to corrupt a Wildmage.

Tiercel shook his head slowly, still reasoning it out in his own mind. "I know that Shaiara keeps talking about Bisochim as if he's Tainted, Har, but I don't know if he *is*—at least not the way the Light-Priests have always talked about Taint."

"Not that they ever really did," Harrier editorialized, and Tiercel snorted ruefully in agreement.

"And in the Elven Histories of the wars that I read in Karahelanderialigor—the ones that Jermayan wrote—he just assumed that anyone who read them would know exactly what 'Taint' was, so they weren't much help either. But Zanattar's army weren't Tainted. They'd just been tricked. I wonder, you know, if what the Dark has managed to do is to convince Bisochim to listen to them long enough so that they could trick him. They'd be lying to him, so that he'd be thinking he was doing something that was right, and they'd be doing . . . the same thing they always do. And he'd have no idea."

Harrier thought about that for a moment. "So exactly what difference does that make?"

Tiercel shrugged. "Not much, I guess. It'll be kind of hard to convince him that he's wrong after who knows what has been telling him who knows what for who knows how long."

Harrier laughed. "Clear as mud." He looked up at the sky. "Ancaladar's coming."

Tiercel punched him lightly on the shoulder. "I know that, you idiot. He's my Bonded."

LATER, THEY SHARED an edited version of their conversation with Shaiara. She was more convinced than they were that Bisochim was actually Shadow-Touched rather than simply being misled, and Harrier found himself in the odd position of being caught between Shaiara and Tiercel, not entirely willing to accept either's belief. On the one hand, Tiercel was a High Mage, and his oldest friend. On the other hand, Shaiara had actually *seen* Bisochim. He decided to do his best to believe both of them at once: there was no harm done in doing that since Bisochim was currently nowhere in sight.

Even Shaiara didn't know where the Lake of Fire was, though—obviously—it was somewhere in the part of the Isvai she called the Barahileth. The three of them had decided this together, just as they'd agreed that Bisochim must be the man Tiercel saw in his visions, the one who stood upon the shore of the Lake of Fire, the one being blandished by the Fire Woman to do something that Tiercel wasn't quite sure of but that must (logically) be meant to bring the Endarkened back. It made sense once you had all the pieces of the puzzle (the ones that Shaiara had and Tiercel had, anyway) and could fit them all together. Shaiara had said that Bisochim had gathered the tribes to him and taken them off into the Barahileth. And Ancaladar had managed to search all of the Isvai *except* the Barahileth— or the part of it that was being shielded by magic, anyway— so if they were looking for Bisochim (and they really couldn't be looking for anyone else, because how could there be *two* maybe-Tainted Wildmages out here?) he had to be in the Barahileth, and the Barahileth had to be where the Lake of Fire was, and Bisochim had to be at the Lake of Fire. And it didn't matter anymore whether or not they knew exactly *where* the Lake of Fire was, now that Bisochim's raiders had blazed a trail that led directly to it. What Harrier and Tiercel couldn't find by magic they could simply walk right to using the evidence of their own eyes.

But not yet.

There was an entire city under the ground here at Abi'Abadshar. Not just the entirely unlikely gardens that had managed to seed themselves and flourish over thousands of years, even through the Great Blight when the Endarkened had scoured all the world east of the Bazrahils—and south of the Armen Plains, for that matter— bare of life, but a *city*. Or the remains of it, built deep into the ground. Legacy of ancient Elven Mages and their dragons.

The Nalzindar hadn't been able to do much exploring. There wasn't any light down there at all, once you got below the level where Shaiara's people lived. Tiercel simply solved the problem by making the walls glow. The small balls of Coldfire that Harrier made tended to vanish after a few hours, which everyone was actually more comfortable with: the Wild Magic was something they knew and understood, though the things they told Harrier about as commonplaces astonished him. Find water and create wells? Turn aside a sandstorm? He wasn't sure how he'd even *begin* to do those things. Fortunately Shaiara's people weren't asking him to do any of them, which meant that Harrier wasn't having to explain anything about being a Knight- Mage. Meanwhile, having Tiercel try to explain that the walls *remembered* having been lit this way—which was why they lit up again now—was almost more than the Nalzindar could take.

It was almost more than *Harrier* could take, when you came right down to it, because neither Ancaladar nor Tiercel could tell him exactly when this Vieliessar Farcarinon was supposed to have *been*. And Harrier had enough trouble wrapping his mind around the idea of things that had happened just as long ago as the Great Flowering. The idea of something happening so long ago that there hadn't even been people (no matter how many times Tiercel told him *Elves* were people—and Harrier smacked him for being picky—Harrier knew exactly what he meant and wouldn't change his words in the privacy of his own mind) was almost impossible to think about. The idea that *things*— cups and coins and wall carvings—had survived from then *was* impossible to think about, so Harrier didn't. He just followed Tiercel around and helped him look at them and tried to figure out what they meant.

At the same time, they did their best to not only fit in, but to reduce the burden their coming had placed on the tiny exiled desert tribe.

HE HAD NO intention of ever telling Harrier this, but Tiercel was grateful that they'd found themselves in Abi'Abadshar, because that meant he wasn't facing Bisochim at the Lake of Fire.

He tried not to think about Tarnatha'Iteru, because he was ashamed of how much it upset him. It was even more humiliating to know that Ancaladar could see what he was thinking, because Tiercel knew that Ancaladar had seen far worse in his long life, and probably thought that Tiercel's reaction was way out of proportion to what had happened.

Now, with the benefit of hindsight, knowing everything that had happened, Tiercel wished desperately that he and Harrier had simply fled the city at the first sign of trouble. But every time he thought that, he thought of what Harrier had told him—that their defense of Tarnatha'Iteru, even though it had failed, had probably saved Akazidas'Iteru—and then he couldn't want that.

But then he thought of the people he'd killed, the Isvaieni who'd died as they'd crashed into his MageShield. And he thought of the fact that he'd only delayed the inevitable for less than a sennight. And he thought of the fact that Harrier had been forced to kill people with his swords to save their lives. And he thought of how the city had *smelled* the night after Ancaladar had rescued them. And he thought of Calling Fire to burn the dead in the morning. And he really wasn't sure whether he could ever use his magic to kill anyone ever again, even if they were an actual real Endarkened, much less if they were only someone who'd been tricked by one.

In order to distract himself, he spent his time trying to

fit into the life of the Nalzindar, and exploring Abi'Abad-shar. Whenever he'd start to go wandering off, Shaiara would insist on accompanying him—not because the tunnels were dark (because they weren't, not any more; he'd meant merely to cast a temporary spell of Magelight on the walls—since the spell could be used to make objects glow as well as to simply form nebulous balls of light—and had ended up making walls, ceiling, and floor glow *permanently* with an eerie full-moon glow) but because she was convinced he'd get lost or into some other trouble. In a lot of ways, Shaiara reminded Tiercel of Harrier.

"SO HOW MANY levels are there to this place?" Tiercel asked.

"'Levels.'" Shaiara tasted the unfamiliar word. "We know not. We have made three descents beyond this—but it is difficult without lamps or lanterns. Or proper torches."

Tiercel looked at her curiously and saw her shrug minutely. "One may not cross the Barahileth carrying aught but what one must to survive," Shaiara said.

"Is that why you . . . ?" He stopped, not wishing to say something that might give offense. He and Harrier had already seen that the Nalzindar had very little in the way of material possessions—little more than the clothing upon their backs and the weapons with which they hunted, in fact.

Shaiara smiled slightly. "We have our lives, by the grace of Sand and Star. In such an evil time, it would be foolish greed indeed to expect more."

Tiercel blinked. "I. Ah. But I know where there *is* more. A lot more. There's a whole Isvaieni camp—tents, and gear, and rugs, and even food—well, you don't need food, but there's wine, and spices, and honey, and *kaffeyah*. We'd been going to take supplies from there to go deeper into the Barahileth once Ancaladar got us some *shotors*, so it's not as if anyone else is going to be using it. He can bring it all here."

It took Tiercel quite some time to convince Shaiara that such an undertaking would be safe, and only Tiercel's calm (and repeated) assurances that he could cloak himself and Ancaladar in veils of invisibility induced Shaiara to finally permit it. The two of them had gone in the dark of the night, after moonset, planning initially for two trips (to bring the most important items first), and using two of the Isvaieni tents themselves as carrying bags. They'd returned with a vast bounty—enough to provision the tiny Nalzindar tribe far more lavishly, in fact, than it had been at the beginning of its flight. In the enormous unwieldy bundles with which Ancaladar returned there was clothing, blankets, jugs of oil and honey and wine, rugs, weapons, spices, herbs and medicines, *kaffeyah* and *kaffeyah*-services—and paper.

This last item was for Tiercel's own use. He'd found paper, writing-leads, and pens among the tents—for the Isvaieni had looted the city almost at random, probably intending to discard anything they found useless at the very last moment—and ink was easy enough to make. While the Nalzindar had little use for paper, Tiercel wanted to make a record of what he found on the walls of Abi'Abadshar so that he could use his notes to help himself decipher the mystery of the buried city.

WHEN ANCALADAR HAD brought back two more tents from Tarnatha'Iteru, you would have thought he was bringing back something *useful,* but despite the fact that they had no possible need of them for shelter, Shaiara's people were more delighted to have the tents than all the *actually useful* stuff they contained, Harrier thought.

When Ancaladar arrived with his first load, depositing it gently upon the sand and then taking off again at once, the twenty or so adult Isvaieni who had been (along with Harrier) awaiting his arrival had all come swarming up the steps. They'd dragged the bundle back down the steps to lay it beside the *Iteru* without unfolding the heavy black cloth from around the bundle of long poles; that surprised Harrier a little, until he realized that they'd want to stay out of sight as much as possible. The sky was dark—Shaiara had forbidden Tiercel and Ancaladar to fly before moonset—and the only light there was came from a handful of stones upon which Harrier had cast Coldfire. As the folds of cloth were thrown back to expose the contents, Harrier saw the normally taciturn Nalzindar look at each other excitedly.

"A tent, Shaiara. The Star-Crowned has brought a tent," a girl about Harrier's own age said. He was pretty sure her name was Ciniran.

"Talk later," Shaiara answered briefly. She picked up an armload of poles, and Harrier hurried to help her, because the poles were long, and no matter how much or how little they weighed, no one person could manage them easily alone.

Everyone worked quickly—down to the youngest children, who took charge of bundles once they'd been brought into the garden-space. The path back to the door was marked with stones that Harrier had cast Coldfire upon—it had taken Tiercel hours of work to quench the Magelight upon the walls of the top level again once he'd accidentally illuminated it, but Shaiara had been as close to upset as Harrier had seen her yet at the thought that they might leave some visible trace of their presence for some outsider to see.

Not "some outsider." Bisochim, who'd wanted the Nalzindar to join the other Isvaieni—and if they had, they would have been outside the walls of Tarnatha'Iteru just like the ones who followed Zanattar . . . or they would have been dead.

They'd barely emptied the first tent of all it contained—as much as a large shipping-crate, Harrier estimated, and a miracle that none of the jugs had broken—and dragged the folds of fabric down into the tunnel, out of sight, when Ancaladar was back with the second bundle.

"No more," Shaiara said sharply, as Ancaladar turned to take off again. "The sun comes."

Tiercel had looked puzzled (and well he might; it was still dark), but: "She's right, Tyr," Harrier said. He spoke as softly as Shaiara did; it had only taken him a day or so to learn the knack of pitching his voice so it didn't carry across the desert. "It's only an hour before dawn. This is the time of day that the desertfolk are out hunting, and you might be seen coming back."

Tiercel had sighed, shaking his head, but he'd nodded, and unbuckled the riding-strap, and Ancaladar had laid down, and Tiercel had slipped from his back. Ancaladar had launched himself into the sky (he would hunt, far from here, and return to Abi'Abadshar after dark), and Tiercel helped Harrier and the Nalzindar carry the second load inside.

There, Tiercel illuminated the garden with balls of Cold-fire, for it was still many hours before the sun would shine down into it, and there was much work to be done. To the surprise of both of them, the first thing the Nalzindar did— even before inspecting all the things Tiercel and Ancaladar had brought—was to pitch the two new tents here in their little campsite, and then to add the extra tent-poles they'd been missing (abandoned at Kannanatha Well in order to save weight in their crossing of the Barahileth) to the one tent they'd managed to keep. Next they unrolled all of the rugs, covering the ground beneath the tents, and taking up the woven mats and animal skins from beneath the original tent to replace them with what they obviously considered to be far more suitable and civilized floor coverings. Only then was the rest of what had been brought surveyed and put into its places, along with everything they had saved in their original crossing and made since they had come here—*shotor* saddles and harness, woven baskets, and cups and bowls of glass and metal that Shaiara had said had come from chambers within Abi'Abadshar.

Though the Nalzindar were a silent folk—and now was

no exception—both Tiercel and Harrier saw expressions of joy on every face as warm cloaks and thick blankets and proper heavy quilted sleeping-mats were unpacked. Marap forgot herself so far as to utter a soft cry of delight when the store of *kaffeyah* was revealed, along with its proper cooking-pan and brazier, and other Nalzindar women had greeted the stores of flour and oil—and cook-stones—with equal joy and relief. Long before the last of the items from the campsite at Tarnatha'Iteru had been inspected and carefully repacked, the garden was filled with savory cook-smells and the scent of brewing *kaffeyah*.

"Ancaladar told me what I ought to bring," Tiercel said to Harrier. "I had no idea." The two of them were standing off to one side, having figured out very quickly that the most useful thing they could do now was stay out of the way of the people who knew what they were doing.

"Looks like he did a good job," Harrier said.

"There's more stuff there," Tiercel said. He didn't sound as if he knew whether to be happy that there was still most of a campsite's worth of stuff available for the taking, or upset that it was there and abandoned.

Shaiara walked over to them, carrying two small wooden cups in her hands. She held them out, and Harrier caught the flat bitter scent of *kaffeyah*. He didn't like the stuff, and he knew that by now Tiercel never wanted to see another cup of *kaffeyah* as long as he lived, but it was good manners, so they both accepted the cups.

"This day you have done the Nalzindar a great service," she said in her soft voice. She smiled slightly, and her eyes flashed with humor. "And you have done me one as well, for now the day is far off when I shall have to learn to spin and weave, and so I thank you." Then her expression sobered and her face grew stern, and her gaze rested steadily upon Tiercel's face. "But you must go no more to Tarnatha'Iteru. It is too dangerous."

"But I'm sure there are more things there that you could

use," Tiercel said. "And they're just going to rot if we don't take them. And nobody will know."

Shaiara's eyes flashed dangerously. "Indeed, you have named yourself a Mage—do you also claim for yourself the power to see the future? What if Zanattar should turn back in his flight to reclaim his lost possessions, and see more of them gone than even the largest caravan of *shotors* could bear away? I will not accept such a risk to my people."

Tiercel opened his mouth again, and Harrier kicked him. "You're right," he said. "It isn't worth the risk. Tiercel won't go there again."

Shaiara nodded, and after a moment she walked away. When they were sure she wasn't looking, both of them poured out their cups of *kaffeyah* into the roots of the nearest tree.

"I still think—" Tiercel said.

"No," Harrier said quietly. "You aren't. What if Zanattar did go back? What if someone else did? What if they went back to Bisochim? What if he started looking for their *stuff*? He's a Wildmage. Any Seeking Spell could find it—oh, not all of it, I don't think a Seeking Spell can be cast except to find a specific object—but what if you happened to take away something that somebody could describe? He could follow it right here."

Tiercel sighed and ran a hand over his hair. "Yeah. I guess you're right. Let's just hope nobody goes back and looks until the rest of the campsite has been completely torn up by predators."

"Let's," Harrier agreed.

OVER THE NEXT days, their lives settled into a quiet predictable routine. Tiercel explored the city beneath the earth, and when Harrier wasn't trekking down into the bowels of the earth with Tiercel, he stayed with the tribe and did useful things, like explaining to Ciniran and the others that the "stone-fruit" was mushrooms, the "fur-mice" were squirrels, the "great-doves" were chickens, the "terraces" were steps, and the mysterious "barriers" blocking so many of the "chambers" were doors to rooms. To Harrier's surprise and faint discomfort, the fact that the Nalzindar knew he was a Wildmage meant that they relied on him. Not in the way they would rely upon one of their own people, but they expected certain things from him, and despite his misgivings, he did his best to provide them. They thought his ability to tell them so much about what was safe to eat in the gardens of Abi'Abadshar was Wildmage wisdom, and after the first couple of days, he'd stopped trying to explain that he knew these things *not* because of Wildmage wisdom, but because these plants and animals were common where he came from in the North, and simply stuck with saying that he *knew*.

Because he *did* know, even when he shouldn't.

They'd been in Abi'Abadshar a few days more than a sennight when Marap brought him a basket of berries. Marap was the Nalzindar healer. She'd told Harrier that she was no true Healer—not like a Wildmage—but she had herb-skill, and she was grateful for his presence for as long as he was willing to grace the tents of the Nalzindar, because she'd long feared another happening that would lie beyond her skills. One of the *ikulas* had been poisoned by the stone-fruit before they had properly understood what they were, and so she hoped he would call upon the Wild Magic now. The Nalzindar had long wondered if these berries might be safe to eat; they had seen the birds and many of the animals eating them, and they looked very fine. . . .

The berries did *look* fine: large and red and almost like cherries, so succulent Harrier's mouth watered just to look at them. "Sure," he'd said. "I'll try one." *What's the worst that can happen?*

He'd picked out a large one and raised it to his lips. It smelled a little like cherries and a little like roses and a little like something he couldn't quite identify. And as he'd opened his mouth, the warning voice in his mind sounded clear and strong.

No.

He obeyed without question, dropping the berry back into the basket. Hunch or intuition or just paranoia? He didn't know. But he knew it was important to *listen.*

"Don't eat them," he said, and Marap had nodded and taken the basket away.

And that hadn't been the strangest thing to happen to him in the past year—if he'd been making lists, Harrier would have run out of numbers a long time ago—but it was kind of strange. He wondered if you got to be a Wildmage— okay, a *good* Wildmage—by just assuming you knew what you were doing.

Meanwhile, if he'd been trying to stop Tiercel from ever going to the Lake of Fire to do whatever he could against Bisochim, Abi'Abadshar would have been a good way to do it. Tiercel kept talking about there being so much to learn here and so much to find out, and about all the ancient races that the Endarkened had destroyed, and about how they'd all always known that the Endark- ened had destroyed so many of the races of the Light in the ancient wars (the things that Tiercel insisted that "everybody had always known" never ceased to amaze Harrier). Down here in the depths of Abi'Abadshar there was proof not only of that, but of the existence of even more of them. The ancient world, Harrier decided, had been very crowded.

And no matter how many times when Tiercel came back at the end of a day's explorations to tell Harrier what he'd learned and Harrier said, "Yes, but where does it say how Vielly Whatsername got rid of them that time?" Tier- cel would shake his head and say, "It isn't that easy."

At least they were getting some useful things done in ad- dition to all of Tiercel's exploring. While Tiercel and Har- rier supervised, Ancaladar had dug out some of the other terraces—what normal people called *stairs*—to clear other entrances to the underground city. Shaiara worried about piles of sand building up on the surface—though Harrier was pretty sure that if Bisochim showed up to see the piles of sand they were already in deep trouble—but Tiercel simply turned the sand into water. He did it at midday, and here in the Barahileth, the water simply turned to steam immediately. Even though Harrier figured that if this Bisochim were even *looking* in their direction they were already in trouble, he was glad to see that the steam didn't make a beacon for anyone to see—he already had a very clear idea of how far away you could see things in the desert. But the clouds disappeared instantly, sucked away by the moisture-starved air. Shaiara fretted constantly about so much water added to the air being an insult to the desert's Balance, but Harrier couldn't see it. Even all the water Tiercel'd made by turning Tarnatha'Iteru to water wouldn't make a dent in the dryness of this place.

And the more excavating Tiercel and Ancaladar did between them, the clearer it became that Abi'Abadshar had been built for dragons as well as, well, *Elves*. It had only taken a day or two after they'd located it for Ancaladar to clear out one of the staircases, and after that, he was able to get into Abi'Abadshar. The outer section—where Shaiara and her people were camped—was relatively small—and the entire top level was built to a human scale, but the further down you went, the larger everything became. The staircase at the very back of the top level was enormous and once they'd excavated it and started going down—all the staircases were huge—and reached the fifth level below the surface, they reached passages where Ancaladar could move around in complete comfort.

"WHY BUILD SO deep? And why does it get bigger as we go down? Why put the dragons on the bottom instead of the top?" Harrier asked.

"They had magic," Tiercel answered absently. He ran his hand over a wall. Harrier found the fact that every single surface—the floor included—glowed bright moon-blue almost as disconcerting as the fact that this place was bigger than the biggest cavern in the Caves of Imrathalion. Except that the walls and floor and ceiling Caves of Imrathalion hadn't all been as smooth and level and squared-off as the rooms of his *house*. And they hadn't all been covered with . . . weird stuff.

"So was it *useful* magic?" Harrier asked. He thought he was being reasonably patient, because they'd been here a fortnight already, and all they really seemed to be doing was finding out how a bunch of Elves who were older than *rocks* had lived.

"Useful to them," Tiercel said, sounding amused. "They defeated the Endarkened, which allowed *us* to happen. And created the Wild Magic as we know it."

"Which is creepy to think about. You know that, right?"

"Maybe," Tiercel said. "But, Harrier, don't you see? This is the very beginning of the relationship between dragons and people. The beginning of dragons sharing their magic."

"The beginning of dragons *dying*," Harrier muttered. He hadn't meant for the other two to hear that, but he'd forgotten how much the stone magnified every sound.

"Yes, well," Tiercel said uncomfortably. "Ancaladar, you want to give me a hand here? I can't see the carvings at the top of the wall."

Considering that the carvings at the top of the wall were at least a hundred feet above Tiercel's head, that was an amazing—and typically Tiercel—understatement.

"Now I am a ladder," the dragon sighed. "Of course." The great black dragon lowered his head, and Tiercel stepped onto it as if he were stepping onto a log. Harrier resisted the temptation to tell the two of them to be careful as Ancaladar slowly raised his head until Tiercel's head nearly brushed the ceiling.

"See?" Tiercel said, leaning in to peer at the wall.

"See what?" Harrier demanded from his position far below both of them. "And don't expect me to catch you if you fall."

"It says here—" Tiercel began.

"You can read that?" Harrier demanded.

"I'm looking at the pictures. And guessing. A lot. What's weird is that the letters look like the High Magick glyphs, only the glyphs are just *glyphs*, they aren't an alphabet, so even though—"

"Light and Darkness, Tyr, don't make me come up there and *hit* you!"

"Okay, okay! I'm *guessing* that what this says here is that the Elves of Great Queen Vieliessar Farcarinon's time weren't worrying about their Bonded dragons dying— except by accident. And the dragons weren't worried about dying either."

"It says all that up there?"

"This is the fifth level we've been on and there have been carvings and writings that were clear enough to read on levels three, four, and five, so, no. It doesn't say *all* of this right up here. Would you like to come up here and look at this section of the carvings for yourself?"

"Um . . . no. How come they put that stuff up there where nobody could read it, if it's so important?"

Even all the way down on the floor Harrier could hear Tiercel sigh. "Oh, *I* don't know, Harrier. Maybe because this was just *decoration* and they had the same stuff written down in a much more useful and accessible way in *books*."

"Okay. Right. So what does it say?"

"You know that—"

"Bonded, it is not that I am becoming tired of standing here . . ." Ancaladar said meaningfully.

Tiercel cleared his throat. "It says that the dragons' Bond was supposed to be a *temporary* condition. I'm not sure I've got that right, but . . . there's something about the Bond, and something about time, and something about a Mageprice being fulfilled, and I can't figure it out. But what I *can* figure out—and I'm sure about this—is this: when the Bond is paid, the dragons will stop dying."

"Yeah, well that time obviously isn't yet," Harrier said before he could stop himself.

"No," Tiercel said, sounding wistful. "I guess it isn't the 'Time of the Three Becoming One' yet."

"I'm not even going to ask what that means," Harrier said as Ancaladar gently lowered Tiercel to the floor again.

"Good," Tiercel said, sighing, "because I don't know. Which three, or how they become one, or what that has to do with . . . anything. Does it mean there won't be any more Elven Mages?"

"You're asking me?" Harrier wanted to know.

"No," Tiercel said, stepping from Ancaladar's head to the floor. "I'm just asking."

"Fine. Now do you—"

"Oh, I really don't think you're going to like this," Tiercel said.

"Look, Tyr, we know they won," Harrier said, caught halfway between irritation and worry.

"Yeah. But I'm starting to think they didn't do it here— as in, they weren't in Abi'Abadshar—um, the name means something like either 'glorious rightful rule' or 'city of the red bones' if you're interested—when the Endarkened were cast out in Vieliessar Farcarinon's time. Okay, you know about the Firesprites, right?"

"No."

"Ancient race the Endarkened killed. But not until a long time after Abi'Abadshar was built. And abandoned, because this was where the Firesprites lived. Here. In the Barahileth, and the Elves made an alliance with them, and one of the provisions was that they would leave."

"And you know this because of the . . . ?"

"Pictures."

"Right. Which they put on the walls because . . . ?"

"They liked putting things on walls? I don't know. The point is that the Elves built this city as part of their war against the Endarkened. They made an alliance with the Firesprites, and turned the war in this area over to them. I think. After which they withdrew from this city."

Tiercel began moving around picking up his gear—which

was scattered all over the place—and packing it up. Harrier wondered if what Tiercel had been hoping to find on this level was the same thing they'd both been hoping to find somewhere here in Abi'Abadshar all along: an answer, directions, some clear instruction on what exactly it was they were supposed to do in order to do . . .

The thing that the Elves and even the Wild Magic seemed to be so serenely confident that Tiercel *could* do: stop Bisochim from calling the Endarkened back into the world. Harrier wondered if it might be as simple as going to the Lake of Fire and finding Bisochim and saying: *"Hey, we don't know what it is you think you're doing, but you really aren't. And calling the Endarkened back into the world is a really bad thing, so please stop now, okay?"* If it were that simple, probably somebody else would have done it already.

"Which means that if there's an answer it isn't going to be here, because this is not only an *old* place, it's an old place from, um, the middle of the war so even though the Elves not only probably wrote everything down and they *definitely* carved it into every flat surface they could find, *these* flat surfaces don't have any information about how the war came out and particularly on how they managed to *win* it." Harrier looked back up the corridor—he supposed he might as well still call it that, although it wasn't exactly. A big enough space to make Ancaladar look reasonable-sized. Enough room for *two* Ancaladars side-by-side.

"Come on, Harrier. We never thought there'd be a real answer here. If there was a perfect solution available here, wouldn't they have used it in the next war? And the next?"

"And the next, and the next, and the next—just how many wars are there going to have to be?" Harrier demanded in frustration.

"I don't think the Dark stops trying, Har," Tiercel said softly. Harrier wondered if Tiercel felt as frustrated by all this as he did. Or maybe even more frustrated—Tiercel was the one who knew all the history, the one who had all the *details* about all the times the Dark had tried to kill all of them. "I wonder what time it is?" he added.

"Time to go." When Tiercel looked at him in surprise and suspicion, Harrier said: "No, really. It's almost time for the evening meal—I mean, considering how far down we are, we've just about got time to get back for it if we start now."

It had surprised both of them to find that no matter how deep below the surface of Abi'Abadshar they went, Harrier always knew exactly what time it was up above. Since Ancaladar did, too, they knew that Harrier was accurate. How and why he could be was something none of them really understood. More Wild Magic stuff, Harrier guessed.

"Yeah, okay," Tiercel said.

"Because I'm not moving down here," Harrier added belligerently.

"I said I was coming," Tiercel said, hefting his bag of gear over his shoulder.

IT WAS ONLY a little odd to be sitting around a campfire underground, Tiercel decided. Odd-but-nice, because at least the Nalzindar and their garden-camp were a lot more normal-seeming than places so far underground it took him and Harrier almost two hours just to walk to them. Abi'Abadshar was so old that when he stopped and thought about it, Tiercel really couldn't get his mind around the sheer *age* of it. Every time he tried to imagine something older than the World of Men his mind just . . . stopped. It was easier to imagine a world that didn't have humans in it any more than one in which there hadn't been humans *yet*. Thinking about it raised so many fascinating questions, and there was nobody to ask—he wasn't sure even the Elves knew the answers. But . . . had they—human people—come from somewhere else? Had the Wild Magic made them out of some other creature, the way the Endarkened had been made from Elves? No matter how much he wanted to know, the answers wouldn't be carved into the walls here, because this city was too old for that. It had been born—and died—long before there had been Men at all.

Tiercel found that he liked the Nalzindar very much. It made him a little sad, thinking that he would have liked the other Isvaieni just as much, and now, because of what Bisochim had done to them, he'd never get to know them. Shaiara's people were quiet and shy, and Tiercel had quickly learned that they would never look directly at him when he was speaking to them, and that it was hard to get most of them to say more than a word or two at a time, either. The most disturbing thing about the Nalzindar was something that wasn't something they were, or something they did, and it had taken him an entire fortnight to think it through and realize what it was and why it was so disturbing.

But Shaiara had told Harrier that this was all of the Nalzindar that there were, and there were only thirty of them, and that included three babies too young to walk and two kids that Tiercel thought were probably somewhere around the age of two and one who was maybe four and a couple who were seven or eight and a boy around twelve who spent all his time staring at Harrier and Tiercel as if he'd never seen anything like them before and hadn't said a single word in their hearing the entire time they'd been here. So there were only twenty-one adult Nalzindar, and only seven or eight of *them* looked old enough to be about the age of Tiercel's father.

And Shaiara wasn't anywhere near that old. She was around his and Harrier's age. Tiercel had wondered at first if Bisochim had killed her parents and that was why she was the chief of the Nalzindar now, but Ciniran—who didn't seem to be as shy as the others—had said that Shaiara had been leading the Nalzindar for years.

Tiercel supposed that someone their age being what amounted to a First Magistrate made as much sense as

Harrier being a Knight-Mage or him being the Light's Fated Warrior intended to defeat the Endarkened. And there was nothing much he could do about either of those things, either. So he took each day as it came, doing his best to become used to the fact that the only sunlight he really saw came filtering down through cracks in the broken stone of the roof, and that if he wanted to see full day and open sky he had at least half an hour's hike to one of the exits to the outside. He spent most of his time a mile underground looking at things nobody had seen for thousands of years, hoping that something he found there would tell him what he needed to know to stop the Dark from coming back this time.

And at the end of each day he did his best to put all of that out of his mind and think about nothing more complicated than the things he'd used to think about when he'd been a student back in Armethalieh: dinner, and a quiet evening, and then going to bed.

The evening meal among the Nalzindar consisted of roast meat, or stew, and fresh-cooked flatbread with spiced oil (now that there was oil; before this, it had been animal grease) and various fruits and vegetables. The Nalzindar were hunters, and when they'd roamed the Isvai, the evening meal had marked the time, several hours after sunset, when the hunters would return to the camp to share their news of the day's success or failure. The Nalzindar, like most of the creatures of the desert, hunted at dusk or dawn, and kept as still as possible in the day's greatest heat. Now—by their standards—they didn't need to hunt at all, but the evening meal still marked the end of their day. There might be some talk of the days' activities—though only, Tiercel had discovered, if they involved something the whole tribe needed to know. At meals, Harrier and Tiercel sat beside Shaiara—honored guests—with a half-dozen of what Tiercel thought of as "senior" Nalzindar gathered around them, although they weren't much older than Harrier's oldest brother. He knew most of their names by now: Marap and Kamar and Natha and Talmac and his brother Turan. Even Ciniran ate with them, although he didn't get the impression she was one of the "senior" tribesmen. Actually, aside from Marap and Kamar and Shaiara herself, Tiercel wasn't sure of the relative status of anyone here.

Even though he was determined to be a good guest— and even though he knew how much worse his situation could be—Tiercel found his evenings among the Nalzindar more boring than he could once have imagined. After the meal they simply went off to sleep. And he couldn't practice his spells. He really didn't dare (considering that a simple spell of Magelight had made the walls light up so brightly, he had no idea what might happen if he cast the wrong spell), and besides, Ancaladar wasn't there to work with him. Ancaladar wasn't even there to talk to, most of the time in the evening, because Ancaladar spent most nights hunting. Desert game was small and sparse, and unless he wanted to leave the desert entirely and fly to a place where he could take larger prey, he needed to hunt every night. And while Ancaladar *could* fly to such a place, none of them really liked the idea of him being so far away from Tiercel, considering what had happened the last couple of times.

At least—in this land of what the Nalzindar called "peace and plenty"—some of them were willing to stay up after dinner just to keep "the strangers" company. (Tiercel got the idea that even if he and Harrier spent the next ten years here in Abi'Abadshar with the Nalzindar, they'd still be known as "the strangers"), because even after a long day spent hiking through the echoing caverns below, neither of the two of them was ever quite tired enough to sleep immediately. After dinner most evenings, Shaiara and Ciniran would walk with them through the gardens for an hour or so, accompanied by floating balls of Coldfire. About a half an hour's walk away from the camp, there was a pool with a little waterfall. The two Nalzindar never grew tired of gazing at the falling water.

There were even fish in the pool, though none of them could imagine how they'd gotten there. Harrier had assured the Nalzindar that fish were safe to eat, and had even offered to catch and cook some, but even though Harrier was a "Revered Wildmage" (and Tiercel would *never* get tired of teasing him about that, at least when they were safely out of earshot of any of the Nalzindar) so far none of the tribe had been willing to take him up on his offer.

Sitting beside the waterfall, they would talk, though Harrier and Tiercel and Ciniran did most of the talking.

"You couldn't be planning to spend the rest of your lives here?" Tiercel asked one evening. "I mean, this is a beautiful place, but . . ."

"Where else should we go?" Ciniran had asked simply. "The Isvai is not safe."

"But there are other places," Tiercel said.

Ciniran stared at him uncomprehendingly.

"Um . . . north?" Tiercel suggested cautiously. "You could go north?"

Shaiara had made a faintly amused noise. She was far-too-polite to ever tell them they were idiots, even when Tiercel suspected they were definitely *being* idiots, but she could convey her mirth at foolishness when it presented itself to her, and frequently did. "Into the Great Cold?" she said in disbelief.

"You make it sound as if it's like—I don't know—thinking about packing up and going off to live in the El-ven Lands," Tiercel protested.

"And why should I consider living in the Veiled Lands, when they belong to the Elder Brethren, who would surely not welcome my intrusion?" Shaiara asked. "Still less would I wish to go to live in a wasteland of frozen water."

"No, no, see, the north isn't like that," Tiercel said, wanting to make her understand. "Well not all the time. No, it isn't even like that in winter—okay, there *is* frozen water—I mean, snow and ice—on the ground, well, snow falls out of the sky, but—"

To his irritation he heard Harrier laugh out loud as he

stumbled through his explanation, and even Ciniran gave a single soft chuff of amusement. But it became clear to both of them—to all of them—that the thought of the Nalzindar traveling to a land where they had no idea of how to survive was only a stopgap at best. It might offer temporary safety, but if Bisochim could not be stopped at the Lake of Fire, that safety would be very temporary indeed.

Twenty-one

A Double-Edged Gift

"IF WE HAVEN'T found anything in the last—oh, how many is this?—six?—eight?—levels, I don't see why you want to keep going down," Harrier complained.

"It's ten levels now. This will be the tenth. And among other things, don't you want to see how far down this *goes*?" Tiercel answered.

It was now a full moonturn since the two of them had arrived in Abi'Abadshar. There were whole stretches of time when Harrier could forget . . . things.

The destruction of Tarnatha'Iteru. The thought that the man who'd given him his swords and taught him all that he knew about using them was certainly dead. The fact that this was only a waystation on their way to destroy the Fire Woman and stop Bisochim—and only when it was very late and he was completely alone did Harrier ever take out and look at the thought that *stopping* Bisochim was going to mean *killing* Bisochim.

He'd killed a man whose name he didn't even know. He'd killed, in fact, several men, and the fact that he didn't know the exact number made him want to cry, if there'd been any place he could have done it without anyone knowing. And it didn't matter *why* he'd done it, or what those men's friends and families had done to Harrier's friends (and would do to his family if they could get at them). Having killed had hurt something and changed something inside him, and Harrier would give nearly anything for those moments not to have happened—and to unknow the knowledge that if more such moments lay in his future, he would not turn aside from them.

So he followed Tiercel as Tiercel looked for answers, and practiced with his swords down in the echoing stone depths where none of the Nalzindar could see him— because he couldn't bear the thought that any of them might see what he was doing and praise him, or want him to teach them what he knew—and did what he could to help the Nalzindar in other peaceful ways, and read his Three Books, and hoped that some solution to their problem would present itself.

But not if it meant that Tiercel intended to descend to the center of the world looking for it.

"No," Harrier said simply. "Either there are answers here, or there aren't. And you have to make up your mind which it is. Because just the *surface* of this place is bigger than Armethalieh. And we do not have time to search every inch of the whole underneath of it, because you know what? I do not think the Endarkened are getting weaker while you are drawing pictures of ancient Elves on *pieces of paper!*"

He hadn't meant to lose his temper. He hadn't meant to yell. But if anybody—or any*thing*—had thought that turning him into a Knight-Mage was going to make him all calm and reasonable all the time like, say, *Ancaladar,* they were a lot stupider than they ought to be, was all Harrier had to say.

"Do not yell, Harrier," Ancaladar said gently. "We all are aware of the dangers that surround us."

"No," Tiercel said reluctantly. "He's right. *You're* right. There's a lot about the spells they used, but . . . Elven Magery and the High Magick and the Wild Magic are three different things, just to begin with. I can't learn Elven

Magery any more than I can learn the Wild Magic. It's just . . . I thought . . . You know . . . I haven't had one single vision since we got here," he finished quietly.

"I know." And Harrier had wondered why that was, because Tiercel'd had them from the moment they'd come through Pelashia's Veil and right up through when Tarnatha'Iteru fell. Never in any pattern. Never really changing.

"So I think this place is shielded somehow against the Endarkened. Come on, Har. If Bisochim was looking for the Nalzindar, wouldn't he have found them? You could— it's a Seeking spell. Remember how you told me a couple of moonturns ago that I had to be careful about what I brought back from the Isvaieni camp at Tarnatha'Iteru in case I brought back something that Bisochim could Seek and use to find the Nalzindar? But he wouldn't need something like that. To See something or somebody you know is a simple spell. *I* could—Shaiara's said she's met him, so Bisochim knows what she looks like, and *I* could find somebody if I knew what they looked like, and so could you, couldn't you? So the only reason he hasn't been able to find them is—"

"Because they managed to hide in the *one place* within a couple of thousand square miles that's full of shields against the Endarkened that *still work* after about a million years?" Harrier said.

"Pretty much."

"Which means you think there might be some other magic here that still works?"

"Pretty much."

"And you didn't mention this about a moonturn ago *why?*" Harrier asked with long-suffering patience. If not for the fact that Ancaladar's head was between him and Tiercel, he would have contemplated smacking him. Yes, it was very wrong to hit someone who was unarmed when you were armed—and Harrier never went anywhere without his swords, just as Tiercel couldn't be persuaded to carry anything more threatening than his wand and his eating knife—but Harrier didn't think those rules could ever have been meant to apply to Tiercel. The people who'd come up with those rules hadn't known Tiercel.

"We haven't found any objects below the fifth level. And all we've found there and above have been furniture, household objects, a lot of gold and jewels. Things that would survive for thousands of years. And nothing remotely magical. The protective shields are probably built into the stone of the city, but . . ."

"But something else might not be," Harrier said, starting to get excited now, "and it doesn't have to be something powerful enough to destroy He Who Is and an entire army of Endarkened, because that isn't what we're dealing with."

"And if there's something here, there's no point in doing a spell to try to find it, either your kind or mine, because the shield-spells will just soak up everything. How do you make a spell to look for something if you have no idea of what you're looking for, anyway?"

Harrier sighed in frustration, his momentary excitement evaporating. Tiercel was right. He leaned back against the wall. They'd have to search every inch of this place now and hope they'd recognize something useful—if there *was* something useful—when they saw it. He stared down into the opening for the steps leading from the Ninth Level to the Tenth. The top few steps weren't dark, because the Ninth Level was full-moon bright, but after that, Harrier couldn't see how far down the steps went, and each level tended to be just a *little* larger in scale than the last. "Is this the last one?" he asked hopefully.

"I have no idea," Tiercel answered.

Harrier sighed. "Go ahead."

"I don't see why you never do this," Tiercel grumbled, gesturing back at the glowing walls.

"Because I don't make the walls light up and glow for sennights or possibly for*ever,* is why," Harrier said inarguably. "Go on. We brought lunch but we didn't bring dinner." He really hated eating down here anyway. It didn't matter how large the space was—and it was huge—or how well-lit it was (and it was actually more brightly lit than the underground gardens in which the Nalzindar were living); Harrier could still imagine the crushing weight of all the rock above him. Somehow it seemed to leech all the savor out of the air itself, and though for some reason the air wasn't damp, it seemed as if it ought to be. At least higher up the passages had been dirty, but this far down the levels weren't even that. There was just a lot of . . . nothing.

He stepped away from the wall—though there really wasn't any reason he needed to—as Tiercel reached out and touched two fingers to the wall. An icy white ring of brightness raced away from the place where Tiercel's fingertips met the stone, expanding in all directions. No matter how many times Harrier had seen it happen, it still fascinated him to watch the bright circle of light as it raced over walls, ceiling, down over the steps, and to see the stone bloom slowly into the familiar blue-white radiance in its wake. It took the leading edge of the spell less than a score of heartbeats to reach the bottom of the stair and race outward, out of sight. It seemed as if it happened both fast and slow while he was watching, because watching an ordinary Coldfire spell (and Harrier realized that in the last year, he'd actually begun to think of some spells as "ordinary") make all the stone in sight glow as brightly as a single object that the spell had been cast on (and the first corridors that Tiercel had illuminated showed no sign of going dark, even a moonturn later) was both weird and fascinating, no matter how many times Harrier got to see it happen.

When the spell had finished its work, Harrier saw—with a sigh of resignation—that it was a really long way down, which meant it was a really long way up. As much as he hated the thought, if they were going to do much exploring below this, maybe they *should* start camping down here, because it had actually taken them more than a bell just to get this far.

"Well that was odd," Tiercel said, staring at his finger-tips.

" 'Odd' is not good," Harrier pointed out.

"No, it's . . . I haven't felt anything when I cast a spell since I Bonded to Ancaladar. But I felt something this time," Tiercel said thoughtfully.

"I felt nothing, Bonded," Ancaladar said, sounding puzzled.

"It's probably the, oh, complete lack of air to breathe down here. Or the fact that we've already hiked ten miles on a breakfast of, um, cold roast goat. You know. Food poisoning." For just a moment—when Tiercel had spoken—Harrier had felt uneasy. But Ancaladar's words chased away his half-formed fear. The dragon's senses (especially for things of magic) were much stronger than his or Tiercel's, and through the Bond he could feel everything Tiercel did. If there *was* something down here, and it wasn't something that bothered Ancaladar, maybe it was what they were looking for.

Maybe they'd have a weapon and a plan by dinnertime.

"You've eaten exactly the same things I have," Tiercel said, laughing, his momentary worry forgotten as well. "No, wait. Why do I even bother?"

"Because you're an idiot. Come on," Harrier said.

"I shall go first, Bonded, Harrier," Ancaladar said firmly. "In case you have sensed something that I could not."

Without waiting for a reply from either of them, Ancaladar stretched out his neck and began slithering down the staircase.

Like all the staircases on the higher levels, this one was curved, so that if you were standing at one end you couldn't see the other. The staircase passages were enough narrower and lower than the open spaces of the lower levels themselves for Tiercel and Harrier not to want to share them with Ancaladar, even though there was actually enough room. The great black dragon slithered quickly down the wide shallow steps—Abi'Abadshar was a place definitely designed for dragons—and coiled his long sinuous body around the bend in the staircase.

Harrier had just watched the tip of Ancaladar's tail flick out of sight, thinking: *he must be almost there, we can start down now,* when Tiercel suddenly fell to his knees with a heart-wrenching scream.

"He's gone! He's gone! He's *gone!*"

"What? Tyr—*what?*" Harrier couldn't figure out whether to grab his swords or Tiercel. Tiercel was thrashing around on the floor as if he'd been stabbed, but when Harrier dropped to his knees beside him, he couldn't find any trace of a wound. *"Tiercel!"* he shouted.

"Ancaladar!" Tiercel screamed. His voice should have echoed off the walls, but nothing echoed down here. The sounds were all flattened and hushed the way sound was against a heavy snowfall.

Harrier sprang to his feet and drew his swords. He didn't know what good he could do against something that could hurt Ancaladar, but he had to try. He agonized for a long instant over leaving Tiercel behind, but he knew there was nothing either here or behind them, and every second might count. He ran down the glowing blue-lit staircase with his swords held out before him. The flat dull sound of his footsteps and the distorted sound of Tiercel's ragged sobbing were the only sounds.

Most of his mind was empty *(to fight, to win, a Knight-Mage did not think, a Knight-Mage reacted)* but a tiny part of it, locked away from the rest, was desperately bargaining with what had already happened. Ancaladar wasn't dead. Ancaladar *couldn't* be dead. If he was dead, Tiercel would be dead, too. They were Bonded: dragon and dragon-Bonded Mage, their lives linked by Ancaladar's magic. When one died, the other would die. That had been true ever since that ancient Elf-lady had made the first bargain with the dragons, even before this city was built.

Down and down and down, and he rounded the curve of the staircase, and now Harrier could see the corridor below. To call it a "corridor" was idiotic when you could drop the entire Main Temple of the Light in Armethalieh into the middle of it with room left over on both sides, but there wasn't anything else to call it.

Behind him he could still hear Tiercel screaming, and the sound brought back memories of Tarnatha'Iteru that made Harrier's heart pound wildly. *No.* He could almost hear the Telchi's voice in his mind. *That will not help either of you now.* He reached the last stair-step and skidded to a halt on it, looking both ways wildly. Ancaladar wasn't here.

"No, no, no," Harrier whispered under his breath. This couldn't be happening. This couldn't have happened. *Dragons do not just vanish,* he told himself, a little desperately.

But this level was different than all the other ones.

The Nalzindar lived on what was pretty much the "ground" level of Abi'Abadshar—what would have been a cellar if there'd been houses, and the houses were still there, and the space the Nalzindar occupied was anything like a cellar at all. This space was nine levels below that.

On all of the levels between where the Nalzindar lived and this one, the walls and even the ceiling had been carved: there were pictures like the ones in the Imrathalion Temple of the Light (but a lot more cryptic); there were rows and rows of things that might have been pictures and might not; still more rows of things that looked like Tiercel's High Magick glyphs and that Tiercel said were writing. But the floor had always been smooth. Here the floor was carved. Except not. It was . . .

Harrier took a backward step up the stairs cautiously, supremely grateful he had not taken that last step down to the floor of the level below. He didn't know what he was seeing, but the floor was ridged and grained like a weathered piece of driftwood. The Magelight didn't glow over its surface evenly, either: it collected more brightly in the grooves, somehow, even though Harrier was pretty sure

Magelight wasn't supposed to do that. The floor's surface seemed to be moving, and he couldn't quite tell whether it really was, or whether his eyes were playing tricks on him.

He walked from one end of the stair-tread to the other in order to be sure he was seeing as much of this level as he could from the opening of the staircase. Since it was just one big long chamber, it was easy enough to see most of it. And they'd explored enough of these levels that he knew that the next staircase should open out and down from the opposite wall at the opposite end of the corridor—which meant he ought to be able to see the opening from here, especially with the walls glowing as bright as a midsummer moon.

And he couldn't see anything like that at all.

Harrier rummaged around in his pockets. Tiercel had laughed at him when he'd picked up some of the coins from one of the treasure rooms, asking him what in the name of the Light he was going to spend them on here, but Harrier hadn't collected them to spend them. They were ancient and strange and pretty and made out of metals he'd never seen before, and somehow they weren't as *disturbing* as an entire vast underground city. He could hold them in his hands and look at them and wonder about the people who'd made them and used them and not feel as if he was about to be crushed by the weight of the entire history of the world since the beginning of Time.

He found one and pulled it out—it was five-sided and sort of bluish, with a cat-headed snake on one side and a bunch of butterflies on the other—and tossed it out into the middle of the floor.

Nothing happened. The coin simply bounced across the stone, making a dull chiming-clinking sound as it skittered, and then came to rest, a darker splotch against the glowing stone. It didn't glow, it didn't vanish, it didn't burst into flames. Harrier shook his head. He still didn't intend to step out there and risk sharing Ancaladar's fate. Because wherever Ancaladar was, he wasn't here.

He turned around and ran back up the stairs. Tiercel

was still lying on the floor at the top of the stairs, huddled into as small a ball as he could manage. He was breathing raggedly, but he'd stopped screaming. At least there was that. Harrier didn't think he could have stood listening to Tiercel make those sounds for much longer and not be able to do anything about it. He knelt down beside his friend again and put a hand on his shoulder.

"Tell me what happened!" Harrier demanded urgently.

"I don't know," Tiercel whispered hopelessly. "He's gone. The Bond is broken."

"Yeah, well, it isn't, or you'd be dead," Harrier said brutally. Sympathy was the last thing Tiercel needed right now—he knew that instinctively. Tiercel already thought this was a disaster; the last thing he needed was somebody to agree with him. Harrier didn't know whether he was telling the truth or not, but he did know that what he was saying was what Tiercel needed to hear right now. And at least some of it had to be true. He hadn't known a lot about dragons until they got to the Veiled Lands, but he'd certainly learned a lot since. And it all boiled down to one thing: kill either half of a Bonded pair, and the other half died immediately.

He pulled Tiercel into a sitting position. He had to admit that Tiercel *looked* half-dead. But that was a long way from *being* dead.

"Is he—Where—" Tiercel said, looking around.

"I looked. He isn't down there. It doesn't look like the other levels, either," Harrier said.

"I have to see," Tiercel said desperately.

He pulled himself to his feet—using Harrier for a prop—and staggered upright. Before Harrier could stop him, he lunged for the staircase and disappeared down the stairs. Harrier swore and followed.

It would have been one thing if Tiercel was actually injured. But it was just shock—at whatever'd happened to the Bond between him and Ancaladar—and it wasn't really slowing him down very much. By the time Harrier realized that, Tiercel had a good head start on him. Harrier redoubled his efforts to catch up, shouting for Tiercel to *stop,* to *wait*—

He was just a few instants too slow to grab Tiercel's arm as Tiercel reached the bottom of the staircase and ran out into the corridor.

"Tiercel!" Harrier screamed.

But nothing had happened.

Tiercel stood in the middle of the strange ridged glowing floor, looking all around. *"Ancaladar!"* he shouted.

Harrier ran out into the corridor after him—certain that at any moment whatever had happened to Ancaladar would happen to both of them. Tiercel turned and ran down the length of the corridor, shouting for Ancaladar as if he were refusing to believe the evidence of his own eyes.

Harrier walked over to the coin he'd thrown and picked it up. There was nothing at all different about it than there would have been if he'd thrown it onto the floor on the level above. It wasn't even glowing—not that it should have been, because Magelight (or Coldfire) wasn't something that was *contagious.* He slipped the coin back into his pocket, then bent down again and ran his hand over the floor. It felt like stone, and it *was* ridged. The ridges were curved and smooth: just as if somebody—like, oh, say, the Elves who'd built this place—had reproduced the smoothly weathered grain of driftwood on a massive scale. He straightened up and took a careful look around from this new vantage point. There was nothing at all on the walls or the ceiling. They were as smooth and featureless as the floor normally was—if you defined "normal" as "the way the floor had been on the previous nine underground levels."

He stood up and walked after Tiercel.

Tiercel had stopped calling for Ancaladar, but he hadn't stopped looking for him. He was moving quickly down along the nearer wall, moving his hands over the surface as if he was checking for hidden doors.

But it wouldn't matter if Ancaladar was behind a hidden door, would it? Ancaladar had been hundreds of miles away—asleep—and he and Tiercel had still been linked in some way Harrier didn't quite understand. Able to communicate in some way so that Tiercel had been able to call Ancaladar to come and rescue them. Because they were Bonded, and that was something Harrier had never really understood—not because he was jealous of the friendship Ancaladar and Tiercel shared, but because Tiercel couldn't explain it and Ancaladar had never tried. The closest Tiercel had ever gotten to an explanation was telling Harrier that knowing Ancaladar was there was like knowing his foot was there, and Harrier had laughed so long and so hard at hearing Ancaladar compared to a foot that Tiercel had never tried explaining again.

But what that meant now was that no matter where Ancaladar was, Tiercel should know he *was* there—if Ancaladar was alive. And if Ancaladar was dead, Tiercel should be dead, too. And Harrier didn't want either one of them to be dead, and he really didn't want Tiercel to be dead, and if Ancaladar *was* dead . . .

What had killed him, and how, and where was his body?

Harrier remembered that Petrivoch had vanished when *he'd* died—Sandalon Elvenking's dragon, who'd given up his life back in Karahelanderialigor to the spell that had Bonded Ancaladar to Tiercel. And he didn't want to think that, because that meant that Ancaladar *could* be dead, and there wouldn't even be a body to find.

But Tiercel should be dead too. That much Harrier was sure of, because Ancaladar had been sure of it. For a dragon to have a second Bondmate was apparently the next thing to completely unheard-of, but it wasn't *completely* unheard-of, and if Ancaladar or any of the Elves who'd suggested it in the first place had thought it would work differently from a regular old Bonding, they would have said so. And if the Elves wouldn't have, Ancaladar would.

There weren't any answers down here to the question of where Ancaladar was or how he'd vanished (Harrier was just going to assume he was alive for now: it was simpler), though it took Tiercel two hours to give up and admit it. By that time, Harrier had established to his own satisfaction that this level was nothing like the ones above: the corridor was less than half as long as the one on the level above, the walls and the ceiling were blank and smooth, the floor was covered with a random pattern of ridges and swirls, and there was no place for Ancaladar to have vanished to.

"Come on," he said finally. "Let's go."

"He's gone," Tiercel repeated numbly, running a hand through his hair. It had come out of its tie a while back and hung down around his face in lank strands. "I don't understand what happened."

Harrier sighed. "Neither do I. Look. We'll go back up, and . . . maybe there's a spell, okay?"

But if he'd been hoping to get Tiercel to focus on the long climb back up to the topmost level, his words had the opposite effect.

"A spell?" Tiercel nearly shouted. "You really don't get it, do you? Ancaladar is gone! The Bond is gone! I'm never going to be able to do another spell *in my entire life!* If you're expecting me to go to the Lake of Fire and defeat Bisochim by magic, you'd better get used to the idea of living under the rule of the Endarkened! Or being *dead!* Because—"

"We will worry about that later," Harrier said, spacing out his words slowly and carefully. "You didn't have Ancaladar when you started out, and—We'll think of something. I didn't have the Three Books, either. We'll think of something. Come on."

He practically had to drag Tiercel over to the staircase, but once they were there Tiercel trudged up the steps under his own power.

The climb back to the garden of the Nalzindar was a long one.

ALL THE NALZINDAR seemed to know that something was horribly terribly wrong the moment Harrier and Tiercel arrived back in the garden. They'd never been the sort of people who gathered around and chattered whenever somebody came back, but the moment he and Tiercel arrived, Harrier saw that all of the ones in sight stopped what they were doing and followed the two of them with their gaze as Harrier led Tiercel across the clearing to Shaiara's tent.

Even though it didn't matter here, the Nalzindar still started their day with the sun—which meant that Tiercel and Harrier did too—so it was only an hour or two past midday when they got back, and the tent was empty. Harrier led Tiercel to their communal sleeping mat and forced him to sit down.

"I'm fine," Tiercel snarled sulkily. "We have to—"

"Think," Harrier said. "And rest, and plan." He dropped the bag of supplies that Tiercel usually carried to the mat and pulled off his heavy cloak. It was as cold as an Armethalieh autumn night in the lower levels, but up here it was baking hot—and humid, too. He could never figure out what he ought to be wearing.

Tiercel didn't seem to notice the heat. He sat on the sleeping mat, still wearing his cloak, with his arms clasped around his knees, staring at nothing. "I'm fine," he repeated.

Harrier knew he wasn't, but he couldn't think of anything to do for him. Tiercel said that the Bond with Ancaladar had been broken—or, to be completely accurate, he'd said that he couldn't *feel* it any longer. Harrier refused to believe that it was broken, because that would mean that he didn't even understand what little he'd thought he understood about magic. And he also didn't want to think about the fact that if the Bond were broken—and Tiercel was, by some miracle, still alive—he might have been hurt by its breaking in some way that no Healer could touch.

He was grateful, though he would never have admitted it aloud, when Shaiara poked her head through the tent flap and he could get to his feet, and leave Tiercel's side, and go over to her. She studied his face as he approached, and backed away without a word to let him exit.

Anyone else Harrier had ever known would have assaulted him with questions and demands until he could barely think. Shaiara simply walked away from the tent in silence allowing him to follow and find his words.

"Something I don't understand happened down on the tenth level," he said at last. "Ancaladar vanished. Tiercel says the Bond is gone, but . . . he isn't dead. There's no place Ancaladar could have gone. The tenth level doesn't look like any of the others. There's nowhere to go from there."

Shaiara absorbed his disjointed explanation in silence. "You saw nothing," she said, after a pause long enough to let Harrier know she'd thought carefully about what he'd said.

"Ancaladar went first. You know the staircases curve."

Shaiara nodded, then looked sideways at him, her expression considering. "No, nothing," he said, just as if she'd spoken. "Not until Tiercel . . . screamed. Nothing from Ancaladar."

"Tiercel was injured?" she asked, after another pause.

"Shocked, I think," Harrier said, frowning. "This is . . . the Bond is forever. For a human's life, or an Elf's, and certainly for the life of the dragon. Ancaladar was never supposed to be Bonded twice. The Elves were only able to do it—they called it transferring Ancaladar's Bond—by casting what they called a Great Spell. It . . . it cost the life of the King of the Elves and his dragon to cast it. That was the price."

If he'd expected Shaiara to be shocked, she wasn't. She simply nodded, and kept walking, as if this was merely more information. "So, if this was not a natural Bond, perhaps it came undone?"

Harrier stopped. That hadn't occurred to him. Did all dragons vanish when they died? Petrivoch had, but had that been natural, or part of the Great Spell? "It wouldn't matter," he said at last. "If the Bond came undone and An-caladar died, Tiercel would be dead too. Because whether it was natural or not, it was real. Tiercel could use Ancal-adar's magic."

Shaiara nodded again. "That is so."

Their footsteps had taken them to one of the stands of bushes that flourished directly under one of the gaps in the roof where the sunlight was strongest. The Nalzindar dried and cured the leaves and used them to make a bever-age that Harrier preferred by far to *kaffeyah*. Marap was squatting beneath one of the bushes, harvesting leaves. Shaiara touched her shoulder to summon her attention.

"Tiercel requires a tea to help him sleep," Shaiara said.

"I'll make him drink it," Harrier said grimly.

WHATEVER HERBS THERE were in the potion of Marap's brewing, the honeyed drink was strong, for Tiercel barely finished the cup before his eyes were closing, and he had not awakened by the time for the evening meal. Harrier simply lowered the inner flaps of the tent for privacy and left him to sleep when the outer flaps were pegged out so that the Nalzindar could gather around the communal dishes. He ate automatically, without any particular ap-petite, although the last meal he remembered was the cold bread and meat of breakfast.

He was a little surprised to find that Shaiara announced the fact that Ancaladar had vanished on the bottom level of Abi'Abadshar today. She spoke of it in the same calm fashion that she would have mentioned that one of the hunters had taken down an especially fat goat, or that to-morrow they were finally going to try eating fish, or that one of the *ikulas*-hounds was expecting puppies.

"—but the Wildmage was there, and has inspected the entire area, and there is no Taint," she finished calmly. "It is merely more work of the Balance that we do not under-stand."

Harrier took a deep breath to deny it, and then blinked. Okay, maybe he *wasn't* the best Wildmage in the world. But he'd been over every inch of the Tenth Level, and there was one thing he was willing to swear to: there was nothing Tainted down there. He hadn't thought about it until now. But just the way he'd known the berries Marap had offered him hadn't been safe to eat, the way he'd known what the Mageprice for healing the Telchi had been and when it had come time to pay it, Harrier knew he would have known if there were anything bad or dangerous down there. Anything . . . *wrong.*

"There is nothing Tainted down there," he agreed firmly, looking at the Nalzindar gathered around the small cookfire.

As for Ancaladar's disappearance being more work of the Balance, Harrier wasn't quite prepared to go *that* far.

AFTER THE MEAL, Harrier looked in on Tiercel as the rest of the camp—it was still hard to think of it as anything else, although, by rights he ought to be able to call it a village—prepared itself for sleep. Ciniran followed him inside and seated herself on the rug beside Tiercel's head.

"I will watch over him," she said quietly.

HARRIER FOLLOWED SHAIARA down to the waterfall. It felt strange to be going without Tiercel and Ciniran—Tiercel to be explaining at great length everything they'd seen today and Ciniran to ask her occasional odd-but-interested questions. Even making a ball of Coldfire—something he'd done dozens of times because Tiercel insisted that he wasn't going to be the only one casting spells around here—didn't feel the same.

When they got down to the pool, he just watched the water for a while in silence.

"I'm not sure what we're going to do," he said at last.

"Without Ancaladar, Tiercel doesn't have the power to cast spells. It's really hard to explain."

"You may try," Shaiara said, so Harrier stumbled through a long explanation about lamps, and lamp-oil, and how without Ancaladar to provide the power Tiercel needed, he had the knowledge, but not the ability.

"—and even knowing as little High Magick as he does—he keeps telling me he doesn't know much, and Ancaladar always agreed—he, well, maybe we had a chance. Now, well, he can still make Coldfire and Call Fire. That's about it. For anything else, he needs Ancaladar's power to draw on. He runs out of power too fast. The equivalent of Ancaladar is . . . well, there's nothing. Not since there were High Mages in Armethalieh doing something neither Tyr nor I understands to make their magic work." Harrier sighed. "We were investigating the rest of the city because . . . Tyr hasn't had any more visions since we got here. So he was guessing that the city had protective wards over it, wards that still worked. It has to be why Bisochim hasn't found you, and why Tyr hasn't seen the Lake of Fire again since we got here. He thought if those protective wards were in place, there might be something else here."

"There was," Shaiara said, and Harrier winced.

"I just can't figure out why any spells set up by a bunch of old Elven Mages would want to hurt a *dragon*," Harrier said, baffled.

"I do not claim to understand the minds of the Elder Brothers, much less the minds of their ancestors," Shaiara said, "but it eases my heart to know that here we cannot be found no matter how eagerly the Tainted One seeks us."

Harrier sighed. "Yeah. But we can't stay. At least Tiercel and I can't. We have to try to stop him anyway. As soon as we can. Because . . . we know where to go. And we know there's no more reason to wait."

There was a long silence, broken only by the sound of falling water. Harrier thought that decisions like this ought to be, well, more *momentous*. In a wondertale he'd be wearing glittering armor and standing in a Light-Temple—maybe in front of the High Altar—and the Light-Priest and the First Magistrate would be there, and all the nobles and the Chief Merchants of the city, and he would announce . . .

That I'm going off to get myself killed—oh, and Tiercel too—by doing something that we have even less chance of succeeding at doing than we had this morning. And we didn't have much chance then . . .

"I will accompany you," Shaiara said.

"I, um, what? No. You can't do that," Harrier said.

Shaiara turned to stare directly into his face. Her black eyes glittered hotly. "Will you tell me I may not make amends for the shame that Bisochim has brought to all the Isvaieni, Wildmage? That I may not set my face against the Shadow as my ancestors did? That I may not keep you and your friend alive in the desert until you reach this place he speaks of? The Barahileth is not the hospitable place that the Isvai is. It can kill in an hour. Less."

It was the longest speech he'd ever heard from her. "There's an, uh, road," he said stumblingly. "And water." *Yeah*, his internal voice reminded him. *And you were counting on Tiercel to be able to make the two of you invisible or something if you ran into anybody.*

Shaiara snorted, outright derision in her tone now. "Spaced a day's travel apart for Isvaieni. Are you certain you can say the same? Do you know to avoid the *ishnain*-wastes, and what to do if you are befouled with the dust? How long is the journey? What will you do if you run out of food? What if you encounter those who look to Zanat-tar? Can you pass yourself off as Isvaieni, even in the heaviest robes?"

"All right!" Harrier said. "We'll take a guide."

"*I* will take you," Shaiara said firmly. "We will depart a sennight from now. The journey will be a difficult one. Much will be required in the way of preparation."

"Wait—look—wait—Shaiara." Harrier couldn't quite

bring himself to touch her, but he lifted his hand, caught halfway between exasperation and a feeling he couldn't quite name. "You . . ." He swallowed hard. "I really don't think we're going to be coming . . . back."

Shaiara's fierce expression softened, and she reached out and placed her hand on his knee for just a moment. "I know," she answered. "Kamar will lead the Nalzindar wisely and well."

Epilogue: Cold as Fire

BISOCHIM COULD DO nothing as he waited for Zanattar's return to the plains of Telinchechitl but attempt to school his unquiet spirit. So many of his people lost and dead! And in battles that need never have been fought—for surely, surely, once the True Balance had been restored, everyone would see there was no need to fight at all? Why fight a battle that was already lost—or won?

He might—at any time—have summoned Saravasse and gone forth in search of Zanattar and his captives, but caution held him back. To broach the spell-wards with his own body would be enough to destroy them, and if the Enemy had gathered Mages and sorcerous Otherfolk in sufficient number against him, such hasty action would bring doom to his Isvaieni, precipitating the vision that he feared. Even a spell of Far-Seeing would be enough to pierce his spell-shield's impenetrability. He could do nothing as he waited save question the Isvaieni who returned. Their stories were all much the same, tales of march and siege and battle, and most of them had not even seen Zanattar's captives.

It was true that Saravasse could pass back and forth through his wards without disturbing them—but of what use was a scout who would not speak to tell of what she had seen? Three times Bisochim summoned her to him and sent her forth, and three times she mocked him with silence upon her return.

But the bitterest blow of all came a fortnight later, when

Zanattar himself returned at last. He did not bring prisoners. He brought a nearly unbelievable tale.

IN HIS EAGERNESS to see the agents of his great Enemy in the flesh at last, Bisochim rode out to meet them, when sentries came dashing into the camp just past dusk announcing that the light of a cookfire had been seen out upon the Barahileth. Bisochim met the returning war-party just inside the white stone markers that denoted the edge of Telinchechitl's spell-wards. The grief and shame upon Zanattar's face the moment he saw Bisochim told Bisochim all that he needed to know.

"Your captives have escaped you, Zanattar of the Lanzanur Isvaieni."

But to his surprise, Zanattar shook his head. "No, Wildmage. They did not escape. They were rescued."

THE BEGINNING OF Zanattar's story was much like thousands of others that Bisochim had heard, differing only in that it had been Zanattar's decision to make this war in the first place, and his planning that had given the Isvaieni's campaign against the String of Pearls much of its success. It had been his decision to keep the prisoners with him at Tarnatha'Iteru and to depart from there last of all the people so that if the captives should have the ability to summon allies after all, he would not have unwittingly led the enemy back to the hiding place of his people. Zanattar reasoned that any prisoner would naturally summon rescue as soon as possible, and hoped that by dallying at Tarnatha'Iteru for sennight after sennight he might goad them into rash action.

In the end, it had not taken so long. Less than a handful of days after the fall of the city, Zanattar and his comrades had been driven in terror from their campsite outside the walls of Tarnatha'Iteru by the assault of a monstrous black dragon. It had spoken to them in a human voice, threatening them with death if they did not flee at once.

Their *shotors* had fled, maddened with fear, and they had fled on foot, without pausing to take up so much as a waterskin in their flight. If not for the fact that another group of Isvaieni had left Tarnatha'Iteru only hours before and been made curious at the dust raised by the herd of fleeing *shotors,* if not for the fact that they had paused to capture them, recognizing them as Isvaieni beasts, and then followed along their backtrail to discover Zanattar and his people, if not for the oath of brotherhood they had all taken that made any aid extended to them not charity, but the help that kin might extend to kin—Zanattar and his comrades would never have been able to return to the Barahileth at all. Zanattar and his band of warriors did not lack courage. Neither the sort that every Isvaieni must have merely to accept life between Sand and Star, nor the bright sharp sort forged in blood and fire, for every man and woman of them had fought their way up the String of Pearls, taking each city by force, and surviving the privations of the long marches between. Yet not one of them had been willing to risk turning back to face the black dragon again, or even to see if it was still there.

"We have failed you, Bisochim," Zanattar said, when he had finished his tale.

"You have not failed me, Zanattar," Bisochim answered, for the length of the tale had given him time to settle in his mind the words he wished to say. "You have done far more than I could ever have imagined possible. Let our enemies recover two of their pawns. It means far more to me that you have come back safely."

Zanattar smiled with relief. "You will need every *awardan* by your side when the People of the North come, Wildmage. I promise you, my warriors will not fail you a second time."

The tale had brought them from the edge of the Barahileth, through the fields and orchards, through the numberless tents of the Isvaieni, to the tent of Zanattar's mother Kataduk, and to the carpet spread before it, where they had sat as dusk became night, eating dates and drinking small cups of bitter *kaffeyah*. Now that the tale was ended, Zanattar rose to his feet to go within, and Bisochim stood as well, turning away to begin the long climb up the steps to his solitary palace. His steps were as heavy as his heart.

Zanattar had spoken of a war to come as if it were not only inevitable, but a joyous thing. The visions Bisochim had seen of such a war had shown him only death. Death for his Isvaieni. Death for Saravasse, as the enemy Bisochim feared knew well that to slay the dragon was to slay the dragon's Bonded as well.

His Isvaieni had destroyed the *Iteru*-cities thinking to deny their resources to an invader. Bisochim had leeched the water from the wells and oases of the Isvai for the same reason. But Zanattar had spoken of a dragon coming to the aid of his captives, and if the enemy army marched with a dragon-Bonded Mage at its head, none of that would matter. The power such a Mage could call upon—twin to Bisochim's own—would allow him to call up water from rock and sand anywhere he chose. Enough to provision an army large enough to destroy all who sheltered here at the Lake of Fire. To destroy everything Bisochim had worked so long and so hard to achieve.

There was only one thing he could do.

He must work faster.

Turn the page for a preview of

The Phoenix Transformed

Book Three of
The Enduring Flame

Mercedes Lackey
and James Mallory

Available September 2009

TOR®   A TOR HARDCOVER   ISBN 978-0-7653-1595-3

One

A Terrible Beauty

THE BINRAZAN WERE one of the largest and wealthiest tribes to make their home between Sand and Star. Fully ten double-hands of tents could Phulda their *Ummara* number when he counted that which the Binrazan held—and swift *shotors*, and flocks of fat sheep, and goats as well—for Binrazan wealth lay not in its hunting skills, as did the Khulbana's, nor yet in its ability to wrest gold and gems from the secret places of the desert, as did the Kadyastar's, nor in its trade in rare spices, like the Hinturi, nor in its harvest of salt, as the Kareggi did. The Binrazan were master rug makers and weavers, whose carpets graced the floor of every tent of every tribe, and the homes of the soft city-dwellers as well, who paid in cloth and glass and *kaffeyah* and glittering sugar from distant lands, in cakes of *xocalatl* and in medicines and in good steel knives and even in gold. Gold bought little among the Isvaieni, but it bought much in the *Iteru*-cities, and so the Binrazan accepted it in trade, for it could be held for a season or full turn of seasons and then exchanged for as much value as on the day it had been given.

For these reasons, and for the need of their flocks, the Binrazan had always kept to the edge of the Isvai, traveling between the Border Cities known even in the Cold North as the String of Pearls for their fabled wealth.

The first time Narbuc of the Binrazan had gone to Elparus' Iteru to say that the Binrazan had come to Rulbasi Well, he had seen eight Gatherings and had just begun his apprenticeship to Curam, master rug maker of the tribe. Then, he had not believed that any people could live as he saw these living, and his elder cousin had laughed, and had told him there were many strange sights to be seen between Sand and Star. Years passed. Master-weaver Curam went to lay his bones upon the sand, and Lacin became the new master, and still Narbuc practiced and learned. His life—as his father's and his father's before him—seemed as unchanging as the Isvai itself.

Then, in the depths of one summer's heat, all changed. At first it was no more than unrest and rumor, and then it became something that Phulda must go and see for himself, and so the Binrazan came to Sapthiruk Oasis when the next Gathering of the Tribes was more than six moonturns away, and there Phulda heard the words of the Wildmage Bisochim, who told them all of the terrible danger they faced.

And when Phulda returned to the tents of the Binrazan to speak of the warning that the Wildmage Bisochim had come to give, Narbuc discovered he had walked all unawares of peril all his days, as the foraging *sheshu* browses unawares of the towering falcon, for Bisochim had come to warn all the Isvaieni that the people of the cities had long ago given up their hearts to false truths, and, as a fool will envy a man who possesses riches that the fool cannot use, the city-dwellers now hated the Isvaieni for having kept faith with the Balance and meant to enslave them.

And so all the tribes—thousands of men and women, and all that belonged to them, down to the last herd-dog and hunting-hound and fat sheep and weanling kid— followed Bisochim into the depths of the Barahileth, upon

a journey that was hard, but not as hard as the yoke of en-
slavement that their enemies prepared for them.

From Sapthiruk to the place called Telinchechitl, that
journey was the work of three moonturns to accomplish,
and without Bisochim to guide and sustain them, many
would have died. But at last he brought them to the place
where—so Phulda had told the Binrazan—they would wait
and prepare for the day they might fall upon those who held
to the False Balance. And if Sapthiruk had been a garden of
impossible splendor, Narbuc did not know how he should
name the Plains of Telinchechitl, with its tall date palms, its
orchards of figs and *naranjes* and *limuns*, its fields of green
barley and sweet green grass and devices which cast water
upon the very wind to slake its fierce heat, just as if water
were something as infinite as the sands of the desert itself.

Yet here, in this place where there was nothing but soft
cool breezes and sweet grass and sweet fruits and endless
water, there came anger and bloodshed between tribe and
tribe before two moonturns had passed. It seemed, despite
Bisochim's wise words, that there would be no end to the
strife, for how could any man avoid a quarrel if there was
nowhere he might go that he could not look upon the face
of his enemy? And it was true that Telinchechitl was the
strangest and most beautiful place any of the Isvaieni had
ever seen, but beyond its boundaries there was nothing but
the stark waterless desolation of the Barahileth. Paradise
penned them in as closely as the walls of the *Iteru*-cities
closed up their inhabitants, and such confinement chafed.

And so it was that when Bisochim spoke to them of
a thing they all knew well—that of all the tribes numbered among the Isvaieni, one was absent from the Great
Ingathering—all the young hunters were eager to turn their
skills to seeking out the Nalzindar wherever they might be.

All, perhaps, save Narbuc.

He was not alone among his age-mates in staying behind
when the men and women of the Isvaieni rode forth, but
nearly all of the others were women with infants too young
to leave. Of all the rest—youths who had barely seen a

dozen Gatherings, grizzled elders of two-score years who might have chosen to remain within their tents—all rode forth. They went in bands of fifteen or twenty—no more—nor did it matter that this one might be Adanate and that one might be Fadaryama, for before they had gone, each who rode had sworn a blood-oath of fellowship to hold all the others as dear as the kin of their own tents.

Had he been needed to defend the people, Narbuc would have gone with the others without question. But Narbuc had no proficiency with *geschak* or *awardan*—or even spear or bow. All his life, Narbuc had honed his skills in the direction that would most benefit his tribe—to gain skill with the loom so that perhaps one day he might win Master-weaver Lacin's place as Master-weaver for the Binrazan. And one more pair of eyes would make far less difference upon the sands of the Isvai than one more pair of hands in Lacin's weaving tent. With the other young men of the Binrazan tents gone, only Narbuc and the elders remained to work the looms and knot the rugs. And there were many rugs that must be made.

It was nearly half a year before those who had gone forth from Telinchechitl returned . . . those who did. Eight thousand had ventured forth. Half that number came back.

To discover that the true wealth of the Isvaieni had been wiped from the face of the future, as the Sandwind scoured the tracks of the hunter from the desert itself, was catastrophe enough. To hear the news that the young hunters returned with made that disaster as small and meaningless as a pot of spoiled dye when one's tent was ablaze. Those who had ridden forth now called themselves warriors—not mere hunters—and claimed they had struck the first blow against the False Balance. They spoke of Demons with the faces of children, of discovering proof that the False Balance had slain the Blue Robes upon whom the Isvaieni depended for protection, of riding in vengeance to pull down the walls of the String of Pearls and burn the *Iteru*-cities to the ground.

It was this last boast which caused words to sit beneath Narbuc's tongue like a burning coal, for many of those who had ridden with Zanattar—who named himself chief-of-warriors without being master of any tent—had never walked the streets of an *Iteru*-city before the day upon which they had entered it to bring fire and death. And the proudest boast of all the new warriors was that they had left none alive behind them—but could all, *all*, down to the unweaned child rocked in its mother's arms, be guilty of fealty to the False Balance?

It was a question for which Narbuc had no answer, and as day followed day another question took its place beside the first: how could Bisochim, the most powerful Wild-mage ever seen between Sand and Star, able to call upon the power of a dragon as other men whistled hawks to their hand and *ikulas*-hounds to heel, have let such events come to pass? If this was truly the will of the Wild Magic, there must be some deep truth that Bisochim might reveal to ease Narbuc's mind.

It was with this hope in his heart that Narbuc set out toward Bisochim's fortress at the top of the cliffs of Telinche-chitl. Narbuc had never been inside Bisochim's great fortress. He did not know anyone who had. He did not know why it should be that a Wildmage—servant of the Wild Magic, an individual who belonged to all tribes and none of them, one of those who by custom called no tent their own—should possess a vast stone house larger than the largest house of the greatest city-dweller. Narbuc did not like to presume to enter such a place. But Bisochim had not been seen upon the Plains of Telinchechitl for many days, and if Narbuc wished to have words of him, Narbuc must ascend to Bisochim's dwelling.

The tents of the Isvaieni were as far from the cliff upon which Bisochim's dwelling perched as a man might walk in the time it took for the sun to turn from gleam of light upon the horizon to a full disk, and Narbuc was grateful for the grass beneath his feet and the decadent waste of water that vanished so quickly into the air, for his journey was made beneath the brutal heat of the noonday sun. He had waited to slip away upon his errand until the people rested quietly in their tents. Only madmen and fools ventured forth at the peak of the desert day. Madmen—or those who were desperate.

In his desire to speak privately with Bisochim, Narbuc's many visits to the *Iteru*-cities served him well. Had he been born to the tents of the Tunag or the Zarungad, he would not have recognized that which led to Bisochim's fortress, or their purpose. But in the *Iteru*-cities he had seen stairs many times, and sometimes even walked up and down them, though in all his visits to the *Iteru*-cities, never had Narbuc seen stairs that climbed so high. After the first few minutes, his legs began to ache at the unfamiliar exercise, and there was still a very great distance to traverse.

His discomfort was only increased by the intense and unfamiliar heat. The Isvaieni were a desert people, used to the desert's merciless heat, but here there was nothing but stone and sun. The air around him shimmered with heat, and the stone beneath his feet was hot enough for him to feel through the soles of his desert boots. The sun of the Barahileth beat down upon his *chadar* as if he wore nothing upon his head at all.

And still he climbed.

At last Narbuc began to feel faint bursts of coolness upon his face—a sensation he was now familiar with—and knew them for welcome droplets of cool water, borne on the wind from fountains in the fortress above. His dry mouth ached with the desire to quench his thirst at such a fountain, and not so many more stairs would bring him to his goal.

But when he reached the top of the pale sandstone stairs, instead of turning left to refresh himself at the fountain he could see beyond the low wall, Narbuc found his steps turning right, leading him forward across the wide flat area at the top of the stair toward a second staircase cut into the wall of the black cliff itself. His mind screamed with terror, but he could not give voice to his fear, any more than he could command his body to turn back. He was as helpless as the *sheshu* in the *fenec's* jaws, and his limbs did not obey his will. Within his thoughts Narbuc wept and begged for whatever power that had taken possession of him to release him, but all he could do was climb higher along the face of the cliff. The heat he had felt before was nothing to this. That had been the heat of the sun. This was the heat of fire.

When Narbuc had unwillingly reached the top of the second stair, he understood. This was no solid cliff as he had thought, but an open bowl filled with molten rock. Never had he thought to see such, nor did he wish to see it now, for the wind of it blew toward his face, causing his skin to tighten and ache with heat. Far below—perhaps nearly level with the desert floor—rock glowed orange and yellow with heat, and flames of fire danced over it as if it were burning charcoal. To touch it would be a death more horrible than death by burning.

But even as his mind framed that thought, Narbuc found his hands clutching at the rock which lay before him, and found himself clambering up and over. To touch the rock was as if he laid his hands upon a cooking stone prepared for flat cakes, yet he could neither cry out nor draw back. The terror that he felt at having his body move without—*against*—his will nearly overwhelmed the pain of his injuries. First one leg swung itself over the lip of the caldera, then the other, and for one hideous moment Narbuc thought his traitorous body meant to leap into the lake of fire. But then it turned itself and began to lower itself carefully down the sloping inner wall.

It was such a cliff as a man might indeed climb, were he careful and lucky. Narbuc had done such things himself many wheels of the seasons before, near the southernmost of the String of Pearls, Orinaisal'Iteru, where the desert was edged by tall cliffs. But those cliffs were smooth stone warmed only by the sun, not a crumbling slope of sparkling jagged shards that tore at his robes and at his seared and burning flesh. Narbuc's hands were work-hardened, calloused from years of working with loom and awl, yet they were cut and torn now by his descent as if they had been the soft hands of a child. He was bleeding from a hundred cuts when his hands and feet finally lost their purchase upon the wall and he tumbled the rest of the way to the bottom.

Had he possessed voice, Narbuc would have screamed then, for the stone he fell upon was as hot as fire, searing him even through his robes, and the stone beneath him was ... yielding. Though his volition had been plucked from him as easily as he might take a toy from a child, he retained all his ability to feel. Every breath he took seared his lungs with its heat and caused him to choke and gag, for the air was foul with the scent of strange burning. Then, as suddenly as the terrible compulsion had come upon him, it was lifted. His shriek of anguish burst from his throat even as Narbuc lunged to his feet to batter at his smoldering clothing with burned and bleeding hands. He scrambled backward to the narrow ledge at the very bottom of the cliff, where the stone was burning hot but at least it was solid.

That was when he saw *Her*. A woman stood upon the surface of the boiling rock. She wore no clothing, and her skin was as pale as if it had never been touched by the sun. It shone with the reflections—orange and gold and white—of the fires she walked through untouched. Her hair was long enough that it might have fallen to her knees, unbound and uncovered as a young girl might go in her mother's tent. It was of a color Narbuc had never seen, and in its golds and pale reds it made him think of metal and fire, though it lofted on the wind like a veil of softest, finest linen upon the desert breeze.

And though the rock beneath his feet seared him, though the agony of standing so close to the scorching cliff wall was only exceeded by the agony of moving away from it, still Narbuc must stop and *see*.

The woman held her arms out to him, beckoning: *Come*.

And Narbuc would not. For nearly a moonturn his ears had been fed upon tales of Demons who sought the lives of the Isvaieni, and he was no boy, too young to have heard every tale from *The Book of the Light* told over by the storysinger of the tribe. Narbuc was a man grown, and more than grown, and had heard every word of *The Book of the Light* spoken out not once, but three times: the great tales and the small ones. And he knew well what creature it was that could steal a man's will with a spell, that could take the shape of a woman yet stand upon the surface of burning stone as though she tarried in a garden of fountains and flowers.

And despite the knowing that he looked upon that which his grandsires uncounted generations removed had fought to send from the world forever, Narbuc still felt within himself the yearning to do that which the Demon desired: to walk out into that lake of death to gain the touch of her hand. He pressed himself against the wall behind him until the pain of burning threatened to overwhelm his senses, but at least that pain was enough to scour the other compulsion from his heart.

Seeing that he would not come to her, the Demon-woman lowered her arms and began to walk slowly toward him. Small puffs of flame flashed up from the burning stone each time she set her foot upon it, and as she walked, she smiled upon Narbuc—fondly, as a mother might smile upon an errant child.

His tears dried in his eyes just as the sweat had dried upon his skin, leaving behind only a stinging pain. Narbuc could not flee: the walls of the caldera were too steep to climb quickly—if they could be climbed at all—and the heat and the foul air leached more strength from him with each heartbeat. In a hundred heartbeats—no more—she would be able to reach out and lay her fingers upon his skin, and Narbuc knew not what would happen then. There was only one thing he might do to save himself.

With shaking fingers from which thick drying blood oozed, Narbuc scrabbled at his waist-sash. There, tied and knotted and folded into its wrappings, was his *geschak* in its sheath of leather and bone. Its brass-and-bone hilt seared his hand as he drew it, as if he clutched a bar of forging iron, but Narbuc did not care.

She was barely a dozen paces away when he pressed the sharpness of the blade against his neck and jerked the knife sharply across his own throat.